Cross-Currents

m. a. heberling

Cover design by Noel Heberling and M. A. Heberling

ISBN-13: 978-0-692-42646-3
ISBN-10: 0692426469

This is a work of fiction in which names, characters, organizations, and incidents are the product of the author's imagination or used fictitiously.

I welcome thoughtful feedback from my readers.
You can connect with me at this address:
islandsofstories (at) gmail.com

For Allen, who introduced me to the beauty of the Thousand Islands in the upper St. Lawrence River

CAST OF CHARACTERS

Residents of Manhattan and/or Toronto in Ontario, Canada

Samantha De Haven: daughter of Tom De Haven and Trisha Stanton Cox

Trisha Stanton Cox: formerly married to Tom De Haven; wife of Eddie Cox; mother of Samantha De Haven; one brother, Gary

Gary Stanton: restaurant owner; brother of Trisha Stanton Cox; uncle of Samantha De Haven

Eddie Cox: married to Trisha Stanton

Felix Silva: private investigator

Residents of Clayton, NY

Jeff Tierney: Border Patrol Agent

Clive Tierney: student at River High School; gifted pianist

Robbie Barrett: son of Craig and Sylvia Barrett (PTA chairperson of River High); two sisters, Shelley and Denise

Jason Larabie: best friend to Clive Tierney; son of Cal and Molly Larabie (owners of a marina); twin brothers, Christopher and Chad

Andrew Zey: piano instructor

Residents of Fishers Landing, NY

Hettie Voss: classmate of Jason Larabie and Clive Tierney; daughter of Jack and Connie Voss; two brothers, Josh and Stuart

Dr. John (aka Jack) Voss: doctor of psychiatry

Other community members

Douglas McIntire: principal of River High School

Cy Froehlich: Sheriff of Jefferson County

Claire Harvey: River High School guidance counselor

Ralph Jacobsen: landlord/vacation property manager; marina owner

Win Crow: social worker for Jefferson County

Darcy Monaghan: Hettie's classmate and friend

Kirsten Teague: Hettie's classmate and friend

Emile Fortier: marina owner in Blind Bay

The River: the St. Lawrence River which runs between Canada and the United States from Lake Ontario to the Atlantic Ocean

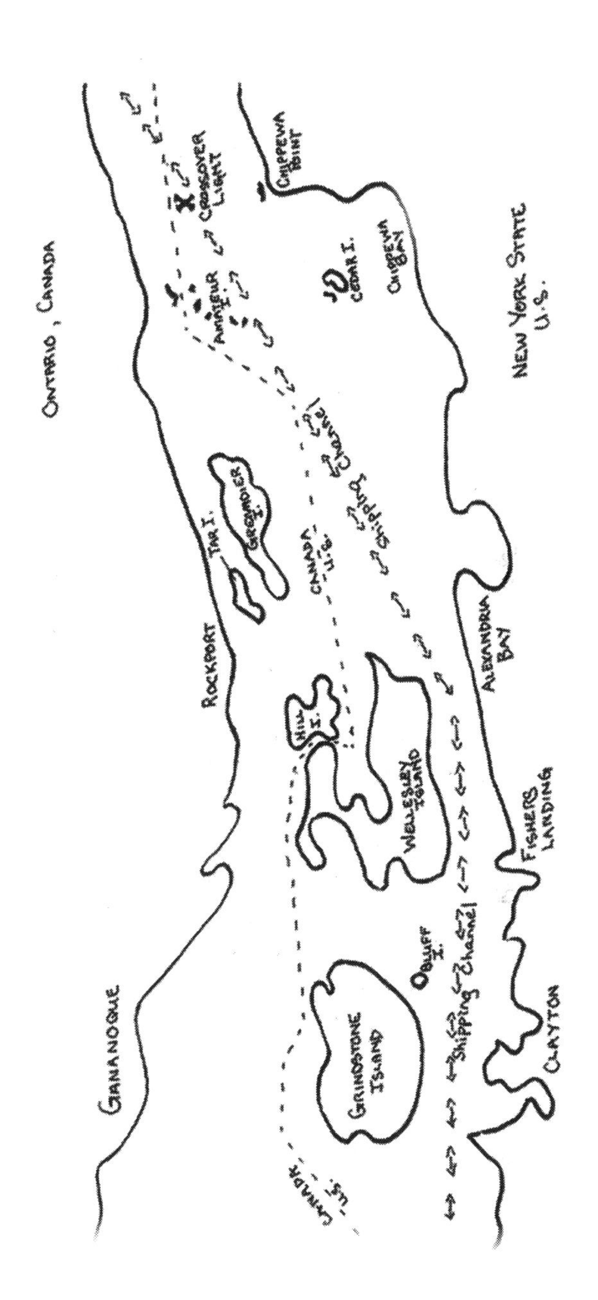
Ontario, Canada
New York State
U.S.
Gananoque
Rockport
Tar I.
Grenadier I.
Canada
U.S.
Hill I.
Wellesley Island
Grindstone Island
Bluff I.
Shipping Channel
Clayton
Fishers Landing
Alexandria Bay
Chippewa Bay
Cedar I.
Chippewa Point
Crossover Light

I. Riverbed: the base of a river

Samantha De Haven: Manhattan

I knew how to keep secrets. After all, I'd been practicing since I was a little girl. I kept them as a way of protecting myself or someone I cared about. Until 1989, that is, when I learned that a secret is like contaminated groundwater. It's buried and silent, but eventually it poisons the life it feeds. I was nine years old when I learned my first life-changing secret. My father was in love with another woman. I don't mean that he lusted after her with the intemperate passion of an illicit affair. He was *in* love, deeply and sincerely.

I remember the first time I met Cecile. Dad and I had the day to ourselves, unfettered from my mother's erratic moods. It was a luminous April Sunday in Manhattan. Tulips stood straight and tall in their row house window planters, like newly opened boxes of crayons. People had shed their puffy, down jackets for lighter pullovers to soak in the sunlight reflecting off the stone buildings that towered over the avenues. My father held my hand as we walked through Central Park. He looked so free from worry, so young and handsome, just like the leading man in those musicals where everyone sings themselves into a state of euphoria.

"You'll like her, Sam. She's kind and she likes children." He explained that we were going to meet his friend for tea. His step quickened and his face brightened as we neared the café where a petite, blonde woman waited beside the glass door with the gold lettering, *Totally Tea*. I'm sure my mother never would've brought me here. She didn't like tea. Cecile briefly caressed my father, then turned to shake my hand as we were introduced. "I've reserved a spot by the window," she said as she directed us inside and over to a round table covered in French blue linen. The waitress handed us each a menu before explaining the different kinds of tea and the specials. I didn't know anything about tea, though I'd occasionally stolen a taste or two of my mother's bitter coffee.

"You can have cocoa, if you prefer," suggested Cecile, "and I thought it might be fun to play a game with the menu." Mom hated children's games. She only liked grown-up ones. Dad chuckled as if he knew what was coming, but maybe he was simply enjoying himself. "Your father's told me what a good reader you are, so you can go first. Pick out a sandwich that you'd like to eat and then your father will have to choose one with a name that follows alphabetically." She must've seen the quizzical look on my face, because she quickly continued. "For example, if you pick out the *Duke of Cucumber* sandwich, your father could choose the *Pickle Dilly* because P follows D in the alphabet."

I studied the unfamiliar selections while thinking that Cecile was nothing like my mother who didn't like tea, who didn't like sandwiches or even lunch, and who most certainly didn't think I'd be capable of reading and ordering from a menu on my own. I finally selected the *Strawberry Cheesewich* which narrowed the choice for my father since most of the other options began with letters that preceded S.

"Now I'm stuck with tuna. I really wanted the *Brie on Pig*."

"You can pass," said Cecile.

"Oh, thank God."

"But I might order the tuna." She winked at me and I laughed while my father stuck out his lower lip to feign a pouty face. "Alright, I'll go with the *Waters of Cress and Melon*." Then she explained that since none of the other selections came after the letter W, we had to start back at the beginning of the alphabet. I chose the *Brie on Pig* partially to please my father, but mostly because I loved bacon. We continued until we had six varieties of finger sandwiches to order.

After the dainty, crustless slivers had been devoured, the teapot had been drained, and I'd slurped up all my frothy cocoa, Cecile commended me. "The sandwiches you ordered were delicious! You chose well, Samantha. Don't you agree, Tom?"

"Yes, she did and so did I." My father beamed back at her while reaching up to cover her fair-skinned hand with his own.

"Daddy, where's your ring?"

My father looked startled by my question while Cecile stifled a smile by biting her lip.

"Out of the mouth of babes," he murmured to her and then added, "I left it at home."

Even at my young age, I knew what had passed between Cecile and my father was not simply friendship. Dad didn't act like that with any other woman, including my mother.

By the time we'd left the café, the sidewalks were draped in shadows. Cecile made sure I'd buttoned up my sweater against the cool breeze that had come up and then tightened my father's scarf for him as she said, "Keep your chest warm, Tom. I don't want your asthma to act up in the damp air." My mother frequently ridiculed him about his bundling up by calling him a sniveling hypochondriac.

I didn't mention the outing with Cecile to my mother because Dad had told me that she'd be disappointed in hearing that we'd had fun while she'd been away visiting my ailing grandmother. I didn't believe that was the only reason, but I didn't want Mom getting angry with my father. I hated to hear her scream at him. He wasn't the target that day, though. Mom was already in a snit when she arrived home, complaining that she'd sacrificed an entire weekend without a single moment to herself, though my grandmother had full-time staff, including a housekeeper and a nurse. I was fast asleep by the time she thought to look in on me, if indeed she thought of it at all.

Nothing seemed out of the ordinary on the morning of my father's final departure from our house. Following the usual routine, he ascertained that I was ready for school with the proper warm clothing, lunch, and backpack. We left via the front door which he locked behind us, as always, while my mother slept in. The letter was found next to the coffeemaker, along with his attorney's business card. This same letter was shoved into my face as I climbed into the back seat of the cab when my mother arrived to pick me up from school. My father had simply written, "I've found happiness elsewhere."

Still seething from what had probably been a half day of rage, my mother whimpered, "How could he do this to me?" As she carried on, I felt the chill of loneliness wash over me and tried holding my breath to push down the sobs welling up in my throat. My mother didn't like children who cried. I crawled into my closet when I got home, emptying my heart into my pillow until I fell asleep.

At first, my mother pursued sole custody in an attempt to punish my father (and me, in turn), but eventually she relented when she realized that a young daughter would be an obstacle to potential husband opportunities. In contrast, visits with Dad and Cecile were always a respite from constantly navigating around the gales and doldrums in my mother's house.

In the ensuing years, I spent more time with friends than either of my parents. I attended a private school with students from other wealthy Manhattan families and was frequently invited to their homes. Fashion was a favorite topic of conversation since we spent five days a week in school uniforms. I loved exploring the closets of my girlfriends who would encourage me to try on their clothes. There were no mother-daughter shopping trips for me. My mother selected all my apparel, usually skirts too long and dated styles. If

Cecile or my father took me shopping, I had to be sure to smuggle the clothes into my closet to avoid another barrage of attacks on my father's sense of appropriate fashion for teenage girls. In truth, I suspected that my developing years, post puberty, frightened my mother. Watching me grow into a woman was the bell tolling away the death of her own youth. Like Snow White's stepmother, she needed to be the fairest in the mirror.

Maybe that's why she fell for Eddie. Eddie Cox pushed his way into our lives like a flashy salesman propping his foot against the door. He came licking after my mother for her money, but she allowed herself to be blinded by his flattery on the rebound from a string of failed relationships. She was, to say the least, a high-maintenance woman who was used to getting what she wanted even if it wasn't good for her.

My new stepfather succeeded in making my less-than-desirable home situation worse by convincing my mother to move to Toronto in 1988, barely two months after they'd married and just as I was about to enter my sophomore year of high school. But my mother was a shrewd woman and wouldn't be held captive in unfamiliar territory. She had refused to sell her brownstone apartment in Manhattan so that she could return there whenever she needed. These trips were frequent and usually didn't include me unless I was to visit my father. Being left alone for days with Eddie would've been unbearable if not, ironically, for his lack of attention. During my mother's absence, he seldom returned to the house before midnight and I often spent the weekend at home alone. My complaints fell on the deaf ears of my mother. I'd begged her to allow me to stay in Manhattan with my father and finish out high school there, but when Dad tried to lend his support, the lid slammed down on my coffin. Mom wasn't going to relinquish the last line of clout over the man who'd walked out on her.

That was the same Fall when I first met Clive and I suppose it's one of the few things for which I can thank my mother. She'd been bored and testy in Toronto, complaining about the weather, the

Canadians, the lack of friends, blaming her unhappiness on everyone and everything but herself. She did know one person in Toronto, though—her brother. My Uncle Gary operated his own restaurant there. Mom made a reservation for the two of us one evening and after we were seated, she asked to speak to him before giving the waiter her order. "Just tell him that his sister is here."

I'd only seen my uncle on rare occasions when he visited my grandparents. I sensed that he and my mother weren't at ease around each other and it was no different on this night.

"You should have let me know you were coming, Trish." He didn't sound pleased.

"We wanted to surprise you." *We?*

"Okay, I'm surprised, but this is the busiest time of the day so I can't sit and chat. Just order whatever you like and it's on the house."

Sounding affronted, she replied, "I didn't come for a free meal, Gary. I just thought it might be nice for Sam to spend some time with her uncle, that's all. She's been looking forward to it." I winced at this false excuse and at what came next.

"Eddie and I need a little time to ourselves and I know Samantha would love to spend a weekend with you."

I could feel my entire face blush with embarrassment while my uncle explained that he'd made plans to spend the weekend at his island cottage.

"Oh, that sounds like tons of fun. Come on, Gary. Eddie needs a break from parenting. It's still new to him."

I couldn't even look at her, or at Gary. *Eddie needs a break?*

"Uh, it's just going to be me and a couple of guys. I don't know if Sam would feel comfortable." *Duh!*

Mom snickered and coughed. Something unsaid hung in the air as she glimpsed in my direction and then back at him. "That wouldn't bother Sam. She's comfortable anywhere. As long as she has a sleeping bag and a couch—maybe even a book—she's happy. Right, Sam?"

How would she know what would make me happy?

Gary was perceptive and kind enough to recognize that refusal would just be adding insult to injury in my case. "Pick you up on Saturday morning at seven. You'll need warm clothing and boots, if you have any."

"All settled, then," added my mother who looked pleased with herself. Later, as a peace offering, she claimed that she'd devoted an afternoon to purchasing my outdoor ensemble consisting of hiking boots, two flannel shirts, corduroys, a fisherman knit sweater, and a waterproof anorak. I imagined her buying the outfit right off the manikins in the display window of a sporting goods store.

Saturday morning was ushered in by a brisk October wind which carried the whispered scent of burning wood from neighboring fireplaces into the cloud-covered skies. I hoped that rain wouldn't follow because I didn't relish the idea of being cabin-bound with strangers for the entire weekend. Eddie and my mother were still asleep when my uncle pulled up in his pickup. The flash of a furry tail in the front seat caught my eye. Uncle Gary had a dog, a black lab, to be precise.

Let's hope it's a female. I could use the company.

I locked up and we stowed my overnight bag in the back of the cab before I climbed in next to Spike who was reluctant to give up *his* favorite co-pilot seat. After a few wet sniffs of my face, he settled down between Uncle Gary and me, squeezing me up against the passenger door, while tolerating my occasional pats on his head.

"He likes having his chin scratched," suggested my uncle.

"I like dogs, but Mom doesn't. She says animals don't belong in houses."

He let out a guffaw. "My sister is a pampered pet, herself." He stopped himself, then, and glanced over at me. "Sorry. I didn't mean to bash your mother. I'm just saying that she's accustomed to a privileged lifestyle."

"What about you, Gary? Why don't you live in New York?"

"You might say that I'm not the favored child. I figured the distance would improve my relationship with my parents. Seems to be the case. It was also easier for me to open an independent restaurant in Toronto than in the Big Apple."

The sun had grown brighter by the time we'd reached Rockport, revealing breathtaking views of a blue waterway ornamented by the enchanting Victorian summer homes sprinkled throughout the densely forested islands. Huge rock formations of pink granite outlined the riverbanks and bordered the highway which ran parallel to the River. Like an explorer on a maiden voyage, I was awestruck by the landscape of the upper St. Lawrence River.

We turned down a narrow road to the harbor from where we would boat across the channel to Tar Island. The morning had stripped off its cloudy garb to reveal a photo-blue background for the brilliant cornucopia of golds, reds, and yellows blazing amongst the evergreens. Uncle Gary backed the pickup down the boat launch ramp alongside the marina, known as Gunther's Boatworks, where small wooden skiffs were built during the early 1900's. After unloading the weekend provisions, he drove back up the hill to park the truck while Spike and I waited on the dock, listening to the water lapping rhythmically against the shore. My uncle had informed me that his friend was coming by boat to pick us up. "We'll be spending the weekend with Jeff and Clive Tierney." Gary noticed the slight change in my complexion and added, "I warned you that it was just me and a couple of guys, but they won't mind the company." I could tell that he was trying to put me at ease about spending the weekend with his friends.

"There they are." My uncle waved at two people in a cuddy cabin craft headed in our direction. There were few other boats on the river since most of the vacation properties had been closed up for the colder months ahead. As they neared the floating dock, Spike barked and rapidly wagged his tail while a gangling teenage boy wearing yellow rubber gloves, jumped out with the bow line and securely wrapped it around a cleat on the dock. The boat's undulant wake rocked the dock up and down forcing me to lurch back and forth to keep my balance while loading our belongings aboard. Gary made the round of introductions which were met with hearty strokes for Spike and terse "hellos" for me. I wondered if he'd told them I was coming.

My uncle pointed out the cottage of sugar-brown cedar shingles and cranberry-red trim as we neared the boathouse located at the edge of a cove. After docking, it was a steep climb up the hill on Tar Island, up the terraced steps and onto the wraparound deck, but not a challenge for Spike who had made three trips up and down the hill before I'd completed my first. The panoramic view out over the river was mirrored by the bank of Grenadier Island peering back at us. "Just put your stuff in the middle bedroom," Uncle Gary told me. "I'm starving, so I'm going to fix us up some lunch."

"What's on the menu?" asked the boy.

"Sunny tuna salad sandwiches."

"Sounds good," I said. So far, the food promised to be a huge improvement over the limited choices at home. I noticed that Clive's father, who had headed back down to the shed near the shoreline, was pulling out a lawnmower while the others disappeared inside. Soon afterward, the roar of the mower was accompanied by the melodic tones of an electronic keyboard. I listened for a bit, astonished at what I was hearing. Was it a recording?

"Is that Clive playing?" I asked Uncle Gary as I entered the kitchen.

"Yup. That's our young maestro. Jeff says he's been playing since he was four years old."

"Think he'll mind if I peek in?"

"Nah, doubt he'll even notice you."

I followed the sound of the music to one of the back bedrooms in the cottage. Clive, no longer wearing the odd gloves, was intently bent over the keyboard which sat under the west-facing window. Against the far wall of knotty pine, stood a single bed covered in a star quilt of navy and red, a simple wooden bureau at the foot of the bed, and a green wicker chair just beside the door. Clive didn't acknowledge my presence, so I remained in the doorway. At one point, he stopped, began again, stopped, and repeated the section. He started to hum while playing the same measures a third time and then continued the piece. As I turned to leave, he stopped again.

"I don't mind. You can stay if you want." He never looked up, but resumed playing while humming along.

I curled up in the wicker chair watching as Clive became lost in his music, more like infusing himself into it, until Uncle Gary came in, clapped his hands and announced, "Food's on. Let's eat!" The music came to an abrupt halt, leaving the complex tonal combinations to hang in the air like an unfinished sentence while Clive left the room without a word.

Jeff was already seated at the long teak table located in front of the full-length sliding doors which overlooked the river channel. I took a seat opposite while Gary served up artfully arranged sandwich plates to me and Clive, who sat to my right. The knotty pine walls of the cottage were attractively accented with touches of orange and rust colors. I'd expected a dark, plaid-upholstered interior bedecked with dusty animal heads and fishing tackle, rather than the light and airy décor of this room. A sand-colored woodstove stood in a stone alcove opposite the doors to the outside deck. Stained wooden shelves were arranged asymmetrically on the wall adjacent to the stove, lined with books, music CDs, and hand-carved wooden decoys.

"Those shelves are beautiful," I said.

"Jeff made them," answered Gary.

I glanced over at the quiet man at the end of the table. "Did you carve the ducks, too?"

He nodded, his mouth full of food.

Gary sat down with a plate piled high and looked at Clive. "This is your lucky day. Instead of cutting down the weeds at the bottom of the hill, we're going to let you take Samantha out for a canoe ride, unless you'd rather do the weed-whacking."

Clive blushed a little, but smiled as he answered. "Tough choice."

"Thanks, a lot," I said. "Me or the weeds?" We all laughed then, even silent Jeff.

After a delicious lunch of tuna sandwiches stuffed with sunflower seeds and sprouts, apple Waldorf salad, and a fudgy mint brownie, Clive pulled on his gloves again before stepping outdoors. I followed him down the hill to the boathouse which was less a house and more a covered dock with storage lockers. We dragged the dark red fiberglass canoe out from behind the structure while Spike, our protector, settled down on the dock. Placing two paddles inside the canoe, we slid it down the bank till it came to rest, half in and half out of the water. Spike jumped up then, barking.

"Stay, Spike. No, you can't come this time." Clive steadied the canoe while I climbed in and perched myself on the webbed seat in the front. He knelt in the stern reaching back with his paddle to push off from shore.

"We'll follow the shoreline till we get to the end of the island," he said. I dipped the paddle in and out of the water, in rhythm to Clive's stroke, and breathed deeply. I couldn't remember the last time my entire body felt so aware, so present in the moment. My senses filled up with nature's messages, the scent of fertile green water, crisp air, pine, the sound of birdsong, paddle against water, the gentle rocking of the canoe as we made our way downriver.

"Wish I'd thought to bring a camera," I called over my shoulder.

He simply nodded and then pointed to a large blue-gray bird standing on a rock near shore. "Look, there."

"What is it?"

"A great blue heron." Clive rested the paddle across his knees letting the canoe glide. "Where did you say you're from?"

I giggled. "Yeah, I'm a born and bred big-city girl, but I can spot a pigeon from half a block away."

Clive began paddling again, from the portside of the canoe. The bow turned outward toward a small island in the middle of the channel. "We'll go around Duck Island," he called out. We paddled progressively harder as we crossed the current and headed back upriver toward the cottage. An hour later we returned to the boathouse and tied up at the dock while Spike, aroused from his nap in the shade, eagerly greeted us. I asked Clive if someone could buy a whole island.

"Of course. Have you seen the castles?"

"What castles?"

"The Boldt Castle, the Singer Castle. They were built in the early 1900's by some super-rich dudes."

"A castle on an island—now, there's an idea for a summer cottage. Like Newport, eh?"

"Newport?"

That led to our first conversation about my family and homelife as we sat on the end of the dock looking out over the River. "Yeah, so my grandparents are loaded and live on Long Island. Their summer place, not quite a Vanderbilt mansion, but still a mansion, is in Newport."

"They have servants?"

"Just three, a housekeeper, a cook, and a chauffeur."

"A chauffeur?"

"Not so unusual in their neighborhood. Kind of handy, actually. He picks us up when we go out to visit my grandparents or when we go down to the shore."

"I thought you lived in Toronto, near Gary."

"Yeah, my mother remarried."

I think Clive sensed my displeasure because he added, "Wow! That must be a huge change."

"Oh, you mean like moving to another country, a new school, no friends, and a stepfather? A piece of cake! Aren't kids—ah, what's the word?"

"Resilient, at least that's what the grownups say."

"I think they say that to make themselves feel better when they screw up our lives."

"Hey, you two," called Uncle Gary from beside the boathouse, "feel like a real boat ride?"

I was hoping he hadn't heard anything I'd said. I didn't want Mom on my case. Whenever I complained to her about Eddie or the move, she'd say, "Nothing's forever, kid. You'll be out of here in a few years anyway."

My usual response was, "I can't wait," followed by hers.

"Be careful what you wish for."

Jeff also accompanied us on the touring ride through the Islands. More talkative now, he began explaining the difference between the American and Canadian channels, where and how to check in at customs. I loved looking at all the vintage cottages, imagining their first occupants. Then came the castles! "Were they living in a fairytale or the Middle Ages?"

"Maybe a little of both," said my uncle.

"They were the barons of the Industrial Age," said Jeff who then proceeded to tell us the story of George Boldt, a hotel owner who had built a castle for his wife on Heart Island. "Unfortunately, she died suddenly and the castle was left unfinished."

"Why would he do that?" I asked.

"Grief," answered Uncle Gary. "Maybe he couldn't imagine living there without her."

Clouds gathered in the twilight and a wind kicked up while we ate dinner back on Tar Island. I watched from the deck as the water peeled off its earthy green coat to reflect the slate-gray clouds above. In the meantime, Gary prepared double-baked potatoes and grilled up succulent steaks along with onions, peppers, and mushrooms. Somehow, this repast here in the near-wilderness tasted better than any of the expensive meals I'd consumed in some of the best restaurants in Manhattan. I knew my mother would never understand if I tried to explain that to her.

Afterwards, I helped Clive with the cleanup while Jeff fired up the woodstove. Gary switched on the radio and declared, "Time for gin rummy, Losers!"

Under my uncle's patient tutelage, I muddled my way through the game. When it ended, we all withdrew to our respective bedrooms, Clive back in his westside den, Jeff and Gary sharing the eastside bedroom, and I in the room opposite the kitchen. I fell off to sleep listening to the gentle patter of rain against the roof and pondering how this day had refuted the preconceived experience I'd anticipated as the only girl marooned on an island with three men.

The next morning, Clive requested permission to take me out on the *Escape* in order to teach me how to fish. Jeff, who'd been instructing him on piloting a boat through the Islands, established strict perimeters—just around Grenadier Island or over to Rockport. We were not to cross over the invisible border line back into the U.S.

"I want you both to wear lifejackets and take the extra can of gasoline. Two hours, no more," cautioned Jeff. Clive, gloves in hand, was already headed out the back door.

"There's fresh bait in the boathouse, Clive, in the little green cooler," yelled Gary from the back room. "And don't touch my red box of lures!"

"I know that already."

Meanwhile, I was still pulling on my sneaks and looking for a sweatshirt.

The storm from the previous night had cooled the temps down a bit, stimulating the hunger of the fish. By 9:30, Clive had caught two good-sized northern pike. I had one little sunfish tickle the end of my hook, but he slipped freely away with the stolen bait.

"Gary will be stoked about this catch! His favorite breakfast is breaded pike with a couple of eggs."

"You seem really close to my uncle. How long have you known him?"

"Six, seven years maybe, but he never told me how rich your grandparents are."

"Well, you've probably spent more time with him than I have anyway."

"Guess so."

"So, what...like you three hang out for a guys' weekend while your mom stays home?"

"No. My mother died."

And, my uncle couldn't have mentioned this sometime during that long drive from Toronto? "I'm sorry. I had no idea."

"It happened when I was a baby." Clive changed the subject, then, as he pulled up the anchor with his gloved hands. "I'm hungry. Let's see if Gary feels like cooking fish."

When we reached the boathouse, we found Jeff tapping down loose nails in the planks on the dock.

"Hey, Dad, I hooked a couple of pike." Clive picked them up by the stringer, the strange yellow gloves gleaming in the sunlight. *Maybe he didn't like the smell of fish on his hands.*

"Nice size. I'll go get my fillet knife while you bring them around back."

By the time the fish guts had been sprinkled back into the River, Gary was in the kitchen mixing up corn muffins. "So, Sam survived the fish slaughter, eh?" he joked.

"Yeah, I'm beginning to feel totally Native American."

"That would be Native North American, to be precise." I could hear Clive in the back bedroom practicing while Gary and I continued with the breakfast preparations and Jeff went back down to the boathouse.

"Uncle Gary, do you think Jeff minds having me up here?"

"What would make you think that?"

"The three of you seem pretty close. I don't want to be a fifth wheel."

"Three wheels plus one is still four, in my book. Two pairs, that is. Sounds kind of even-keeled."

I wasn't sure his answer was comforting, but he did smile at me so I decided to ask another question to avoid a second foot-in-mouth moment.

"What's up with those gloves that Clive wears?"

"He wants to be a concert pianist and worries about his hands."

"Is he worried about germs?"

"Not exactly. Let's just say he's more relaxed with them on than with them off."

Sunday afternoon passed too quickly and my mood descended sharply by the time I climbed back into the pickup for the return trip to Eddie's house. After riding for about an hour, Uncle Gary cleared his throat to ask me a question. "Your mother and I aren't exactly close. We stay out of each other's business. I think we both prefer it that way, but it was nice to spend some time with you this weekend.

"Thanks. I had fun."

"I need to ask you for a favor, though. Well, I'm just wondering, could you keep Jeff and Clive out of your conversations with your mother?"

I almost laughed. Conversations with my mother were usually focused on herself, her wants, and her moods. I seldom mentioned my friends to her to avoid interrogation as to their backgrounds. "On the rare chance that she asks about the other weekend guests, I'll just say they're some fishermen friends of yours. Will that do?" It was déjà vu. Again, a man in my life was asking me to keep something from my mother, a woman who took little notice of what went on in my life. I was curious, though, why Uncle Gary cared whether or not she knew about his friends.

I don't remember if it was my Uncle Gary or Clive who decided to invite me back to Tar Island that Fall, but I was grateful. I soon came to realize that Jeff and my uncle were the only family Clive had. My affection deepened for these people who shared their island refuge with me, away from the growing tension in the place where I lived, a foreign place, not a home in any sense of the word. My stepfather's concept of family time meant spending an evening at a casino or an expensive restaurant with an expensive wine list. I hated every ticking second of those occasions listening to his exaggerated stories about himself, his double entendre remarks to my mother, and hearing her crass responses. The whole time I'd be thinking, *just take out a mixing spoon and gag me!* It never failed that he'd recognize some supposed business associate, then order a bottle of wine for the "client's" table and when acknowledged for the gesture, take the opportunity to swagger over to the table and insert himself into the conversation. Eddie was a gamer, alright. My mother would grow inpatient and angry at his neglect and leave the table before finishing her meal—or her third cocktail—expecting me to realize (or not caring) that she was headed for the front door, stopping to ask the Maître d' to call her a cab. We'd ride back in silence, my mother barely able to sit still, feet tapping, fingers clenched, unclenched, clenched. I knew how the rest of the night would go. I'd hole up in my room with my stereo turned up while my mother drank herself into a fury or unconsciousness, depending on when and if Eddie returned that night. Either way, no one was worried about how I felt, or how I'd sleep.

After the cottage was closed up at the end of October, I didn't see Clive for another six months. My mother and I spent the Christmas holidays with her parents in Florida which provided us with a brief break from the longest and bleakest winter either of us had ever experienced, a subject Mom frequently grumbled about with the added overtone of martyrdom. Though I spent Spring break with my father and Cecile, I eagerly awaited another invitation to the cottage on Tar Island.

Trisha Stanton De Haven Cox: Manhattan

After Samantha was born, I made sure there'd be no more babies swelling up my fingers, ankles, and belly, causing me to puke for nine long months. I can't remember ever having the slightest tingling of maternal predilection. My role model had spent most of her married life in her separate bedroom, rendered almost immobile by bouts of depression, and had delegated the child-rearing to a series of au pairs. Other times, she had run away from us, back to her parents in Georgetown. More than likely, she'd been running away from my father. We all did.

He was a workaholic investment banker. His self-importance increased with every rub up against an expensively-clad elbow attached to a hand buried inside a deep pocket. I'm sure that's how he met and married the daughter of a politically-influential public relations executive. Lloyd Stanton's conduct as a father was nothing more than that of supervisor to subordinate. He gave orders and my brother and I were expected to follow. Praise and fun were rationed out like hardtack to starving sailors lost at sea.

In high school, I had fun by spending my parents' money. "I need to buy some art supplies." Or, "I need to get a gift for Kate's birthday." I spent the lies on alcohol and drugs. It was the late '60's and I had plenty of company in my excesses. If word got back to my parents, I'd be subjected to a diatribe about disgracing the family or damaging the likelihood of my acceptance into a prestigious school, but I knew that my father could buy his way out of those scenarios. While he dished out his reprimands with heaping spoonfuls of disgust, I'd focus on the reddened vessels underneath the blotchy skin of his face, urging one or more of them to burst open with dark, angry blood. His abhorrence spurred me on in my mission to break every last one of his cherished rules.

I didn't love Tom De Haven, but he was convenient. I snagged him and married him in City Hall before he or my parents became aware of my pregnancy. Though the fait accompli had circumvented their authority, my parents insisted on throwing a lavish Manhattan wedding reception to curb unflattering conjecture as to the real reason for my hasty marriage. Besides, Tom was the perfect son-in-law, in line for a position with his father's commercial development firm. Their esteem for him irritated the crap out of me.

Tom loved Sam from the first kick, never suspecting that she'd been conceived before I'd ever met him. She loved him back, too, with an easy and open comfort. It must've taken all of his courage to leave her. Tom's non-confrontational nature enticed me to chip away at him until he roared back. I mocked him, I ignored him, I lied to him, and I cheated on him. He didn't roar. He didn't fight. He left quietly and he left first. I was stunned and humiliated when I discovered that he'd left me for another woman. It was also a sign that I was beginning to lose control.

So, I struck back by attempting to deny him time with Sam. I knew this would hurt him more than any monetary demands, but I capitulated after my attorney warned me that pursuing sole custody could lead to hanging my dirty lingerie all over the society page. I didn't give a rat's behind about my father's image, but I didn't want people snooping around in my drawers, so to speak. Eventually, I saw the advantage of sharing custody of her with a parent residing at a separate address.

Eddie was brash, vulgar, slick, and ungoverned by social mores. He was everything Tom wasn't. Like me, he was a flagrant liar and a very large thorn in my father's side. He was entertaining. He could make me laugh, especially when he'd been drinking and oh, how he could arouse my animal instincts. Blonde, with piercing blue eyes, a solid jaw line, broad shoulders and over six feet tall, Eddie was photogenic and knew how to use his good looks to charm the ladies. He convinced me that the younger women he'd known could never match my appetite for sexual exploration. Eddie was a great salesman and for a while, sold me an image of youth and vitality.

I met him at a wedding reception on a private estate in Newport, R.I. He'd cozied up to the groom, a wealthy son of one of my father's investment partners. Dustin was trying to decide what to do with his trust fund and Eddie was doing his best to represent both their interests. Fortunately for Dustin, he introduced Eddie to me and saved his coffers for future folly.

"So, I hear you're Daddy's little girl, all grown up," he began.

I laughed. "Where did you get that line? I don't think those modifiers have anything to do with me or my father."

"Modifiers? What are you, a school teacher?"

"Again, your description is off the mark."

"Oh? Why is that?"

"Let's just say, my nickname isn't Prudie."

He laughed and grabbed another drink for me as the waiter passed by. From across the lawn, the heat of my father's disapproving scowl ignited my recalcitrant pride like a school boy's dare. I took Eddie's arm and said, "Why don't I show you around the estate." We finished out the day by driving into Manhattan for a night of bar-hopping and ended up in a hotel room by sunrise.

Eddie had told me very little about his family, only that his father had left when he was about six years old, leaving his mother to raise him and his brother in Canada alone. He'd been on his own since he was eighteen.

"I have a daughter, you know," I answered after his first proposal.

He stopped kissing me. "Really? How old is she?" Oh, how I wanted to lie, but assumed that Eddie already knew. He was very accomplished at digging up information about his wealthy contacts, especially the sordid tidbits.

"She'll be fifteen soon."

"So, she's practically on her own. What's a few years? Then it'll be just the two of us, Babe. Come on, marry me."

I hadn't given much thought to Sam's future and his response unsettled me.

"I'll need time to get her used to the idea."

"What about your old man?"

"He'll never get used to the idea," I laughed. "That's why we have justices of the peace!"

Three months later we were married; Sam and I moved into Eddie's townhouse. Next to New York, Toronto seemed provincial. Since Eddie kept late hours with his business partners, I was frequently on my own for the evening and restless. Sam was unhappy with the move, too, but I knew she'd be busy once school opened. My brother had moved up here years ago to open his own restaurant, so although we'd never been close, I called him when I wanted company. If I begged and whined that Sam needed a family connection, he would agree to stop by with a luscious meal. He seldom stayed long, though, claiming he had to get back to work. I knew that was an excuse since we had little to talk about after all the years of distance, especially anything pertaining to family. We'd chosen separate cures for our genetically defective hearts and our paths had seldom crossed until I married Eddie.

I didn't even know Clive Tierney existed before I opened that letter.

Gary Stanton, Toronto

Growing up in the fifties and sixties, I watched all the TV shows about middle-class suburban families where one of the kids would do something stupid where he'd get himself into a predicament, eventually confess the deed to Dad and be forgiven. The parents always talked things out with the kids. I didn't know families like these, certainly not my own, except for the fact that my father was the Chief Executive Officer of all matters, business and domestic. No need for thinking or opinions in this household. All was decided for us and orders were to be carried out in his absence, long hours of absence. "Who do you think puts food on the table, clothes on your back, and provides a life of leisure for your mother?" We weren't middle class like those TV families, either. My mother had a housekeeper and a cook. And she wasn't well, but we didn't talk about that.

My sister fertilized my insecurities with her favorite torment. "You're not my real brother. You're adopted." *Adopted?* Did I miss that episode of happily-ever-after-families? I spied on my parents in an attempt to find out the truth. I hid behind sofas or chairs to observe; I sneaked around corners to eavesdrop. I studied them, looking for shared attributes to confirm I belonged to them. Nothing. Except for my mother's chestnut hair and—I hated the thought—my father's small, beady green eyes. But those hardly qualified as unique, distinguishing characteristics. I believed my sister up until I came to the conclusion that I must've been a mistake. My mother couldn't look at me without despondency pooling in her deep-set eyes. Perhaps she'd been deserted by her lover, my real father, and that's why she was repeatedly dragged under by a melancholic undertow for weeks at a time, mourning for him—not despondent over the very existence of me. I craved physical contact, but my parents were untouchable. Like a puppy, I was trained not to jump up on them, not to snuggle with them. "Mommy doesn't feel well today." How was it that these two anesthetized people had conceived children? I continued to search for the hidden passageway into their frozen hearts until I was old enough to find substitute gratification.

Puberty convinced me I was a charlatan in my own skin. I was in love with food and sprouted the flab to show it. I hid inside those folds of flesh so no one would guess my secret. My father ordered the cook to restrict my diet. After my raids on the kitchen were discovered, the cook was directed to keep the pantry under lock and key. I countered by going on a hunger strike, liquids only. That earned me a rare compliment from my father for my stamina and determination to lose weight and that's all it took for me to reverse direction and begin eating again. I promised the cook to be on my best behavior if she'd teach me her culinary skills and soon, I was preparing the dishes I wanted to eat. When my father threatened to ban me from the kitchen, I took up the practice of daily regurgitation to keep my weight down. Up and down, up and down, I ate; I emptied. I didn't learn that from those TV shows, either.

In high school, I did what it took to be my father's son and keep him off my back. I kept my grades up and made it onto the tennis team. I preferred hanging out with friends from the school orchestra. I played the cello (remarkably, my mother never missed a performance). On a rare occasion, I caved into peer pressure and asked a girl out. I avoided serious relationships.

When I announced to my parents that I intended to enroll in a culinary arts school instead of a traditional Ivy League institution, they dismissed the idea outright. "Unacceptable! You're not kitchen help! You need to work in a field that's going to earn some real money, a respectable occupation for a man." So, to assuage my father's fears that I wouldn't make loads of money or that I wasn't a real man, I explained that there were plenty of respectable chefs who were also men, and that I planned to open a restaurant of my own. I knew entrepreneurship appealed to him.

Out from under the strict control of my parents, I evolved. An empty plate was my blank canvas to paint with flavors, aromas, and textures. The creative possibilities exhilarated me and the process of crafting culinary masterpieces totally engulfed me. As my technical abilities grew, so did my confidence. It was time to find out more about myself.

I'd been careful about avoiding liaisons with classmates and tended to find my partners off-campus, yet during my final term, I fell in love with one of my instructors. This lasted nearly four months until I discovered he was having an affair with another student. My bitterness led to an impulsive outing of myself to my parents during a heated squabble about my plans for the future. Their disgust was almost tangible. The word, *homosexual,* hung in the air while my father tried to slap it off my face. My mother wept silently. In the end, I wasn't disowned, but bought off. My father wanted me miles away from his powerful network, afraid that I might smudge his shiny suit of prominence. I moved to Toronto to work as a chef and eventually used my father's bribe to open my own restaurant.

My sister had married and divorced Tom by that time. I felt nothing but pity for Tom from the day he said, "I do." That was another of her coup d'états, getting married in City Hall and then dropping the news on my parents the next day over dinner. She smiled, my father blustered, my mother picked up her cocktail and silently retreated to her room. Tom tried to step in to take the blame, but Trisha belittled him for it. "Give that white horse routine a rest, will you?" That was just the beginning of her abuse. He endured it for nearly a decade, probably for Samantha's sake.

Eddie—now there was a car wreck anyone could have seen coming. Another misdirected cuff to Lloyd Stanton. Anyway, that was one wedding no one was interested in celebrating, let alone mentioning. That's probably why she agreed to move to Toronto. She knew her social group smelled Eddie for what he was, a huge windbag of manure. Getting him back to Canada meant she'd be free to hang out solo with her do-nothing gossip circle in Manhattan whenever she chose to visit. Underneath Trisha's rebellious veneer, she was a lot like my mother, an escape artist.

In the meantime, I'd fallen in love with a man I'd met while catering a wedding for one of my colleagues. Jeff was older by nine years and had a son. He'd tried living a straight life by getting married, but his wife had been killed in a car accident shortly after Clive was born. Tragically or maybe even mercifully, Jeff had been spared years of trying to make the unsuitable union work. By the time we met, we'd both been accustomed to living covert private lives. Except for a few trusted friends, we kept the nature of our relationship secret. When I made the decision to buy the cottage on Tar Island, I insisted that we have a talk with Clive. Jeff was concerned that his son was still too young (at that time, eleven years old) to keep such a thing to himself and might inadvertently expose us to the bigotry of nosy parkers from his tightly-knit community. It wasn't easy to ask a child to keep a secret such as ours, a love so misunderstood and vehemently condemned by so many. No, it wasn't easy and I'm not sure it was the right thing to do, but what was the alternative? There were a lot of us back then who were afraid to walk out into the light.

Robbie Barrett: Clayton, NY

I was a mean kid, the one and only son of a mean man. My old man loved to say, "What can I do? God gave me three girls." I had two sisters. He beat toughness into my hide and taught me that boys don't cry. By the time I was five, I'd learned my lessons. I was a good liar and knew how to put the blame on others. To cover my tracks, even my own mother would lie for me. I had the superpower to intimidate others which kept me invincible for years.

A kid named, Clive, lived across the street from me. He wasn't around much until we got to the fifth grade. Then his dad must have decided he could stay home alone after school instead of going to the latch-key program. He was an easy mark. People thought he had a kind of superpower, too, but it was more like a big dose of talent. Some of the teachers called it a gift. I made it my job to show him that he wasn't special, just another little kid. But I never did make him cry. Clive pretended he didn't hear me if I called him names like, *sissy* or *orphan*. I was a whole lot bigger than he was and older by a year, even though my mother said no one knew that. Every time he ignored me, it was like a challenge to see when I could get him to crack. Out on the playground, I'd shove him off a swing or kick sand in his face and he'd just walk away like a wimp!

Once, my mother got it into her head that I should ask him out to play. She probably just wanted to get me out of the house. I walked across the street and banged on his door to let him know where he stood.

"Hey, Chives. Answer the door! It's Robbie." I had to shout over the loud piano hammering.

He finally came to the door. "What do you want?" I knew he didn't trust me.

"*I* don't want nothin'. My mother made me come over here to ask you to come out and play. Don't you want me to play with you, Chivehead?" He knew what I meant.

"I'm practicing."

"That what you call that awful racket?" Clive shut the door in my face and after a few seconds, I heard him playing the same loud crap.

"Clive is practicing, Mom. I don't think he likes me." I lied to my mother, too. She didn't like it when other people snubbed me and said so while she loaded a plate with Clive's share of her homemade cookies added to mine. If I ate these in front of my old man, he'd be disgusted.

"Geez, Robbie. You're fat enough! Lay off them cookies! I'm not takin' you anywhere, lookin' like that." That was okay by me. Going anywhere with him meant putting up with mean stares, head slaps, and more put-downs. I showed him, though. By the time I was seventeen, I was head and shoulders taller and more muscular than he'd ever been.

I'll never forget what happened after that Friday night football game in 1988. It was snowing, but huffing and puffing up and down the field kept me and my teammates good and warm. It was a close game on the field of the other team who broke the tie by scoring the final touchdown. For the ride home, my friends and I had smuggled booze into our thermoses so we were all feeling mighty fine by the time Nick pulled into the driveway behind my father's truck which was still running.

"Hey, Robbie, there's your dad! Ditch the thermoses, boys!"

I stepped out of the car and stumbled toward the house, but my old man jumped out of his truck, grabbed hold of my arm, spun me around, and started to slap me in the head.

"What were you doin'?" he growled. I dropped my gear to hold my arms up in front of my face. He started kicking me in the groin, bringing me down on my knees. "You let that Filkins kid score a goal in the last five seconds of the game? You loser! What college coach is gonna want a loser on his team?"

"Dad, Dad! Stop."

By now, my friends had poured out of the car. "Hey, Robbie, you alright?"

"I don't want to see your whining face around the house

tonight. You got that? You find another place to sleep, Loser Boy!" He landed another kick into my lower spine just when we heard a loud thwack from behind us.

"Touch that boy again and I'll have to take you down, Barrett." I rolled over to see Clive's father wielding a billy club in his hand. He slammed it against a hubcap.

"Lay off my truck!"

"Step away from the boy."

"This is none of your business, Tierney. Get off my property!"

"I'll go when you go." Jeff Tierney wasn't budging, so my father climbed into his truck, put it in gear and backed over the lawn, avoiding Nick's car as he skidded into the road while cussing out Clive's dad.

I boiled with hatred for my old man. Pain brought tears to my eyes when my friends helped me to my feet. I don't know if I was more ashamed that I'd taken a beating in front of them or that they'd seen what kind of man my father was. I could only manage a nod of thanks in the direction of Mr. Tierney. Nick helped me back into his car while Jonesy picked up my gear. No one spoke as my neighbor watched us drive away.

Usually, when I didn't show up at home by midnight, my mother would start calling my friends. There were no phone calls that night and I didn't go home until the next afternoon, hoping my father would be working his Saturday bartending shift. Coming into the driveway, I saw that I'd called it right. No truck.

"Thanks, man," I said to Nick.

"No problem. Call me if you need a bed tonight."

Due to the game, a night of drinking, and the bruising, I was still walking a bit stiff-legged and inwardly licking my wounds as I entered the kitchen. I was surprised to find no one there.

"Mom? Denise? Shelley? Anybody home?" I figured they must've gone out shopping, so I headed upstairs to take a shower. I was still stinking from the night before. When I reached the landing, I heard a door close and some shuffling.

"Mom? You in there?" I opened her bedroom door and gaped.

"Your sisters are staying with friends." I stood speechless, staring at her swollen eye and the dark, purple bruises. "It was my fault, Robbie. When your father told me what he'd said to you, I became very angry."

My fists tightened. "Mom, this is not going to happen again. Son of a bitch!"

"Let it go, Robbie. Your father loves his family and takes good care of us. He's just under a lot of pressure."

"And how long before he goes after Denise or Shelley?"

The tears fell from her wounded eyes. "He promised. He promised," she sobbed.

My father's shift didn't end until one a.m. which gave me plenty of time to plan. I was waiting in the driveway for him when he got home. He looked none too pleased to see me when he opened the driver's door. "Robbie, go back in the house!" Anger surged through me as I kicked the door which sprang back and caught him in the face, knocking him off balance. Flinging the door open again, I dragged him out of the truck and landed a punch squarely into his right eye. He whirled back against the door and I yanked him up by the collar, spun him around and threw him against the hood of the truck. He collapsed onto the ground where I kicked and kicked and kicked until he lay still. I trembled with rage while I stood there trying to decide whether or not to run over his body with his truck.

"My old man taught me not to cry," I spat, then turned and walked back to the house.

Jason Larabie: Clayton, NY

Music and puniness, that's what cemented Clive and me as best buds. He was already some kind of Boy Wonder at the piano before I'd had my first cello lesson. Two big instruments for two small children. Clive was a celebrity by the time we finished third grade, a freak of a kid who could play like Chopin. Heck! I thought he was

Chopin till I found out he'd died centuries ago. A lot of kids called him, Chops, but he didn't mind. He didn't go looking for attention, but he stood apart. He was marked with extraordinary talent and he was the only one in our class whose mother was dead. I think he would've preferred being typical. I would've preferred having more of his talent.

Maybe that's what made him a prime target for Robbie Barrett. Robbie was large and wide for his years and liked to play human snowplow over anyone smaller, anyone except girls. He usually left them alone. Some of them even liked him! Our defense strategy was avoidance until that day in the fifth grade. We were in the school cafeteria eating lunch and Robbie was seated right across the table from us.

"Hey, Chives," Robbie began sarcastically. "Is that something your mommy made?" Clive had just bitten into a chocolate marshmallow cookie, continued to chew, and waited for whatever would come next. "Oh, that's right. You don't have a mommy, do you? Maybe that's something a dog left on your lawn." That got a laugh from other kids, so Robbie reached across the table and pounded the remaining cookie into mushy chunks with his huge fist.

No one laughed, but I shouted at him. "Hey, moron, knock it off!" As soon as the words slipped out of my mouth, I knew I was going to pay for the insult. Robbie's face morphed into a twisted scowl as he picked up his milk carton and flung it at me. The spectators erupted into elongated "Oo-ohs" and more laughter.

"What's going on here?" The lunch monitor looked over my shoulder.

Clive spoke up first. "He tipped over his milk." I knew he was trying to preempt further acts of revenge. The lunch monitor's warnings of discipline consequences didn't faze Robbie. A visit to the principal's office might have earned him a missed recess or a coerced, insipid apology, but that was no immunization against further abuse. Robbie just sat there with a smug grin on his pudgy face until the monitor moved out of earshot, but before he could utter his threat, Clive jumped up and tipped over the entire table. I was flabbergasted, but was I ever proud of him. All of our classmates seated on the opposite side of the table, including Robbie, were now drenched in lunch leftovers and fuming! Clive was sent to the office where he spent the next two weeks eating his lunch. I spent them trying to stay away from Robbie.

I was still worked up when I got home from school and made that serious misstep of telling my mother what had happened. She insisted on calling Mrs. Barrett to discuss Robbie's behavior. Mrs. Barrett, chairwoman of the PTA, was always parading around like a self-appointed superintendent while peddling the latest fundraiser or running one of the school activities. Whenever she entered the classroom, an immediate transformation came over the teacher. A stern face and tone automatically cracked into a fake smile and brown-nosing chit-chat. "Oh, look who's here, boys and girls! Can you give a nice, warm hello to Mrs. Barrett?"

Robbie's victims despised the woman who had spawned him, the same person who defended all of his bullying, but a disingenuous salutation would be regurgitated by all, including the dissenters. "Good mo-orrr-ning, Mrs. Brat," we mumbled, combining the syllables of Barrett into one.

"You're sure it was Robbie, right Jason?"

"Positive. You can ask Clive."

"You let me know if this happens again and I'll have a talk with your teacher and Mr. McIntire." That was the last thing I wanted and I'm sure that Clive felt the same. We wanted to stay out of the line of fire.

It wasn't easy to hook up with Clive after school. His dad was usually working and Clive had to practice. They were away a lot on weekends, too. Occasionally, though, I could convince him to come home with me on the bus, if his dad agreed. His first visit was on a Friday afternoon and as soon as we hit the door, I took him up to my room to show him my cello. I showed him how to sit with it between his knees and how to hold the bow. He stroked one of the strings and hummed the note before naming it.

"How'd you do that, Clive?"

"My dad has a friend who plays cello. I know about strings and chords, but it's hard to pluck the right notes and hold onto this at the same time."

"You don't have to tell me. I'm hoping I'm a foot or two taller by the time my skill kicks in."

"Jason? Jason, come down here with your friend so I can meet him," my mom called from the bottom of the stairs.

My mother was a petite woman with an uncanny ability to read the minds of children. She also had a truckload of patience being the only female in our house. She knew how to keep us busy, too. "I thought you two might like to do the cooking tonight." I spotted the warm twinkle in her eyes, but Clive looked over at me not knowing what to say.

"Like what, Mom?"

"How about pizza?" Clive lit up at this, so my mom pulled a round pizza pan out of the drawer beneath the oven. "The dough is ready, so you can start by shaping it." I'm sure we looked like some slapstick act as we tugged, pounded, and stretched the dough to fit it into the pan. The countertops, our hands, our shirt fronts, and our faces we're dusted with flour as if we'd been laboring away in a talc mine. "You can look in the fridge and the pantry to choose what you want to put on your pizza. Dad is picking up your brothers and they'll be home in about a half-hour."

After my mother left us on our own to complete the work of art, Clive asked, "How old are your brothers?"

"Eight."

"And? You have two brothers, right?"

I nodded.

"Oh, I get it. You have twin brothers!"

"Yup! And watch out because they're identical and they're tricky. I'll let you figure out how to tell them apart."

Clive and I piled pepperoni, cheese, green olives, and chocolate chips onto the pizza. The chocolate melted into the cheese a bit as it baked, producing a marbled effect. The rest of my family arrived just as my mom removed our hideous sculpture from the oven.

She had that same twinkle in her eye as she said, "Looks yummy, boys. Grab your plates and dig in!" My father came through the door, then, carrying two boxes of large pizzas from the shop in town.

"Hey, I thought we were cooking tonight," I whined.

"Oh, my mistake," answered my dad, but I noticed how he glanced over at my mom with a smile. He set the boxes down on the counter and then helped himself to a piece of the chocolate, green olive, pepperoni masterpiece and gulped down a generous bite. "Not bad, not bad at all for beginners. This might actually become a family favorite."

"No way! That stuff looks worse than a school lunch," chimed in my brother, Chad.

We all laughed and I could see that Clive was enjoying himself. After dinner, his father showed up to collect him and my dad invited him to stay for a cup of coffee. Mr. Tierney said he'd just gotten off of work and wanted to get home to clean up.

"It's been nice to finally meet Clive. I hear he's a very talented boy," said my dad. I could tell he was trying to get a conversation going.

"Thank you. He works hard."

"Hope you'll visit us again, Clive." The Tierneys simply waved in unison as they headed out the door.

"Big talkers, eh?" quipped my dad just as my mother charged past him to make sure that our leftover marbled pizza went home with Clive.

Hettie Voss: Fishers Landing, NY

I don't think I ever totally understood Clive. He was eccentric and he was introverted. He was a mystery. That's probably what attracted me to him. I liked puzzles and maybe without realizing it, I was trying to decode him. I didn't think about what that would do to me, though.

We were just entering our junior year of high school in 1988 when his pheromones zapped me into an altered state. He was tall and thin, slightly bent forward as he walked. No stagger, just a quiet, moderate gait. He was so *not* the jock-type. His lean face with its narrow nose and sharp chin reminded me of a hawk, always observant with deep set mud-puddle eyes. I'd get lost in them, hunting for the pupils which were just a slightly darker shade of mahogany in the midst of the mud—like finding hidden pictures. He must've thought I was an attentive listener while I searched, but there were times I completely checked out while he was rambling on about a classical composer. His dimples were the bigger challenge. They slayed me each time I managed to coax them out into the open, not an easy task. Getting Clive to smile was like watching time elapse photography. His face would slowly transform as if in pain, his lips extending outward, then slightly upward, his cheek bones rising, until the hidden crevices revealed themselves. Smiling almost seemed alien to Clive.

Nothing about him was open. He passed through the hallways like a shadow, covered in dark layers right down to his fingers in those Dickens-like gloves which raised a major stink with some of the faculty until they eventually backed off. Not so for the simpletons of River High, though. Clive was a target for their dissing practice. "You take a pee with those gloves on, Chives?"

No one, regardless of IQ, could dispute that Clive had exceptional talent. We were struck dumb whenever he performed. Performed isn't the right word, I'm sure, for what came out of him. Watching him play was like observing a séance where the spirit of Mendelssohn or Chopin spoke through his fingers. Sometimes after he'd finished a piece and dropped his hands into his lap, the auditorium sat in complete silence for an extended moment as if we'd just heard the voice of God and couldn't believe it. Then the applause would start and Clive would take a quick half-bow, only from the shoulders up, before he walked offstage. He didn't have a big head about his talent and didn't brag. He didn't need to.

Language was one of my strong suits. I started flirting with Clive in our German class. It struck us funny that the German teacher had a French name and by the way, the French teacher had a German name. Or, maybe it was Dutch. Anyway, Herr LaPointe sat on a stool behind a podium and worked right out of the textbook which meant a lot of conjugating verbs and building sentences, boring drills. Boredom made me restless. I'd volunteer to read passages aloud and break out my Hitler impression, mimicking his public speaking voice—that dramatic, frenzied crescendo meant to incite a crowd of listeners. The class laughed, but they paid attention. I think even Der Herr enjoyed the comic intermission. Maybe he was just as bored as we were because he'd come to the realization that his students weren't ever going to use what he was teaching, year after year. (Hello! The Germans now spoke English while Americans were translating everything into Spanish.) Clive and I used to joke that Der Herr only got excited when he stayed up late with his mistress to read from erotic German novels and role-play until they succumbed to their arousal. That brought the dimples out along with a rare, loud guffaw. The Herr looked up then, but Clive recovered with a fake coughing spasm, a trick he learned from me, I might add.

He's the first friend I had who didn't have a mother. Well, that's not exactly true. I mean, everyone had to have a mother in order to be born, but his died when he was a baby—killed in a car crash. My own mother had been a mostly stay-at-home mom since my older brother had come into the world, even though I maintained that he was dropped out of a B-52. I mean, he was Mr. Gee I Wish I was a fighter pilot. But that's another story.

When Clive came home with me for the first time, he was fascinated by all the family photos decorating the walls of our large dining room. My mother was an avid photographer and collector of portraits from the family tree. She'd say, "I'm intrigued by faces. Each is a different topographical map and the eyes are the key." That would bring out the sarcastic streak in my brothers.

"That's not a zit on your face, Stuart. It's a volcano!"

My younger brother was quick with his comeback. "Better than having a head shaped like a butte or a brain like a butt."

"Ah, but …" My father took a dramatic pause here. "That which we call a nose by any other name would smell as sweet." We groaned. Shakespeare was Dad's favorite author and he never missed an opportunity to prove it to us.

Clive was impressed by the size of our extended family. "I don't have any photos of my mother."

That was a stunner. "Seriously?"

"Dad said he didn't keep any reminders. He wants to live in the here and now, not the past."

"Do you have cousins?"

"Not that I know of. Dad says he didn't get along with his family. I haven't met them and he won't talk about them."

"No Grammy and Grandpa? You can borrow a couple of my wacky uncles, if you want." I was floundering for something to say and feeling out of my depth. I don't think either one of us was comfortable with the conversation so I skillfully segued to the cookie jar.

Before he left that afternoon, Clive asked if he could come over again. I nodded nonchalantly, trying to hide my excitement and hoping that this was a sign of mutual attraction.

When I returned to the kitchen for another cookie, my mother asked, "Is that boy alright?"

"What do you mean?"

"Seems a little gloomy."

I laughed. "He's not gloomy, Mom. He just dresses in black."

"Be careful, Hettie. I don't want you getting serious about a boy. You've got a lot of years ahead.

"Get real, Mom. We don't even date." *Yet.*

II. Tributaries: streams which flow into a larger body of water

Andrew Zey, Piano Instructor

I was surprised when Jeff Tierney asked me to take on Clive as a piano student. I'd only met him once through his friend, Gary, who often came to hear me play and always made a point of talking with me on a break to say how much he enjoyed my performance. This was a solo gig so I got to choose the tunes, but I preferred playing with other musicians, good ones, that is. They kept me on my toes and I almost always learned something new. Anyway, Gary introduced Jeff and told him that I had a classical training even though most of my professional work was in jazz. Yes, siree. Went to the Eastman School on a scholarship thinking maybe I'd end up in an orchestra or on tour. That train got derailed when I started hanging out at some clubs to listen to jazz artists. It wasn't long before I started jammin' with different groups, then got hired by a band, dropped out of school, then joined another band … and so the story goes until I ended up in New York, hoping to make it into the ranks of the rich and famous. Never scored those billings, but I had steady work, paid the rent on my studio apartment, and was able to put a little into a savings account. I lived the urban life for a couple of decades until my grandfather passed away and left me his place just outside of Clayton. Memories crept into my days about the great summer vacations I'd had with my grandparents on the River. Guess the inheritance showed up at the right time. I don't know if I'd grown tired of city life and hustling for gigs or if I'd just become cynical, but I was ready for a change. So, I upped and moved. No mortgage; can't beat that. I still did gigs, locally or otherwise. And if I went out on the road for a bit, I got one of my river rat buddies to check on the place and feed the collies (yeah, I'd rescued a couple of border collies to keep me company in the country).

I didn't have a whole lot of experience with little kids, but Jeff was anxious to find someone since Clive's former teacher had recently moved away. The kid was eleven years old when I met him and was quite accomplished for his age. If I played a few measures of a simple melody, he'd hum it first before playing it back. This intrigued me. So, we started out by ear before we ventured into more demanding pieces, testing a frustration threshold in need of a serious adjustment. He wanted to be able to play a piece flawlessly by the second lesson and that just wasn't going to happen, especially at this level. I tried to explain that even the composer made several attempts and revisions before he was satisfied with an opus. During one lesson when I'd misjudged his level of readiness, Clive had a major meltdown. I'd been demonstrating how to improvise with a classical piece, but he couldn't handle getting off the page. He banged on the keys, crumpled up the sheet music and shot it against the wall. The collies started barking and he told them to shut up. Jeff came in from the den where he usually sat during the lessons, took two strides across the room, and picked the kid up off the stool. Clive's arms were flailing as his father took him back into the den. I heard him speaking in a controlled voice to the boy. "Calm down, Clive. No, I'm not letting go of you till you calm down."

"I want to go home!"

"Okay, we'll go home, if that's what you want, but not before you calm down." The boy was sobbing now. "I know you're upset. We've talked about this before. Not everything comes easy. This was followed by a few minutes of quiet. "No more banging and wailing. Still want to go home or try again?"

"I want to go home."

"Okay, but not until you apologize to Mr. Zey." (I'd given the kid permission to call me Andy.) "Tell him you won't bang on his piano anymore and that you're sorry for scaring the dogs."

Jeff called a few days later to let me know that Clive was practicing his chops daily and didn't want to give up. He also explained that he wouldn't be staying for the lessons anymore, hoping that would discourage Clive from acting out in front of me alone. I told him that I knew where the frustration was coming from, that Clive needed to cut himself some slack. He was still just a little kid.

"But not a typical little boy, Andy." I couldn't disagree with that, but then I wasn't the typical piano teacher either.

Clive and I developed a pretty good relationship over the years. I think he thought I was cool. I had a few tats, an earring, dressed like a rocker (even though I played jazz), and sounded like one when I spoke (a gravelly voice from too much smoking, not from singing). I wouldn't be the first choice for most parents when shopping for their kid's music teacher. Clive liked my dogs, too—Scotch and Whiskey—and they liked him since he quit telling them to shut up. I wasn't soft on him, but I didn't need to be tough since he did a good job of that on himself. Sometimes, we just spent the lesson listening to various pianists play the same piece and discussing the differences in style. He dug it as much as I did.

He wasn't a Mozart and he wasn't a Thelonious Monk, but he did have talent. When Clive was a junior in high school, I took him to the amateur classical piano competition which is an annual event up here. Afterwards, he was pumped up. He wanted to know what he had to do to enter the competition in '89. Performing is one thing, competing is another. Clive had been performing solo since his formative years, but hadn't been judged against others of equal ability or better. There were already too many Big Egos in the world vying to be the best, especially the young ones. That kind of focus can eat your heart out. It took me years to figure out it was healthier to focus on learning the art of making music rather than trying to shine brighter than all the other stars. Clive had set the bar high for himself and wasn't happy with less than what he considered perfect. That was bad enough, but now he was determined to win his first competition. What if he didn't?

Sylvia Barrett, PTA Chairperson at River High School

When Jeff Tierney moved into the house across the street, I gave him a few days to get settled before I went over with a welcome basket of home-baked muffins. I only put in a half-dozen since I hadn't seen anyone except him and an infant move in. "Maybe the wife's in the hospital or closing up their last place," I said to my husband, but Craig wasn't interested in neighbors and told me to mind my own business.

When Jeff came to the door, he didn't invite me in. I was curious about the baby, so I mentioned I'd seen him with the little one.

"Yeah, my son."

"Oh, how old is he?"

"Just a few months."

Now, isn't that just like a man? A mother would tell you precisely how many weeks or months old the infant was. "You and your wife must be very proud. My son, Robbie, is just a little older than yours."

That didn't get any more information out of him, though. He gave me the brush off. "Nice. Thanks for the basket. I need to get back to the unpacking before the baby wakes up." There were scarcely any chats after that first meeting and there was no wife, no mother that I ever saw. The child must've been dropped off at the sitter's or daycare when Jeff went to work. I'd see him leave the house in his uniform and not see him home again until after six. Not till Clive was in the fifth-grade, that is. We knew then the boy was home by himself after school because we heard the piano. I sent my Robbie over a few times, but Clive never wanted to play with him. I don't think he had any friends or ever played outdoors; just stayed cooped up in the house and played the piano for hours. It sounded good, but I thought he should be out playing with other little boys.

I talked to a few other PTA moms to see what they knew. Apparently, Jeff was a widower and worked for the Border Patrol. Clive played piano in the school concerts and you couldn't help but be impressed by his talent. His father showed up for the concerts, but never once came to a PTA meeting.

On weekends, they were gone. I wondered if Jeff had a lady friend or if he really was a widower. Maybe the boy was visiting his mother on the weekends. They weren't around much on holidays, either, so there must have been some out-of-town relatives somewhere.

It was in middle school that Clive started wearing those weird clothes, everything in dark colors. He wore a long, woolen overcoat while most kids wore ski jackets, especially on sub-zero winter days. The older he got, the stranger the clothes got—and gloves all year round! Robbie told me he'd been written up for not wearing shorts in P.E. class, but was given permission to wear gloves. I didn't understand why the rules were bent for him.

He was an odd duck from the beginning, just like his father. The boy needed a mother.

Douglas McIntire, Principal of River High School

I was a brand new principal when I met Clive. Being a principal has few pluses and more negatives than I care to list. Clive could be either one, depending on the day. I don't know what bothered me more, worrying about when I'd say something to get me fired or worrying about kids like Clive.

I'd moved up to the administrative level after ten years as a P.E. Teacher. Though that position had less arenas for conflict, I just couldn't picture myself pumping up basketballs, running drills, and standing out in cold, wet fields for the next twenty years. Besides, my family was growing and I needed more income. Usually, I got along well with parents, but that changed as soon as I moved out of the gym and into the Main Office. Principal McIntire saw less smiles than Coach McIntire when he was speaking with parents. Come to think of it, there were less smiles from the students and faculty, too. Someone always had a complaint, no matter what decision I made. In all, the kids griped less than the grownups and frequently, the squeaky wheel got the oil just to shut it up. Clive was no squeaky wheel. His waters ran silent, deep below the surface.

Maybe that's not entirely true. There was the issue with the dress code for P.E. When Clive was a junior, he refused to wear shorts for the class. He argued reasonably that longer pants made sense in subzero winter temps and I never suspected he had another motive for his refusal. This suggestion had been brought up before, but the current teacher had been concerned about the droopy-drawer look where the male students let their boxer-covered behinds hang halfway out of their sweatpants. This time, we agreed to establish rules about appropriate coverage and non-inhibiting freedom of movement, i.e. no crotch-at-the-knee pants. (Principals and phys. ed. teachers have the same approach to conflict reduction—stick to the rules.) A final recommendation was included that students not walk around all day in the same clothing in which they'd perspired during their exercises. The formal letter to parents was later drafted and sent out after review by the board of ed.

The next point of contention centered around Clive wearing his gloves to class. The P.E. teacher pointed out that the gloves could be hazardous when working with any gymnastic apparatus and slippery when gripping sports equipment. With maturity, Clive conceded that he'd replace his knit gloves with athletic ones during the gym classes. His priority was protecting his hands from injury. "I'm going to be a concert pianist, Mr. McIntire. That's my dream."

And that's why I get up on Monday mornings and go to work. Here was a student who showed promise. He was intelligent, well-spoken, had a gift, and had a dream! He was the type of student every teacher wanted in a classroom, regardless of what kind of funny get-up he chose to wear.

Hettie Voss

We knew something was up when the alarm went off in the middle of German class because we wouldn't have been sent outdoors for a practice drill in that type of weather. Winter lingered in the background even in April. We could smell snow in the air as we filed out under the gray clouds. A few more degrees upward and maybe it would only sleet. Any higher and we might get rain. Either way, there was a bite to the wind that made us pull the hoods up on our sweatshirts and our sleeves over our fingers. We couldn't stand still while attendance was taken.

Clive had tucked his sketchbook under his arm just before we exited the classroom, as he did every time the fire alarm rang. I think his sketchbook meant as much to him as his piano. He could say a lot with pictures.

After about fifteen minutes of shivering out on the soccer field, we heard the sirens. Not only did the firetrucks show up, but so did a pile of cop cars and a vehicle transporting a bunch of heavily clad officers carrying large duffel bags and a couple of German Shepherds. Rumors began to fly then, along with plenty of off-color jokes.

"I hope they're sending the dogs into the cafeteria to sniff around. I'm sure the food is lethal."

"Maybe they found the secret stash of weed in McIntire's office."

"Nah, they're making sure that there are no magazines in the library that any healthy male would want to read."

Groups of girls began to huddle together in tight circles like

Antarctic penguins to protect themselves from the wind. Others began doing jumping jacks to stay warm. Clive was leaning against the goal post with his sketchbook open and the pencil was moving. No one was teasing him about his gloves now.

Another forty-five minutes passed before the buses arrived for an early dismissal. We weren't allowed back into the building. Students who had driven to school offered rides to others. Some walked home in the cold. Just before I boarded my bus, Clive stepped in next to me. "Do you mind, Hettie? Could I come home with you?"

This took me by surprise since he'd only been to my house once before, but I wasn't about to say no. "Of course, but only if you give me a peek at what you were drawing out there." He agreed on condition that we look at it in private.

My mother was at the front door as soon as she heard the bus pull up in front of our house. "It's been on television and radio. A bomb scare? I hope they find the knucklehead who called this in." Then she noticed Clive. "Haven't seen you in a while." Mom looked over at me with her eyebrows arched.

"Bomb scare? Are you kidding me?" Josh repeated. "This is my lucky day. Physics test postponed. Ha!"

"It's not my lucky day," said Stuart. "I was supposed to try out for pitcher this afternoon." He stomped upstairs, punching the wall on his way.

"That'll be enough, young man! Didn't think I'd see the day when one of my sons would be disappointed that school had been canceled."

Josh threw himself down on the sofa and cheered. "No homework, either!" Suddenly, he jolted back up. "Dang it! I've got to work today. Mom? Mom, did you wash my uniform?"

"Who else? Maybe you can manage to get it out of the dryer on your own, though." Josh worked at the small airport near Alex Bay. His uniform was nothing more than a navy blue shirt with a logo and an insulated navy-blue jacket with *maintenance* written across the back. He was a senior trying to earn money for flight time before going off to study aviation in the Fall through one of the military academies or an ROTC program. My father had paid his own way through med school by serving in the navy, but he didn't see the need for Josh to do the same. No one was going to talk my brother out of his dream, though. He had his whole life planned out. First, he was going to college, then on to life as a superhero battling evil forces, then on to Washington. I told him not to expect any campaign donations from me until he changed his hawkish, conservative views.

I took Clive out into the kitchen where I made us some hot tea before we settled down in front of the woodstove in the family room.

"Okay. Time to settle up. Show me the sketchbook."

"No, that wasn't the bargain. I'm going to show you what I drew while we were out in the field today." Clive opened his book to the two-paged scene of faces sketched in front of a mushroom of flame and smoke. Some of the faces were looking back over their shoulders, some were weeping. In each of the corners of the sketch glaring down on the crowd, were the malicious faces of four gargoyles pouring out laughter, one of which held a glaring resemblance to Robbie Barrett. This wasn't a caricature or a cartoon. It wasn't meant to be funny. The representation of what could have been was disturbing.

"Geez, Clive. You think there really was a bomb?"

"I doubt it. Probably just a stupid prank."

"Will you let me look at some of your other stuff?"

"Maybe," but he closed the sketchbook and placed it beside him on the rug.

After our tea mugs were emptied, I asked Clive if he wanted to help me with a puzzle. My family always had a puzzle in the midst of assembly somewhere in the house. The challenge was to be the person who inserted the final piece in order to win the jar of money. We'd started at a quarter a piece when we were little, gradually increasing the amount as we grew older to a dollar, then five, and now ten. Stuart had once stayed up all night to finish a large puzzle just to earn back what he'd lost the previous four times. Clive and I had just about completed the 1000-piece photo of the Lake of the Isles, which probably hadn't been touched in weeks, when my mother interrupted.

"Clive, are you staying for dinner?"

"Oh, I should probably get going. My dad doesn't even know I'm here."

"Why don't you call him? He's probably heard the news by now and might be worried about you."

I heard Clive apologizing to his father on the phone and reassuring him that he was fine before he got the okay to stay for dinner. My brothers entertained him with jokes about the bomb scare while we ate, but my father, a doctor at Bayview Medical Center, wasn't amused. "I don't think we're prepared up here for a serious medical emergency of those proportions. If this had resulted in hundreds of injuries, we would've needed the assistance of the National Guard or the military to fly people into Syracuse. I hope they catch the bloody clotpole who pulled this prank. Maybe he should work a shift in the emergency room, cleaning up puke and human bowels."

"Jack! We're eating!"

"Alright, unruffle your skirts, Constance."

"What kind of a doctor are you?" Clive asked.

"A Doctor of Elizabethan Profanity." My brothers and I rolled our eyes as my father smiled slyly.

"Or so he thinks," I said.

"He's a shrink," said Stuart. "That's why we're all so well-adjusted," he added while clenching his butter knife like a spear to stab his peas.

After the bomb scare, Clive was inclined to come home with me more frequently whenever he could afford to sacrifice some practice time. Music came first with him. He had set his sights on qualifying for the amateur piano competition and he wanted to win. He'd be competing with other young pianists from all over the world and a win for Clive would be a win for many of the locals who depended on tourism for their livelihood. The publicity could bring in new customers for the businesses located along the upper St. Lawrence River.

Yet as the weeks went by, I became increasingly impatient for Clive to reveal how he felt about me. I'd given up waiting for him to make the first move and had established a routine of greeting him with a quick hug and a peck on the cheek which he tolerated, but didn't return. And the whole glove thing was beginning to get on my last nerve. Was I just another threatening germ to him?

"Clive, don't you want to feel my hand in yours?"

"What do you mean?"

I picked up his hand and held it up in front of his face. "Ah, the gloves ..."

He just shrugged.

"Are you worried about germs? Or, that I might hurt you?"

"No, not really. I'm just over-protective of my hands, I guess. They ache after a few hours of practicing."

I didn't buy that, but I let it drop. Blind, stupid love.

One afternoon while sitting out on the porch to listen to another dead composer Clive liked—Scriabin or somebody—I tried pushing the envelope and leaned over to kiss him on the lips, but he pulled away. Immediately embarrassed, I shot up out of my seat and bolted out the back door, blinking back the tears. Clive turned off the music and followed me out to the garage, wearing his backpack. I picked up the push broom and attacked the floor while he stood there watching. For my dignity and Clive's safety, I had to keep moving, but then he spoke.

"I like you, Hettie, I do. I just have a lot going on right now and I don't want to ... well, I don't want to make things complicated."

I turned away from him, sweeping more furiously. *Complicated? Give me a break! We're not even dating!* And then he opened his mouth and made it worse.

"I'm glad you feel that way about me, but I don't think I can give you what you want right now. It's a lot of things. It's my music; it's just me. Not you."

I kept sweeping, trying to decide if his words were comforting or insulting. There was only the sound of the broom swooshing the floor between us until I heard Josh drive up. Before he could make a wisecrack, I spoke up. "Hey, Clive needs a ride home. He's got some practicing to do."

I didn't look at Clive and Josh didn't sound one bit pleased as he climbed back into the car. As soon as they disappeared from sight, I threw down the broom and raced back into the house up to my room before my mother or Stuart noticed me. There was no phone call from Clive that evening and I knew I wouldn't see him again until Monday morning since most of his weekends were spent at his father's cottage on Tar Island.

I managed to avoid him throughout my morning classes until lunch. He didn't waste any time getting to the point. "Hettie, don't be upset. I want to stay friends with you." I'd had plenty of time to stew over the weekend and cook up wounding remarks, but my courage escaped me as soon as I looked at him.

"So, that's what we are? Just friends, right?"

"Good friends, I hope. See me hanging out with many other people? Well, there is Jason, but I'm not sure he can be classified with Homo sapiens."

That prompted an involuntary smile from me, despite my injured feelings. "So, should I ask him out on a date?"

The dimples were showing now. I started to melt. "I might have to come along as a chaperone, though."

I was left in limbo, but held out hope that once the competition was over, Clive might open up. We continued the dance at school and I even asked him if I could come over to listen to his practice session. He said his father didn't allow visitors while he wasn't home, but I suspected Clive just didn't want the distraction. Or, was he hiding something?

Cy Froehlich, Sheriff of Jefferson County

When a kid decides to pull something like a bomb scare, he—or she—doesn't usually put a lot of thought into it. I don't see the humor in it, but it's one way to get out of school. I don't imagine the caller cares what it cost the community to pull employees off of other duties, to haul out the trucks and equipment, spend an hour or two combing the interior and exterior of a building, no matter what the weather, while simultaneously getting everyone evacuated and to safe ground. The strange thing about that call was the lack of scuttlebutt. The year-rounders up here are a close-knit community. Most of us know each other and know more than necessary about the other guy's business. Usually, kids brag about their stunts, but nobody was talking this time and that's what made me think the caller might not be a student at all.

The team went in with the dogs to carefully search the premises. In the meantime, arrangements were made for early dismissal of the students. The employees were allowed to leave as soon as all students had been accounted for. No bomb or the like was uncovered. After hearing our report, Principal McIntire looked relieved and then joked that we should check underneath his car. "Already done," I said.

The next day, I assigned a couple of officers the task of investigating the whereabouts of each absentee student at the time the threat had been received and again later, during the time the building was being evacuated. That job sapped up a chunk of man-hours since there were fifty-five names on the list. We began our inquiries with the students who were absent from class before moving on to those absent from school. Being caught skipping class could make a kid nervous, but being caught and interrogated by police was like injecting the kid with caffeine. Eyes blinked uncontrollably, hands were in constant motion, and there was obvious difficulty with constructing a coherent sentence.

"So, where were you during third period?"

"I cut. Didn't do the homework."

"That's not answering the question."

"I didn't do it. Bomb scares are stupid."

"Still not the question."

"I went to the band room and zonked out till the bell rang."

Other responses reinforced a similar lack of academic dedication and my cynicism about the future of this country.

"I went out back for a smoke." I didn't pursue what was being smoked.

"I was out in my car."

"What were you doing out in your car?"

"Just chillin', you know."

"Easy to do in this weather. That's all?" Turns out this one had a girlfriend who was sitting in the car with him when the alarm went off. I don't think they'd noticed the cold.

The student interrogations turned up no clues. Most of those who hadn't attended school on the day of the bomb threat claimed to be sick, some had written excuses, the rest played hooky. Nothing stuck to any of them. We didn't get far trying to trace the call either. It came in from a phone booth near a convenience store and we were unable to locate a single witness who may have spotted the caller. Like I said, this stunt didn't fit the M.O. of the typical, dumb high school prankster.

Robbie Barrett

After giving my father a taste of his own medicine, we stayed out of each other's path like two barges loaded with dynamite. He kept his distance from my mother 'cause he knew I was watching him and Mom watched my back the only way she could—by standing up to anyone who questioned my behavior, anyone except my old man.

I played football and hockey, two sports that encouraged me to hurt others. A fight on the rink was just part of the sport. I liked the adrenalin rush I got from the first slam into another player. If I drew blood with a jab to the face, it was even better. A short rest in the penalty box was all it cost. The coaches and the spectators expected the violence. They cheered when I came onto the ice.

One of my English teachers got it, though. She assigned a debate topic about contact sports. First, she wrote something on the board like, *Professional football players can weigh close to three hundred pounds. If someone was threatening to crush you with nearly a thousand pounds of weight (like with a three-man tackle) wouldn't that be considered illegal? Why, then, isn't football an illegal sport?* The class erupted. Strong opinions were thrown back and forth until the teacher boiled them down into pros and cons. I thought it funny that she'd recognized the abuse disguised as sport. My old man probably had another name for abuse, too.

Teachers can come close to the truth sometimes. I bet some at River High had figured out that my family was whacked, but Mom was good at acting like a model parent. So good that she became head of the PTA. It gave her a way to hide the stench of the family laundry. It also guaranteed my freedom to be the Number One Bully on campus.

I don't know if any teachers knew the truth about Clive, though. My mother was right. He was odd, but not the way she meant. He didn't care what others thought about him. I kept up my ambushes because I wanted to crack him, just like that time in the cafeteria.

P.E. Class was the perfect time to home in on him. Like I said, I could disguise a shove as just part of the sport. Clive had gotten himself some kind of waiver to wear his geeky gloves in class, the kind used in commercial gyms. Score one for the misfit. We were told that it was okay for any of us to wear sport gloves to P.E., but most of us thought it was sissy.

"Chives, what kind of athlete are you? Afraid to get your hands dirty or did you just have your nails done?" Like usual, Clive ignored my dissin' him.

We headed outside to the field and that's when Jonesy took a turn. "Did you make those gloves yourself or did your Mommy buy them?" That brought him to a stop. He stared at Jonesy.

I put my arm around Clive. "Don't mind my dumb friend, Chives. He can't remember his own phone number, nevermind remembering your mom is dead."

"Oh, dang, Chives. I did forget. Sorry, man." Jonesy stuck out his hand to shake with Clive.

I tightened my hold around his shoulders. "Come on, Chives. It isn't polite not to shake his hand after he's apologized." I could feel him tense up, but he stuck out his right hand. Jonesy yanked it with a jerk, then twisted his body around so that Clive slammed into his back as he whipped off Clive's glove.

"What? What's this?" Jonesy threw the glove away in disgust and held Clive's hand up in the air. Clive was flailing at him with his free hand, but I pounced on it and pulled off the other glove.

"Whoa, Chives. What have you done to yourself?" Some of the other guys stopped to stare. "You been filing your nails with sandpaper?" We all gawked at the bloodied skin on the ends of his fingers.

"You're a mean nail-biter, man!"

"Why don't you try just sucking your thumb?"

Just then, we heard the coach's whistle so we took off while Clive hung back to pick up his gloves. They were back on his hands when he caught up to the class, but he never said a word to the coach.

Jason Larabie

I turned a corner that day when I watched Clive walking out to the field with his head down, tugging on his gloves and wiping at his nose. "Hey, Larabie, I think you'd better take care of your girlfriend," called Jonesy nodding in Clive's direction. Clive looked away, blinking back tears of embarrassment. My adrenalin surged as I gulped down the bait.

"Geez, Jonesy. You must've been a real star in your biology class. Seems that gender identity is still giving you a problem."

"I don't have no problem, but Chives, there, needs you to give him a serious manicure."

"Shut up, Neanderthal!" I seethed, feeling the safety in numbers on the field, even though a few of those numbers were now snickering and pointing at Clive.

"What'd you call me?" Jonesy spun around with a threatening stare.

"Oh, trouble with the vocab, too?" I was throwing caution to the wind, now. Jonesy didn't appreciate being the butt of his own medicine. The coach's whistle drew our attention and the inevitable was delayed while we were assigned to relay teams on the track field and, as luck would have it, I was placed in the fourth and last position right behind Robbie. Our team was sandwiched between Jonesy's on the left and Clive's on the right with four others beyond that. Jonesy was pushing his way to the end of his line to position himself opposite me.

"I'm gonna beat you, Wastin' Jason."

"You've got poetry mastered, I see."

"I ain't talkin' about speed, here, Dude. I'm gonna give you a bruisin'."

I felt Clive look our way, then. "Is that a threat?" I said loudly.

"What's going on over there?" asked the coach.

"Yeah, cut it out, guys. Focus on your team," came the hypocritical voice of Robbie. The whistle blew and the first runner of each team took off, baton in hand. Robbie turned to face me. "You'd better watch yourself, Larabie. You've upset Jonesy." The batons were handed over to the second position runners and Robbie moved up to the line, focused on the race, now.

"Yeah, that's right. You'd better watch yourself. Heh-heh." Jonesy had a groveling chipmunk kind of laugh, but I didn't respond, hoping for a chance to wipe the stupid grin off his face. The third place runners took off from their lines. Jonesy and I moved into position alongside each other, eyes on our teammates. He received his baton seconds ahead of me. My anger propelled me forward to quickly overtake him as he accelerated to keep pace. I pulled my arms up and out to advance, but he kept up and suddenly lurched to his right, forcing me to skip around him, my left foot in front of his right ankle. Jonesy tumbled in front of me and I leapt over him. Our classmates erupted in laughter and applause as I crossed the finish line. Jonesy exaggerated the role of an injured victim, claiming that he'd been tripped, which only prompted more ridicule. Even Robbie scoffed at him. I glanced over at Clive, expecting a sign of approval, but he simply stared back at me with a concerned look, knowing I'd just signed up for retribution. I knew I hadn't made things better, but for the first time, I felt a wave of confidence flow through me.

Andrew Zey

After Clive decided to enter the piano competition, we agreed to meet twice a week for lessons. I was alarmed when his hours of practice showed up on the ends of his fingers. "What are you doing to yourself, man? Your fingers look like ground beef."

I don't feel them," he answered, looking somewhat embarrassed.

"How much woodshed time are you putting in at the keyboard?"

"I don't keep track."

"Looks like you've overdone it. If you keep this up, you might wear out your fingertips, or worse, get some kind of infection. Then what?" Clive shrugged. "I'll tell you what. You'll be out, out of the competition, that's what'll happen. Is that what you want?" He was looking at me, but not saying anything. He was a stubborn kid.

"You need to get yourself to the doctor's. If you don't do something about this, I will. Either I'll take you to the doctor myself or I'll withdraw my endorsement of you for the competition." Now the alarm was on his face. I was peeved. I was losing patience with this kid's idiosyncrasies that took up way too much time and space. Worse than that, Clive was beginning to look unhealthy.

"Okay, I'll cut back on the practice." I didn't respond. "I just can't stop, sometimes. I keep hearing the way I want the piece to sound and I go over and over it till my fingers play it the way I hear it."

"You've got to get a life, man. Put something else besides music on your schedule, something you can't dodge. Make time for friends, join a club, sign up for a sport. And eat something! You don't look like you've been eating. Are you sleeping?"

"More on the weekends, I guess."

"That's not good enough. You need to be healthy. Brains and skill aren't the only things you need to win this competition. It takes endurance. If you get sick, you won't finish on top; I can guarantee that. I've seen enough sick musicians burn up from bad habits and unhealthy living." I'd been headed down that path myself once.

"It's just hard to shut it off."

"You're living up in here in God's country, aren't you? Get outside." I closed the keyboard and handed him his music. "We're done for today." I whistled to Scotch and Whiskey. "Boys, take Clive for a walk!" I handed him their leashes and led the way to the door. "Don't bring 'em back till they look good and tired." That would take a while. My border collies liked to run.

Hettie Voss

It wasn't like Clive to ask for help and even more uncharacteristic for him to be talking about bulking up.

"Are you alright? What have you done with the real Clive?"

"Seriously, Hettie. My piano teacher thinks I need to exercise."

I began to laugh, but stopped just as he was about to walk away. "Wait, I just want to be clear here. You know we're both nerds, right? I mean, I'd rather read a biology book than jog a mile and you'd rather practice a polonaise than kick a ball around. Are you trying to change your image?"

"Sort of ... I thought maybe your brother, Josh, could show me how to build up my muscles." Now, I couldn't help myself. I laughed so hard I cried. Clive looked exasperated, but didn't give up. "Are you going to ask him or not?"

Josh, Mr. Military, loved working out in our garage on the weight bench which my father had purchased shortly after my brothers were born. "By my beard, we're growing men, here, Connie. We've got to have man space!" Josh and my father were competing to see who could bench-press more weight. They both loved the competition. Stuart, on the other hand, preferred team sports, especially baseball.

I broached the topic one evening with Josh while he was in the midst of his workout in the garage, making it sound like it was my idea. "Who? Clive? Oh, you mean that musical geek you hang out with? You're not serious."

"But *he* is. You can't hold brains against him."

Josh lowered the weights and turned to look at me as if he were about to say something sarcastic but thought better of it. "You've got a point. Brains don't guarantee brawn, though."

"That's why he needs you. Maybe he's trying to fit in. Maybe he's just trying to keep some guys off his back. Come on. Just help him out a little by showing him what to do."

"Why doesn't he ask his father? Isn't he a cop or something?"

"A Border Patrol agent, but I don't think he's home much or maybe Clive's embarrassed. Besides, I'm asking you."

"Oh, yeah, right. Okay, but I've got a busy schedule. Can he do Sunday afternoons?"

"No, he's never home on weekends."

"What? Where is he?"

"His father's got a cottage on Tar Island. If they're not there, I think they go visit relatives in Toronto."

"Well, then it's going to have to be Monday evenings. That's the only time I can spare and make sure it's okay with the folks."

I did more than that. My mother agreed that Clive could come for dinner, as well. On the night of his first lesson, I was setting the table for dinner when Josh came through the dining room. "So, are you ready, Coach?"

"Ready? For what?"

"Oh, don't tell me you forgot!"

"How *could* I forget? You've only reminded me every day for the past four. Don't worry. I'll make a man out of your boyfriend."

"Please, please, Josh. No teasing. This isn't the usual sort of thing for him. And don't use the 'boyfriend' word because he won't like it."

"Your sister is too young for some pox-faced younker to come courting," called my father from the kitchen.

"Now look what you've done!"

"Alright, alright. Don't have a cow. I've got to go out and find the five-pound weights."

"Mom! Tell Josh and Dad not to tease Clive or me tonight, please."

Clive arrived just as dinner was placed on the table. He was dressed in his sweats and his sports gloves. I caught my brothers staring at the gloves just after grace was finished, waiting to see if he'd remove them. To my relief, he did. I also noticed that his fingertips were a bit red, but I was grateful that no one commented.

"So, Clive, I hear that you're preparing for the piano competition. That sounds like quite a challenge," said my father.

"It is."

"Which composers have you chosen?"

"I'm trying to narrow it down, but definitely Chopin and Scriabin.

"I imagine you spend a lot of time preparing. Is it just a matter of practicing?"

"Well, first I listen to recordings of various pianists playing the piece, making notes where I would do things the same or differently. Next, I choose the recording I like the most and listen to it over and over."

"Clive can hum almost all of the pieces he memorizes," I interjected.

"It's like making an audio-recording in my brain, something for my fingers to follow."

"Do you have a photographic memory?" asked Stuart.

"I don't know if you can call it that. My brain can remember sounds before it remembers individual notes so it's not like a skill that helps me ace a science test." Was it fact or just modesty? I think Clive was trying to tell my brother that he didn't have supernatural powers. The rest of the dinner conversation continued like most other nights, my father debating the latest political event with my oldest brother.

"No dessert for Clive and me, Mom," announced Josh when he felt he was losing the argument. "We've got some work to do, first. If he's still breathing after my Boot Camp, he can have his pie, but he's got to earn it."

I wasn't allowed in the weight room while Josh and Clive were working out. In the meantime, I tried to concentrate on some homework, but kept watching the clock. The boys had agreed to forty-five minute sessions. The minutes crawled by for me while I anxiously worried that Josh would make Clive feel like a wimp and that I might never see him again. When the clock read 7:45, I flew down the stairs to sit and wait on the bottom step. I thought I heard Clive laughing while Josh talked. Was this a good thing? The back door opened and they both came in wearing smiles. I looked from one to the other. Neither one spoke.

"Well?" I finally asked.

"Well, what?" answered Josh.

"How did it go?"

"What happens in a man's garage stays in the garage, you know that L'il Sister. How about that pie, Clive?"

Josh Voss

Clive Tierney. He wasn't on my radar range until he started hangin' with my sister. First impression? Artsy-fartsy type. Definitely wouldn't have considered him an athlete. He dressed in Goth; most kids around here preferred flannel and denim. I thought he was either an imitation artist type trying to attract chicks with the Mr. Lonely act or, he was missing a Y from his chromosome deck. (I wasn't the only one who thought that.) He looked like someone whose own shadow could beat him up. Well, yeah, there was that musical thing; couldn't deny that. He had chops, but I would've preferred hearing something more hip than Beethoven or Beethoven's dead friends.

So when my sister asked me if I'd help him out, help him beef up, I laughed in her face. I thought it was a ruse to get close to her and I didn't want to waste my time with him. Didn't think I had the patience to train someone who looked like he'd spent more time under a book than lifting books or anything else for that matter. I could tell she was sweet on the kid, though, and I didn't want to wilt the bloom of her first crush, so I caved.

"Okay, I'll take him on under one condition. If he turns out to be a whiner or a wimp, he's out. I don't do girlie workouts." I was already bench-pressing one seventy-five and working my way up. I doubted that boy could bench-press my sister's backpack.

And then the scrawny nerd shows up in sport gloves, jeans, and a long-sleeved T-shirt hot off the ironing board (all in black, of course). The sleeves had creases in them, for crying out loud! "Don't you own any sweatpants?"

"Guess I didn't think."

"Think about it for next time, if there is a next time. You're going to be moving and sweating in here if you do everything right. Obviously, you thought about your hands." We were standing out in the weight room my dad had built onto the back of the garage. He'd installed heat and electricity so we could use it all year round.

Clive just stood there, staring at the weights as if they were a rock collection.

"What got you interested in building muscle?"

"I'm entering the piano competition. My piano teacher thought it'd be a good idea."

His piano teacher? Who was he trying to kid? "I don't get the connection."

"Endurance. When you play a long piece, you need endurance."

I wasn't buying it, but the walking skeleton seriously needed muscle. The real reason for the sudden interest was probably none of my business.

Well, I've got to say that Clive astonished me. Goes to show you can't judge a book by its cover. He was hefting seventy-five pounds to begin with and told me he did a lot of outside work over on Tar Island. I would've never guessed that and I couldn't help but wonder what kind of gloves he wore for those chores. Soon, we were meeting three times a week. He'd show up after my work shift or ball practice for a forty-five minute session. We were both drenched in sweat by the time we finished. Afterwards, he'd hang with Hettie for a while before he jogged home. If the weather was too wet or cold, he'd call his father for a ride or I'd give him a lift. Not once did he ask me into his house, though. I'd just drop him off and leave.

Clive earned my respect during those workouts. He wasn't a quitter and liked being challenged. Maybe that's why I got so burned up about what happened to him at the Spring Rally. Have to admit, I was a Big Senior on Campus—part organizer and part performer that day—and I had big plans for the future, so I got involved in anything that was going to move me forward, anything to get me out of small-town America and into the big league of international political power. That's where I was going and I needed to scoop up awards and get my name on the scoreboard.

The band played a Souza march as the students of River High piled into the bleachers in the gymnasium. When the color guard paraded in with the flag, everyone stood while a trumpet player performed the national anthem. Principal McIntire spoke a few words of commendation about the band and the athletic department before explaining the importance of good sportsmanship, both on the field and in the stands. Not that anyone wanted to listen…they were happy just to be out of the classroom. As captain of the baseball team, I was introduced next. I wanted to psyche everybody up. "Who's going to state championships?" I yelled into the microphone.

"The Eagles!" echoed the students in unison.

"I can't hear you."

"Eagles! Eagles!" the crowd chanted.

Out came our mascot, Bodacious the Eagle (a ninety-eight pound freshman named, Eric, who played the glockenspiel in the marching band), to do his swoops and cartwheels, chase a few cheerleaders, and throw buckets of wrapped candy at the spectators. Next, I introduced the varsity and JV team members, including my brother, Stuart. As our team filed off the floor and into the bleachers, the tennis team filed in. That's when I noticed Clive sitting directly behind the area reserved for my teammates, so I slapped him a high-five before I sat down. The enthusiastic crowd ramped up the sound and the silliness as the rally continued. In the row behind Clive, I heard the loud, obnoxious crowing of Robbie Barrett.

Robbie was a royal pain in the backside; just a punk. He only chose the weak and timid as his victims. He'd mistakenly identified Clive as one of them since Clive chose to ignore him. Robbie's lackey, Derek Jones, was a misfit type. I don't think he had the grades to participate in sports or the social skills to attract friends. He walked around like Robbie's clone, putting others down. No one considered him a real threat; they sized him up as a joke. I think he was loyal to Robbie because he was the only one who paid any attention to Jonesy.

One of the coaches was speaking when the taunts began. "Hey,

Chives," said Jonesy, "get your nails done, yet? Did you try out for the cheerleader team? You'd look good in a skirt." (Our cheerleading team did have a couple of guys, gymnastic types, who wouldn't be caught dead wearing skirts.)

Robbie followed up by trying to disguise poison ivy as an olive branch. "Don't pay attention to Jonesy. Let's let bygones be bygones. Shake on it?"

Clive was sitting right behind me. I looked over my shoulder at him, but he sat tight and didn't even glance back at Robbie and Jonesy.

"What? Afraid to shake my hand?"

"Maybe he's been chewing his nails again," quipped Jonesy.

Suddenly, everyone stood to applaud as the cheerleaders pranced out onto the floor. That must've been when Jonesy grabbed hold of Clive's pants. Down they came! I heard someone yell, "Hey! What'd you do that for?" When I turned around, I caught a glimpse of Clive's thighs covered with several red, crusty cuts. Clive quickly pulled up his pants. Robbie and Jonesy were howling now.

"Man, your thighs look as bad as your nails!"

"Been sleeping with the barn cats?" asked Robbie.

Those nearest Clive were upset with these juvenile delinquents. "Shut up, you two!" Clive was now working his way off the bleachers and out the nearest exit. Robbie and Jonesy made weak attempts to muffle their laughter.

I heard someone whisper, "Did you see those cuts? What's going on with Clive?"

My blood was boiling. I wanted to pummel those two, but decided it was better to check on Clive first. I followed him out into the hallway. "Hey, you okay?"

A bit red in the face, he answered, "Yeah, fine."

"Those two have always been jerks. Just a waste of space. Don't let 'em get to you."

"I try not to."

But it wasn't over. My brother raised the issue that evening at the dinner table. "Did you see Jonesy pants Clive today?"

"What?" exclaimed Hettie. "When did this happen?"

"At the rally. You saw it, too, didn't you, Josh?"

"Yeah, I saw it."

"Didn't you talk to him?"

"He didn't want to talk about it. He was pretty embarrassed."

"Somebody said his legs were all cut up."

My father tuned in now. "What do you mean? Did something happen to Clive?"

"Just a stupid prank, Dad. This dumb jerk pulled Clive's pants down during the rally today."

"How did he get cut up?" I could tell that Dad's professional nose was sniffing the air.

"I don't know. The cuts were there already and Clive wouldn't talk about it," I repeated.

"Self-wounding is something to be taken seriously."

"Dad, you don't think Clive is cutting himself up, do you?" Hettie asked.

"Either that or someone's abusing him." Dad stated this as a matter of fact, not realizing that it was scaring my sister.

"I'll talk to him. Maybe I'll talk to my guidance counselor, too. Something needs to be done about Robbie and his sidekick."

"You'll probably make things worse for him, Hettie," added Stuart.

I agreed, but I'd already hatched a plan of my own.

At 7:30 that evening, a crowd gathered on the football field for part two of the Spring Rally, the bonfire. This brought out a lot of people from the community. It was something to do on a chilly night. The spring sports teams gave a few demos, the band played, and the chorus sang a couple of tunes while the fans sipped hot cocoa or coffee. Local firefighters kept the bonfire under control. Once it was lit, I went searching for Robbie and Jonesy. Divide and conquer was my strategy.

It wasn't difficult to find them. I simply listened for the familiar sound of Jonesy's howling. I stepped up behind them. "Pretty funny prank you two pulled on Clive, today."

Jonesy let out a crass honk. "Yeah, what a geek that kid is."

Robbie eyed me a bit suspiciously.

"You two want to have some real fun?"

"Like what?" asked Robbie.

"Like a drinking party over on Bluff Island. Thought you might like to join in."

"Yeah, if you're bringing the beer," said Jonesy.

"Got it covered."

"How are we getting there?" asked Robbie.

"You can boat over with me." It had taken a half hour of debate to convince Dad to let me take the *Nevermind*. I told him it was safer than driving his pickup (not yet a year old) through a parking lot of drunken teenagers.

Robbie wasn't biting, yet. "Who else is going?"

"My brother, a couple of my teammates, and some of the cheerleaders we know." The mention of girls was the hook, line, and sinker for these two. We headed off across the field toward French Creek Bay where the boat was docked. After untying the boat lines, Robbie pushed us away and I put the boat into gear, heading out across the bay. It was a clear night and I had no trouble navigating. I'd been going out there for as long as I could remember. My grandfather owned a small cabin out on the island and had given a key to my father which was now in my pocket. As we neared the shore, I slowed the engine and tooted the horn to alert Stuart and company who'd been dropped off earlier to begin the preparations.

The guys had the music cranked up to full volume in the cabin and paraded back and forth in front of the windows to make it seem like the place was packed with partiers. There were indeed a few of our teammates in there, but no cheerleaders. Jonesy noted this as soon as we stepped inside.

"Hey, where are the girls?"

Since Stuart had been the one to suggest using cheerleaders as bait, he was quick to answer. "They should be here any minute," he lied. "One of the guys went over to the mainland to pick them up." Gabe, one of my cohorts, handed each of them a beer.

"Let's get the game started."

"What game?" asked Robbie.

"It's called, Survivor," said Stuart.

"What's that?"

"First, we each take turns telling why we'd be the best candidate to survive an island challenge," said Gabe.

"Yeah, and no one knows what the challenge is until after we've all had our say. The challenge is inside of this sealed envelope," I explained as I held up a large manila envelope.

"I thought we were waiting for the girls," complained Jonesy.

"This game isn't for chicks," I said dismissively. Gabe, Stuart, Ben, Robbie, Jonesy, and I sat down around the large oak dining table. "Who wants to go first?"

"I'll begin," volunteered Ben. "I'll survive the challenge because I'm an Eagle Scout." Both Robbie and Jonesy hooted at this. "I know how to start a fire and I'm a good swimmer."

"Okay, how about you, Stuart?"

"Well, I'm not an Eagle Scout, but I've grown up on the River and I know how to fish. I can start a fire and swim, too. On top of that, I know how to use Morse code to signal for help."

Robbie and Jonesy cracked up again.

"Jonesy, you're up next."

"Ah, well, I'm a swimmer. I'm strong. I can kill birds, squirrels, and rabbits. Even killed a dog once." No one responded to this. Stuart rolled his eyes at me.

Robbie spoke up. "This is stupid. We don't know what the challenge is. All I can say is that I can whoop any of you at anything."

Gabe was the next to list his qualifications. When it came to my turn, I had to explain that because I'd written the challenge, I wasn't an eligible candidate, but I could still vote. I pulled out a small notepad and handed each player a piece of paper and a pencil. "Write down the name of the person you feel is most qualified to be the survivor."

"Hold up." I could tell that Robbie wasn't sold on the whole idea, yet. "What's the point of this game? Is there some kind of prize?"

"Now that you mention it, yeah. If the survivor is successful, he gets a six-pack of beer and he gets to write the next challenge. If he fails, he gets bounced from the island. No party for losers."

"Hey, you didn't say nothin' about this when you asked us to come out here," whined Jonesy.

"Wanna go home?" challenged Gabe. Jonesy didn't have the guts to admit that.

"Okay, let me have your votes." After all the ballots were folded and placed in the middle of the table, Stuart scooped them up and began to read them aloud. "Robbie. Robbie. Jonesy. Robbie. Jonesy." Stuart took a dramatic pause before reading the last name. "And, another for Jonesy."

"Looks like a tie," announced Ben.

"First time this ever happened," I claimed. "What should we do?"

Robbie and Jonesy looked at each other with confusion. Obviously, one had nominated the other for the test, but hadn't expected this outcome. *Even better.*

"Why don't we leave it up to the contestants, I mean, the men." suggested Stuart with some added emphasis.

Robbie stared at Jonesy until he spoke up. "I know you want to show these guys you're the best, Robbie. You take it."

I pulled a quarter from my pocket. "We could flip a coin."

Robbie warily eyed the coin. "How about we read the challenge first?"

"Nope, against the rules," said Gabe.

"That's right," echoed Stuart and Ben.

"I insist, Jonesy, you go."

Jonesy looked around the table nervously. "I can't."

"What do you mean, you can't?" boomed Robbie.

"I lied. I can't swim."

"What a friggin' wimp!"

"Now, wait, boys. We don't know if the challenge involves swimming," I said.

Everyone stared at Robbie, waiting for his answer. "Okay, coin flip. Winner gets to go."

"I got heads!"

"Okay, heads for Jonesy," I repeated as I tossed the coin into the air, caught it and slapped it down in the center of the table, tails side up. The guys refrained from letting loose with triumphant cheers while Jonesy sighed with relief, slumping deeper into his chair. Robbie glowered and looked away, his hands tightened into fists.

I picked up the sealed envelope and tore it open to slide out the hidden instructions which I'd written out only an hour before. "The Survivor will be dropped off on Grindstone Island where he'll find a canoe. The challenge is to paddle back to Clayton in less than two hours from the start time. If he succeeds, he'll be awarded with a six-pack of beer. If he's unsuccessful, he's banned from the island."

Robbie's face tensed a little, now. "Paddle back to Clayton in the dark?"

"That's what makes it challenging." I knew he was feeling the pull of pride. "Let's get going."

We headed for the door while Stuart stayed behind with Ben to clean up and lock the cottage. Gabe and I stifled our grins and remained expressionless as the duo of tough guys settled into the rear seats of the *Nevermind*, the sound of the boat blower amplified by their tense speechlessness. Just as I switched on the engine, my brother and Ben jumped aboard shouting out, "Yeah! Let's do this!" We pulled away and I pressed the throttle forward, steering out into the open channel. The night sky was speckled with stars, but without cloud cover there was no protection against a cutting wind which had grown strong enough to whip up whitecaps on the dark surface of the water. We crouched down lower into our seats to get out of the chill.

"Oh, now, who put the canoe over there?" I asked, pretending to be surprised as we neared the larger island. "There's no dock so you'll have to wade into shore to pick up the canoe."

"What? Are you crazy, man? It's freezing out here."

"Giving up before you've begun?" asked Gabe.

"Yeah, come on, Robbie. You're the King," coaxed Jonesy.

"Shut up, pantywaist!" barked Robbie as he slapped Jonesy in the head. Jonesy cowered back into his seat.

I circled about with the boat. "Last chance. Going or not?" I asked. Robbie squinted out at the shore, then stared down at the water.

"Where's this canoe? I can't see it out there."

Gabe clicked on a large, handheld spotlight and beamed it toward shore. "See that big oak tree? Right beside it is the canoe."

Robbie nodded, hesitating again. He looked around at each of us, a bit of the tough bravado fading from his face. He slowly reached down and pulled off his sneaks and socks, one at a time, then rolled up the cuffs of his jeans. Without another word, he slipped over the side, suddenly up to his thighs in the choppy water.

"Awww! Son of a B ..."

"Just keep moving," called Gabe. "There's a sleeping bag in the canoe to keep you warm and a flashlight, too!"

"Yeah, go Robbie! You can do it, man," the others cheered. They played their parts well.

Robbie began crashing forward, occasionally cursing after stubbing his toe on a stone. He hobbled onto the rocky shore and stepped into the canoe, shivering as he hurriedly pulled off his pants and unzipped the sleeping bag to climb inside. He clicked on the flashlight and we watched as he rummaged around inside the canoe.

"Hey," he called out. "Where's the paddle?"

"Isn't it in the boat?"

"No, I don't see it anywhere."

No one answered. We waited, stifling our laughter, while Robbie used up a month's worth of profanity frantically scouring the area around the canoe by swinging the beam of the flashlight back and forth in wide arcs. "Maybe a bear took it," teased Gabe.

"Cut out the crap! What are you pullin' here?"

"Okay, here's the deal," I finally said. "You and your pal, here, are to leave my friend alone and just maybe I'll give you a paddle to find your way back home."

"What kind of bull is this? You guys know who you're foolin' with?" yelled Jonesy.

"Sit down, weasel," I commanded.

"What friend?" stammered Robbie as he shivered.

"You go near Clive again, you touch him, or you so much as breathe on him and you're going to find yourself and your weaselly friend up a bigger river without a paddle. Got that?"

No response. I revved the engine and dropped the prop again.

"Okay, deal!" called Robbie helplessly.

Ben picked up a paddle, attached it to a tow rope, and hurled it towards shore. It hit the water with a smack, then popped up and started drifting downriver as Robbie clambered out of the sleeping bag in his undershorts, leapt over the side of the canoe, and splashed back through the icy water to chase after the runaway paddle. About waist high, he caught hold of it and untied the line.

Ben retrieved the tow line and I turned the boat about. "Just follow the shoreline till you get to the southside of the island. From there, it's a straight shot across to Clayton. If you paddle hard enough, you'll warm up and get there before midnight. If you can't make it, flash a distress signal in the same direction. Somebody will come fetch you."

Jonesy sank deeper into his seat, barely glancing over the side of the boat. He knew his one and only friendship had been thrown overboard that night. I knew I'd judged these two characters correctly.

"Watch out for freighters!" I shouted out as we headed southward.

Hettie Voss

I searched for Clive at the bonfire, but couldn't find him. Not surprising considering he'd been mortified in front of his classmates at the rally, but I finally cornered him Monday morning during a second period study hall. "Clive, I didn't see you at the bonfire. How are you?"

"I was at the cottage with Dad."

"That's not what I asked. People are talking about what Jonesy did to you and no one thinks it's funny."

"You got that right. It wasn't funny."

I dropped my voice to a whisper then. "They're also talking about the cuts on your legs."

Clive looked up at me, then away. "I don't want to talk about that."

"Is someone hurting you, Clive?"

Looking perturbed, he started to pack up his books and said firmly, "Stay out of this, Hettie." He picked up a hall pass and went out the door. I was miffed that Clive left so abruptly, basically telling me to mind my own business, but more than that, I was worried. What if he was being abused? Who would he tell? I knew I wasn't going to be able to concentrate on anything academic, so I signed out wondering if I should have used Benedict Arnold's name.

"Hettie, I haven't seen you in here since we filled out your class schedule. What can I do for you?" Ms. Harvey, my guidance counselor, was a tall, athletic woman with a husky, energetic voice that could boost the morale of a frozen muskie. She'd told me once that she'd been the captain of her field hockey team in high school. Not hard to imagine.

"Well, I'm not here about me. I'm worried about a friend of

mine." She came out from behind her desk to close the door. No doubt she'd heard a lot of unpleasant stories over the years, just like the ones my father heard, the kind of stories buried inside dysfunctional homes.

After she was seated again, she encouraged me by saying, "Being worried means you really care about this person, Hettie, so I'm sure you're not in here to gossip. Why don't you just start with the reason for your concern."

"A friend of mine got pantsed at the rally last week."

"Pantsed?"

"Yeah, some stupid kid pulled down my friend's pants."

"Okay … that must have been embarrassing."

"For real, but that's not all. I didn't see it, but my brother, Josh, saw what happened. He said that my friend's legs were covered in cuts."

"Cuts? Like scratches or knife cuts?"

"Like I said, I wasn't there, but it sounded more like cuts. Maybe they're scratches, but when I asked my friend about it, he told me it was none of my business."

Ms. Harvey tapped her pen while she thought a minute. "Hettie, if you were telling me this about yourself, I'd have to report the information to someone who would interview you. If you tell me your friend's name, I can speak with him myself and then determine whether or not further investigation is warranted."

"If I tell you who he is, he might never talk to me again." Tears quickly clouded my vision.

"You told me he was humiliated in front of others, right? I could say it came from them."

"Would you mention my brother?"

"No, no. I'll just say that a few students who were in the gym that day came to me and described what happened. It wouldn't be the first time someone has complained about bullies and I think I know just who they were." She handed me a tissue.

I wiped my eyes and nose, feeling like I'd stabbed Clive in the back. "I don't want anything worse to happen to him, Ms. Harvey. He's not a trouble-maker and he's a very private person."

"You're speaking about Clive, aren't you?"

"How did you know?"

"I've seen both of you together and I know a little about him, quiet but talented." I simply nodded in agreement as the tears spilled out. Ms. Harvey brought me some water from the cooler in her office. "Hettie, you've done the right thing for your friend and don't worry. I'll handle this discreetly. In the meantime, you can hang out here and sort the recent college brochures for me or I can give you a pass to the Ladies' Room till you've collected yourself."

I thanked her, grabbed more tissues, and quietly slinked out the door.

In the days that followed, Clive made no mention of his conference with Ms. Harvey and I was anxious to find out if he was getting help while, at the same time, worried that he may have pegged me as the messenger. A couple of weeks went by before my curiosity got the better of me. I'd stayed after school for a yearbook meeting and then wandered down to the auditorium to see if the orchestra had finished rehearsing. I found Clive sitting in the back by himself as others were packing up their instruments. We had about ten minutes before the buses arrived so I sat down beside him and jumped right in, keeping my voice barely above a whisper. "So, I've been meaning to ask you if your legs have healed."

He looked startled by my question, but there was no going back. "What are you talking about?"

"You know. Those cuts on your legs."

Even in the dim lighting, his blush was visible. "Did your father tell you about it?"

"Tell me what?"

"That I'm seeing him."

I was confused, at first, and then it struck me. Clive was seeing my father, a psychiatrist, as a patient! I wasn't sure this was good news for me.

"I had no idea. That's the truth. My father's not allowed to share confidential information about his clients. You know that, right? But why him? Couldn't you see someone else?"

"The school recommended your father and my dad thought it a good idea for me to talk to someone I already knew. He was right."

I dove right into the deep end now. "So, you've been cutting yourself?"

He nodded. "You think I'm nuts?"

"It scares me. Why do you do it?"

"Your dad is helping me to figure that out. It's something I do when I feel kind of stressed, I guess."

Impulsively, I gave Clive a hug. He didn't resist.

"You aren't going to tell Josh, are you?"

I didn't want to saddle him with another layer of humiliation by inflicting the truth on him. "No, I won't tell my brother." I didn't have to. Josh, along with other witnesses, had instantly known that something dark had been exposed that day when Jonesy had pantsed Clive and I wasn't sure I felt relieved to learn that it wasn't Mr. Tierney hurting his son, rather than Clive himself.

Robbie Barrett

I should've listened to the hairs that pricked the back of my neck when Josh Voss told me about that party. I couldn't believe I fell for such a stupid trick! Why would someone like him, the Banner Boy of River High, ask me to his party? And Jonesy—what a loser! If it hadn't been for that old guy from over on Wellesley Island coming down the River and giving me a tow, I would've been frozen stiff by the time I reached the mainland. Had to thumb a ride home, too, without my sneakers! Those showed up on my front lawn, but whoever owned that canoe wasn't ever going to see it again. I set her loose after slamming some sizable rocks into the hull.

No way was I going to let that stuck-up bunch intimidate me. They hadn't grown up with my old man. I'd make sure Clive knew how pissed off I was, too. Funny thing, I never did hate that kid. I'd just been playing with him before the Voss brothers stepped in. Now, he was bait.

McIntire hauled me into his office on Monday. He looked more testy than usual so I got the sense I'd been tried and convicted already. That Amazon woman, Ms. Harvey, was sitting in there, too, all ready with her eye-witness statements. I managed to put the blame on Jonesy, though. "I didn't tell him to pants the kid. Jonesy pulled that prank on his own. Is it a crime to laugh when something is funny?"

The Amazon trotted out that old line, "What if someone had done that to you?" *Like anyone could.* She was talking down to me like I was in the third grade. I wanted to tell her I'd beat the crap out of anyone trying a stunt like that with me. I knew that's why Jonesy felt safe hanging out with me, until the Voss brothers got a hold of him, that is.

"I know. I told him not to touch Clive and I felt bad, but it seemed funny at the time."

McIntire spoke next. "I expect more from an upperclassman. Graduation is only another year away. It's time you start thinking about that and take matters more seriously."

I was off the hook, but Jonesy got an in-school suspension. The isolation probably bothered him more than missing classes. I made sure he knew we were finished, though.

"Geez, man. I'm sorry about Friday night. How did you get home?"

"No thanks to you, Loser. I'm sure you were snuggled into bed with your mama before I made it to shore."

"You shut your filthy mouth, Robbie!"

"Or what? What are you going to do?"

Jonesy turned red and stomped off down the hall.

I didn't need him. I didn't need anyone. I'd learned that a long time ago. Still, McIntire's words were needling me. Exactly *where* was I headed?

Samantha De Haven, Toronto

During the long, cold months of that first winter in Toronto, my mother's drinking had increased to the point where I barely saw her awake and sober. There were times when I worried that I'd come home from school and find her dead. Occasionally, I'd creep into her room and stand beside the bed, listening for her breath before creeping back out.

She and Eddie were frequently arguing whenever the two of them were at home together. From what I could determine, it sounded like Eddie was in some kind of financial trouble and wanted my mother to bail him out. My mother's trust fund was her lifeline. Without it, she'd be dependent on my grandparents because there was no way she'd go out and get a job to support herself or for any other reason. Goals and dreams weren't part of her vocabulary and even if they were, where was she going in her current debilitated state? Sometimes their fights became physical; my mother was usually the first to strike. This would either lead to a raucous romp in bed, as if I didn't exist—*ugh, gag me*—or Eddie would storm out the door, sometimes absent for days.

I think Mom also suspected him of cheating on her. *No duh!* I wondered the same about her, doubting the probability as she grew more frail, more wasted. I don't know what her mirror was telling her these days, but she didn't like hearing from me that she looked like the walking dead. My pleas for her to quit drinking or seek help would set off a nasty tirade against me, my father, Eddie. I couldn't stand on the sidelines and watch her drink herself to death, so I began to secretly pour her stash of booze down my tub drain—little by little, bottle by bottle—whenever she was asleep or away from the house. Eventually, I emptied an entire bottle at a time. My mother stored her liquor in bookcases, dresser drawers, the linen closet, any place where she thought Eddie wouldn't find it. It's not that Eddie disapproved of her drinking. She didn't want to share.

Dad and Cecile were aware of the situation and though they

had two preschoolers of their own, they repeatedly reminded me that I was welcome to move in at any time. My father and I both knew that wasn't going to happen without a major battle. Besides, I had to admit that I dreaded what would happen if I abandoned her.

Guardian by night and high school student by day, I lived in two different worlds. I made sure that I was a model student so that school authorities had no reason to contact my mother and I surely didn't want her contacting them. To avoid going home any earlier than necessary, I signed up for several extra-curricular activities and soon made new friends, but none that I confided in. How could I explain my mother to anyone? Most of the girls I met lived in modest homes with mothers who worked or did their own housework and didn't consume copious amounts of alcohol. Though I was often a guest in their homes, I never returned the favor. These same mothers would want to meet my own if their daughters came for a visit. That wasn't going to happen, if I could prevent it.

I was contemplating whether or not to let Uncle Gary know what was happening to my mother when an incident occurred which decided the matter for me. On a late Thursday afternoon in April, I came through the front door and was met by Anna, our housekeeper. She stood dressed in her hat and coat, ready for an early departure.

"Your mother's gone over the edge! I can't reason with her and she's frightening me."

"What's going on?"

"She's searching every cupboard for her liquor and screaming at me. She thinks I've stolen it! I don't drink that poison."

"Anna, I know it wasn't you."

"You'd better call someone. She's going crazy!"

After she'd gone, I cautiously approached the kitchen where Mom was slamming about. When she spotted me, she screeched, "Where's that thieving hag? She'll never get another job after I'm done with her."

My mother's hands were shaking uncontrollably as she brought a cigarette to her mouth. Unable to steady her hands enough to light it, she tossed it into the garbage disposal.

I was shaking, too, as I confessed, "Mom, it wasn't Anna. I poured out your liquor."

"Don't lie for her, Samantha."

I stepped forward, trying to swallow my fear. "Mom, Mom, you're sick. You need help. I've been worried so I ..."

The slap came so suddenly and so hard that I tumbled backwards, falling against the corner of the tile countertop. I reached up to feel my lip bleeding.

"You don't tell me what I need, you lying slut! I know you've been waggling your sweet little behind in front of Eddie, too!"

I was horrified at the accusation. "Mom, you don't know what you're saying!"

The second slap caught me in the right eye. As I fled the kitchen, I heard the sound of breaking glass. I ran upstairs to my room and shoved my desk in front of the door. Her vulgar shrieks echoed from below as I dialed Uncle Gary's work number. While I waited for him to come to the phone, I heard what sounded like an entire shelf of glassware being thrown around the kitchen, followed by a painful scream. I dropped the phone and ran back downstairs to find my mother sprawled on the floor in the midst of broken shards of glass. Blood was streaming from her face.

I picked up the kitchen phone to begin dialing 9-1-1 without realizing that I hadn't hung up after the previous call until I heard my uncle's voice shouting from the receiver, "Sam, Sam, are you there?"

"Uncle Gary! Mom's hurt. She's bleeding. I think she needs an ambulance."

"Okay, call the paramedics, but don't let them take her anywhere till I get there. I'm on my way, Sam."

A Toronto police officer was the first to ring the doorbell within five minutes of my call, the paramedics shortly after that. One of the paramedics inspected my lip and my eye while the officer asked me how I'd been injured. My mother, who was being examined by the second paramedic, had now regained consciousness, but had to be sedated so that she wouldn't resist the aid. I was asked how long she'd been in this state and what events had preceded her fall. "She drinks a lot." They didn't respond to this; it was not the first time they'd encountered a drunk.

Uncle Gary came through to the kitchen. "Is my sister going to be alright?"

"The cuts from the glass don't appear to be serious, but we'd like to take her to the hospital to be sure."

"Is it safe to keep her here if I get someone to care for her?"

"Sir, look at your niece's face. It isn't in her best interest to allow her mother to remain here. Besides that, an incident of violence will have to be reported since a minor is involved," stated the officer. I could tell that my uncle wasn't happy with this decision. "Will you be assuming custody for your niece?"

"Yes. Yes, she can stay with me."

"And how about her father? Where is he?"

"Not in the picture, at the moment," was the only information Uncle Gary offered.

The paramedics had finished applying gauze bandages to the several cuts that covered my mother's forehead and arms before lifting her onto the portable gurney. She looked so tiny beneath the white cotton blanket and much more vulnerable than just a short hour ago. My uncle hugged me while she was loaded into the ambulance. We gathered up our coats to follow in his pickup.

Mom refused the detoxification treatment recommended by the hospital staff, but Gary said he'd urge her to enroll in a private program near the home of my grandparents. After the situation was explained to both Eddie and my father, it was agreed that I'd spend the next few weeks with Uncle Gary.

Since the slap to my eye left me with a conspicuous shiner, Uncle Gary kept me under wraps at his home until I healed. He drove to my school to explain that there'd been a family emergency and that I'd be absent for several days. My teachers gathered assignments for me which were sent back with him.

Uncle Gary's townhouse spoke home in every detail of décor. A large, floor-to-ceiling bay window faced the street and brightened the cozy parlor. The sofa and chairs, upholstered in white, stood out against the walls of persimmon. Parquet flooring continued on through the dining room until it met the terracotta tile in the kitchen which overlooked the garden awaiting Spring planting. Upstairs there were three bedrooms, one of which would be mine for an entire month. Every afternoon, the guest retreat welcomed me with its sun-drenched, butter-yellow walls and fern-green accessories. This house of color stood in stark contrast to Eddie's with its nude tones of apathy.

Throughout Uncle Gary's home, paintings and photographs were tastefully displayed. The majority of the photos captured scenes of the River, often including Jeff and Clive in the forefront.

"Do they come to visit a lot?" I asked.

"Who?"

"Clive and his father."

"Ah, mostly during the winter months."

"So that's why you have the piano."

"How do you know that I don't play?"

"Well, I've been here for three days and haven't seen you open the keyboard cover, but there is sheet music on the stand in front of that cello," I pointed to the honey-colored wooden instrument leaning against the wall in the corner near the bay windows.

"Quite the detective, aren't you?" He set a tray of sandwiches down on the coffee table which sat in front of a woodstove inserted into the fireplace.

"I notice things, I guess."

"Like what?"

I hesitated, feeling myself blush. I wasn't sure how to continue, but Uncle Gary appeared to sense that I wanted to raise a forbidden subject.

"Samantha? Did you want to tell me something?"

"It's none of my business."

"Sam, what are you trying to say?"

"I don't want another black eye."

Uncle Gary laughed. "I can't remember the last time I hit anyone. Come on, out with it."

"It looks like Jeff usually stays in your room whenever you two are together."

Uncle Gary sat back against the cushion in his chair and sighed, looking up at the barnwood rafters lining the ceiling overhead. "I knew you were smart. You do know that I'm gay, right?"

I nodded. "At first, I wasn't sure, but I caught you two hugging each other when we were up at the cottage."

"Did you talk to Clive about it?"

"I didn't know how to bring it up. How's he feel about it?"

"Clive has grown up with us. He understands."

"But what about Clive's mother?"

"What do you mean?"

"Well, Jeff was married once, right?"

"Yes."

"And now he loves you."

Uncle Gary let out a hearty laugh before he answered. "It happens, Sam, especially given how homosexuals are treated. Some of us try to act out what others see as normal behavior for a while, possibly for a lifetime, even if it doesn't feel normal to us."

"Is that why Clive doesn't talk about it?"

"Probably, but you should ask him. I do know that Jeff has stressed to him that our relationship shouldn't leak out into their small, insular community. Given past experiences, Jeff doesn't want to expose himself or Clive to the harassment of intolerant minds.

"So, is Clive's mother really dead?"

"Yes. She was killed when the car she was driving slid under the back end of a tractor trailer on the Thruway. Any more questions?"

"Just one. Why didn't my mother ever mention to me that you're gay?"

"Probably because she won't even talk about it with me. We've always led separate lives, at least, until now. I've never talked about Jeff or Clive with her, either."

"Neither have I. Besides, you asked me not to, remember? And I don't talk about Clive with her because I don't want her sticking her nose in and ruining our friendship." I impulsively bounced up off the sofa then, to give my uncle a tight hug, nearly falling into the chair with him. "I'm so glad you've come into my life," I said, choking back my tears.

Jeff and Clive did show up that weekend. When he saw my bruised eye, Jeff's reserved facade melted and he gently embraced me, whispering, "I'm sorry, Sam," as if he understood what I'd been through. I had the distinct impression that Gary had filled them in on the recent events, including our discussion of his relationship with the man who now appeared less reticent about showing his feelings.

"So, now you know why my father has stayed single," said Clive when we were left alone to wash up the dinner dishes.

"I suspected, but I didn't know if you wanted me to know. I guess I thought my uncle and Jeff might want it kept secret."

"A lot of people don't understand. You hear how kids talk about it. It doesn't bother you?"

"Clive, my mother's a crazy alcoholic and my stepfather is a con man. I've felt more love being with the three of you than I ever have in my own home." That was the first time Clive kissed me—a sweet, spontaneous, short smack on the lips. I tried to pretend it was not a big deal, hoping he'd kiss me again and soon.

Trisha Cox

The first two weeks of my treatment were a journey down a rabbit hole. I was having a tough time distinguishing what was real, other than the vomiting. I was given drugs to calm me down and drugs to prevent convulsions and when I was lucid, I kept thinking about having another drink. A drink would fix everything. I'd feel like myself, again, or at least, the only self I'd known since my early teen years.

After those initial weeks, the fog cleared a bit and I remembered hitting Sam. I'd never struck her before and this was one of the few times in my life when I felt sincere remorse. I wondered if she'd ever trust me again.

Eddie came to visit me twice. The first time, I was in the full fury of withdrawal and he wasn't allowed in to see me. The next time, Day 22, he brought me a lush bouquet of irises and day lilies. I saw genuine pity in his eyes. "Oh, Baby, I hate seeing you like this. You've lost a lot of weight. I bet it's been a nightmare."

"What are you doing here, Eddie?" Eddie didn't do anything kind without an ulterior motive.

"I know things have been rough between us, but I do care about you. You gotta believe that. I want to take you home, Baby, whenever you're ready."

"I have to think about it. I'm not sure we're good for each other."

"Good for each other? You're the *only* good in my life, Baby. Come on. Give me another chance. Let's take a second honeymoon after you check out of this place."

"Like I said, I'll think about it. I need to spend a little time with Sam, first. Have you seen her?"

He spun his excuses. "I've been pretty busy and she's either in school or at your brother's. I don't think he wants me visiting."

After a short stroll through the dining room and out to the enclosed veranda, Eddie kissed me good-bye, and made a show of helping a young female aide hang a plant near the window before he left. She beamed back at him as she asked, "Is this lucky man yours?" It wasn't just the fertilizer in that planter I smelled.

I sipped my coffee slowly and stared out the window. I knew it was time to call Sam to see how bad the damage was.

"Mom? How are you feeling?"

"To be frank, like crap."

"You sound stronger." The inflection in her voice implied a question, perhaps hope, instead of an observation.

"Sam, I called to apologize. I shouldn't have hit you."

"You weren't yourself, Mom. It was the booze."

"I'll make it up to you when I get home."

"Will that be soon?"

"I'll be talking with my doctor tomorrow to see if he'll release me sometime next week."

"Don't push it on my account, Mom. I want you to be well. I'm okay. I'm enjoying Uncle Gary's cooking."

It would be another three weeks before I returned to Toronto. Eddie picked me up from the airport and brought me back to the townhouse. He'd gone all out—set the table with linen and candlelight—and behaved like a perfect gentleman. As soon as I sat down, I wanted a drink. Just being in his house made me want to scream. It was like being locked in the tomb of a marriage gone to dust. I needed to get out, but for Samantha's sake, I swallowed my anxiety that evening with a club soda and a tranquilizer while Eddie poured himself a glass of wine.

"Eddie, I'm worn out. I'm going to sleep in the guest room tonight."

"Sure, sure, Baby. We're going to get you better. How about I take you shopping tomorrow?"

Meaning, how about we go spend some of my money instead of his? "I'll probably sleep in a bit. I'll let you know when I feel like going out."

That didn't stop him from disappearing for the evening, leaving me to watch some mind-numbing TV while trying not to think about the half-consumed bottle of wine he'd left behind. Sam would be home the next afternoon and I needed to be sober.

Gary Stanton

My sister was difficult to love. Not sure I ever did. She was selfish. She was a master manipulator. And, she was a liar most likely by the time she'd learned to speak in full sentences, a by-product of parental neglect. How else could she get what she wanted when she wanted it in a household where the interaction between parent and child lasted no longer than a transaction with a bank teller? Her addiction problems had deep roots. But I was more concerned about Samantha. I'd become very fond of her and worried that my sister would take Sam down with her.

Jeff's family had been dysfunctional, too. Probably another reason we understood each other so well. He'd grown up in a tumultuous home where his domineering stepmother had favored her one biological child over him and his younger sister. They'd been left in her care after the untimely death of his father when Jeff was just seventeen. A year later, he enlisted in the military, leaving his sister to fend for herself. She ran away from home and Jeff never heard from her again. After being discharged from service, he took a job with the Border Patrol and moved to Watertown where he met Clive's mother. Shortly after her death, Jeff and his infant son moved to Clayton.

I think both of us were looking for a family, so we became an island family, away from the conventions and judging eyes of the mainland. The cottage was our refuge. The rhythms of the River massaged away the stress from the work week and numbed our worries. Hours passed by in a leisurely pace, but at the same time, our weekends together were too brief.

Eventually, Jeff relaxed around Samantha. He knew that Tar Island was her safe haven, too. The day before Trish was due to come home from her rehab, he brought Clive to Toronto for a visit.

It had been six weeks since Sam had seen her mother.

"Gary, how do you feel about her going back to your sister? I mean, how do you know Trisha won't go off the deep end again?"

"What choice do I have? I'm not her legal guardian."

"That guy your sister married is a snake."

"You think so?"

"Why isn't Sam living with her own father?"

"That battle's already been fought. My sister isn't giving up control; it would be like admitting defeat."

I didn't sleep well that night. I doubt Sam did, either. On the drive back to Eddie's house, she barely said a word. "You okay? Nervous?"

She nodded. "I never know what I'm in for. I hope she's still asleep when I get there."

"We'll go in together."

Sam hugged Spike, who sat between us, then looked up at me. "I wish she hadn't forced my father out. He would've stayed, you know, if she'd been good to him."

"Would you rather live with him?"

"Yes and no. He's got a new family. Mom doesn't have anyone."

"She's got Eddie." I shouldn't have said it.

"He's slime! Mom shouldn't have married him."

"She probably knows that. Give it time. She'll leave him."

"And then what? Back to New York? Back to her looking for another man?"

"Maybe, but would it be so bad if you moved back to New York? You've got friends there, a school you like, and grandparents. It's okay to do what's right for you, Sam."

She quieted down, becoming less agitated. "But when would I see you?" She wiped away a tear.

"And when would you see Clive?"

Samantha started to sob. I pulled the truck onto a side street, then over to the shoulder of the road and kept the engine running while I reached around Spike to hug her to me. "I hate my life, Uncle Gary!"

"I wish I could fix it for you. I could ask your mother if you could stay with me a while longer."

"No, no," she choked. "That isn't fair to you. Maybe you're right. I should move in with Dad, but who would take care of Mom?"

"Okay, let me do this. I'll try to get her to see that she needs to leave Eddie or let you move back to Manhattan, for your sake. And don't worry, you can still vacation with us at the River or I'll bring Clive down to the city."

She fell into my arms again, sobbing loudly. "I love you so much, Uncle Gary."

"I know. I love you, too, Honey."

Jason Larabie

It was obvious that Robbie and Jonesy had had some kind of falling out after the pantsing incident, but most of us figured it was because Jonesy was the only one saddled with the blame. He became pretty much a loner afterwards and didn't show up for school functions for the rest of that year. I'd seen him working at the local grocery store, though. That didn't mean we'd be spared any future run-ins with Robbie, especially since his athletic season had ended, leaving him with plenty of time on his hands for mischief. Clive didn't say much about the incident, but I noticed a change in him. He was bulking up. "Dude, look at those muscles? What's your secret?" I gave him a friendly punch in the biceps.

He smiled. "I've been doing some weight training with Hettie's brother."

"You mean, Josh? Think he'd let me join in?"

"I can ask him."

I can probably thank my mother's side of the family for the fact that I was barely five-foot seven inches and weighing in at only a buck thirty. Most of my free time was strummed away on my cello or more recently, my electric guitar. I had visions of fame, or at the very least, being a professional musician and I figured that playing music would impress the girls. Maybe muscles would do the same while giving the old ego a boost. I made the false assumption that Clive had similar goals.

Spring is a short season in this neck of the woods. April would thaw out the last of the frozen riverbanks and May would spruce them up with blooms of color. I was busy with school, orchestra rehearsals, and the chores my father assigned. To prepare for another season of boaters and vacationers, my brothers and I were expected to help out at the marina. Memorial Day weekend was a hectic one for the business, but each of us was allowed one afternoon off and I was looking forward to time on the River with my friend.

"Are you going over to your cottage this weekend, Clive?"

"My dad's got to work on the holiday, so we'll be coming back Sunday night as usual."

"Awesome! Why don't you come boating with me, then? We could ask Hettie to come along, too." I was secretly infatuated with Hettie but realized that she only had eyes for Clive.

"I've got to practice in the morning."

"That works for me. I'll pick you up at the town dock around noon. You going to ask Hettie or should I?"

He smiled. I think Clive knew how I felt about Hettie. He patted me on the back and said, "You ask her. You're the cruise director."

On Monday, I boated over to the pier in my runabout, the *Spit in the Wind*, to pick up Clive and Hettie. Mom had made sure the boat cooler was stocked with plenty for us to eat. My father, in the meantime, had given us a full tank of gas and orders to return by 4:00. This was one of the busiest weekends of the year when people drank too much and accidents happened both on and off the river. By midday, heavy boat traffic had churned up the waters beneath a clear blue sky. Private yachts, center-consoled fishing rigs, sailboats, and noisy high performance boats flew by as we headed downriver. A few brave souls in swimsuits crashed about on jet skis in the ice-cold channel. We laughed when Hettie was doused by a spray of water as the *Spit* smacked down hard over the crests of the waves on the choppy surface.

I eased back on the throttle as we neared Rock Island. Its mid-nineteenth century lighthouse was no longer in service, but it was still a popular spot for recreational boaters and site-seers. As Clive swung the anchor overboard, I noticed he wasn't wearing his gloves. The skin of his fingertips showed no signs of the raw, chapped ugliness he'd tried to hide from his classmates. Hettie, who had also noticed, looked over at me and nodded before peeling off her bulky sweatshirt. I felt my breathing seize up as she bent over in a tropical-patterned orange bikini top to pull a tube of sunscreen from her backpack.

She tossed it to Clive. "Can you put some on my back?"

Without hesitating, Clive pitched the lotion to me. "My hands are cold. You take care of it, Jason."

Just the thought of touching Hettie elevated my internal temperature to the liquefy level. I could feel heat spreading from my flip-flops up through my ball cap, turning every inch of my skin a deep red and pouring sweat into my fingers. Hettie stuck out her tongue at Clive and said, "Come on, Jason. I'm not going to bite." *Be still my heart.* I spread thick globs of lotion over her smooth, unblemished skin, hoping that she couldn't feel how clammy my hands were. I was too nervous to rub the cream in until it vanished and as a result, Hettie basked in the sun unaware of the huge, visible smears of white sunscreen finger-painted up and down her back.

I broke out the lunch and we settled down in the aft of the boat to eat. Nothing like being out on the water to make me hungry. We watched as a cargo freighter passed by and carved a fat, undulating wake that shoved the *Spit* into a rock 'n roll carnival ride. Hettie laughed as she raised both hands in the air. "Whee-ee!" The

American channel is deep, but narrow. Cargo ships from the Atlantic Ocean travel upriver on their way to Lake Ontario and into the other Great Lakes. It takes experienced pilots to navigate the passageway, especially when two freighters are passing each other.

"Oh-oh, here comes another one." I pointed downriver to a Dutch vessel headed our way. Suddenly, two jet skis, one following the other, roared out from behind the ship in our direction, then sharply turned about to jump the wake. We watched as both skiers jumped back and forth a few more times before steering directly at us again.

"What are they doing?" yelled Hettie.

"Showing off."

"It's Robbie Barrett," said Clive. "Who's that with him?"

"No idea," we both answered.

Robbie and his follower swished in closer to us and began circling the boat. "Should I pull up the anchor?" asked Hettie nervously.

"No! Don't touch it!" Clive hollered over the roar of the machines.

"Hey, back off," I commanded.

Robbie veered closer to the *Spit* cutting his engine. His companion followed suit on the opposite side of the boat. "Chives, what are you doing out in the bright sun? Aren't you worried your pretty little hands will get sunburned?"

"Robbie, don't you have something better to do than track me down on a holiday?"

"Not at the moment. I'm chasing freighters with my cousin, here. Brian, meet Chives." Brian didn't respond.

Hettie pulled her sweatshirt back on. "Aw, you're not going to hide those beauties from me, are you?" he chided.

"Shut up and crawl back under your rock," she answered.

Robbie grabbed hold of the anchor line. "Maybe I'll take you guys for a ride."

"Not a good idea," said Clive as he grabbed a paddle from the floor of the boat.

"What are you going to do? Swat me with a paddle? Or, maybe you're going to tell your buddies to gang up on me again."

"What are you talking about?"

Robbie looked at Hettie and said, "Ask your girlfriend."

I reached into the toolbox in the front of the boat and pulled out my father's fillet knife. "Let go of the rope, Robbie."

Brian spoke up. "Yeah, let's go. I want to head back to the Bay."

Robbie leaned toward the *Spit,* staring directly at me. "Don't go threatening me, boy. You don't know what you're dealing with."

"If you don't let go of the rope, I'll simply cut it loose, you horse's ass."

"I'm out of here," said Brian as he started up his jet ski, swirled around the *Spit* and headed back downriver.

Looking at Clive, Robbie threw out the last word, "Someday." He dropped the rope, switched on the engine and tore off after his cousin.

"I'm so sick of his crap!" I yelled.

"He's out of control," said Hettie as she crossed her arms over her chest, "and he gives me the creeps."

Clive dropped the paddle and looked at Hettie. "What did he mean, my buddies would 'gang up on him again?'"

Hettie bit her lip and looked away. He tugged on her arm till she faced him. "Tell me."

"I hate how Robbie humiliates you. You haven't done anything to provoke him, but you never fight back. After the pep rally, my brothers and I talked about it at home. That's all I know, honestly."

"I don't like it either, Clive. At least, Jonesy seems to be out of the picture, but Robbie enjoys being a bully."

"I can take care of myself. He's mostly talk."

"Have you told your father about any of this?" asked Hettie.

"A little. He doesn't want me adding fuel to the fire."

"What if the fire spreads?" I asked.

"I know you're trying to help, but don't. I've got bigger things to focus on."

Hettie shook her head at me, but let the subject drop. Clive pulled up anchor as I started up the engine. "I'll take you for a ride through the Lake of the Isles before we have to head back. Settle in." Hettie, irritated with Clive, took the front seat next to me while he sat astern. I dared to reach over and pat her knee in sympathy.

Josh Voss

My family always throws a big potluck picnic on Memorial Day in our backyard. Dad grills up burgers and sausages and everybody else brings the deviled eggs, chips, dips, desserts, and more than enough potato and macaroni salads. Clive showed up just after the friendly, but seriously competitive volleyball game. He filled a plate and pulled up a lawn chair next to me. Seemed odd that he didn't look for Hettie first.

"Dang! You must be hungry," I said. "I've never seen you eat so much."

"Must be the fresh air."

"And?"

"Oh, and the great workouts I do with my coach."

"That's what I like to hear."

Clive quietly chomped on his burger for a few more bites before saying, "We ran into Robbie Barrett today, out on the River."

"So?"

"He said something strange."

"That's not unusual."

"No, I mean he implied that I'd sent a couple of my friends after him."

"Did you?"

"I don't have those kinds of friends, that I know of. That is, not unless *you* know what he's talking about."

"What makes you think I'd know anything about it?"

"He told me to ask Hettie about it."

I put down my fork and looked him in the eye, ignoring his

deduction. "Has he been bothering Hettie?" The mention of her name was like bouncing back my sister's sonar ping; she immediately closed in on us.

"Are you two talking about me?"

"Did you have a run-in with Robbie today?"

"Jason took us out in his boat and we were anchored off Rock Island when he and his cousin showed up on jet skis and started buzzing around us. Then Robbie grabbed hold of the anchor line. Jason took care of him, though." She said the last part with a bit of a snit in her tone, but didn't even glance at Clive. I got the feeling she was disappointed in him.

"Clive, how do you plan to get this monkey off your back?"

"Are you suggesting I beat him up? Or, maybe get some friends to do the job for me?"

"Maybe we need to be smarter."

"What do you mean?" asked Hettie.

"Something like giving him enough rope."

Clive didn't look pleased. "Just leave it alone, will you? I think it bothers the rest of you more than it bothers me. I've got enough pressure on me right now."

Hettie looked apologetic, then. "Okay, you've got a point."

After Clive's father picked him up, Hettie and I started in on our cleanup chores. She hadn't dropped the bone, though, and raised the issue again. "What did you do, Josh? Did you threaten Robbie?"

"That's on a need-to-know basis only, Sis."

"Don't pull that military stuff with me. I don't want you making matters worse for Clive."

"I'm just watching his back."

"You two cleaning up or arguing?" my father called out.

"We're talking about Clive. Robbie Barrett is still bullying him and G. I. Josh wants to do something about it."

"Stay out of it, son. You have enough on your plate. And no pun intended," he remarked as he eyed the trash bag full of paper plates I was about to cram into the trash bin.

"Dad, does Clive talk to you about Robbie?" Hettie asked. My father finished scraping grease off the grill with a brush, closed the lid and pulled the rain cover over it. "You know that's off limits. I don't divulge information entrusted to me by my patients. In fact, I'm not sure I'm comfortable listening to you discuss him."

"Then tell us how to get Robbie to stay away from Clive."

"You won't like my suggestions."

"Watch out, Hettie. He's going to tell you that you and Robbie should exchange friendship bracelets." She landed a sharp punch into my bicep.

"No way! You can't tell me you would want your only daughter hanging around Robbie Barrett!"

Fright instantly transformed my father's calm veneer; he was speechless. Hettie and I busted out laughing until he'd regained his composure. "All I can say is that some problems take years to correct. It's possible for wild kids to grow up to be responsible adults. People can change."

"I'm not sure I'll live *that* long," I said.

Jason Larabie

On the following Saturday, Hettie unexpectedly showed up at our marina where I was manning the gas pumps. "What are you doing all the way over here on your bike?"

She leaned it against the wall of the shop and walked out to me. "I need to talk to you about Clive."

A pang of disappointment flashed through me, quickly replaced by alarm. "Has something happened to him?"

She looked out over the water. "Not yet, but I don't trust Robbie. He's out to get Clive."

I put a hand on her shoulder bending to look into her eyes which were clouded with tears. "Hettie, Robbie is just a lot of talk, maybe some push, but he's never really hurt anyone. Besides, Clive can take care of himself if he needs to."

We walked out to the end of the dock, away from the men going in and out of the shop for parts and supplies. "I'm not so sure. You saw him out there. You were the one who got Robbie to back off."

Feeling proud, I confessed, "What you and Robbie didn't know is that my old fillet knife is about as dull as my thumb."

She laughed and wiped her eyes. "I want to go talk to his father, but I've never met him."

"Are you asking me to go there with you?"

She nodded.

"I'm not sure Clive will like that. Besides, he'll most likely be there if his father's home."

"Not if one of us makes sure Clive has somewhere else to be."

"Oh, so that's it. I'm part of a conspiracy. Tell me which part."

"Like I said, I don't know Mr. Tierney so I'd be pretty uncomfortable meeting him for the first time and telling him what's been going on. He knows you're Clive's best friend, though, so maybe we could go together? You know, like when Clive's at my house working out with Josh?"

I could tell she'd been whittling away at this plan for the past few days till it took shape. "Great! I get to be the messenger. Hope I don't get shot."

"For sure, Mr. Tierney knows who Robbie is since he lives right across the street from him and he probably knows what happened at the pep rally. I just think he needs to know that it's not over."

"How do you know Clive hasn't already told him that?"

She gave me that girlie, teary-eyed face again, melting my resistance. "I'm really scared, Jason. I just have this bad feeling that Robbie's going to do something reckless, something that will hurt Clive." I moved closer and put my arms around her. She didn't resist. She smelled like honey mixed with a cool, Spring breeze. I buckled.

"Okay. Okay. While Clive is at your place on Monday evening, I'll play Paul Revere for you."

"Not for me. For Clive."

"Oh, right. Where do we meet up?"

"Clive works out with my brother between seven and eight, so I'm going to tell my parents that I need to go over to Darcy's after dinner to work on a project for school. Instead, I'll meet you at the corner of his street around 7:15. We have to be out of there before Clive gets back to his house."

Just then, a boat pulled up to the pumps and I went over to gas it up. Hettie hung around for a bit longer until the traffic picked up and I got busier. "I'd better get home. Thanks for the help, Jason."

"Nothing to thank me for, yet. I'll expect something in return, though."

"Like what?"

"How about going fishing with me tomorrow?"

"It's Sunday. I've got to go to church in the morning with my family."

I didn't want the opportunity to slip off the hook, so I proposed another option. "I have to work most of the afternoon. How about we go kayaking after that?"

She smiled and said, "It's a deal."

Just before she hopped on her bike, I called out, "And wear that bikini top!" She turned and stuck out her tongue. "Or not," I laughed.

I didn't like the idea of going behind Clive's back. He'd been crystal clear about Hettie and me staying out of this business with Robbie and now we were going to tell his dad all about it. Most times, I only saw Mr. Tierney when he picked up Clive at my house or after a school event, but occasionally he'd taken Clive and me out for pizza to reciprocate for all the times Clive had eaten with my family. He liked hearing what went on at school. He told me a couple of stories about Clive when he was first learning to play the piano and I told him that I wanted to be a professional musician, too.

"I hope you're planning on college first. Go while you're young. I should've used my G. I. tuition benefits to get a degree, but I had a young son and needed to work."

"You could still go to school, Dad. It's not too late."

"Probably, but things are good. Working for the Border Patrol is a decent job."

I asked him how many people he'd arrested.

"I don't count and unfortunately, it's a job that's never done. Some people have to be locked up to keep others safe."

"I'd like to see Robbie get some of that," I said.

"I think he's got his own bag of troubles," was all Mr. Tierney had said on that subject, but that was well before things had reached the boiling point.

I agreed with Hettie that something needed to be done about Robbie, but I didn't think the adults were going to take effective action. Telling Clive's father seemed like something a six year-old might do, tattle on the brat in the neighborhood. It hadn't worked in the past. What could Mr. Tierney do about it? If he talked to Robbie's parents, I doubted that Robbie's attitude would be adjusted for the better. Nevertheless, the damsel in distress had called and I was willing to give Hettie moral support or just about anything else she asked for.

Hettie was already at the corner of Marion Street on Monday evening when I arrived, but she wasn't alone. Robbie Barrett was perched on the seat of her bike, riding in the street while Hettie ran along the sidewalk. "Get off that, you jackass!" Robbie continued to ignore her, steering in and out of driveways, popping a wheelie or two. I pedaled faster, passing by Hettie and pulling alongside of Robbie.

"You heard her, get off the bike!"

He ignored me, turning in the direction of his house.

I rode faster, catching up. "Stealing bikes from girls, now, Robbie?"

He stopped abruptly, forcing me to veer out of the way. Turning around, he headed back toward Hettie, but passed her by while standing up on the pedals to move faster. Hettie threw up her arms and stopped chasing him. I slowed down.

"You alright?"

She nodded and said, "Let him go. If we don't chase him, he'll either have to come back with the bike or he'll ditch it somewhere."

"What do you want to do, then? Go ahead with the plan?"

"Definitely. I don't want to waste any more time. Clive will be heading home soon."

I dismounted and walked my bike alongside Hettie.

"He showed up while I was waiting for you, probably on his way home. I couldn't get him to go away and I told him I was waiting for someone. I think he thought I was waiting for Clive."

"Maybe this isn't a good idea, Hettie. We might only make things worse."

"Things are worse, Jason!"

Just then, we heard his loud voice. "Aw, look at the cute couple. Does Clive know you're cheating on him, Hettie?"

Hettie turned beet red. I didn't know if the comment simply embarrassed her or if there might be a whiff of truth in it.

"Are you two going over to Clive's to tell him all about it?"

I threw my bike down and grabbed the handlebars of Hettie's bike. "No, we were going to wait at your house till you came back with this."

"You keep away from my place!" he hissed, leaning into me.

"Or what? I'm sure your mother will want to know why we're waiting for you."

Robbie glared back at me, then looked at Hettie. "Your tire's flat. Better get your boyfriend to fill it up for you." Robbie leapt from the bike and shoved it into me before huffing off to his house with his middle finger raised in the air.

I checked my watch. "Hettie, it's 7:35. Do you think we still have enough time to talk to Clive's father?"

Hettie's hands shook as she took hold of the handlebars of her bike. "I can't do it, now." Her eyes filled with tears. "Thanks for ..." Her lips began to quiver as she looked down at the deflated tire.

"Here, you ride my bike and I'll walk yours down to the gas

station to use the air pump." I bought a soda for her after filling the tire and we sat for a bit on the curb. The sun had gone down and the streetlights had come on.

"We'd better get going. I've got a longer ride than you do. Guess this was a dumb idea," Hettie said.

"Not dumb. You had good intentions, but I don't think Clive would have thanked us for it."

Hettie Voss

When Jason first pulled out that fillet knife, I was terrified that he was about to do something reckless. That whole boating incident with Robbie left me with the foreboding sense that something more sinister than high school bully pranks was going on. What reason did he have to hate Clive? Or, was he more mentally unstable than any of us realized? I contemplated discussing what happened out on the water with my father, but was worried that I'd be barred from future outings with Clive or Jason. I doubted that would be the case if I were a son, instead of a daughter. Do most fathers assume their sons can take care of themselves whereas their daughters need taking care of? Anyway, this wasn't about me.

I couldn't go back to Ms. Harvey, either. So far, any school discipline actions against Robbie had proven useless. I wouldn't put it past him if he'd been the one to stage the bomb scare or if he'd manipulated Jonesy into doing the dirty work. He was that kind of street smart and now he'd stepped up his bullying by threatening Clive off-campus; nothing the school officials could do about that. Telling Clive's father was out, too. *Cuts on his legs?* After sticking my nose into that business, I was uncomfortable with the idea of showing up on Mr. Tierney's doorstep to give him the latest news. I also wanted to keep my brothers out of this since their previous preemptive strike had only fueled Robbie's motivation to harass Clive. He wanted revenge. Seems like it all came back to Clive to stand up for himself, but if he ever did, what would the outcome be?

My worry about his well-being conflicted with my exasperation about our stagnant relationship. It seemed like I was spending more time and thought on it than Clive. Maybe his head was just too far under the lid of his piano. I decided to put him to a test.

This time of year, Clive spent the weekends with his father over on Tar Island. That meant he seldom attended any Friday night or Saturday school functions unless the orchestra was involved. Clive was still working out with Josh, though he'd missed a couple of sessions right after the rally. Outside of class, I saw him at lunch or caught him in the hallway, but we hadn't had an official date, yet, and there'd been no physical advances on his part. It was time to find out where he stood and if he was interested in being more than friends. The Final Fling dance was scheduled for a Friday night and I wasn't going to wait any longer to see if Clive would ask me to go with him. Deciding not to risk the possibility of public rejection, whether in front of my classmates or my family, I chose the phone as the least uncomfortable approach. I called his house around 4:30 in the afternoon, but when the answering machine came on with his father's greeting, I hung up, then redialed. This time, I left a brief message with no details.

"Clive, please call me back. I need to ask you something."

I waited and waited and waited, barely able to concentrate on anything else. I'd purposely chosen a day when Clive was not expected for his session with Josh, again to avoid any humiliation. No mention was made of the phone call in school the next day until dismissal time when I stopped at his locker.

"Did you get my phone message last night?"

"No, why?"

"Well, I called."

Clive finished packing up his backpack, closed his locker door and latched the combination lock. "Why didn't you say something earlier?"

I hesitated and cleared my throat. *Was this what guys went through to get a date? I always thought they held all the cards.* My heart was pounding so hard I wondered if Clive could hear it. As we headed for the exit, I knew it was now or never. "I wanted to ask you something in private."

"I told you I didn't want to talk about it."

"No, this isn't about you. I mean it is, but … I don't know how to do this." I was about to bolt.

"Then, just spit it out. The buses are lined up."

"Will you take me to the Fling on Friday night?"

He looked like he was about to laugh. I wanted to run, but then the dimples showed up.

"You want to go to a dance?"

Well, duh! I could feel my face burning, but I couldn't speak. I looked toward the door and saw that the row of buses had begun to move forward. Clive and I hurried out the exit.

"I don't know. I'll have to talk to my dad."

We parted and ran to catch our buses before they pulled away from the curb.

As soon as I arrived home, I ran past my brother, Stuart, to the front door and flew up the stairs to my room, closing the door behind me. The tears I'd held back on the ride home were now streaming down my cheeks. I threw myself face down on the bed to stifle my sobs in the pillow until anger crept in to dry my tears. My thoughts were spinning and I couldn't lie still a minute longer. I picked up the loose clothing that was scattered about my room and tossed it into a laundry basket. I tore off the bedspread to tuck in the blankets and sheets. *Why was I even interested in Clive? So what if he was Mr. Gifted Musician; that didn't make him God's gift to women! Neither did his good looks.*

My banging around drew the attention of my mother who knocked on my door before poking her head in.

"What's gotten into you, Hettie?"

I tossed a magazine across the room, bouncing it off the edge of the waste basket. "I'm cleaning up this mess!"

"I can see that. Kind of unusual for the middle of the week."

Nothing got by my mother. She had some kind of mother-daughter ESP allowing her to pick up the scent of a disturbance from a mile away. Perhaps being the only two women in a household of men strengthened the silent signals between us.

"Yeah, well. It'll help me concentrate."

"By the way you're throwing things around, seems more like target practice. Who's the target?"

There it was; her mother's lens had zoomed in on the core. I felt the tears coming again and collapsed on my bed. She sat down beside me. "What happened?"

"I'm so embarrassed, Mom. I don't know how to do this boy-girl thing."

My mother smiled as she said, "Oh, you mean the boyfriend thing?"

"Yeah, but I'm not Jessica or Alicia or one of the popular girls. No one is going to ask me out. I'm more like the kid-sister or tomboy friend."

"You still haven't told me what happened."

"I tried to ask Clive to the Final Fling. I knew he wasn't going to ask me."

My mother didn't respond. I sensed a hint of disapproval.

"You think I shouldn't have asked, right?"

"Not for the reason you might assume. I just know that Clive has a lot going on."

"Oh! I'm so tired of hearing about his music competition!" I pulled away from her and winged a pillow into the closet. "As if the rest of us are mere mortals of servitude."

"I wasn't referring to that."

"What do you ...?" I stopped as soon as I realized what she meant. "Oh, you mean that you don't want me dating one of Dad's patients. That's just great! Should I call him up and tell him that I can't talk to him anymore because my parents think he's nuts?" My anger was reignited.

My mother kept her voice controlled. "I'm just concerned that you're getting overly involved with a boy who may need help that you aren't qualified to give."

BAM! I slammed a book across the room and yelled, "Nice, real nice, Mom. So, I should just dump him and tell him sorry, can't be friends with a psycho!"

"Now, you're over-reacting. All I'm saying is that you shouldn't push him. You two seem to have a very nice friendship. Boys need more time to mature and he might not be ready for a girlfriend."

"You're telling me."

"I'm not saying that you can't go to the dance together; just don't put all your eggs in one basket. There may be someone else out there who has eyes for you."

"I won't hold my breath."

The next morning, Clive came to my locker before the homeroom bell. He didn't waste any time on small talk before bringing up the matter. "Hettie, I can't go to the dance." Reading my look of disappointment, he added, "But thanks for the invite." I hesitated, waiting for him to give a reason, then began to walk away without a word. He caught up to me. "Are you angry?"

How was I supposed to answer that? I didn't want to explain that I felt slighted, felt as if he didn't care, felt that I came last in his book. "So, you can't go, or you don't want to go?"

"We're going over to the cottage. Dad doesn't want to go back and forth across the border or wait in the Saturday morning lines at Customs."

"If I ask, you could probably stay at my house for the weekend."

"I can't do that. We're having company."

Looking for an escape, I suddenly called out to Darcy as she passed by us. "Wait up!" I ran after her like a dog chasing a squirrel. I didn't look back.

I gave Clive the cold shoulder for the remainder of the week. That's probably why he didn't show up at the house to work out with Josh and when my brother asked me about it, I played dumb.

My anger was fueling my suspicion that Clive was hiding something from me. Was he really spending his weekends on Tar Island or was there someone else?

Samantha De Haven

I was barely speaking to my mother and I'm not sure she cared. She was drinking again. She'd never be able to stop as long as she lived with another drinker. I'm sure that her loser socialite friends in Manhattan were also drunks who, just like Mom, hadn't evolved. I think mornings must've been the worst part of the day for my mother and would've induced an instant enema if she hadn't slept through them. How could she bring herself to get up and face another day of nothing? By the time she did put herself together, it was nearly evening. I tried to avoid eating dinner in the same room with her because I couldn't stand to watch her refill a glass while she asked me stupid questions.

"Where were you after school today?"

"Not sleeping. Not drinking." I didn't even try to be polite about it anymore.

"Don't speak to me like that! You need to show respect. I'm your mother."

That's usually when I left the room. *Respect?* What was left to respect? I could've been drinking, smoking dope, doing a lot of stuff that she wouldn't have noticed, but there was no way I was going to allow myself to turn into *her.*

She'd made one major decision, though. Mom had finally agreed to let me move in with my father and Cecile at the end of the school year. For the most part, I was excited to be returning home to my friends and my former high school, but I wasn't sure I'd be any less frustrated with my mother or less worried. I couldn't figure out why she didn't just dump Eddie and move back to Manhattan for good. Like a second divorce was unheard of in her social circle? Yeah, right! Or, maybe Eddie had some kind of hold on my mother.

Did she give him money? She didn't love him; she couldn't. Was she afraid to leave him? Darker thoughts frequently crossed my mind. I worried that my mother had given up on herself.

I was going to miss Uncle Gary and Clive. My uncle had been picking me up almost every Friday night since my mother's return home. Once the final thaw had cleared away the ice of winter, we spent the weekends at the cottage on Tar Island. Heavy spring rains had raised the water level in the River and by mid-June, heat and humidity thickened the air. Weekend boat traffic was heavy. After lunch one Saturday, Clive and I sat on the end of the dock to soak up the sun and dangle our feet in the water.

"I'm moving in with my father after the Fourth of July weekend. Uncle Gary said he could bring you down to the city sometime to visit me, if you want."

"Yeah? Awesome." He looked pensive for a moment. I don't think either one of us wanted to talk about being apart, especially during the summer months. "I've never been to the Big Apple. All our vacations are here. Well, except for trips to Toronto to visit Gary or watch a Blue Jays game."

"You could get tickets to a Yankees game in New York, or the Mets. There's a ton of stuff to do there." We spent the afternoon erasing the reality of the looming separation by laying out different weekend itineraries for Clive's visit. He opened his sketchbook to map out his favorite choices including, the Metropolitan Museum of Art, the Empire State Building, the Hayden Planetarium, and Carnegie Hall.

"I'm going to play there one day," he mused.

"Can you get me a front row seat?" He laughed and I continued in my travel agent voice. "You won't want to miss the new museum that's opening up next year on Ellis Island. My mother's grandparents came through there. My grandfather keeps the family tree up on a wall in his den."

I saw a distinct change in Clive's composure as his eyes returned to the River. He spoke quietly. "Dad won't talk about his family. I hardly know anything at all about my mother."

"Do you know her name?"

"Veronica Wallace. Dad told me they eloped and her parents weren't one bit happy about it. I think she was already pregnant and they didn't like my dad. At least, that's my guess. Otherwise, why would they be upset? I've never met my grandparents."

"I don't know which is worse. Not having much family or not wanting the one you have." Clive reached for my hand then, and gave me a hug.

"Hey, you're not wearing your gloves!"

He smiled at me. "I've been told that I need to be a little less obsessive compulsive. Guess it was kind of crazy to wear them, like carrying around a rabbit's foot or a garlic necklace."

Clive was opening up. We'd arrived at the point where we both felt safe to tell each other the secrets in our lives.

"And don't think I haven't noticed those muscles," I gave his arm a squeeze. "You've been working out! You must be a chick magnet at school."

Clive's face turned pink, but he flexed his bicep for me. Then he leaned down and kissed me tenderly on the lips. "I'm not looking for chicks," he said as he pulled away, while locking his steady gaze on me. I hugged him back and gave him another lingering kiss.

"I'm going to miss you, Clive." We sat quietly in a warm embrace, staring out over the river, afraid to make promises which might be broken.

On Sunday morning, we all rolled out of bed early for an excursion into Kingston, a city in the province of Ontario, where Uncle Gary wanted to sample brunch at some place called, The Bucket in the Well. He had a standing invitation from the chef there for a complimentary meal. The two had been discussing the prospect of opening another restaurant together in Ontario. The steamy air and clouds in the western sky forewarned of a possible thunderstorm, so Jeff snapped the canvas canopy onto the *Escape* for the trip to Rockport where the boat would remain docked for the day. From there, the drive would take about a half-hour.

After parking on a side street, we walked down the hill toward the harbor. Kingston is a small city located where Lake Ontario pours into the St. Lawrence which flows in a northeasterly direction. The city once served as a British military site during conflicts between Great Britain and its former colonies. Like many buildings in the city, The Bucket in the Well was constructed from the native gray limestone, giving it that indestructible, fortified look. We walked through the awning-covered entrance from East King Street into a dimly lit, crowded dining area with wood-paneled walls and beamed ceilings. A potent aroma of eggs, sausage, beef, and potatoes wafted through the room, stimulating our appetites. At Uncle Gary's request, the hostess seated us in a booth near the kitchen. "Please let Chef Jonathan know that Gary Stanton would like to say hello when he has a moment." We'd just begun to browse through the detailed brunch menu when a large man with a loud voice burst forth from the kitchen and bounded over to our table.

"Gary! You're here, at last! I can scarcely believe my eyes. How are you able to get away from work?"

"I keep telling you, it's all about delegation and paying your people well."

"I'm working on it, but I have to find time to sit down with you to get more information."

"I think I'm going to have to drag you over to Tar Island in order to accomplish that."

"So, who are these fellow diners you've brought with you?"

"This is my niece, Samantha, my friend, Jeff, and his son, Clive. Got any recommendations for us?"

"Stay away from the hash. Eat something exotic and expensive." We all laughed at this, but Jonathan continued, "It'll be my pleasure to feed you, compliments of the house. You've certainly fed me enough times."

Our eyes widened larger than our stomachs, prompting us to

order more than we could consume, all except my uncle, that is. Eating for him was not only a pleasure, but a business mission. I had crêpes stuffed with berries and whipped lemon ricotta, while Clive ordered an asparagus and crab omelet with a side of Canadian bacon. Jeff chose a trout dish with eggs Benedict and Uncle Gary went for a hearty sausage tart with a beet and goat cheese salad. When we couldn't swallow another bite, Clive asked if he and I could stroll down to the harbor to walk off the feast while Jeff and Uncle Gary joined Jonathan for a private drink.

We stepped back outside into the sauna-like heat intensified by the absorbent stone walls of the tavern and the concrete sidewalks. Holding hands, we walked along King Street, then turned down Market toward City Hall and the harborfront. A small breeze drifted in from the water, whispering a brief breath into the humid air as we sat down on a park bench to watch some of the smaller sailing craft. A cruise ship the size of a city block was berthed in port just west of the park.

"Where do you think she's going?" I asked.

"Could be headed back out to the Atlantic and down the coast."

"Nothing like a vacation with thousands of strangers. Oh, wait, that would be like a vacation with some of my relatives."

"At least, you have relatives."

I stared at Clive a minute before saying, "That really bothers you, doesn't it?"

"My father doesn't tell family stories. I don't have a family album with photos of Grandma and Grandpa, no sense of who came before me. Do I have my grandfather's hands? My grandmother's talent? My mother's eyes? I mean, I have Dad and Gary, but it just doesn't seem enough. What's it like to have brothers, sisters, cousins, and the whole family tree with roots and limbs? I feel more like the broken branch left behind after a flood washed away the tree."

"You're talking to the wrong person about family trees. Mine has root rot or something. I don't think my mother ever wanted me.

At least, my father's planted in healthier soil."

Clive put his arm around me then. "It has to be better when we're adults, doesn't it? I mean, we'll get to choose the people we bring into our lives."

I was silently analyzing whether or not Clive meant we would do this together, but I was afraid to ask. I knew plans could be interrupted, bonds could be broken. "Thought you wanted to go on tour. How are you going to keep up with friends if you aren't home?"

"Guess I'll just have to make loads of money so I can bring my friends with me."

I wondered if I'd be one of those friends or maybe someone more than a friend. "Your friends will have lives, too, with jobs and families. It might be lonely out there, Clive." I stopped myself from saying more, suddenly worried that I'd scare him off if he thought I was getting too serious about him, but he sidestepped the issue.

"I'm used to being alone, but I need to play. I hear music all the time, in my head. I have to play. It's not really a choice, at this point, so I want to go out and travel while I'm doing it. When I get tired, I'll come back here to the River."

I switched gears to lighten things up, or maybe I was being just the tiniest bit sarcastic. "I know. You could live on a cruise ship and be the nightly show!"

Clive began to tickle me. "You mock me?"

I wormed my way out of his embrace and began to run across the park. While glancing back over my shoulder at Clive, I ran smack into Eddie! Dazed, I stumbled backwards into Clive who'd caught up with me. Eddie stared at both of us. "Eddie! What are you doing here? Is mom with you?"

Eddie hesitated a moment before turning his eyes to me. "No, she's not. I'm on business." A broad-shouldered, tall man in a dark suit stood behind him exhaling a puff of cigarette smoke. He held up a hand to acknowledge me.

"So, who's this?" asked Eddie, nodding in the direction of Clive.

I resented the question. Eddie had earned no points as a stepfather and I didn't want him nosing around in my personal life. I'd been careful not to talk about Clive around him or my mother. While Eddie continued to gawk at him, I mentally clicked through my multiple choice answers, choosing the shortest.

"This is Clive." I glanced over at Clive who looked sideways at me and then back at Eddie with a blank gaze. He'd heard my disparaging critiques of Eddie's character and could sense that this encounter was unwelcomed.

Eddie's curious stare was suddenly interrupted by a fleeting look of alarm. I turned to see Uncle Gary and Jeff approaching. My stepfather quickly recovered and put his pretentious mask back on.

"Hey, Gary."

"Eddie, what brings you here?"

"Just business."

An awkward moment passed before Uncle Gary said, "This is Jeff." Even he sensed the need for simplicity.

Eddie stuck out his hand and gave Jeff's a hearty shake. "Haven't we met before?"

"I don't think so," answered Jeff curtly. A discernible awkward moment passed between the two men.

"Well, we've got to catch the next ferry, so I apologize for not staying to chat." Then, looking at me, he added, "I promised to take your mother out for a nice dinner when I get home. You could join us, Sam."

Not for a second did I believe that Eddie had made such a promise and for sure, his invitation was no more genuine than he was. He was just playing to the crowd. "I've got homework to catch up on."

Eddie smiled at the others. "Always the scholar, this one. See you later, Kid." The four of us watched the two men walk off in the direction of the ferry landing.

Finally, Gary gave me a quick hug and asked, "You okay, Sam? You look a bit nervous."

"He gives me the creeps, Uncle Gary. I just don't trust him."

Clive spoke up, then. "Something about him seems familiar. Maybe I've seen him somewhere."

"Been reading some bookie sheets?" my uncle joked.

Clive looked confused, but I wanted to put Eddie out of my mind, at least for the rest of the day. "Nevermind. You don't want to know." But he did. Clive wanted to know why I was upset. We allowed Uncle Gary and Jeff to get further ahead of us as we sauntered back to the car.

"I don't want Eddie in my business. I don't even want him in my life! And, I certainly don't want him telling my mother anything about you."

"Why not, Sam?"

"She'll start asking me what kind of person you are so she can take charge. She'll want to know if we look right together. She'll want to know about your family." I saw hurt swim into his dark eyes. "I'm sorry, Clive. I didn't mean that your family is something less than what it should be." I hugged him and kissed his cheek. "I just don't want her ruining our ... our friendship."

"So, I'm something to hide?"

I felt myself perspiring, battling off a sense of shame. "Not something, someone! Would you feel better if I told her all about you, all about your father and Gary? She would break us all apart. That's what she's good at!" My voice had risen in volume. Gary and Jeff looked back at us.

"Alright, Sam," he whispered. "Calm down. Just promise me that we won't keep secrets from each other. Sam? "

I nodded silently even though I knew that promises, like secrets, possess the potential for hurt.

Sheriff Cy Froehlich

By the start of the summer season, a curious series of incidents deepened my suspicion that the bomb scare was no high school prank. My officers had been called out to a break-in over at Fineview. A window on the vacant cottage had been broken from the outside, but there were no other signs of damage or stolen property, later verified by the owner. Another call involved suspected arson of a dilapidated barn on a property in LaFargeville. A third call sent us over to Evans Mills to investigate a report of domestic violence, but the location again turned out to be vacant. We began to cross-reference the dates of these calls with reports of smuggling from the Customs and Border Patrol authorities and found that the date of the bomb scare corresponded with an arrest made on the same day. A significant amount of drugs were confiscated from a buyer, but the smuggler hadn't been apprehended. I didn't rule out the possibility that illegal trafficking of goods had taken place on the other dates. After further discussions with representatives from Border Patrol, U. S. Customs, the Coast Guard, the Royal Canadian Mounted Police, and the Ontario Provincial Police, we developed a plan of surveillance to include a River watch when suspicious calls came into the Jefferson County Office.

Smuggling was not new to the River. Back in the days of Prohibition, alcohol was illegally transported into the States by boat. Nowadays, contraband included black-market cigarettes, narcotics, and even human beings. Over 1000 islands in the upper St. Lawrence gave smugglers plenty of hiding places for their goods. People in my line of work are trained to look for something out of the ordinary, but it's been my experience that criminals come in all shapes and sizes. So, what's ordinary?

We knew there had to be a local link to the smugglers, another link in an organized criminal chain of supply. Each of the questionable calls had originated at phone booths at various locations around the county. I put surveillance on the phone booths, hoping the perp would be dumb enough to use the same phone more than once. If we were lucky, we'd find a set of prints attached to a previous record. Real lucky, that is. A phone booth could be smeared in prints, but would contain none from a person who wore gloves. In a rural community with limited resources, tracing numerous prints was no simple task. We had an old-fashioned, homestyle communication advantage, though. A change in someone's habits or bank account could bring unwanted attention. Our ears, as well as our eyes, were open.

John (aka Jack) Voss, Doctor of Psychiatry

Clive was referred to me by the nurse who worked at River High. He was an intelligent introvert who favored fine arts. There was evidence of self-wounding and some obsessive compulsive behavior, both of which I believed to be caused by anxiety and his focus on perfectionism. I explored Clive's relationship with his father, but felt he was holding something back that I'd hoped would come out in a future session. It was startling to discover that he knew next to nothing about any other relatives, including his deceased mother.

In the first consultation with Jeff Tierney, I delicately broached the subject of possible sources of apprehension for Clive. He was taken aback and jumped to a conclusion. "Listen, there's nothing harmful going on in our household, if that's what you're thinking." This reaction wasn't unusual and didn't signify guilt or innocence. I deemed it probable that a Border Patrol agent would be sensitive to an inference of physical abuse.

"Something is upsetting your son, enough to pull out a knife or a razor blade to cut himself. I'm sure I can help him find a better way to cope if I can identify the triggers for his behavior." That brought him up short.

"You're right. I'm sorry. I had no idea about the … about his cuts until the school nurse phoned me. My son is smart, but he thinks too much. He's hard on himself, always has been, but I had no idea that he might be unhappy. I know he worries a lot about his hands and he's had nightmares about injuring them."

"That's a start, anyway. How about his mother? Does he express any grief over her death?"

"He barely knew her. She died when he was an infant."

"Have you told him much about her?" I asked, knowing that he hadn't.

"There's not much to tell. It was a short-lived relationship. Veronica and I knew each other for only a few months before she became pregnant and then, shortly after Clive was born, she was killed in a car accident."

"Clive has mentioned he has no relationship whatsoever with any grandparents."

"Neither do I and it's going to stay that way." Jeff held my gaze, implying this was a dead end, but I wasn't deterred.

"And why is that?"

"A whole lot of bad history, Doctor. None of them has an ounce of goodness in them."

Rather than dig deeper into his own past, I kept the conversation focused on Clive's current environment and let it go for the time being. "Do the two of you socialize much? Entertain guests?"

"My work and Clive's activities don't leave a lot of time for that. In general, Clive spends most of his free time preparing for the piano competition. Otherwise, he's at school or with his friend, Jason, or with your kids."

No smile lit his face or his eyes. Was he the worried parent or hiding something? "And the weekends?"

"We're over on Tar Island. A buddy of mine joins us sometimes."

I didn't respond, letting a minute or so go by. Silence often yields more information when people try to fill the gap in a conversation. Nothing, though. Jeff Tierney was a closed book, for now, but in the end, he demonstrated his concern for his son by scheduling another appointment.

"I appreciate your efforts, Dr. Voss. I'm doing the best I can to be a good father." That statement did little to assure me that Jeff Tierney would bare his soul in the future.

As for my daughter, Hettie, I could tell she was infatuated with this conflicted young man. My wife and I had mixed feelings about it. On the one hand, Clive might come out of his introspective turmoil as he matured into adulthood. On the other hand, he was a complex person who wasn't wired to be easy-going. Neither was Hettie. Connie and I were hoping this was a teenage crush which would be swept away as soon as the new school year began, but even a psychiatrist can be naïve and overlook the impetuous nature of his own daughter.

Josh Voss

"Mom! Mom! It's official." I darted up the front steps with the acceptance letter in my hand and ran straight through the kitchen out to the back porch. I spotted her in the rock garden and leapt out the back door. "I'm in! I've been accepted to Annapolis!"

She stood up slowly, shading her eyes from the sun. "Josh? Oh, Josh! Congratulations Honey. I know this is what you want."

I saw the concern in her face. "Don't worry, Mom. War's not on the horizon. Maybe I'll even go to law school." I knew that wasn't my plan, but I wanted her to be happy for me. "Hey, did you hear that?" I held a hand up to my ear, pretending to hear something. "The doors are opening, Mom." I gave her a big hug, lifting her off her feet to make her laugh. I didn't want to see any tears.

"I know I'm being a baby. You're the first to leave the nest. I'm not sure I'm ready."

"You're going to love visiting Annapolis. All that old architecture, the Chesapeake, the history. Think of all the great photo shoots you can do there." That got a smile out of her. "Hey, can I take your car? I want to go over to the hospital and see if I can find Dad to tell him the news."

"Fine, but you'll have to pick up Hettie from school around 3:30.

She's staying late for a review class."

I was already headed back through the house. "Okay. Will do."

"Don't forget!" she hollered.

I backed the car out, cranked up the radio and rolled down the windows. I let a few loud whoops out the driver's window. "Good-bye, Fishers Landing. Hello, Annapolis! Joshua Voss is headed for the Big World." I'd grown up on a mighty River and now I'd be heading off to adventure on the high seas, a dream come true.

I parked on the street, sprinted up the steps to the main entrance and headed down the hallway to the rear elevators. Dad's office was on the fourth floor in a section overlooking the River. Mrs. Hutchins looked up from the reception desk as I entered the waiting room. "Josh! Haven't seen you in a while. To what do we owe the pleasure?"

"Just stopped in to give my dad some good news."

"Good news, eh? Well, that's a real treat in this office. What's going on?"

Even though the waiting room was empty, I whispered. "I've been accepted into the Naval Academy."

"Joshua Voss! A sailor? Congratulations!"

"A sailor and a pilot, I hope."

"Let me check to see that your father has finished with his conference call." She picked up the phone and I heard her say, "Your son is here to see you, Dr. Voss. May I send him back?" She replaced the receiver and nodded her head as she pointed towards the door to the inner offices. "You know how to get there."

I thanked her and started down the hall. Another psychiatrist and a couple of counselors who weren't medical doctors had offices in this corridor, too. One of them waved at me while talking on the phone. The last door on the right was open and Dad was standing at the file cabinet.

"Josh! What are you doing here? Everything okay?"

I took the letter out of my shirt pocket. "Here it is, Dad. I'm in."

My father took his time reading the letter. I thought I caught a touch of dampness in his eyes when he came around the desk to give me a hug and slap me on the back. "I can't believe eighteen years have gone by."

"You sound like Mom. Don't get all mopey on me, Dad. You know this is what I've been working for. It's going to be fantastic!" I exclaimed.

My father pulled a pen from his pocket protector and walked over to his wall calendar, summoning me. "I want you to write that on this calendar. I want us both to remember what you said, today, at 1500 hours."

I wrote the words in a large sprawl and then Dad launched into a discussion about my savings, supplies I'd need for Plebe Summer, about staying in touch. "Okay, Dad. It's not like I'm going tomorrow. I've got to go pick up Hettie. See you at dinner."

After saying good-bye to Mrs. Hutchins, I jumped back in the car and took off for the high school. When I pulled into the parking circle in front of the building, I scanned the groups of waiting students till I spotted Hettie. Some guy next to her suddenly threw down his backpack and stepped up into Robbie Barrett's face. Things looked like they were about to get ugly. The challenger was outweighed by about sixty pounds and the cocks were circling each other on the sidewalk within an arm's length of a brick wall. Yeah, this wasn't going to be pretty to watch, so I swerved over to the curb and parked. Grabbing the keys from the ignition, I raced over to my sister. Robbie already had Jason Larabie pressed up against the bricks by then.

"Hey, Robbie. Who's your dancing partner?" I knew this would throw him off balance for a minute. Robbie turned to glare at me while Jason slipped out of his way.

"Robbie needs to shut his filthy mouth!" said Hettie. My fists tightened when I saw the angry tears puddling in her eyes.

"Are you picking on girls, now, Robbie? I didn't think that was your style."

"Maybe your friend here ought to put his pants back on, instead of loaning them out to your sister."

I leaned in toward him, just waiting for him to make a move.

"Josh! No!" screamed Hettie. "He's not worth the trouble."

I knew Robbie was itching for the fight, hoping for some payback after what had gone down out there in that canoe. Hettie's voice had caught the attention of others, including a few parents who were waiting to pick up their teenagers. "My sister's right," I said. "You're a zero. Get your pack, Jason. I'll give you a ride home."

"Yeah, later, Fags!" Robbie called from behind our backs.

Jason punched the back of the seat after getting into the car. "I've had it with that clown! I want to belt him in the mouth!"

"I'd like to kick him in the balls!"

"Tell me what happened back there."

"Just the usual bullcrap. Robbie started running his mouth. First, he insinuated that Jason and I were an item, cheating on Clive. We told him to buzz off, so he continued and insinuated that Clive swings both ways, playing both Jason and me."

"He didn't insinuate, Hettie. He used graphic vocabulary to spell it out, loud and clear, for everyone to hear." Jason punched the seat again.

"Take it easy back there," I said. "This is my mom's car."

"I'm sick of him talking trash like that about Clive, about any of us. He's got such a fat mouth! Just like the rest of him, fat!"

"Josh, don't tell Dad about all this. He'll just give us the lecture about sticks and stones or talking to McIntire. When has that ever done any good?"

"Listen, you two have to start using your heads. You're a lot smarter than that numb-nut. I'll think on it, too."

"Oh, no you don't, Joshua. You're not going to pull any more secret ops stuff. It didn't fix the problem last time."

"Well, I'm not putting up with any more of his bullying," Jason added.

We dropped Jason off at his house and on the way home, Hettie opened up about her fear. "This is getting serious, Josh. I'm begging you not to pull anything on Robbie. At some point, someone's going to get hurt."

"Okay, I'll talk to him tomorrow."

"Him? Who do you mean? Clive?"

"Yeah, Clive."

"Clive isn't a fighter and he wants us to butt out. There's got to be a way to stop Robbie without anyone getting beat up."

"Well, until we figure that out, it doesn't hurt to know how to defend yourself." We pulled into the driveway and parked.

"No, Josh. We're not in the military and neither are you, yet."

"Oh, haven't you heard?" I filled her in, but she wasn't impressed.

"Great! Just what we need in the family, a hawk!"

III. Cast Off: to untie the lines which secure a boat to a dock

Hettie Voss

Clive showed up for the first time in over a week to work out with Josh. I didn't bother coming downstairs until I heard him in the living room talking with my brothers.

"A bunch of us are going to camp out on Cedar Island this weekend. You're coming with us. It's going to be another step in your training."

"Watch out, Clive. Josh has gone military. He wants to start his own little boot camp before he gets to Annapolis," said Stuart.

"So, you got accepted? Congratulations!"

"Thanks. I'm really looking forward to it. You can ride over with us in our boat. Make sure you and your sleeping bag are here by 5:30."

"Don't you mean seventeen hundred thirty hours, Admiral?" cracked Stuart.

"I've got to check with my father, first. Sounds good, though."

I walked through to the kitchen without saying hello, poured myself a glass of lemonade and took it out to the back porch where my parents were sitting to escape the heat of the house. "Did you tell Josh and Stuart they could camp out this weekend?"

"We did. Your brother wants to invite some of his buddies in lieu of a graduation party," said my mother as she eyed me closely. I could tell that her ESP antenna was up again.

"Sounds better than grilling burgers in the backyard," added my father, "and it saves me the food bill."

"And he gets the boat, too? You haven't ever let me take the boat out alone. When do I get my chance?" I saw my mother look over at my father. He stood up and crossed over to look out the screen door.

"You may have a point, but I thought you wanted to work on getting your driver's license, first."

"Why can't I do both? I'll be taking driver's ed in the Fall, but I only have the summer to take the boat out."

"First of all, you're the one who put off getting your driver's license till your senior year. Secondly, if you want time in the boat, we'll make time, but it doesn't have to be this weekend. What is this really about?" asked my mother. "Are you upset about your brother's campout or about being treated unfairly in some way?"

There it was. She'd seen right through me, again. I didn't answer her for fear she'd make the connection that I was angry with Clive for refusing my invitation to the dance. Instead, I stomped back through the living room which was now empty. Mom followed me.

"Hettie, why don't you ask some of your friends over here for a girls' night? No brothers around." I knew she was trying to soothe my quill-like feathers, but her suggestion didn't sound like the remedy I needed.

"I'll think about it."

Two days later, it was Stuart who gave me the news. "Hey, Clive's dad is going to let him camp with us. Aren't you surprised?"

Surprised? Burned, red-hot and singed, was more like it! Clive was choosing my brothers over me. Boys against girl, eh? We would see about that. Josh wasn't the only leader of the pack.

By Friday, I'd gathered my troops. I'd convinced Darcy and Kirsten to accompany me on my mission of counterinsurgency. Kirsten, whose father was a charter boat captain, had her own tin can, or in other words, an aluminum runabout with a motor on the back. She'd been handling boats since she was old enough to hold onto an oar or a tiller. The girls were excited about the prospect of crashing in on my brothers' boot camp party because, as I was aware, they both had crushes on Josh. Kirsten and I told our parents that we were spending the night at Darcy's in Alex Bay where Kirsten would meet us in her tin can and bring us over to Cedar Island. Darcy told her parents that we were going for a short boat ride before going into town to have pizza. We were told to be off the water by sunset.

The warmth of the day still hung over the water with the sun well above the horizon at seven o'clock in the evening. Dressed in our dark hoodies, bathing suits and shorts, we filled the boat with our ammo—rifle-sized waterguns and backpacks loaded up with water balloons which had been filled from a tap at the dock to avoid being questioned by our parents. Darcy and I tossed our lifejackets in next to the two Kirsten carried with her. I untied the line from the dock cleat as she tugged on the starter cable two or three times before the motor kicked over and I jumped aboard. We glided through the sparkling crystal current, steering in the direction of Chippewa Bay. Tourists had already arrived to welcome in another weekend of boating, waving happily at us as we sped by.

"We can't just pull up to the dock without being seen," said Kirsten.

"We'll have to find another place to pull in, or we'll anchor off shore." I was determined to see this through.

"Yeah, but how do you know where the campsite is?" asked Darcy.

"We'll just have to circle around till we spot them, or hear them. Remember, we don't want to be seen first."

"That'll be tricky," said Darcy, "unless there's some tree coverage."

"Put your mission face on, girls. We're going to get the drop on them!"

They laughed at this as Kirsten directed the boat around the backside of the island to avoid being spotted by our targets. She skillfully guided the little boat to a location just northeast of the park, beyond a rocky point. We anchored about ten feet offshore in thigh-high water and waded in with our backpacks held over our heads, giggling uncontrollably. When we entered the dense brush, we were suddenly attacked by swarming mosquitoes. Swinging our backpacks over our shoulders, we pulled up our hoods and tightened the drawstrings. Our cone-headed trio pushed forward, slapping at our exposed legs to beat away the bloodthirsty insects. I knew I had to keep the sinking sun on my right to find the way to the park.

Darcy spit out a couple of gnats as we emerged from the trees into a clearing a short distance from the campsites. Instantly, our noses were greeted by the tantalizing aroma of grilled burgers and hot dogs wafting our way from some of the campsites. "Yum! I could use a hot dog," she said.

"Hey, Soldier! We're not here to eat."

"Not unless the boys are cooking," chuckled Kirsten.

We loosened the hoods, but kept them on as we followed the outer path at the edge of the tenting area.

"Maybe they're down by the water."

"Must be. I don't see Josh or Stuart."

"What about Clive, Hettie? Lovely C-li-ve," teased Kirsten as she sang his name in three melodic notes.

I'd confided to my friends how frustrated I was with Clive. Darcy had sympathized while Kirsten had suggested that I should find someone less caught up in himself. "You know, someone more fun, someone who'll make you laugh."

"Wait! There's the campsite! Isn't that Stuart?" exclaimed Darcy.

"Yeah, that's him alright. Looks like he's walking away. Alright, girls, we've got to approach their tents without calling attention to ourselves. Let's continue around and come in from the west. Keep voices to a whisper." My orders just made them titter all the more until we stopped to get a grip on ourselves. We had a few false starts before the laughter was held in check.

As luck would have it, the boys had pitched camp in a spot surrounded by shrubbery, affording them some seclusion and providing cover for us. We crouched down low, trying to muffle the mosquito-slapping, while we scanned over the area.

"I don't think anybody's home," observed Kirsten.

"Just in case, let's creep up behind the tents and check them out first," I suggested, fully immersing myself into the leadership role. We slowly tiptoed forward in a horizontal line with waterguns ready. When we reached the three tents, we each squatted low behind one, lifting the edge carefully with the nozzles of our guns to peek inside. All were vacant. I signaled for my soldiers to circle around to the front of the site which was also deserted.

"Doesn't look like they've eaten, yet."

"What now?" asked Kirsten, sounding a bit disappointed.

"All the way here for an empty camp?" whined Darcy.

"We can still pull a prank. Let's see what's in their backpacks. Maybe we can mix them up."

"Oooo-ooh. That's bad," mocked Kirsten.

Without hesitating, I dashed forward to Josh's tent, taking delight in getting one over on him. How would he feel to know that his sister pranked him while he was off playing commando with his homeys? I hurriedly emptied out two backpacks, noting that deodorant and clean underwear must've been missing from the checklist and thinking these boys were going to smell like a locker room by the next day. Josh had thought to bring a Swiss army knife and a mag lite while the other, probably Gabe, brought two decks of cards, a bag of chocolate chips, and some bug repellent. I figured the chocolate was up for grabs.

"Hettie! Hettie!"

"Hurry up! I see Josh headed this way!"

I stuffed the chocolate into my sweatshirt and dashed back outside.

"Hey! What are you doing here?" yelled Josh.

"Quick! Balloon attack!" I hollered.

We dropped to our knees and unzipped our packs, launching the water balloons at the approaching band of six. They ducked and laughed, but kept advancing, forcing us to snatch up our packs and waterguns as we sprinted back into the woods. The boys tore off after us.

"Faster! Don't let them catch us!" I urged.

Kirsten turned back for a moment to unload her gun on Stuart who had forged to the front of the pack. She doused his face and head, compelling him to stop as the others pulled forward.

"Run!" screamed Darcy.

We dropped the waterguns on the riverbank and dove in, swiftly swimming out to the tin can. Kirsten pulled herself aboard and immediately began yanking the cord to start the motor. I pushed Darcy over the side and hollered for her to pull up the anchor before clambering in next to her.

Four of the boys were now in the water, wading out in our direction. Darcy and I grabbed the oars from the bottom of the boat and began slapping the water to splash the oncoming avengers. Kirsten leaned hard on the tiller to spin us about, tossing us off our seats as we raced off to the backside of the island. Hearing the sound of an approaching boat, I turned to see Josh and Clive quickly gaining on us in my father's boat, the *Nevermind*. The chase was on!

To avoid a freighter headed upriver, Kirsten guided our craft through a cluster of small islands to the northeast of the park. The sun had just slipped below the horizon, leaving a dusty afterglow of daylight. We merged back out into the channel ahead of our pursuers and crossed over the wake of the freighter. BAM! BAM!

"Yahoo!" yelled Darcy, as we smacked down over the wake.

"Look out!" I warned from the front. BAM! This drop threw water over the bow, bouncing Darcy off her bench. Kirsten decelerated each time we climbed the crest of a wave, then gunned it again to steer the boat across the path of the wake. I looked back to see Josh gaining on us, the *Nevermind* able to skip over the top of the waves more swiftly than the tin can. We headed down the channel beyond Chippewa Point.

"We'll go into the Amateur Isles and sort the men from the women!" she bellowed over the growling motor.

"There are lots of sunken rocks in there!" I answered. It was dark now and difficult to see what was beyond the front of the boat.

"Grab the flashlights from the storage chest to spot them out for me!"

The *Nevermind* was gathering speed in the open water. We needed to find a hiding spot before Josh caught up with us. A sudden warning thought flashed through my mind. *Whatever you do, Josh, don't bang up Dad's boat.*

"Okay. Get ready."

Darcy and I knelt down in the bottom of the boat, flashlights panning from side to side over the water off the bow.

"Point to the rock and I'll steer in the opposite direction or around it." Kirsten slowed the engine.

"What if they're on both sides?" asked Darcy, always the pessimist.

"Just pay attention," I ordered.

"Hey! It's dangerous in there, Hettie! Come on out and face the music!" hollered Josh.

"You'll have to come in and get us."

"You're getting close to the border. Can you see the lighthouse, yet?" he warned.

"Turn off the back light, Kirsten," said Darcy.

They giggled with excitement. "There! Watch out!" I whispered, pointing toward a barely submerged rock. Kirsten quickly steered to the port.

"Hettie, NOT, I repeat, NOT a good idea," sang Josh.

We muffled our laughter while Kirsten focused. "We'll head for that inlet." She slowed the motor, almost to an idle, and allowed the current to carry us into a grassy cove.

"Another rock!" cautioned Darcy.

I could barely hear the *Nevermind,* now, as Kirsten clicked off the engine and threw the anchor over the side. We turned off our flashlights. The sky was clear, but the air was cool, raising goose bumps on my legs. We had drifted within fifteen feet of one of the larger islands.

"What do we do if they find us?" asked Darcy.

"Good question," said Kirsten, "but I doubt they will, so we'll hightail it home if they don't show up in about fifteen minutes."

"Wait! What's that?" I asked.

"They're on the other side of that island."

"How'd they get past us?" Darcy asked.

"I don't think it's Josh and Clive. Listen!" I said.

"Sounds like a couple of guys arguing," Kirsten observed.

"Are we in Canada?" asked Darcy.

"I'm not sure," replied Kirsten. "The border runs between the islands, I think."

"We had a deal!" exclaimed a man in anger.

"You'll get the rest on the next trip," someone answered.

"I've taken a risk here. How do I know you'll deliver?"

"Hey, Chum, we're all taking risks."

Just then, we heard the *Nevermind* slowly approaching from the other direction.

"Hettie! Het - tie!" called Josh.

"Are you in there?" added Clive.

"Who's that?" barked the angry man, followed by the rumble of a large engine turning over.

"Get down!" hissed Kirsten. We flattened ourselves in the bottom of the boat, legs entangled. The giggling started again, but stopped abruptly as we heard the thunder of another engine. The first engine sound, loud at first, soon dwindled to a distant drone while the other craft puttered slowly along the opposite shore of the island which separated us from the unknown boater. I heard my brother's voice off to the west of us.

"Clive, do you hear that engine?"

"Yeah, but it doesn't sound like Kirsten's."

"Hope it's not Customs. Which side of the border are we on?"

"Hard to tell in the dark, but it runs through here somewhere."

"Okay. I'm turning around. Maybe the girls have headed south."

We let out our breath and kept quiet a bit longer, still listening for the mysterious boat which continued to slowly troll in our direction as if waiting for the *Nevermind* to move out of sight.

"Let's get out of here before he sees us," I said.

Kirsten popped up and tried starting the motor. It coughed and whirred. "Weeds!" she said. "Weeds are wrapped around the prop!"

"I see his lights!" warned Darcy. "Do you think he knows we're here?"

Kirsten was busy pulling up the prop. "We've got to clean it off, but I'll need some light."

"Wait! I can't hear his engine anymore." We turned to stare into the darkness of the island. Suddenly, we were blinded by a spotlight.

A deep, raspy voice yelled out, "What are you doing in there?" We could see only the silhouette of a man wearing a cap low over his eyes. Instinctively, we threw ourselves to the floor of the boat, remaining silent. Fallen branches and twigs cracked as the figure crept toward the water's edge.

"What do we do?" asked Darcy.

Kirsten held a finger to her lips, shushing us, and pointed with her other hand to the oars. *Was she suggesting we use the oars to defend ourselves?* My thoughts were disrupted by the familiar whirr of the *Nevermind*, entering the cove from the north. Josh and Clive must have circled around when they didn't spot us. I peeked over the edge of the boat and saw the spotlight click off.

"I think I hear him running away," said Darcy. We popped up like three chipmunks, peering once again into darkness.

"Hettie! Where are you? No more games," commanded Josh in a parental tone.

"We're stuck in the weeds!" I replied disappointedly.

Once more, we heard an engine turn over and all five of us remained silent as Josh and Clive coasted nearer and the sound of the mystery boat floated off into the distance toward the American mainland.

Stuart Voss

Hettie almost ruined our camping trip. She seemed to have some kind of bug up her behind about Clive going camping with us. I wasn't sure inviting him was such a good idea in the first place, but I didn't say so to my brother because I was blown away by the fact that he'd included me that weekend. I'm three years younger than Josh, two years younger than Hettie. Together, they were my extra set of parents, only more bossy. Since my sibs were born with the bulk of the competitive genes from the family tree and happiest when in charge, they frequently butted heads. Me, I just liked watching them take center stage in front of Mom and Dad. Gave me a chance to fly under the radar.

Josh couldn't do anything just for the sake of fun. He always had an agenda, an objective, or a goal. The campout couldn't just have been about sleeping under the stars, cooking some hot dogs, and hanging out. That wouldn't have been enough for my brother. No way. He planned some kind of mini-Olympic feats for us and didn't bother to fill anyone in till we were out on the water.

Clive and my brother's three best buds—Gabe, Troy, and Ben—all arrived at our house around 5:30 on Friday evening. We hauled three tents, an ice chest, a duffel bag, and our backpacks down to the *Nevermind* docked out back. When we reached Chippewa Bay, my brother killed the engine and dropped anchor near Oak Island, then switched into his military act.

"Okay, men, your first challenge of the night is right here.

You're going to swim to that island and back." He pointed to a small island about a quarter of a mile from us. "The ten bucks I collected from each of you to cover food is now in the booty bag for a total of fifty and the first one back is Keeper of the Booty till the next challenge. I'm acting as lifeguard and referee. Any questions?" The guys were up for it, including the piano player. I was amazed that the kid was willing to get wet; even more amazed when he pulled off his security-blanket gloves. The rest of us took off our sneaks and t-shirts, but Clive kept his shirt on, tucked it inside his swim trunks that reached almost to his knees, and tied the drawstring with a double bow. Weird. I caught Troy and Gabe trying to hide their smirks.

"Isn't your shirt going to slow you down?" asked Ben. Clive looked embarrassed, but just shrugged.

"Ready?" Josh blew the whistle that hung from the cord around his neck and we all dove in. The first smack of chilly water stole my breath away for a minute, then I got moving to stay warm. Troy and Ben were already out in front. Gabe and I were next with Clive bringing up the rear. After five minutes, the three of us overtook the first two and now, I was out in front! I held this lead until after we made the turn for the home stretch. My arms began to feel like lead weights and I could feel my lungs begging for more air. Gabe passed me first, then Clive. Like punching a power-surge button, he hauled on by Gabe and busted into an impressive butterfly stroke for the last few yards. We were all blown away that it'd been Clive who'd defeated us. He was a dark horse, alright.

While we dragged ourselves back into the boat, Josh stood there beaming like some kind of proud papa as he remarked, "Guess all those workouts in the garage are paying off."

"Dude! Why aren't you on the swim team?" asked Troy.

"Might hurt my nerdy, misfit image, don't you think?" The guys laughed, but I wasn't certain if Clive was mocking himself or us for making assumptions about him. Either way, we showed our respect with high fives as we stumbled around in our towels and my brother pulled up anchor.

After docking at Cedar Island, we lugged all our gear over to the campsite and set up the tents. Just as we were about to get comfortable, Josh announced the next challenge.

"For the next task, I have some fishing line and hooks. First to catch a fish is ..."

"Keeper of the Booty," we shouted.

"Right!"

"Where are the rods?" asked Clive.

"Well, that's up to you. Look around. You'll find something useful."

"No way!" said Gabe.

"I'm starving," I added. This didn't sound like fun; it sounded more like a lame waste of time. "You better have food in that cooler."

"This is about survival, men. Step up to the task."

"I haven't eaten since lunch," complained Troy. "What if we don't catch any fish?"

"I've got soda and chips, a jar of peanut butter and some bread." Groans all around.

"Okay, here's what I'll do. We'll put a time limit on this—maybe an hour—and you can take the chips with you." He pulled out two large bags. I tore into one of them and Ben ripped open the other. We dug in by the handfuls while Josh cut a six-foot line for each of us and passed around the hooks. He blew the whistle and the guys took off. I hung back to eat more chips and sneak a look inside the cooler to see how seriously I had to work at fishing. Just as I'd suspected, my big brother had a stash of hot dogs buried underneath the soda and ice. I took my sweet time finding a stick before strolling on down to the dock to do some fake fishing. By then, I'd totally lost interest in winning the booty. I just wanted to eat.

But that's when all hell broke loose. We'd all given up on trying to hook our dinner and started back to the campsite when we spotted Hettie and her friends snooping around our tents. We tossed the homemade rods and raced after them while they bombarded us with water balloons. I heard Josh yell out, "Clive, follow me! We'll head them off in the boat." The rest of us sped after the girls. I'd nearly caught up to them when I was ambushed by a Niagara Falls gush of water from the biggest squirtgun I'd ever seen. The girls dove into the woods and we dashed after them. By the time we'd scrambled through the mosquito-infested trees to the shore, the girls were already in the water making their way out to Kirsten's boat. We peeled off our t-shirts and sneakers and dove in, but they managed to climb aboard and get the motor running before we reached them. The *Nevermind* rounded the bend just as the girls turned about. We watched as they tore off into the sunset.

The four of us swam to shore and hoofed it back to camp to dry out and cook the hot dogs over a nice warm fire. After we'd eaten, we began to wonder if something had happened to Josh and Clive or the girls. One of the guys suggested we ask another camper to help us search for them.

"It's dark and we don't have a clue where they went," answered Gabe.

"Maybe we should contact the Coast Guard," added Troy.

"What's up with your sister? Is she trying to crash the campout?" Ben sounded annoyed.

"She's probably burned that we're having guys-only fun. I bet my parents have no idea she's out here."

"Isn't she dating Clive?" asked Gabe.

"I don't know. I think they're just friends."

"Yeah, right," said Ben. "Like that ever works between a guy and a girl."

"I thought he was some weird dude who likes to cut himself up," said Troy.

I didn't answer that. Clive had spent a lot of time at our house with my brother, my sister, or my father, so it didn't feel right to talk about stuff like that behind his back. Besides, it was one of those things I'd rather not know about. None of my business.

"Well, he sure can swim," said Gabe, "even with his shirt on."

Then I heard the buzz of a boat engine resonating over the water and gradually growing to a quiet purr as it reached the docks. Gabe and I ran down to make sure that it was Josh and Clive.

"What took you so long? Where's Hettie?" I asked.

"She's in deep manure, that's where!" growled Josh as he cut the engine and Clive tied up the boat.

"What happened?"

"Kirsten drove into the Amateurs and got stuck in the weeds!"

"You didn't go in after them, did you?" asked Gabe. "There are too many rocks in there."

"We might have bumped a few. Hope the prop didn't hit."

As we walked backed to the tents, Josh filled us in. "I think something funny was going on out there. There was another boat, maybe two, in the area and the girls said that some guy came looking for them after Clive and I pulled out of the inlet."

"How did you find them?"

"I didn't see them out in the channel, so I circled back around."

"Are you going to tell Dad?"

"Not if I can help it, but I'll let her sweat it out."

"Your sister's got a lot of moxie," said Gabe appreciatively. "Sounds like she gave you two a run for your money."

"Maybe I should give her the booty," said Clive.

"Not on your life!" yelled Josh. Ben and Troy cooked up the remainder of the hot dogs for the hungry warriors. Clive washed his hands with a towelette packet that he pulled from his pocket. We noticed, but didn't laugh.

"We left you some of the macaroni salad and a couple of cookies, too."

"Yeah, thanks for not betting on us to catch fish," joked Troy.

Josh and Clive were quiet while they wolfed down their food. Meanwhile, the campfire had started to die, so Gabe and I threw more logs on. I tried stirring up the cinders, but there wasn't enough heat left for the wood to catch fire.

"That was supposed to be the next challenge," Josh said.

"What was?" asked Troy.

"I was going to see who'd be the first to start a fire from scratch."

"I'm done with challenges for this night, boys. I'll stick with matches," I said.

"Except there's one problem with that," continued Ben as he pulled an empty matchbook from the pocket of his shorts. "I'm out of matches."

"Lucky for us, I brought some, too." Snatching up the flashlight Josh had carried up from the boat, I crawled into my tent and unzipped my backpack. At first, I thought I'd picked up the wrong gear. Shining the light to the other side of the tent, I noted the sack of a dark-green color with a boondoggle chain on the zipper clasp, Clive's bag. I crawled back outside and asked, "What's going on? Did one of you guys put your stuff in my backpack? Or, did I pick up the wrong one when we unloaded the boat?"

Five blank faces stared back at me as if I'd spoken some alien language.

Troy spoke up. "I've got a black backpack. Let me see that one." I brought the bag closer to them. "Nope, that doesn't belong to me."

"Maybe you picked up mine," said Josh. We both had the same kind. He checked the contents, taking out a t-shirt and a small flashlight.

"Hey! That's my stuff!" declared Clive as he stood up and grabbed the bag from Josh.

"Hettie!" said Ben and Josh in unison.

We emptied the backpacks near the firepit in order to sort through the belongings and return them to their respective owners. I noticed Clive looking upset after everyone had repacked. "What's up, Clive?"

"I can't find my sketchbook."

Gary Stanton

Jeff was talking even less than his usual taciturn self and avoiding me. Ever since our trip to Kingston, he'd been preoccupied. Something was bugging him and he wasn't saying what. I knew he'd rather work off whatever it was than discuss it. It's just the way he was. That could mean anything from carving a decoy to replacing the docks. I'd seen him chop up three full-grown, dead evergreen trees in one day on the island after one of his coworkers had been shot to death. He never did tell me what he knew or what he felt about it.

The week after that excursion to Jonathan's restaurant, he called me to explain that Clive was going on an overnight camping trip with friends. I suggested that this would be a great opportunity for us to have some time alone sans teenagers, but he said he wanted to use the time to catch up on chores around the house. When I pushed, he stonewalled.

"What aren't you telling me, Jeff? Are you short on cash? Got a health issue?"

"No! Nothing like that. Just got a lot to do, that's all. Got to repair the back deck and do some trimming around the yard."

"You sound irritable. Would you like some help? I can come disguised as the gardener, or better yet, I can send over a crew to take care of the deck."

"That's all I need. That nosy Barrett woman would be on me like a vulture on roadkill to find out how I paid for it."

"You mean the neighbor with the abusive husband?"

"That's the one."

"Tell her to buzz off."

"Look, I don't have time for useless conversation. I'll call you later." Click. He didn't call back that day or the next, or the day after that.

Clive brought it up. The two of us had an established routine for calling each other a couple of times a week, sometimes more. I didn't like being an absentee parent who missed out on the daily scoop, but that's just the way it was. Jeff was reluctant to move to Toronto or try to sign up with a Canadian law enforcement group and I couldn't move my restaurant to his location. Clive called me two days after the camping venture.

"Dad's been a major grump, lately."

"Did you ask him what's got him wound up?"

"Yeah. He just says he's got a lot on his mind. I think it's work."

"Did he get the deck work done?"

"What are you talking about?"

"You know. The back deck. He said he had some repairs to do."

"He was on duty this weekend."

Something wasn't lining up. Seems Jeff either got called into work or he'd told each of us different stories. I didn't want to pass on the bad vibe I was getting to Clive so I let the matter drop.

"Heard you went camping. Did you have a good time?"

"Yeah, it was great."

"Who did you go with?"

"The same guy who's been helping me with the weight training."

"Sounds like a good buddy."

"Yeah, pretty nice. He's graduating this year."

"The year's almost over, Clive. By the way, I'm bringing Sam up for the Fourth of July before she moves back to the big city. Anything special you want to do?" It was quiet on the other end of the phone. I waited a bit before continuing. "Clive? You still there?"

"Yeah, just thinking. Should I get her something?"

"That's up to you. Maybe something to remind her of the River. Why don't you frame one of your sketches?"

"Hmm-mm. Maybe." His response was lukewarm, but I figured he was just glum about Sam's move back to Manhattan.

"Don't worry, Clive. I'll make sure you get to visit her." I knew the separation would be hard on both of them, but they had years of shifting relationships ahead of them. I hoped that Clive could handle it. Jeff had filled me in about a recent humiliating incident at a school rally which had revealed that Clive had been wounding himself. *Cutting? With a knife? Razor blades?* This news had caught me totally off-guard. Drugs, maybe, or even alcohol wouldn't have been nearly so unexpected. *But cutting?*

"He's seeing a counselor. Something to do with obsessive compulsive behavior."

Over the years, we'd both been concerned about Clive's fixation on perfection and his hands—*the gloves*—but we figured it was an eccentricity that he'd outgrow as he became more accomplished. Neither one of us suspected it was a symptom of something more serious.

"You've seen how frustrated he gets when he thinks something isn't just the way he wants it, like when he practices the same section over and over again. And remember when he was little? He wouldn't wear the same shirt two days in a row and he'd make me cut the labels off his clothing so they wouldn't tickle his skin."

"He's sensitive, Jeff. He needs to learn how to tell you what's bothering him. He plays it out in his music, sketches it out on a piece of paper, but doesn't say it. Who's that sound like?"

Jeff ignored the question. "He used to ask me if my job was dangerous or if the bad guys were going to shoot me."

"What did you tell him?"

"I told him I'm always careful and that most of my days are pretty boring."

I laughed. I knew that Jeff's job could be unpredictable and stressful. He'd seen the ugly side of people, like those who tried to smuggle someone into the states in the airless trunk of a car. He'd also seen children kidnapped by one of their own parents or someone more sinister. Drugs, on the other hand, were a common form of contraband.

"Clive sets the bar high for himself, higher than most mortal humans."

"We're not the typical family."

"Is that what you think this is about?"

"Maybe." Jeff said he'd keep me updated on the counseling.

In the meantime, I broached the subject with Clive during one of our weekends at the cottage. "I heard what happened at the rally. Guess it was pretty embarrassing for you."

Clive looked away. His eyes teared up a bit.

"So Dad told you about it?"

I rubbed his back gently. "You've got two dads, remember? You can tell me anything."

His lips trembled. He wiped the tears away and struggled to gain control. "I … I just don't fit anywhere. I feel like I'm on the outside looking in."

"What do you mean? At school? At home?"

"Mostly at school, around other kids."

"What about Samantha?"

"She's different. She gets it. Look at what she's going through with her mom." He looked up at me. "Sorry, Gary. I know she's your sister."

"No apologies necessary. I have no illusions. She's a piece of work. But as far as not fitting in, well, that pretty much sums up my teenage years."

"Why do people hate homosexuals?"

"I've been grappling with that most of my life! I think it has something to do with changing beliefs. Sometimes it takes centuries."

"Dad just tells me not to worry so much about what others think and just be who I want to be."

"Easier said than done and he ought to know." I wondered if our own struggles had made us any wiser as parents.

Samantha De Haven

I couldn't wait to get out, out of the dead space of Eddie's house and away from Mom. I was being snuffed out by her addiction;

there was no air left for me to breathe as long as I shared space with her. As far as I could see, there'd never been a good reason for her to become a drunk. Was her childhood all that bad? It wasn't like she was born into a Dickens narrative—not by a long shot—and it certainly didn't sound any more painful than mine. And why wasn't I, her only child, reason enough to get sober? I couldn't find a reason to feel sorry for her and I was at the point where I was finding it difficult to love her. I had to get out. I tried to imagine my life free from her, but worried that the tiny, fine hairs of guilt would cling to me and prick my skin like nettles after I'd abandoned her.

On the last day of the school year, my last day in that school, I skipped home looking forward to packing. I'd be moving out and moving on. As soon as I opened the front door, I heard Mom's bellows. She was screaming at someone on the phone. It soon became apparent that someone was Eddie.

"I want to know what this is all about. Is this woman trying to blackmail you? Is that where my money has been going? Don't you hang up on me, you son of a bitch!"

I closed the door quietly, hoping I could sneak upstairs before the dragon turned its head to breathe its fire onto me. Just as I reached the top landing, I heard DING and then a splintering sound of the phone smashing against a wall. My mother's foul mouth ratcheted up to the red zone, carrying all the way up the stairwell as she climbed the steps. I slipped into my room, shut the door and leaned against it, not daring to move. *Don't come in here,* I silently pleaded, but then I heard her tumble back down. *No friggin' way!* I didn't want to play this game anymore. I waited by the door, cracking it open ever so slightly to listen for movement. *Come on, get up! Don't do this again!* I crept out to the landing to peek over the edge. At the foot of the stairs, Mom lay crumpled in the fetus position, her eyes closed, with her left arm curled beneath her rib cage. She was moaning, but still conscious. For half a second, I imagined myself stepping over her and running out of the house, but I knew I had no choice.

I squatted down beside her to brush away the dry, fragile strands of highlighted hair that had fallen over her face, surprised to find large patches of gray underneath. Her trips to Manhattan had always included a visit to her expensive hair stylist. Had she missed an appointment? How long had it been since she'd left the house? She was still in her robe and nightgown which hung loosely around her skeletal frame. There was no color, real or cosmetic, on her cheekbones. The drinking had finally triumphed over vanity. How had this frail ghost ever managed to intimidate me?

"Mom? Mom? Are you hurt?" She groaned and slowly turned her head towards me, her eyes closed.

"Hmm-mm. My arm."

"Your arm hurts? Mom?"

She didn't answer. I placed my hand beneath her head to feel for blood or a bump, relieved to find neither. Gently, I pressed my fingertips here and there on her neck, shoulders, ribs, and legs to see if she felt pain anywhere else before attempting to move her.

"Samantha, stop. Help me up."

Carefully, I slid my arm behind her neck to raise her. She groaned when the weight of her body came up off her left arm, her gauntness unnerving me as I shifted her to a sitting position. Grasping her about the waist, I repositioned her so that she could rest her back against the wall, then ran to the kitchen, kicking away pieces of smashed phone to get to the freezer. I packed a small plastic bag with ice and filled a glass with water before retracing my steps.

"Here, Mom. Drink a little water." Her right hand came up slowly, shaking spasmodically, barely touching my own. Her skin felt cold. I held onto the glass as she sipped. "Point to where your arm hurts." She cupped her left elbow in her right hand.

"Can you straighten your arm?" She nodded and sluggishly flexed her forearm up and down while pressing her lips tightly together. Setting down the glass of water, I pulled her right hand away to give her the bag of ice, but she let it drop to the floor.

"Too cold." I returned to the kitchen for a tea towel and wrapped it around the bag of ice.

Scurrying back to her, I asked, "Do you want me to call 9-1-1?"

She shook her head. "Not going there again."

Once more, I picked up her trembling free hand to slip it between my own and the ice pack. She held onto it this time while I helped her take another sip of water. Her eyes were open now. "Do you think you can stand up?" She nodded. I stood in front of her and placed my arms under her armpits to lift while thinking that this was the most physical contact we'd had in years. She used the wall to prop herself into a standing position, but she wasn't strong enough to stand on her own. I shifted around behind her to help her move into the living room and sat her down in an overstuffed chair, placing her feet on the matching ottoman. I snatched a tapestried accent pillow from the sofa to place under the ice bag and her elbow. A tinge of color began to fill her cheeks.

"Get me a glass of scotch, Sam." My bloodstream immediately filled with white-hot wrath, as if she'd stuck me with a syringe of malevolent elixir.

"No."

"To kill the pain."

Instead, I went upstairs to her medicine cabinet to find a simple over-the-counter painkiller, but I should've known better. The cabinet was filled with unpronounceable prescription drugs, mostly empty containers. *Maybe one sound thrash to the head would put you out of your misery.* Nixing that thought, I found myself choosing between two evils before I dashed back to the kitchen for the liquid anesthetic.

After the first drink, she revived a bit. "So, Samantha, I've just learned that you have another stepbrother."

"Is Cecile having another baby?"

"No! Please, no! I mean Eddie's got a son."

I didn't want to hear this.

"He's got a son, a gifted one it seems. Ha! Here, see for

yourself." With her bony, shaky fingers, she picked up a newspaper clipping from the end table beside her chair and handed it to me. I glanced at the headline, *"Local Teenager to Perform in the St. Lawrence Classical Piano Competition."* My throat went dry. The article went on to mention that Clive would also be performing at the upcoming graduation ceremony at River High School.

"Where did you get this?" I whispered, barely hearing my own voice.

"Came in the mail. Read the back."

Scrawled in blue ink across the other side of the article were the words, *"Eddie, guess we should have hung on to our baby boy."* It was signed simply, *"Veronica."*

No! No! This had to be a dream, a nightmare. The gentle, perceptive boy I so loved couldn't be the offspring of the repulsive Eddie Cox. I was suddenly overcome with nausea and rushed to the bathroom. The vomiting relieved the pain in my stomach, but didn't stem the flood of tears. This couldn't be happening. My mother's toxic marriage to Eddie had leached into the one beautiful haven in my life, like spilled tea seeping into white linen. Was her self-absorption going to stain Clive, too? I heard her voice croaking my name from the other room.

She wanted a refill. "Absolutely not," I answered coldly. I no longer cared about her pain. The endless Trisha Cox Show had drained me of sympathy.

"Why should you care how many children he has?"

"I don't care about the boy, but Eddie had better not be making a fool out of me with this woman. Son of a bitch!"

I stormed off to my room to avoid listening to her. The jig-saw pieces of Clive's family history weren't fitting together. Hadn't Veronica died years ago? Wasn't Jeff Tierney Clive's father? Why would Jeff lie to Clive or to Uncle Gary? These questions were tangled up in worry that my mother would say something to my uncle or worse yet, to Eddie. *Do I tell Clive?* I couldn't see what good it would do him. But did I have the right to decide what was best for him, or did Clive have the right to learn the truth even if it meant the contamination of his trust for the man he believed to be his father?

Trisha Cox

So, Eddie had a love child. Gigolo! He and this *Veronica* thought they could make a fool out of me? And live the high life on my dime? Well, they'd be feeling the sharp end of that stick soon! After all, Sam was moving in with Tom and Cecile and the happy little family. I didn't need her fawning over me, treating me like a child. She didn't need me; she wanted to leave. Probably made sense for her to get back to her friends while she still had some. I knew what that was like, but one day she'd find out that trust and love are fairytale dust. Can't count on family, friends, fathers …

I'd show Eddie and his girlfriend that they couldn't hide anything from me. It was time to hire a private detective and search through their closets. Oh, I was going to enjoy this!

Hettie Voss

After our escapade, we'd spent the remainder of Friday night at Darcy's, both laughing and fretting over the impending fallout. "Did you see Stuart's face after I soaked him?"

"You think Josh will stay angry?"

"I'm dead if he tells my parents."

"Who was that guy in the boat?"

"Should we tell anyone about him?"

The unexpected encounter with the strangers out on the River taunted our imaginations.

"Maybe they were dumping a body out there," suggested Darcy.

"I didn't hear a big plop into the water," replied Kirsten.

"Could be smugglers. Think it's anyone we know?"

"What if it is and he's still looking for us?"

"Come on, Darcy. Why would he be interested in us? We don't know what he was up to."

"Yeah, but he doesn't know that. He might think we saw something." Darcy's thrill had quickly deflated into worry.

"I don't think that's likely. What's he going to do? Gun down three high school girls in Clayton, New York? That would turn up the heat."

"The heat! Listen to us!" We giggled until we cried.

"I'm worried that Clive might not want to talk to me on Monday," I confided.

"What do you see in him? Why don't you go for Jason? He obviously likes you," Kirsten needled. "Clive's kind of a dweeb."

"I think he's cute," Darcy said.

"I hope your brothers aren't going to rat us out. Think they'll forgive and forget?"

I hadn't given much thought to that, being more concerned about Clive's reaction. My parents wouldn't be happy to find out I hadn't told them the whole truth about this evening's plans.

Darcy changed the subject. "I'm starving. You girls want junk food or something like a sandwich?"

"Wait!" I shouted. "I've got booty!"

"Booty?" the girls echoed with glee.

I pulled the bag of chocolate chips from the pouch of my sweatshirt.

"Yum!"

We munched quietly for a moment before Darcy confessed, "I've got booty, too." She unzipped her backpack and pulled out a sketchbook, Clive's sketchbook. My good mood tanked immediately. I knew that this was a special possession, as private as a diary.

"Oooh—gimme!" urged Kirsten as she grabbed for it. Twinges of guilt gripped my stomach.

"I ... I don't think we should look in there," I said weakly.

Kirsten had the sketchbook in her hands and began to flip through the pages. "Just a peek. Hey, who's this?" Darcy and I sat on the floor next to Kirsten, staring down at a curious sketch showing two men with their backs to us as they embraced at the edge of the River. Was this Clive and his father? Two brothers? Maybe more than brothers? The next page turned up what was obviously his self-portrait, his profile with a magnified cranium filled with fingers! All kinds of fingers—wrinkled with dirt under the fingernail, what looked like a baby's thumb in a pacifier, a woman's with a wedding band and polished nail, a finger dipped in a glass of wine. Darcy thought it was blood and let out a scream.

Kirsten chimed in. "He's one strange dude."

The face was shaded out in fine crosshatch markings and Clive had drawn hands to cover the ears. The rest of the page was wallpapered in musical notes with pieces of a heart scattered throughout.

"That's creepy," observed Kirsten. "Is he having one of those out-of-body experiences?"

"Like maybe he does drugs?" asked Darcy.

Kirsten waved her hand over her head to show that her comment had exceeded Darcy's comprehension level. She continued to turn the pages, several of them filled with portraits of young women. "Who are they?" One of them, appearing to be about my age and blonde, smiled back at me.

"I don't know." I seized the book and slapped it closed. "But I don't think we should be poking around in his business." Noting my own hypocrisy in that statement, I maintained a principled tone of voice to cover up my fear that Clive might have a secret girlfriend. "Now help me figure out how we're going to get this back to Clive."

After a groggy, quiet breakfast the next morning, I headed home to face the music, quickly seeking the safety of my room. I was in the middle of a sound nap when Josh came barging in. He lit into me right away. "What got into you? You couldn't let Clive have a little fun without you, could you? I don't think he was impressed by your antics!" Josh closed my bedroom door and stood over me. "You're lucky no one got stuck in that cove and that nothing happened to Dad's boat."

When his rant finally broke through my deep sleep, it took me a moment to realize I was in my own bed and it was still daylight. Rolling over, I came face-to-face with my brother staring down at me. Instantly incensed over his trespassing on my privacy, let alone my need for sleep, I screamed at him. "Get out of my room!"

"Hand it over, now, Hettie!"

"What are you talking about?"

"The sketchbook! Clive's pissed that you took it."

"I don't have his sketchbook!" Josh started tossing things off my desk and pulling out the drawers of my dresser. I sprang from the bed to slam them shut. "Get out of here!"

"I thought you liked Clive. Why would you steal his sketchbook?"

"I told you I don't have it! Maybe he lost it. Why do you think I took it?"

"After you and your friends switched up the stuff in our backpacks, Clive couldn't find it."

"Well, I don't have it. How about one of your pals?"

"You think I'm stupid? Check with your partners in crime. Somebody walked away with it and you know what it means to him. This little prank may cost you a boyfriend." Josh slammed the door behind him on his way out.

I was dumbfounded by his reaction. After all, he was the King of Pranksters. Now that I'd won the upper hand for a change, he was behaving like Mr. Righteous. Perhaps he didn't like being bested by a female, let alone his little sister. Who was I trying to kid? Josh was right and I'd lied to him because I knew that the theft of the sketchbook was a deplorable breach of trust. If Clive was angry with me, I needed to mend the situation before the wounded feelings had a chance to fester.

Robbie Barrett

I saw my chance and I took it. As simple as that. The Voss brothers thought they could threaten me? A lucky coincidence allowed me to score a double-hitter to even things up. When I walked out of my Monday morning exam, I ran smack into Hettie. Her books flew across the hallway. Like the gentleman I am, I helped her pick them up and insisted on carrying them for her till we reached her locker.

"Okay, Robbie. Give me my stuff."

"I'm just waiting for you to open your lock, you know, while you've got a free hand."

She looked sideways at me as she spun the combination dial. "Alright, it's open. Try watching where you're going next time."

"Now, is that any way to thank a person? I'm trying to be nice, here. Hey, look how neat you keep your locker."

"Just give me my books, Robbie. I've got to catch my bus." Somehow, the books slipped from my hands and fell to the floor. As Hettie squatted to pick them up, I nosed through her locker.

"Hey, what's in here?" I picked up a sketchbook and flipped open the cover. *Yummy.*

"Get away!" She lunged at me. "You can't have that!"

"Don't worry. I'll take good care of it!" I tore off down the hallway while she shouted insults at me, but I didn't look back.

Later that afternoon, Nick and I drove into Alex Bay to get burgers and eat them down by the waterfront. I showed him Clive's sketchbook.

"This dude can draw," commented Nick.

I turned the page and found a drawing of two men with their arms around each other. "What's this? Think Clive has a boyfriend?"

"I can't tell who that is."

The next several pages were filled with portraits of girls or older women I'd never seen.

"Why do you think Hettie had this book in her locker?"

"Maybe he loaned it to her."

"With all these pictures of chicks? I bet he doesn't know she has it, or had it, that is."

"Hey, stop. Isn't that you?" Nick started laughing and I stared harder at the page. Clive had me dressed up as a laughing gargoyle looking down on some kind of last-day-on-earth calamity. I suddenly felt the blood pounding in my temples.

"Look at the date. Isn't that when we had the bomb scare?"

"That wasn't my doin'!"

"Hey, you don't have to tell me." Nick laughed again. "Look what he did to your mouth!"

I jabbed Nick hard in the ribs. "It's time to teach Chives a lesson he won't forget. Come on. We're going back to school." I tore out the page with my face on it, crumpled it up, and tossed it into the River.

Jason Larabie

I'd just stepped through the main entrance on my way to my locker, when I heard the commotion. Hallways were never this loud on the morning of an exam. I picked up the pace a bit to turn the corner. A crowd of students was staring upwards at some kind of art exhibit covering the walls above the lockers.

"What a freak!"

"Weird. Is that his brain on drugs?"

"Hey, what's up with those fags?"

It only took me a few seconds to realize that I was looking at Clive's work, that is, photocopies of Clive's art work. I kept moving through the packed corridor until I came to Hettie's locker. Multiple sketches of women were plastered all over the outside of her locker door. I began to remove them when I suddenly heard her call out my name.

"Jason! What are you doing? How? What?" Then she looked up.

"Oh, no." she whispered. Her eyes instantly filled up with tears and her lips began to tremble. I put an arm around her shoulders and she dropped her head into my chest. "This is all my fault."

"People! The bell is about to ring. You need to move along to your exam rooms!" Mr. McIntire was plowing through the throng, followed by the custodian. "Let's go. Show's over."

I continued pulling the drafts off Hettie's locker and helped her get it open. "Jason, do you think Clive has seen this?"

"I don't know. I haven't spotted him, yet." I was about to ask how these pictures got here when Kirsten interrupted us.

"He's in the office." We turned to look at her. "Clive was here when I came in, trying to snatch some of the drawings off the wall and tear them up. I think he's really upset, Hettie." I could tell by the guilty looks exchanged between the girls that there was more to this story. "Darcy's in the office, too." Kirsten added. "I came to find you so we could help them explain this mess."

Hettie covered her mouth with one hand and nodded. The girls walked away just as the bell rang.

Douglas McIntire, Principal

Nothing gets my goat more than seeing a nice kid tormented by the thoughtless behavior of an ignorant bully. Now I had two weepy students sitting in front of me, one apologizing and the other one coming apart.

"I'm so sorry," blubbered Darcy Monaghan. "I meant to get the sketchbook right back to you. I don't know how the drawings got up on the walls." She broke into sobs then, while Clive sat silently in a nearby chair, rubbing a gloved hand over one thigh and trying to wipe away tears with the other. We were interrupted by my secretary.

"We have two more confessors that would like to speak to you."

I rolled my eyes at her as Hettie Voss and Kirsten Teague joined the sob party. Hettie was already in tears. This morning was off to a soggy, painful start. Kirsten stepped forward, looked me straight in the eye and got the ball rolling. "We knew about the sketchbook heist. Hettie was going to return it yesterday, but Robbie Barrett stole it from her locker."

Right to the point, that's what I liked about Kirsten. "How did he steal it from your locker, Hettie?"

"He, he … I had the locker open and he reached in. I'm so sorry, Clive. I didn't mean for this to happen." Clive looked like the flood of hurt was about to wash him over the side of the dam. I had to get this group shored up in a hurry and back into test mode.

"So, Robbie's behind this then?" All except Clive nodded in agreement. "I guess I don't need to tell you about the Law of Unintended Consequences and how pranks can go awry, do I?" More shaking of heads. "Alright, which of you is taking a Regents Exam this morning?" All raised their hands. More flies in the soup. "Well, I'm going to suggest that you try to collect yourselves and take your exams today. If you don't think you're able to do that, then you'll have to take the make-up in August. The catch with that is your report card may reflect an incomplete or a failing grade. Unfortunately, we don't have a lot of time to make the decision."

These were good kids, high achievers, and I had to think of something comforting to say in the next five minutes to help re-engage their prefrontal cortices in order for them to demonstrate their skills and knowledge to the New York State Board of Regents. In my best principal-speak, I suggested the way forward. "To put your minds at rest, I'm not holding any of you accountable for this unfortunate situation. Instead, I'm leaving it up to you, as friends, to work this out. As you can see, Clive's privacy has been violated and trust needs to be restored. I hope that he'll allow you to make amends, too. If you ladies are ready, I want you to report to your exam room." The girls were excused and it instantly felt like there was more oxygen in the room. I took a seat beside Clive.

"Look, I know this stings and it's going to sting for a while. The good news is that there are only a few days left to the school year.

The summer vacation will give you time to let all of this simmer down and for the friendships to heal. I can assure you I will deal with Robbie Barrett, but I'm going to ask you to do something. After you finish your exam, I'd like you to stop in to see Ms. Harvey. That is, if you feel up to taking the test. I'll inform your proctor that you'll be taking it here in my office." Clive didn't answer, continued to rub his thigh and finally, nodded in agreement. I handed him a box of tissues, wishing I could hand us both a stiff drink instead.

I left Clive alone to work on his English regents after going over the directions and setting out crackers and water on the credenza for him. To confirm that all was quiet in the junior locker wing, I did a walk-through. The custodian had just finished removing Clive's artwork from the walls as I came down the hallway. He handed the sketches to me. "I'll take another look around. If I find any others, I'll drop them by your office."

"Thanks, Frank. I appreciate it."

"Sad, huh, Doug? This kid is talented, but these drawings show some muddy waters."

"Maybe. Maybe not. Keep your eyes open, will you? I expect the graduating class is planning some monkey business of their own doing. I want to keep the lid on till they all go home for the summer."

I didn't look at the drawings on my way to Claire Harvey's office, but I gave her time to browse through them before I started to explain how they ended up on display that morning. "I think it was a fairly impetuous prank on the part of the girls. They didn't mean anything malicious by it, but Robbie …"

"Not again." Claire shook her head at the mention of his name.

"Anyway, he pinched the sketchbook from Hettie's locker before she could return it to Clive and now they're all upset, all except Robbie. He's playing innocent. So, who do I call first?"

"Clive's got talent, I have to say, but a few of these illustrations raise some questions in my mind. Take a look at this one." She passed it over to me as she continued, "It's labeled as a self-portrait."

"If this were my son's, I'd be nervous and might wonder what he was ingesting. Should I share this with his father or will that do more damage than good?"

"Let me talk to Clive, first. I'll call his father after that. In the meantime, I think you need to deal with Sylvia Barrett."

"Glory! That'll be a waste of time."

"Time to lower the boom, Doug. He's been hiding behind his mommy's skirts for too long."

"It's exam week. Can't suspend him and there's not much else going on except for graduation."

"You could ban him from attending; maybe consider isolation for the remainder of his exams. You might also want to find out if he used the staff copier for all the photocopies."

"I can't lock everything down and put the burden on the staff."

"Just keep in mind that the number of students who see Robbie getting away scot-free is growing."

"Is he, really? That boy's only got but one friend and he has to live with Sylvia." Claire laughed aloud.

I took the long route back to the Main Office, peeking into a few classrooms to watch the student body hard at work. Such a dichotomy—one minute all was peaceful and scholastic—the next minute, a hormonal hurricane of teenage sturm and drang.

Sylvia Barrett

"Are you calling my son a thief?"

I heard Principal McIntire clear his throat over the phone before he tried to cover his behind with his silver tongue, saying that wasn't exactly what he meant. I knew what he meant! He was always on Robbie's case about something. As if my boy didn't have enough pressure at home.

"Robbie took things a bit too far, Mrs. Barrett. A student's private work has been made public, but what also concerns me is that he broke into the school after hours."

"How do you know that?"

"The hallway was covered in the drawings. If students and staff had been around, someone surely would've noticed the person hanging them up and reported it."

"So, what you're saying is that there weren't any witnesses. Then, how do you know it was Robbie?"

"Another student identified him as the one who reached into her locker to take the sketchbook."

"*Her* locker? Was it her sketchbook?"

"No, as I've explained. The sketchbook belonged to her friend and she'd planned to return it to him that day."

"Let me get this straight. You're telling me that Robbie took a bunch of drawings from some girl's locker and hung copies of the drawings in the hallway. And you say this girl is telling you the truth, but that my son is lying. Couldn't it be the other way around?" I wasn't about to back down. Sure, Robbie was a little impulsive at times, but I couldn't see why he'd be interested in somebody else's drawings.

"Mrs. Barrett, I'm not taking this lightly. Property has been damaged and a student has been humiliated."

"Whose sketchbook is it?"

"I don't feel that's relevant to the outcome."

"How can you say that? Maybe this kid has been antagonizing Robbie. Maybe I should speak with the parent. Robbie will tell me who it is."

"It's the same boy we spoke about after the Spring Rally incident, Clive Tierney."

"Not that oddball! I want you to know that Robbie has tried on several occasions to be nice to him. That kid is a loner. You can tell by the way he dresses that there's something weird about him. And don't get me started on his father who doesn't have a friendly bone in his body."

"Mrs. Barrett, let's try to stay focused on your son's actions. I'm afraid I'll have to bar him from campus activities for the rest of the week, other than taking his exams, that is. His report card will be mailed home."

"So, my son takes the blame with no proof of his guilt."

"I've made my decision."

"It doesn't sound to me like a fair decision. You told me yourself that Robbie said he's not the one who destroyed the sketchbook."

I heard the sigh before he answered. "Students saw Robbie run off with the sketchbook and your son told me that someone took it from him after that, but I have no corroboration to support his claim."

"We're right back where we started. You're calling my son a liar and a thief! How do you know Clive didn't do this himself?"

"Listen. Clive is upset. It's uncomfortable for him to have his private thoughts and feelings exposed to the entire student body. He wouldn't have done this to himself. I've made my decision based on the information in front of me."

"And I'm telling you that you don't have the whole story. I'll talk to Robbie when he gets home, but you haven't heard the last of this!" I slammed down the phone.

I didn't want this trouble brought home. Craig had been putting in extra hours at the tavern, or so he said, and was cantankerous around the house. I didn't want to give him an excuse to tear into me or Robbie. I'd been constantly cleaning and cooking up his favorites to placate him, but he'd flare up like a match dropped on brittle-dry pine needles if he got wind of Robbie's latest scrape. The two of them barely spoke to each other these days. It was left to me to boost our son's self-esteem, make him feel he was worth something, and as far as I could see, the school had done nothing to help. I made another phone call before Robbie came home.

He came drifting in around dinner time when his friend, Nick, dropped him off. Craig had already left for his shift at Tully's Tavern over in the Bay. The girls had eaten and were out in the kitchen cleaning up, so I sat down with Robbie while he ate. "Mr. McIntire called me today."

"Yeah, I knew he would," he said with a mouthful of mashed potato.

"Robbie, swallow your food before speaking." I didn't want my son to grow up eating like his father who slumped over his plate and shoveled the food in faster than he could chew, letting the excess dribble back down his chin. He'd wipe it off on his sleeve and I'd be the one to clean out the stains. A pig of a man!

"What's all this about? Did you take Clive's sketchbook and tear it up?"

"Mom!" He stopped to swallow. "Mom, I told him I didn't do that."

"But you did take it from a girl's locker."

"Yeah, I took it and left it on a table in the cafeteria. When I went back, it was gone. I was going to give it back."

I knew this wasn't the whole truth, but I didn't press. McIntire had doled out punishment enough. "I thought I told you to keep away from Clive. You can see that boy's got his own problems."

"I didn't go near him."

"You're to finish your exams this week and that's it. You can't be hanging around the school after that since you've been suspended for the last day."

"I know. It's not fair."

"Maybe not, but I've found you something else to do in the meantime. You're going to work for Mr. Jacobsen over at the marina where your father docks his boat."

"You got me a job? Might have been nice if you'd asked me about it first." He dropped his fork onto his plate, his face dark with anger. I was startled to see my husband's scowl on my son's face. I had to make him see that this was good for him (and safer than having him home when his father was around).

"Look, this is a way to earn some money over the summer. You could start saving for a car or college. Earning money of your own will make you feel good."

The scowl faded slightly. "Geez, Mom. I don't know. What's he going to have me do?"

"You'll be pumping gas at the docks, maybe minding the store, or doing errands. He agreed to give you a try, Robbie. You start on Wednesday afternoon. Don't let me down."

Without another word, Robbie stomped off to his room. I cleared up his dishes and happened to glance out the dining room window just as Jeff Tierney pulled into his driveway. I'd never seen him volunteer one minute of his time at school, yet his kid got all the sympathy while my son got none. Robbie was right. It wasn't fair.

Andrew Zey

Clive did something he almost never does; he called to reschedule his lesson saying that he wasn't feeling well. There'd been times when he'd hauled his sorry self over here feeling sicker that a kennel cat, so I knew this had to be serious, but he hung up before I could ask him about it. When I saw him the next night, he looked notably haggard. "You're looking wrung out. Are you okay?"

"Just tired. I need you to listen to the Mendelssohn piece I'm going to play for the graduation ceremony." Yeah, Clive was trying to be sly by changing the subject.

"No, we're not going there yet. Tell me what's going on with you, man. Did you pick up a virus at school?"

"It's finals week. I just need this week to be over."

"Oh, right. Exams. I forgot. Why don't we postpone lessons till next week?"

"But I need help on this piece. The ceremony's on Friday night." So, I listened. To give him some space, I moved over to an armchair and sat with my eyes closed. After his first play-through, we went over a few measures where I thought he could improve the phrasing and dynamics. After that, we talked through it some more before he played the entire piece again, while I watched and listened.

"Much better. Your audience will be impressed." Clive didn't smile at this. He looked away. "Something's going on with you. Want to tell me about it?" My people barometer was telling me he'd just been rejected by a girl or his dog had died, but I knew he didn't have a dog. Or, did he? It suddenly occurred to me that I really didn't know that much about him.

It came out slowly. "High school's a drag. The kids there are mostly ..."

He didn't seem to know what to say. "Just dumb kids?"

"I don't know. I don't fit in."

"Every kid feels like that in high school."

He almost smiled. "I doubt it."

"Well, maybe I can't speak for them all, but I certainly didn't know who I was then." Still thinking a girl might be at the bottom of this, I added, "I didn't know anything about girls." That was one way to put it.

"How'd you figure it all out?"

"Life figured it out for me. You've got to do what works for you, what's comfortable for you, and throw the rest away. It's like trying on shoes, you know. Sometimes you can tell by looking at them that you're not going to like them, other times you have to wear them for a while to figure out they're killing you. After some trials and errors, you learn which ones are a good fit. You can't let someone else pick out your shoes for you, Clive."

That got a laugh out of him, but I couldn't tell if I was hitting the mark. If he had his heart set on being a professional musician, he was going to need shoes with tough soles.

Dr. Jack Voss

Was I more upset with Hettie or myself for this foul imbroglio? I should've known better than to take on a family friend as a patient, though that is a circumstance difficult to avoid in a community like ours where low population density tends to breed familiarity among those who've put down roots. The bands of such a relationship were bound to stretch, until someone was snapped in the face and I should've applied sounder judgment.

I'd just put the phone down after speaking with Jeff Tierney who'd called to explain that there'd been an episode at school involving Clive's sketchbook and public humiliation. Jeff wanted to know if I thought this kind of thing would throw his son off the rails i.e. cause him to harm himself. (He's not the first to have mistaken me for a fortune teller rather than a psychiatrist.) I reiterated my conclusion that Clive was somewhat obsessive compulsive, a worrier perhaps, but that he'd given me no reason to think he was a serious danger to himself. (In fact, he was more mature than most of his peers who barely gave a thought to the next day, let alone the future, before they acted.) That being said, I cautioned Tierney to keep the lines of communication open with his son and informed him that he could call me at any hour if Clive needed my assistance.

It's what came next that perturbed me. Tierney explained that he was going to engage the services of another physician due to Hettie's involvement with his son. I assured him that no professional lines had been crossed on my part, but he told me that it'd been Clive's decision. Disconcerted by this, I pressed him for more information. He was reluctant to tell me about Hettie's role in the latest development, but finally related what he knew. I offered my apologies and promised to forward a copy of Clive's records for his next physician.

I put the phone down and took time to collect my thoughts. As a professional, I'd frequently given advice about anger management.

As a father, it was a different matter. This was my daughter we'd been talking about! After a few minutes of pacing in front of the window in my office, I walked to the bottom of the stairs and took a deep breath before going up to knock on her bedroom door.

"Hettie, may I come in?"

"Sure, Dad."

She was seated at her desk which sat in front of a window overlooking the backyard. My daughter had a fondness for the décor de désordre—in other words, clutter. She'd been collecting paper and books of all sorts since she was a preschooler. Like her mother, she also collected photos, many of them tacked to the wall by one means or another. I hated to think what kind of wall repair would be involved in order to repaint the room. River scenes and artifacts dominated the muddle.

"Studying?"

"Uh-huh." The open notebook on her desk contained her handwritten chemistry equations.

"Tough year, eh?"

"Yeah, can't wait till this one's over."

"Only a few more days. I need to discuss something with you, but maybe we should wait until tomorrow afternoon. You sound tired."

She looked up at me and I noted the redness of her moist eyes and drippy nose. I brushed a strand of caramel-brown curls away from her face. "I know what happened to Clive. Is that what has you upset?" She covered her face with her hands and began to weep aloud. Her tears doused my smoldering choleric. A woman's tears are the most powerful of magical charms to alter the nature of a man, even more potently effective on a father's disposition. I bent down to hug her.

"Why don't you tell me the whole story so I can help you through this."

We sat side by side on her rumpled bed as she held onto a frayed, stuffed bear—one I'd purchased for her during the Cape

Festival just before she was born—and thereby added a wild pansy or the eye of newt (hard to tell which) to the potion that yanked on all my heartstrings. She sniffled her way through the saga. "I didn't know Darcy had taken his sketchbook until we were all back at her place. I felt bad about looking at his private drawings, so I was going to return it to him on Monday, but Robbie stole it from me before I could get it back to Clive."

It's unpleasant to admit that your only daughter hasn't always been one hundred percent truthful with you. In my line of work, I've seen many parents struggle to understand the secret lives of their children, but this seemed to be a case of spontaneous behavior without malicious intent. "I can't say I'm pleased about your crashing in on your brothers' campout or your lack of candidness with your mother and me."

"I know. I know. I made of mess of things."

"Well, I don't think you meant to hurt Clive. Did you tell anyone that Robbie had taken the sketchbook?"

"I was thinking about it overnight, trying to decide whether to ask Josh for help or go to Ms. Harvey."

"Josh? Why would you get him involved?"

"He can stand up to Robbie and make him back down."

"How do you know this?"

Hettie bit her lip. "Well, you know Josh. He takes command and he's tough."

I sensed that there was more to this story, but I let it go to avoid going off on a tangent. "I'm afraid that the fallout from this whole comedy of errors has resulted in my loss of a patient, too." She looked alarmed. "I think Clive's right to choose another physician outside his circle of acquaintances, but I hope that the two of you will be able to mend your friendship." My daughter collapsed into my arms again, sobbing.

"Hettie, it's not irreversible damage. Just find a moment to talk with Clive and apologize. Tell him exactly what you've told me."

"How will he ever trust me again?"

I patted her back and smoothed her hair. "Step by step. Reconciliation is accomplished one step at a time. First, you apologize. Second, you wait."

"Wait? For what?"

"Forgiveness."

"I don't know, Dad. If the roles were reversed, I'm not sure I could do the same."

"This is one of those tests of character."

"And, if he does forgive me, what's the next step?"

"Rebuild."

Ralph Jacobsen, Marina Owner

The wife and I didn't see much of her cousin, Sylvia. Not since she married that no-good clout, Craig Barrett. They'd been teen parents and anyone with eyes or ears that worked could've seen that guy didn't have both oars in the water. Bent he was and a drinker besides. Gossip had it that he cheated on Sylvia, but she never breathed a word about that business to us. Some said he knocked her around, too. Just kept it all to herself, she did, that is if it was true, while she doted on her three kids.

So, when she'd called the wife to ask for help, there wasn't nothin' I could do but give the okay. First off, my wife's got a heart big as this continent; I can't say no to her. And secondly, I guess I felt I'd been a pretty lucky fellow myself and maybe I could do somethin' for the boy. His old man had a fire in his belly that no one could put out, short of puttin' out his lights for good, sorry to say. I heard tell some of his fire had spread onto his son and I guess I was thinkin' maybe I could change the boy's outlook, teach him that not all men are louts.

I started fixin' boats almost thirty years ago. When I came into property, after my father passed, I built the docks and opened a small marina with twenty slips. Then I started rentin' trailer space to the summer residents. Eventually, I added cabins. Some years were better than others on account of the weather, but all in all, River life had been good to me. Never had a hankerin' to go anywhere else, not even in the worst of winters.

My own sons worked right alongside of me. We were a team, so I told them we'd play it by ear. If Robbie proved to be a good worker, we'd keep him on for the summer. If not, we'd make the decision together when to cut him loose. He came in here that first day wearin' an attitude all over a face droopin' as low as his drawers. Probably didn't like that his mother had signed him up for work. I decided to dangle the carrot before I put the saddle on his back by talkin' dollars and cents. Then I planned to keep him busy, too busy to do any bellyachin'.

"Well, son, you're gonna have some money to put in your pocket this summer if you do what I tell you. I'm gonna start you out at minimum wage, but if you work hard and your work's good, I'll boost that up in a few weeks."

"What kind of hours do I work?"

His question carried a surly edge.

"Don't be speakin' to me in that tone of voice. I'm older than you and I'm your boss. Mind your manners." He stared harder. "Everybody here works on Saturday and we alternate Sundays. You can have Tuesdays off and your hours are ten till six-thirty with a break for lunch. You need to see Mrs. Jacobsen before start time every day to check your schedule."

No smile. No response. He just kept diggin' the toe of his sneaker into the grass, lookin' down at the ground, now.

"Let's head on over to the pumps. Seth's gonna show you how to gas up a boat."

"I know how. I've helped my dad."

"Good, then you can show me. Just a word of caution, though. Not all boats are the same."

One of my customers had just come in with his sport boat and Seth was givin' him a hand to tie up. Robbie grabbed the nozzle from one of the pumps and said, "Someone's got to stand on the front." I climbed onto the bow myself, happy to see the boy knew what he was doin'. This boat's engine was in the back of the boat, along with the gas tank, which meant that someone had to stand on the bow during the fuel up in order to distribute the weight and level out the fuel tank so that the indicator would accurately read, *full.*

"No spillage, that's important. Can't be washin' those dollars away or pollutin' the River." The customer handed his cash payment to my son who took it inside to the register.

"Did you hear Seth ask if there'd be anything else? Some of the customers need an extra can of gas for other tools or smaller boats out at their cottages. Askin' that question could bring in another sale."

My son returned with the change for the boat owner and untied the mooring lines from their cleats as the engine turned over.

"There are always jobs to be done even when there are no customers to wait on." I led him into the repair shop and directed Robbie over to a craft which had just been taken out of storage. "The owner's comin' up this weekend. We've just removed the shrink wrap and need to get this boat cleaned up. That includes inside and out." Robbie wasn't sayin' much; I just kept on talkin', explaining what materials he'd need to get the job done. "You hear another boat pull up to the pumps, though, you drop what you're doin'. That customer is your first priority." He nodded and picked up the rubber gloves and the pail of cleaning solution.

His first day was a slow one at the pumps, being kind of overcast on the River. Robbie did a fair job of cleaning up the boat, but when I asked him to bring her around to the pumps, he appeared hesitant.

"Haven't driven one before?"

"Sometimes my friend lets me take the wheel of his when we're out on the water."

I untied the lines and hopped in to give the boy a real lesson on boat piloting. We had to back out of the slip in the boathouse first.

"Easy on the throttle as you move in reverse. That's it. As you come out, look around for incoming craft." He turned her about and pulled up to the fuelin' dock with a gentle hand. "You sure you've never done this before?" He looked a tad embarrassed, but I could tell that he appreciated my words. After fillin' the tank, I suggested we head out for a test drive, lettin' him handle the wheel.

The rain had started by the time we returned to the docks. When we pulled in, we noticed Craig had pulled his boat from her slip up to the pumps. He nearly did a double take when he saw his son drivin' that beauty of a craft. Craig owned a beat-up cuddy which needed a good scrub and a tune-up, but he wasn't gonna spend the time or the money. In fact, the "t" had been missing from the *Footloose* for more than a couple of years and he hadn't bothered to paint it back in.

"I'm gonna get the canopy on. Why don't you give your father a hand with the fuelin'?"

I watched Robbie out of the corner of my eye as he skipped onto the bow of the *Footloose* to level her off. "What are you doin' ridin' in that boat with Jacobsen? Why aren't you in school, boy?"

"I'm working."

"Workin'? What do you mean?"

"I've got a job here for the summer."

Craig replaced the fuel pump and tightened the gas cap. "Well, that's the best idea I've heard, yet. You gettin' paid in cash?" Robbie shrugged his shoulders while Craig glanced over at me.

"Where you going, Dad?"

"It's none of your business where I'm goin'. When you finish up here, you get yourself home, that's all you need to know."

I saw the boy's shoulders slump as he stepped back onto the dock. I went on over to collect for the gas.

"Twenty-eight fifty, Craig." He reached in his pocket and handed me thirty dollars. "Your son's done a good job today. I think he'll work out just fine."

"Why wouldn't he work out?" Craig asked gruffly.

I just shook my head and went back into the shop to get his change and my rain parka. Craig had already pulled away from the dock by the time I came back out. It was rainin' harder now and I couldn't help but wonder to myself why he'd be out on the water in this weather, but then he never did have much sense. I gave the dollar-fifty to Robbie. "See you tomorrow, ten a.m. You need a ride home?"

Robbie Barrett

What was my old man doing out there on the River in the rain? When I sat down to dinner, I asked my mother where he was and she said he'd been called into the tavern early. I didn't bother to tell her otherwise because I didn't want his lies to leave any bruises on her, physically or emotionally.

Good thing I had work the next day since I was done with exams and since McIntire had finally managed to suspend me. I didn't want to be stuck at home. Mom dropped me off at the marina just before ten o'clock. The River was calm. The rain and wind from the day before had spun out and the hot sun was burning off the haze. I walked past the docks and noticed that my old man's boat was not in her slip. Was he already out on the water? Sometimes he spent the night in a room over the bar at the tavern. Mom didn't object; she didn't dare.

I stopped into the shop to see what Mrs. Jacobsen had on the schedule for me. Looked like I'd be unpacking and shelving inventory.

"The truck just pulled out, Robbie. Start with anything that requires refrigeration."

Just as I'd finished restocking bags of ice, I heard a boat pull up to the docks. I closed the ice chest and headed on out to see if a customer wanted refueling. That's when I saw the *Footloose* pulling into her slip. The boat was buttoned up tight in its canvas canopy except for where my old man stood to peer out over the windshield while he steered. I walked over to help him tie up thinking I'd get a better look at whatever he was hiding. When I grabbed the bow line, he snapped at me. "I can get that!"

"Just thought I'd give you a hand."

"I said no need. Aren't you workin'?"

"Yeah."

"Then, get on with it."

I threw the line back up on the bow and left him to it. Back inside the store, I got busy breaking down some empty boxes, then carried them out to the dumpster. By then, my father had driven his truck down to the shoreline and was lugging a big marine cooler up from the boat. The top was taped down and there was a number scrawled on it, written in fat green marker. Must've weighed plenty 'cause my old man was strong, but he was gruntin' and groanin' as he shoved it up into the back of his truck. Since when did my old man catch that much fish? I couldn't remember the last time my mother had cooked fresh fish that he'd caught himself. That got me thinking. I wondered how long a person would stay locked away in a prison cell if he was to get nailed for smuggling.

The next morning, I woke up at my usual going-to-school time before I remembered I'd been suspended and still had a couple of hours till I had to be at work. Work—that word was taking on a whole new meaning for me. School was boring every day. Learning was 2-D. Everything was in a book, on a worksheet, on writing paper, on a screen, or a chalkboard. There was no action. At Jacobsen's, I was *doing* a job, real work, not sitting in a chair all day staring at print or listening to some boring teacher drone on and tell me how important it was to pay attention to stuff I didn't care about. I could look at the shelves in Jacobsen's shop, the grass, the boat I scrubbed, and see what I'd done. Even better, I was getting paid for what I did. Maybe McIntire had done me a favor.

Feeling hungry, I got out of bed, pulled on my jeans and a clean t-shirt, then went downstairs to scramble up some eggs.

"Robbie! You're cooking?" Denise gawked at me when she

came through the kitchen to grab some on-the-go food for school. "Are you feeling alright?"

"A working man's gotta eat."

"You've got a job? What did you do with my real brother?" She hightailed it out the back door before I could answer.

My sister, Shelley, wasn't a morning person. I'm not sure she was an afternoon person either. She wasn't a girlie girl like Denise and a lot of other girls in my high school. No makeup covered her red pimpled face and her nappy hair always looked like someone had just sheared a sheep and stuck a dingy wad of the fleece on top of her head. She shuffled around the kitchen like a silent zombie, picking up the tea kettle and filling it with water.

"What are you doing, Shelley? It must be 80 degrees outside already!"

She didn't answer, but just shot me a look that said, "Drop dead." Since I was in a good mood, I offered her some eggs, but she made a gagging face before snarling, "Don't leave a mess in here for Mom. Dad's home this morning and I don't want any of us catching crap for something you did." Shelley filled her thermos with black tea, then slammed the door on her way out. She'd thrown a dirty, wet rag over the start of the day. I gulped down my breakfast, washed up the dishes, wiped down the counter and the stovetop. To avoid my old man, I decided to ride my bike over to the marina early, leaving a note for my mother so she'd know where I was.

Seth Jacobsen was just climbing aboard a large ride-on mower when I pulled up to the bike rack outside the store. "You're early! We haven't opened up the store, yet."

"Guess I'll wait unless your father has something for me to do."

"He's gone to Watertown to run some errands." Seth looked about for a minute, then turned back. "You could give me a hand with some mowing."

"You're going to let me drive that rig?"

He smiled and shook his head. Seth was his old man on a diet, same broad-shouldered build minus the potbelly. Talked like him, too—real polite without a lot of cuss words. "Nope. Not today. Got a hand mower for you, though. You can do in-between the cabins with it, but start along the walkways so we can give the lodgers time to have their morning coffee."

We walked to the barn where boats were stored for the winter along with tools and equipment for the marina. Seth pushed back one of the vehicle doors to fetch a mower, signaling for me to snag a gas can. "You gotta remember never to fill the gas tank when the mower is running. It could explode on you and turn you into fried flesh. Always turn it off before cleaning out a clog or clearing the blade, too."

"I do the mowing at home."

"That's all well and good, but I just want to make sure you know the rules. My dad's big on safety around our marina. You'll find some gloves hanging on the hooks just inside the door, there. Grab a pair for yourself. You may want to wear a hat in the future, too, to keep the sun off." I could tell by the way Seth was taking care to give me instructions that he'd never been knocked around by his father.

It took me all morning to finish the mowing with occasional interruptions by customers wanting to refuel. My forearms were already darkened by the fierce sun and I had to douse my head twice under the hose near the dock before I'd finished up. Mrs. Jacobsen called me into the shop shortly after noon and told me to choose something from the refrigerator aisle for lunch.

"Now, as long as you check with me first, it's fine if you pick up a meal here. If you don't see something you like, you can bring your own. Just make sure you drink a lot of water on days like this."

I sat under the big elm tree by the riverfront to eat my ham and cheese sub. A heron swooped down onto a rock and waited for his own food to swim by. The smell of the fresh cut grass filled the air behind me. I listened to the river tap a soft slap-slap-gurgle, slap-slap-gurgle against the shore in front of me. I didn't feel restless just sitting there by myself like when I'm at home or sitting at a desk in school. After finishing my sandwich, I leaned back against the tree to watch the current until I was distracted by a large pickup hauling a boat trailer. The driver backed down the short, sloping concrete ramp to lower the craft into the water. He'd done this before, I could tell. He set the brake and left the engine running while he stepped out of the cab to wade in and release the boat. He climbed aboard and his wife moved over into the driver's seat of the truck. After a couple of sputters, the man got the boat engine running and signaled to his wife. She threw it into gear and pulled the empty trailer out of the water. They sure knew what they were doing; they had this down to a smooth routine. I heard a cheer from the back seat where two little boys were watching their daddy from the rear window of the cab. I wondered what it was like to take a family vacation. I'd never been further than Syracuse and that was when my mother took us to the State Fair. My father was fuming over the money she'd spent, but I think he was more pissed that we'd had fun. That was the first time he split my lip open. I was seven years old.

At quitting time, I went home to shower. A hamburger and potato salad were waiting for me when I came downstairs.

"So, how's the job going, Robbie?" This wasn't idle talk. Mom was fishing for information.

"It's okay."

"I spoke with Mr. Jacobsen, today. He said that you've been working hard."

I tossed my burger back onto the plate. "You aren't going to be checking up on me, are you?"

"I just want to make sure that he knows I'm grateful for giving you an opportunity."

"No, you don't. You want to make sure I'm not screwing up. If you keep butting in, I'll quit."

She sat down across from me, arms folded on the table. "You'll do no such thing. I'll stay out of your way as long as you don't give me a reason to suspect anything is wrong. I want you to earn some money this summer, Robbie."

"You want me out of the house."

She sighed and glanced out the window. We both knew that the less time I spent at home when my old man was around, the better. I changed the topic.

"Nick is picking me up soon. We're going to hang out in the Bay."

"I want you home before midnight."

"I'll try, Mom, but I'm going to be a senior this year. Time to loosen up those apron strings." I shot her a smile, but saw tears pool in her eyes before she stood up to rinse my dish in the sink. How would she survive once I left home?

Samantha De Haven

I called Clive the day after school ended. "How were your exams?"

"Too many Regents exams."

"And how was the campout?"

"The campout wasn't bad until some girls crashed in and stole my sketchbook."

"You're kidding! Did you get it back?" Clive took his time explaining how his sketchbook had been ruined and how all of his illustrations had been posted on the walls of his school. I knew how much the collection meant to him. "What are you going to do?"

"I guess I can put the recovered sketches in a scrapbook or a file."

"No, I mean about your friend and his sister. Think you'll hang out with them anymore?"

"I really don't feel like seeing anyone right now, except for you, that is. Sam, you're the only one I trust."

A pang of guilt shot through me. I was still struggling with whether or not to tell Clive about Eddie. We'd promised not to keep secrets from each other, but I wasn't convinced that Clive was Eddie's son. Maybe I was just holding onto doubt as an excuse not to make things worse for him, but these thoughts were interrupted by his next bombshell.

"I saw your stepfather again."

"WHAT?"

"Hey, I can hear you just fine. I said that I saw Eddie again. He was at the graduation ceremony."

"You spoke to him?" I was frightened that Eddie might be trying to establish contact with Clive and that this could bring down both our worlds.

"He came up to my father and me out in the parking lot. He introduced himself again and told me that he enjoyed my performance."

With a groan, I sat down hard on the floor of my bedroom.

"Sam? Sam? You still there?"

"I don't like this, Clive. I don't like it one bit. What was Eddie doing over there?"

"He didn't say and we didn't ask, but I wondered, too. Dad didn't say much because he was in a hurry to get home. I get the feeling he doesn't like Eddie."

The clock was ticking down to decision time, but I didn't want to tell him over the phone. I'd wait until Fourth of July weekend, unless something else happened in the meantime.

"Clive, I'm telling you. Eddie is not to be trusted. Stay away from him. You can tell your father I said that, too."

"What can he do to me, Sam?"

Trisha Cox

Private Investigator, Felix Silva, was worth every red cent I paid him. In fact, he was worth more. His background check on Eddie shoveled up lots of dirt. Besides his frequent affairs with other women, he had a string of unpaid debts, most of them from gambling. His slimy business partners had dubious backgrounds in the—ahem—import-export business. Like I didn't know what that meant. He was also under investigation by the IRS. That would explain not only the reason for his move back to Canada where he was born, but also why he'd been eager to marry me—and my money—so quickly. Even though he'd been implicated in a few questionable business dealings, Eddie had so far escaped criminal charges that stuck. Someone must've paid for his sleazy lawyer or paid off a judge.

I met with Felix at The Loon's Inn to discuss his findings over cocktails.

"So far, I haven't found any adoption records for the boy."

"What does that mean?"

"Well, could be Eddie's not the father. Or, could mean he and this Veronica just gave the baby away."

"That sounds too generous for Eddie. Is this Tierney man married?"

"Never has been, that I can find."

"So, if this boy is Eddie's son, he just handed him over to some single guy?"

"Or, Veronica did. Then, again, we could be reading this all wrong. Hard to tell with so little evidence."

"Have you been following Eddie?"

"That's why you pay me. Your husband took a curious trip last weekend. He drove over the border to Clayton, a speck of a town on the St. Lawrence, and attended the high school graduation. Afterwards, I observed him talking to a man and his teenage son. The boy played the piano during the ceremony and his name just happens to be Clive Tierney."

"The boy in the newspaper article. Got anything on the man with him?"

"Jeffrey Tierney works for the Border Patrol. That's all I've got for now."

"The Border Patrol! Now, that's intriguing. See if you can find out how the boy came to live with him. I need to know what Eddie is up to."

Felix set an envelope on the bar before leaving. Included inside were labeled photos of a few of Eddie's cronies, Eddie himself, Jeff Tierney, and the young boy named, Clive. I gazed closer at the teenager, looking for resemblances. How could a creature so beautiful be related to this contemptible excuse of a man?

Gary Stanton

I picked up Samantha early Saturday morning. Before we even hit 401 East, the silence filling the cab of my truck was almost as suffocating as the humidity outside. Sam was staring out the window, trying to ignore Spike's nuzzling, and devouring the fingernail and cuticle of her right index finger.

"Something up, Sam? Did you and my sister have a fight?"

"No."

Okay. So, it was going to be twenty questions. "Aren't you looking forward to fireworks and grilled steak at the River this weekend?"

A brief smile, followed by more silence.

"Alright. You don't have to tell me what's on your mind, but I do hope whatever it is won't spoil your time with Clive."

"I'm worried about him, Uncle Gary. Did you hear what happened?"

"When?"

"At the campout."

"Clive told me he had a great time."

"Did he say anything about his sketchbook?"

Now, who was playing twenty questions? "No." I heard the distant ping of a warning bell go off in my head.

"Apparently, some girls stole it from his tent and somehow his sketches ended up on the walls of his school. Clive is really ticked off about it."

"He should be. Why would someone do that?"

"Some kid's been bullying him and that kid stole the sketchbook from one of the girls. A lot of kids made rude comments about his drawings."

"Like what?"

"Like he's gay or a perv."

I felt my stomach flip. The bullying had escalated. "I'll talk to him about it this weekend. Sounds like Jeff is going to have to get involved."

She was quiet for several minutes before she added, "There's more."

"More? More what?"

"Clive told me that he saw Eddie again."

The alarm bell rang louder now.

"Where?"

"At the school, after the graduation ceremony."

CLANG! CLANG! CLANG!

"What was he doing there?"

"I'm not sure, but he walked up to Jeff and Clive and complimented him on his piano performance." Sam was chewing her finger again. "I think something bad is going to happen, Uncle Gary. I don't know if I should tell you the rest, but someone has to look out for Clive."

"Wait. Give me a chance to pull off the road somewhere."

I exited the highway near Gananoque, and found a small gas station where I purchased an iced coffee for me and a soda for Sam, not that it was going to calm my nerves. We walked to the edge of the parking lot so that I could let Spike out for a nature break and give him a drink of water. This weekend was promising a soar in the heat index; possibly in my blood pressure, as well.

"Okay, Sam. Spit it out."

"A letter came to the house for Eddie, but Mom being Mom, opened it. It wasn't a letter, really. It was a newspaper clipping about Clive performing in the piano competition and at the graduation ceremony. I should've torn it up before Eddie saw it, but I knew that Mom had already blown up at him about it over the phone."

The alarm bell exploded into a pounding migraine, now.

"On the back of the clipping was a note saying something about how they shouldn't have given up their baby boy. It was from Veronica and I think she was referring to Clive."

Dread spread through my veins, forcing the pain to pulse through my head as if it was clamped into a vise which tightened with each word she spoke. I held the cold drink to my forehead, trying to force logic up through the fog of discomfort and rising nausea.

"Veronica Wallace!" She was shouting, now. Hot tears puddled in my eyes. "That means she's not dead!" I tried to silence her with a wave of my hand, but she ignored me. "If Eddie is Clive's real father, maybe Veronica was already pregnant when she married Jeff. Maybe Jeff doesn't even know that Clive isn't his."

Was it the headache blurring my vision or were Sam's hands shaking as she raised the soda to her lips? I pushed Spike's leash at her and sprinted to the restroom. My stomach wasn't going to hold. After the retching ceased, I rinsed my face and held the cup of ice to my head again while I walked back to the truck to retrieve some painkiller from the glove box.

"Are you alright, Uncle Gary?"

"Massive headache. Here, take this, will you, and buy me a cola. I need something carbonated." Sam took the five-dollar bill into the convenience store while I jammed the key in the ignition to start up the air conditioning and leaned back in the seat beside Spike who licked at my ear. It wasn't the first time he'd seen me buckle under a stress-induced migraine. Questions mingled with the throbbing pain. Had Jeff *lied* to me about his son? Was his recent distracted behavior due to his encounters with Eddie? Had Jeff and Eddie previously known each other? I pounded the steering wheel. "He wouldn't! He wouldn't lie to me!" Spike barked in response to my wail.

Sam returned with the large, icy beverage. I slurped greedily, trying to dull the aching and the doubts.

"Are you okay to drive?"

I nodded. "It'll subside soon."

"Here. I bought some mints to help your stomach." As she handed me the small tube of peppermints, I couldn't help thinking what an accomplished caretaker she'd become, growing up with my needy sister.

"Maybe I shouldn't have told you. I didn't know what else to do. If Clive finds out about all this, what will happen to him?"

"I don't want to swear you to secrecy, Sam. You're carrying enough around. I'm just asking that you not say anything till I've had a chance to talk to Jeff. If it turns out that ..." My voice broke then. I could barely get the words out. "If it turns out that any of this is true, Jeff will have to decide how to tell Clive."

"I hope it's not too late, Uncle Gary."

IV. Maelstrom: a turbulent current

Hettie Voss

Friday and Saturday were packed with relatives and graduation honors for Josh. It was hard to imagine what the house was going to be like after he left for Annapolis. He was the Master of Ceremonies, bringing home most of the activity and excitement, even if he tended to boss Stuart and me around like he was our commanding officer. Since Josh's scolding of me, the air between us had remained cold and silent. It wasn't anger I felt, though; it was more like heartache. I didn't want him to go.

I missed Clive, too. We hadn't spoken since the sketchbook ordeal when I'd barely been able to verbalize an apology to him in McIntire's office, but I cried all the way through his performance at the ceremony. How was it possible for him to lose himself in the music in front of the same people who one minute could scoff at him and the next, applaud? I needed to know if Clive had lost all trust in me.

A week after graduation, I pedaled my bike to Clayton. Jason had become a confidante in my troubles with Clive. Maybe he was becoming something more. I wasn't sure, but he was the only person I knew who might be able to tell me what Clive was thinking. Did he hate me? Was he ever going to speak to me again? Was this the end of whatever we had before it even got started?

I found Jason clearing out a utility shed full of old boat bumpers, tangled boat lines, some garden tools, gas cans, and a multitude of spiders. "Are you being punished for something?"

He laughed as he slapped dust from his jeans. "Looks like it, doesn't it? That's what happens when you work for family; you work from the bottom up. None of that favoritism you might have heard about. What about you? Don't you have to work today?"

"My lifeguard shift starts after the Fourth."

"Lucky you. So, what are you doing for the holiday weekend?"

"I don't think my parents have planned anything. They're still trying to recover from graduation weekend."

"No plans of your own?"

"Well, that's sort of why I'm here."

"Aha. I thought so."

There was a note of disappointment in his voice, but I pretended not to notice. "You've probably guessed that I came to find out if you've talked to Clive."

"And if I did?"

"I just want to know if he's ever going to speak to me again."

"I think he's pretty upset and needs some space."

"Should I call him? Go to his house?"

"He's not home. His Dad took this week off and they're over on Tar Island."

"I've got to see him before he leaves for music camp. How can I fix this, Jason?"

"Look, I'm sure Clive is thinking this all out. He knows you weren't the one who stole his sketchbook and he certainly knows what Robbie did."

"I don't think I can wait a whole month to clear this up, though."

"You may not have a choice. Not unless ..."

"Unless what?"

"We could try to visit him."

"You mean, on the island?" I suddenly felt very excited, almost lighter, about the possibility of setting things straight. "Does that mean you would take me over there? Could you? I'll pay for the gas. I'll pack a picnic. I'll even help you clean out this shed!"

"That's a deal. You do know that cleaning out this shed includes sweeping out spiderwebs and mouse dung?"

I immediately picked up the push broom from amongst the garden tools to get to work. "So, which day do you want to go over there?"

"I'm off on Sunday."

"We have to cross the border, you know. What will you tell your parents?"

"That I'm going to visit Clive, of course."

"Oh, have you done that before?"

"No, but I cross the border whenever my family goes to visit my grandmother. Didn't you know that my mom is Canadian?"

"She is?"

"She's also Algonquin and French."

"How come I didn't know this?"

"You never asked. There's a lot you don't know about me."

I again sensed that Jason was getting at something deeper, but pushed the thought away as he stomped on two more Daddy Longlegs.

"Including your arachnophobia!"

Trisha Cox

"Apparently, Tierney and his son spend weekends in Canada, somewhere in the area of the Thousand Islands. I'll follow up on that later in the week," said Felix.

"So, what more have you learned about this Veronica Wallace?" I asked.

"I found her sister, Rosalinde."

"And?"

"Apparently, there's no love lost between the siblings."

"What do you mean?"

"Well, Rosalinde is upset with her ex-husband, her boss, the world, and her sister for not treating her better. She has sulky teenagers and debts to which, she says, her sister has turned a blind eye and a deaf ear."

"What does this have to do with Eddie?"

"After complaining to me that her stingy sister lives in a big house in a posh neighborhood with her current stuck-up husband, Rosalinde went on to tell me that the hubby has no idea that Veronica sold her first-born child."

"She *sold* him?" I screamed into the phone.

"So Rosalinde says."

"Were Eddie and Veronica ever married?"

"According to the sister, they took the money and ran. After the money disappeared, so did Eddie and penniless Veronica returned home with her hand out, a hand which, at that time, lacked a wedding ring."

I hung up the phone thinking this was the best news I'd heard in a long time.

Gary Stanton

Samantha's revelation about the connection between Eddie and Veronica Wallace sat on my chest like a pile of wet sandbags. Sam and I didn't talk much for the rest of the drive to Rockport, each of us separately sifting through thoughts, feelings, targets of blame. I barely remember any of the miles between Gananoque and Lansdowne where I stopped for groceries. My stress level could've been measured in the pounds of food I purchased while trying to overcome the feeling that the earth was about to split open under my feet.

Clive and Jeff were waiting for us at the bottom of the hill when we pulled into Tar Island.

"You've brought enough to feed the families of a platoon, Gary! Who's going to eat all this?"

"Guess I'm used to buying in bulk." If Jeff noticed the curtness in my tone, he didn't say. I had all I could do to keep from lambasting him right there on the dock. I kept moving, lifting baggage and food boxes from boat to dock, from dock up to deck, leaving Sam on her own to veil her conflicting emotions.

After all the provisions were shuttled up to the cottage, Clive and Sam went out for a canoe ride. I started slamming things around the kitchen, stowing the refrigerated foods and looking for the alcohol. Jeff slipped out the back door, down the hill to the toolshed. He wasn't going to ask what was eating me; he probably hoped it would blow over. He was skilled at putting up a barricade to his own thoughts. Up until now, it had never occurred to me that he could've been hiding more than just his thoughts. I chugged a double shot of whiskey nerve before heading into the ring.

Jeff didn't risk coming back up to the cottage until he saw me out on the deck with cocktails and a platter of vegetables, strawberries, melted brie, and mini-toasts. Maybe he mistook the appetizers for a truce. "What's all this?"

"I need to talk to you."

"Aha. The elephant in the room," he muttered as he picked up his drink and sat down on the deck chair. "You still pissed I didn't spend that weekend alone with you when Clive went camping? I told you I had a lot to do."

Lie. Li-ar. My body temp rose another five degrees. I couldn't look at him. I clenched my glass tighter and forced myself to take a deep breath before I took the first swing. "I heard that Eddie was in your neighborhood for the graduation ceremony."

Jeff's hand halted in mid-air, glass in hand. He carefully measured out his words. "Where'd you hear that?"

He *ducked.* I took another swing. "Clive said something to Sam about it. Why do you think he showed up?"

"Guess he knew one of the graduates."

"Guess he also knows Clive."

Jeff set his glass back down on the table without making eye contact.

"Kind of a coincidence, don't you think? He shows up in Kingston, then in Clayton. He's also married to my sister and that, in itself, is bad enough. I don't want Eddie getting close with the people I care about."

"Well, he came to a graduation, heard Clive play, and stopped us in the parking lot to tell Clive how much he enjoyed his performance."

Oh, if only I could believe it was as simple as that. Time to hit him between the eyes. "I want you to be upfront with me; no more cat and mouse. Does Eddie want something from you?"

"What would make you think that? Because we've seen him twice? If anyone has brought Eddie closer to us, it's you because you decided to include your niece in our family time."

A sucker punch! I suddenly exploded. "I'll tell you why! A newspaper clipping about Clive's entry into the piano competition was mailed to Eddie, but my sister opened it. A woman named, Veronica, sent it to him with a note which implied that she regretted giving up *their* son." I watched as the color drained from Jeff's face. "You've been lying to me all these years." In that moment, it was as if all molecular movement had ceased in the space surrounding us, freezing us in still-motion silence. *Ten, nine, eight ...*

Finally, Jeff nodded. He wouldn't look at me; his eyes on the River. "Yes. Clive is Veronica's son. She was pregnant when I met her."

"And Eddie's son?"

He nodded, barely whispering. "Yes."

"So, she didn't die in any car accident."

"No. She left me."

"And you knew who Eddie was when you saw him in Kingston."

"Yes." He stepped up to the railing of the deck, then, and pounded on it. "I got up one morning and found that she'd left. No note, nothing. It was just me and Clive after that and no one came looking for him." He turned around to look at me. "I've always loved Clive as if he were my own."

"I'm not questioning that, but why did you let me think he was your biological son?"

"Look! I didn't mean to lie to you. I just didn't think I'd ever cross paths with Eddie again, so I convinced myself that he didn't matter, that it didn't matter. He hasn't been a father to Clive."

I wasn't satisfied with the answer, but a new fear suddenly struck me. "So, has Eddie come to claim his son after all this time?"

"No, he's come to bargain."

Samantha De Haven

As Clive guided the canoe eastward along the shoreline, I couldn't help but wonder what my uncle was saying to Jeff. Would the questions surrounding Clive's paternity poison their relationship? I didn't want to believe that Clive had any of Eddie's corrupted DNA. If it were true, I felt that this was one secret worth keeping.

"Let's go around the whole island," Clive suggested, looking back at me to see if I approved.

I tried to relax and concentrate on paddling, but even the magical balm of the River couldn't ease my anxiety. I was living in a horror movie in which my mother's descent into addiction had somehow exhumed some wicked spirit out to destroy Clive and the only two parents he'd ever known. An ominous feeling smothered my senses, preventing me from yielding to the serene beauty that surrounded me.

"What are you thinking about, Sam?"

There was no way I was going to answer that truthfully, so I steered the conversation to my own situation. "My mother, mostly. I wonder if I'll ever have a good relationship with her, one where I actually get to be the daughter instead of a powerless parent."

Clive stopped paddling. He turned back to look at me just as the floodgates broke open. *I hate to cry in front of people!* I think I was crying more for him than myself.

"I don't think I've ever seen you so upset."

"Yeah, maybe it's time for me to start drinking or do drugs. I don't think my mother would even notice." I wanted the tears to stop.

"Don't say that. You don't mean it, do you, Sam?"

Clive picked up the paddle then and steered us toward the shore on the backside of the island. When the canoe bumped up against land, he stepped out into the water. Grabbing the line, he waded up onto shore to pull in the canoe and tie the line to a young maple sapling. I didn't want to look up at him while in a weepy state, afraid that I'd blurt out the real reason for my meltdown. He took my hand then, and led me over to a sunny, half-submerged granite outcropping. We sat down and he put his arms around me, while I silently begged the sun to dry up my tears. He spoke quietly.

"Think about it like this. Addiction is holding your mom prisoner. She probably wants to be free of it, but she doesn't have any strength left. She can't fight back. She gives in."

"No, no, you don't! You don't get to have sympathy for her. She's ruined my life! She'll ruin other people's lives, too. My mother only cares about herself!" I heard my shouts reverberate across the surface of the water into the limber cattails waving from the opposite bank. A startled red-winged blackbird fluttered up into the air.

Clive was taken aback by my reaction, but gently began to stroke my hair. His caresses felt so warm, so comforting. I wanted to dissolve into him as the sobs poured out of me. He held me tighter and waited until my blubbering subsided.

"Sam, I hope you'll never get addicted to anything."

I looked up at him. Something in the grave tone of his voice alerted me that he wasn't just referring to my mother.

"You know that I'm obsessed with music and my hands. As

much as I try to reason with myself, I can't turn the music off in my mind. I keep hearing measures over and over, wanting my fingers to play it the way I hear it, flawlessly. When other things bother me, it's the same. Thoughts go round and round in my head and somehow work their way into my body until I'm desperate to find a way to shut it out with pain, a physical pain."

Straightening up, I turned around to face him. "What do you mean?"

He pulled up his shirt then to show me some fine, crusty, red slashes on his chest. I covered my mouth to stifle my alarm; then he told me about the cuts to his thighs. "The kids at school found out and I was sent to a counselor. He's trying to teach me some healthy ways to cope, but he's also trying to figure out what triggers my anxiety. It's not just the music, Sam. Do you ever feel like you're living a fake life?"

"Almost every day, except when I'm here."

"Exactly! When Dad, Gary, and I are on the island or out on the River, we're not pretending. I feel like no one is watching and we're free to be ourselves. I'm totally chill on the island."

"The same for me; that's why it's so hard to leave. I'll be so far away from you after I move in with my father and I don't know when I'll get back here, back to the River."

"Your father sounds like he's okay, though. I mean, he's happy, right? And he doesn't lie to you?"

"Do you think Jeff is lying to you?"

"Not exactly. It's more like a feeling that he's not telling me something, something about my mother. He doesn't talk about her. He hasn't kept anything of hers. If he really loved her, why did he bury everything he knew about her?"

"Maybe he's like George Boldt when he walked away from his storybook castle. Maybe your dad can't bear the grief of remembering her." I didn't like covering for Jeff, but this wasn't the moment for truth, especially not after what I'd just learned about Clive. Besides, Uncle Gary had asked me to wait until he'd spoken with Jeff.

"But don't I have a right to know something about my mother?"

I wasn't sure how to answer that. "Is that why you hurt yourself?"

"That might be part of it, but now it's a habit. When something starts to bother me, I want to make a cut, feel a physical sting to distract myself. Then I want to make another and just one more even though I know I shouldn't. I keep telling myself I can stop, but I don't. Not yet, anyway." He reached out to touch my hand. "Are you repulsed by me, now?"

"Not repulsed; maybe a little shocked. Have you ever tried to...?" I couldn't finish the sentence, couldn't say the word, my fear rising into my throat. He already suspected that something was being kept from him, but if he learned the truth, would it throw him over the edge and lead him to injure himself more seriously?

"No. I won't lie to you, though. There have been a few times I've thought about it, but only when the buttheads at school get to me. As much as I'm obsessed with music, it keeps me going. I want to win the competition. I want to go around the world."

"Seems like our parents saddled us with their baggage, the things they did or didn't do, the things they said or didn't say. How can we get out from under?"

"We don't keep secrets from each other. I trust you, Sam, and it helps to know that I can tell you anything without being put down."

As we paddled the rest of the way around Tar Island and back to the cottage, I mulled over what Clive had shared. Besides the need for my understanding, Clive had proven that he could keep his promise not to hide anything from me, but I didn't reciprocate. Now I had the burden of his disclosure added to the weight of the unspeakable truth that Eddie Cox was his father and the story of his mother's death was a lie. The lies, the truth, the worry had sapped all my energy.

When we stepped onto the deck, Clive paused for a deep inhale before opening the door to the cottage. "Yum! That smells so-oo good!"

"We aim to please," replied Uncle Gary in a somber tone as he closed the lid of the grill. Clive looked back at me and shrugged his shoulders. I didn't respond.

We found Jeff napping on the sofa, so I went to my room to change clothes while Clive retreated to the back bedroom to practice, keeping the volume turned down. I lay down to listen, my body still feeling the rocking motion of the canoe, the weariness from my weeping. I drifted off to sleep, waking after an hour to the sound of raised voices carried in from the deck.

"You need to listen to your father on this, Clive!" commanded Uncle Gary. I'd never heard him speak to Clive in such a stern manner.

"I don't want you talking to that thug ever again. I'm not sure what he's up to, but I think he's some kind of con man. Maybe I'll ask for a background check on him," added Jeff.

"What about Samantha, though? She's still living in his house. She has to talk to him."

"She'll be out of there soon enough, but you're not to get involved," said Uncle Gary.

"Okay, chill out! I get the message."

Uncle Gary came back inside just as I was filling my plate with the grilled food. "Did you talk to Jeff?" I whispered.

"Yeah," he answered brusquely.

"Are you going to tell Clive?"

"Not yet."

I carried my plate out to the deck. When I sat down, Jeff glared at me, then turned his gaze to the River, then back to me, as if he wanted to speak, but thought better of it.

"Hey, feeling better?" I nodded back at Clive as he got up from the table, plate in hand. He didn't look happy, though.

I took a few bites of tonight's special, Uncle Gary's fajitas, my appetite dampened as Jeff watched me closely. I was trying to figure out if he wanted to ask me something or if he was irritated with me, so I decided to take the first step. Gently setting down my fork, I reached over to touch his hand and looked directly into his eyes. "I promise not to tell Clive. Eddie doesn't deserve to be his father." I meant every word.

Jason Larabie

I felt uneasy about taking Hettie over to Tar Island. First of all, I'd never been invited over there although I had a pretty good idea where the cottage was located. Secondly, I'd talked with Clive the day after all the crap went down about his artwork. I'd never seen him so ticked off, mostly with Robbie, though.

"That asshole has crossed the line," he said. The number of times I'd heard Clive cuss was probably about the same as the number of times I'd caught him listening to heavy metal music. "I'm not going to put up with this shit much longer. After the competition is over, he'd better stay out of my way."

"Or what, Clive? You going to beat him up? It always comes back to the same question with Robbie Barrett. No one has the power to do anything."

"Maybe Josh was right; he needs to be set up. This bully needs to step in his own manure."

Although I felt bad about the circumstances, I had to smile at this new Clive. "So, you're going to talk to Josh?"

"Maybe, I don't know."

"You still training with him?"

"Not lately. We've both been too busy."

"Have you talked to Hettie?"

"No."

"It wasn't her fault, you know. Even Kirsten and Darcy admitted that."

"If she hadn't shown up at the campout, none of this would have happened."

"Women! I think she was bugged you didn't take her to the Final Fling."

Clive gave me an intense look as if evaluating what he was about to say. "Between you and me, Jason, I don't feel the same about her as she does about me. I mean, I like her, but it's more as a friend than a girlfriend."

I tried to fake a look of sympathy, but Clive saw right through me.

"I know you like her.

"I wasn't trying to steal her away."

Clive laughed and the resentment was gone from his voice when he said, "I've got enough on my plate with music camp and the competition. Besides, Hettie requires more attention than I can give her. I think you should ask her out."

"Are you going to tell her? I mean, are you going to let her know that you aren't going to be more than friends?"

"I've tried before, but I don't feel like talking to her at the moment. Plus, if I tell her now, she'll just think it's because my sketchbook was stolen."

"Do you think I've got a chance then?"

"Well, this would be the time to find out."

Maybe it was good that Clive would be away for most of July, but I wanted to be sure that Hettie had snuffed out the torch she carried for him. I knew if the air between them wasn't cleared before he left, her guilt feelings would cloud the way for me to enter her heart.

Humidity and high temperatures rolled in on that hazy morning, but the River would need a few more weeks of sweltering heat to warm up its waters enough to please the tourists. Not so for the local river rats who would brave a brisk dip sooner than later, knowing that rapidly changing weather patterns altered the mood of the River, one day radically distinct from the next. A cold front or a thunderstorm could come through and blow the heat off in a matter of hours. I'd just changed into my swimming trunks when Hettie showed up with picnic basket in hand along with a cash offering.

"Hettie, there's no need to pay for the gas. My father's already impressed with your dust-busting skills. He said that the shed hasn't been this clean since my grandfather first built it."

"So, I made you look bad, eh? I think you'll get over it once you've tasted my mom's walnut chicken salad and my own specialty, mocha chip brownies."

"In that case, let's eat first. We could anchor over in Goose Bay before heading over the border." She agreed and we loaded up the *Spit in the Wind*. I was procrastinating on the visit with Clive, worried that it might suck the fun out of the rest of the day. I knew he wasn't going to be thrilled to see Hettie, but how could I tell her that?

She hopped into the copilot seat and we set out, passing through the narrows and under the bridge. The channel between Alex Bay and Wellesley Island was congested with holiday traffic. The Fourth was a major vacation week for boaters, campers, and cottage owners. I proudly demonstrated my skill at navigating between the tour-guide boats and expensive yachts piloted by amateurs.

"They'll sell a boat to anything that waves a wallet, no license required," I said, quoting my father.

"Damn tourists!" she answered, throwing me a warm smile to make my heart flutter and other parts yearn.

As we neared Goose Bay, I eased back on the throttle to slowly glide through the narrow passages between smaller islands in the bay. We anchored some distance from other boaters who were already soaking up the intense sun rays slicing through the haze.

"I'm getting wet, first," announced Hettie as she stripped off her shorts and T-shirt revealing not the bikini of our prior outing, but a one-piece racing suit instead.

I couldn't help but laugh. "What, are you in training or something?"

She made a face, stuck out her tongue, and then took two steps onto the bow of the boat before expertly diving off the front. I was impressed and followed suit by removing my sandals and shirt and performing my best cannonball entry leap. She rewarded me with applause before breaking into the crawl stroke to swim wide laps around the *Spit in the Wind*. I didn't attempt to keep up, deciding to work on my dead man float instead.

After drying off with the towels Hettie had packed, we settled into the rear seats of the boat to eat. "You're right. Your mom makes a mean chicken sandwich." I looked up and noticed the wrinkled brow. Oh, no! Here it comes, I thought—she's rethinking her little plan.

"Jason, what if Clive doesn't want to see me? What if he's not happy about my showing up?"

Had she been reading my mind? "We don't have to go over there." I was hoping that backing out was a genuine option.

"I don't think I'll be able to sleep until I know that Clive has forgiven me."

"Okay, then. All engines ahead, come what may." I started to pull up the anchor without sharing my own misgivings. Hettie closed up the cooler.

We bounced over wake and wave without another word until docking at Rockport to report in at Customs. Hettie waited nervously in the boat, barely noticing the throng of tourists from the charter buses lining up for the boat tour. By the time I returned, she'd gathered herself into a ball, hugging her knees to her chest, as she sat with her feet propped up on the dashboard.

I untied the bow line myself and hopped in beside her, reaching over to give her a comforting squeeze on the arm.

"Nothing horrible is going to happen, Hettie. It's Clive. Either he'll be there or he won't. He isn't going to explode at you." At least, that's what I hoped.

She simply nodded as we pulled away from the dock and headed toward Tar Island. There was significantly less traffic between Tar Island and its larger neighbor, Grenadier. A one-man sailboat tacked across the passage ahead of us while a pair of kayakers explored the shoreline. In the distance was a motorboat which veered to our portside as it passed by the buoy out in front of a cottage built up on a sandhill. At the base of the hill, on the edge of an inlet, was a small boathouse where a large powerboat sat idling between the two docks. The man in the boat was speaking to Clive while a blonde girl was trying to quiet a belligerent black Labrador.

"Well, looks like Clive has company. What do you want to do?" I asked.

"I want to get this over with. Let's pull in." She was a girl who made up her mind quickly.

As I guided the *Spit* into the cove, I caught the tense look on Clive's face. He glanced over at us and motioned for us to pull up alongside the dock at the outer edge of the boathouse. The dog's barking grew louder, but he stuck close to the attractive girl. While we tied up the *Spit*, I heard the stranger say, "Okay, Chum. Just tell your father that I stopped by."

Hettie stopped dead in her tracks and whispered, "That's him!"

"Who?"

She signaled for me to be quiet as the man continued to speak. "And Sam, let Gary know I was here, too."

The engine of the other boat turned over with a thunderous rumble as the visitor backed it away from the docks and headed upriver. The two faces that rounded the corner of the boathouse stared apprehensively after the departing figure. Sensing that our unexpected arrival was going to up the ante for a warm welcome, I started babbling.

"Hey, Buddy, nice to see you! I promised Hettie I'd take her on a river tour today in return for helping me clean out the toolshed at the marina. She wanted to see where my grandmother lives, so we came over this way after having a picnic in Goose Bay. Hope we haven't come at a bad time."

"Just passing by, huh?" I wasn't fooling Clive.

"I didn't know you had a dog."

"Spike belongs to my uncle," the blonde said.

"This is Samantha," Clive began. "These are my friends, Jason and Hettie." Clive didn't look at Hettie as he made the introductions, but I noticed the slight tightening of her lips at the mention of *friends*. We stood there looking at each other, then at the River until Hettie broke the ice, or more accurately, refroze it.

"So, do you have a cottage over here, too?"

"No, I live in Toronto."

"Oh, really? How did you two meet?" Clive shuffled from foot to foot and avoided looking Hettie in the eye. Hettie shifted her gaze from the girl to Clive, looking quite smug. She was not letting him off the hook.

"I hang out with my uncle on weekends and sometimes he comes over here to visit Clive's father." Apparently, Samantha wasn't feeling the cold snap behind Hettie's questions, so I stepped in to ward off the frost-bite.

"Are you going over to the Bay for the fireworks on Tuesday night?"

"Probably not." Clive didn't elaborate and he didn't smile.

I decided it was time to reverse engines before the brier patch between Clive and Hettie grew any taller. "Well, we should be on our way to finish the tour and get the boat home on time. I have to work most of tomorrow while the rest of you are on vacation."

We said our brief good-byes, including some rambunctious barking from Spike before pulling away in the *Spit*. Turning upriver, I hit the throttle mid-channel, just about the same time Hettie melted down into a waterfall of sloppy, soggy tears and loud sobs. We passed between Hill Island and the mainland and over the roiling waves which flowed beneath the Canadian bridge. Cutting back on the speed, I worked the *Spit* through the channel and along the outer shore of Wellesley Island, looking for a quiet spot to put down anchor.

As the engine came to a still, so did the sobbing. Hettie had buried her face in her arms which rested on the side of the boat. I went aft in search of cold drinks from the cooler. I set hers in the cupholder on the dash and opened my own, sipping it in silence. I knew she'd speak when she was ready.

The gentle rocking of the boat seemed to calm her waterworks. Eventually, she lifted her head and dried her eyes on her shirt sleeves. "I shouldn't have gone over there. Seems all my plans end in a nose-dive." I knew it was best to say nothing and wait. "Why didn't he tell me there was someone else? Why let me make a fool of myself?"

"I didn't know about her, either, if that makes you feel any better."

"Not really. Why should I apologize to him now?"

"It was just bad timing, Hettie. I think that other dude upset Clive."

Suddenly animated, Hettie exclaimed, "That's the guy! He was the one arguing with another man out in the middle of the River the night the girls and I got stuck in the weeds over in the Amateurs!"

"What were they arguing about?"

"Money, I think."

"Could they have been smugglers?"

"It sure sounded like they knew each other, so it wasn't just a chance meeting out on the water."

Then, in a quieter voice she asked, "She's pretty, isn't she? I've seen her before, too."

I knew she was talking about Samantha. "Where?"

"In his sketchbook. He drew a portrait of her. All this time, I've been so stupid! I knew he was hiding something; I just didn't want to think it was another girl."

"So, what's it going to be then? You want to stay home and pine away for Clive Tuesday night, or do you want to chase some smugglers?"

I saw the high beams flash on in Hettie's eyes.

Sheriff Cy Froehlich

Working this job changed the way I felt about holidays. They can be the saddest days of the year. Fourth of July is my least favorite, right up there next to New Year's Eve and Halloween. Liquor sales go way up and so do the number of DUI arrests, brawls, property damages, and highway fatalities. Independently Stupid Day is worse because it's celebrated during the summer season, bringing in people from both sides of the border. We were always spread thin on the Fourth in anticipation of reckless or criminal activity. As luck would have it, we received a call reporting a grass fire out on Grindstone Island, just prior to the start of the fireworks exhibition. Yeah, at night. The Clayton Fire Department was notified and dispatched immediately. Turns out that the fire was spreading towards the beach so reinforcements were sent over. Eyes were diverted from River traffic. I felt something slip through my fingers.

Hettie Voss

I hadn't expected to wake up with a sense of relief on Tuesday morning, the same kind of feeling I get after a high fever breaks. My eyes were clear; my thoughts had stopped running in circles. It'd taken me until then to recover from the initial hurt and recognize that the guesswork was over. I finally knew where I stood with Clive. More likely, it was meeting Samantha that had grounded me again. It was useless for me to continue to force a relationship which simply wasn't a good fit. The effort would've worn us both out. Why not try on the one who actually showed interest? The longer I thought about him, the more I realized that Jason was less secretive, less hung-up, less self-focused—well, just plain less Clive.

Remembering the reason for Sunday's visit to Tar Island, I climbed out of bed to pull my backpack out of the corner where I'd tossed it the night before. I took out the brightly wrapped leather-bound sketchbook, bought three days ago, and lobbed it into the waste basket next to my desk. "Let Samantha heal your wounds," I said aloud. "I'm done with feeling bad about you." I continued the cleansing by gathering every item on which I'd written his name (including my German class notebook), every puny souvenir or photo of our time together, placing it in an empty shoebox, taping it shut, and shelving it in the back of my closet. "Just in case you do become famous, Clive Tierney."

By the time Jason was due to arrive that evening, my bedroom had been thoroughly de-cluttered and dusted. I put on a clean T-shirt and a pair of ripped denim shorts, tied my unruly mane of curls up on my head and grabbed an oversized heather-gray sweatshirt. Stepping out the back door, I was suddenly filled with dread when I spotted Josh and my father standing on the dock watching Jason pull up in the *Spit*. I stepped up my pace, hoping to intercept before anything embarrassing seeped out of their mouths. I reached them just as my brother asked, "Jason! What brings you over here?"

"He's here for me."

My father raised his eyebrows in surprise. "Where are you two going?"

"I've already cleared the plans with Mom. We'll be back by eleven-thirty," I said, trying to eke out an extra half-hour on my curfew.

"That didn't answer the question."

"Dad, it's a famous holiday. What do most Americans do on this night?" Yeah, I was leaving out essential details again.

"Still dodging," he said curtly.

"I'm taking Hettie over to the Bay for pizza, Mr. Voss."

"That place will be filled with every kind of bloody miscreant pickled in drink who can't find his backside in the light of day, let alone a way out of the Bay!"

Ignoring my father's Renaissance vernacular, Josh spoke up. "Jason's been on the River since his cradle days, Dad. He knows how to handle a boat." This olive branch was unexpected since we'd barely spoken to each other all week.

"That may be the case, but the blasted tourists don't know how to handle an oar let alone a vessel with an engine!"

"So, they wait till the crowd clears before heading back, right Jason?"

My father squinted into the orange glow of the sun as he struggled to find an objection. "I guess that's a reasonable plan," he reluctantly admitted, although I knew that was not *the* plan.

My father scowled at Jason while I climbed aboard the *Spit*. "Well, tell your father I said hello, young man, and don't do anything with my daughter that he wouldn't want to hear about."

And there it was, the seepage.

An hour later, the sun was just slipping below the horizon when we came out of Moor Pizza after stuffing ourselves and the Bay was crammed with boaters waiting for the start of the fireworks display.

"What makes you think there'll be any smugglers out tonight?" I asked.

"Look around, Hettie. Most of the attention is over here on this crowd, so if I were a smuggler, I'd take a chance on conducting my business somewhere downriver, somewhere where there might be less patrol during the show."

"That doesn't mean the same people will be in the same spot as before."

"You said you heard these guys over in the Amateurs, right? The border runs through those islands providing good coverage and the shoals over there make it difficult for Customs to chase anyone. I think it's a good bet that if there were smugglers out there before, they'll be back."

As we walked out onto the dock, we spied Nick and Robbie sitting in the boat docked behind the *Spit*. I tried to avoid making eye contact. The last thing I wanted was another confrontation with that brute, but he just couldn't resist the temptation to open his oversized mouth.

"Well, well, look at the lovely couple," exclaimed Robbie. "Does your boyfriend know you're both still two-timing him?" Nick rewarded him with a hyena laugh.

"And who's *your* date for the night?" I was astonished at my own audacity while I glared at both of them. This time, no one laughed.

"You better tighten the leash on that bitch, Jason."

"Watch your mouth, Robbie! There are families here." That seemed to stifle him, so I began to untie the lines and Jason hopped into the boat to start the engine.

Nick threw a parting mock at us. "You're not leaving on our account, are you?"

"Why, no, you don't count at all," answered Jason. He backed out cautiously, turning the *Spit* into the channel while Robbie waved at us with one finger.

Heading up past the Summerland Group, we followed the seaway along the southside of Grenadier. When a sudden BOOM announced the opening of the evening's celebration in the Bay, I looked back to see a golden starburst appear in the dark sky. The sound of the exploding fireworks diminished as we made our way downriver, guided by a three-quarter moon which occasionally broke through passing clouds. I had little expectation of a second sighting of smugglers, but was thrilled by the possibility of spending time alone with this boy who smiled at me. I had his full attention and I didn't have to fight for it. It felt good to be desired.

Jason eased back on the throttle to slow the engine as we neared the Amateurs. "Whereabouts did you hear the smugglers?"

"Well, if they *were* smugglers, they were on the northside of the largest island, up that way."

"I'll swing around from the east end of the group. I think we should anchor off one of the tiny islands and swim over to the big one to keep the boat out of sight."

"I didn't wear a suit," I complained.

"You can stay in the boat if you want, skinny dip, or go as you are. Up to you." I looked down at my thin T- shirt and shorts and then over at Jason to see him grinning back at me.

"I've got a better plan. Let's just circle around. If they're already out there, we'll just buzz on by like any tourist would. If not, you can drop me off on the island, then go anchor the boat."

"Okay, have it your way, but I'm a little fuzzy on where the border runs through here. Keep your eyes peeled for Customs. I don't want to get pulled over and questioned."

After we floated in as close as we dared to land, it became readily obvious that I was going to have to get wet, so I searched the side pockets of the boat for a plastic bag to protect my rolled-up sweatshirt and sneakers, tied it shut and carried it in my teeth as I waded through waist-high water to the shadowy shore. Being that the night air was much cooler than the surface of the water, small islands of mist began to gather over the River. I shivered as I crawled out of the water and up onto slippery rock. I quickly threw on my sweatshirt and sneaks before taking shelter from the breeze behind some shrubbery. Jason turned the *Spit* about and pulled away from my hiding spot. I watched his running lights disappear out of sight and waited for the sound of the engine to come to a halt, peering through the darkness to check for signs of another boater before calling out. "Ja-son! Bring the spotlight!"

There was no response, but I heard the steady whirring of an approaching boat so I refrained from calling out again. I scanned over the water which was now partially clouded by the floating mist. The mystery boat slowed, then came to a stop about a hundred yards offshore. What were the chances we'd be lucky enough to bring about a déjà vu encounter? I listened harder for Jason. Nothing. I darted up from my lookout cover and picked my way through the shadowy trees to the other side of the island, compelled to keep moving in order to warm up. "Jason! Where are you?" I whispered. I was growing anxious now. Had something happened to him? Did the *Spit* run over a submerged rock? In the distance, I heard the approach of another boat. It slowly skirted the outer edge of the Amateurs headed in the same direction as the first craft. I rushed back to my stakeout position, praying Jason had shown up.

Two quick flashes of light cut through the patchy surface fog, followed by one longer flash from the other direction before the second engine switched off. I could hear the rush of water against the shoreline as the wake of the boat dissipated. A voice spoke in a low tone, but I wasn't able to make out the words. Another voice, the one I'd heard through the trees on this very island more than two weeks ago, spoke a bit louder, "What do you mean, this is my last trip?"

A muffled answer came, but I couldn't hear it clearly.

"This isn't the kind of business where you can go around firing people."

The fog parted for a minute and I spotted him, the same man in the powerboat who'd been talking with Clive—and his girlfriend—over on Tar Island. His voice suddenly rose to an audible level and carried just three words across the water, "a new partner."

The first man, his back to me, sounded more irate. "You're cutting me out?"

The snap of a twig from behind startled me and before I could turn around, cold, clammy hands clamped down over my eyes. "Yow!" I screamed.

One of Jason's hands quickly shifted to cover my mouth. A spotlight swung in our direction and we threw ourselves down on the ground. The light oscillated left and right over us. At the same time, I heard a loud splash, followed by the roar of an engine. The powerboat sped off toward the Canadian mainland. The light went out and the second engine turned over, accelerating upriver.

"Why did you do that? You spooked them!"

"Sorry, it was an impulse."

"I saw the same guy who was at Tar Island on Sunday, but I couldn't see the other man. I could hear him, though, and he sounded angry about being cut out of something, something about a new partner, but then you made me yell and they took off!"

"I said I was sorry. I didn't realize that both smugglers had already shown up."

"What took you so long anyway? And why aren't you wet?"

"It took me a while to inflate the inner tube."

"Inner tube? You were sitting in your boat, blowing up an inner tube while I was over here soaking wet, freezing my butt off?"

Jason smiled at me, then grabbed my face between his two hands and gave me a smoldering kiss on the lips, sending a surge of delicious, moist heat throughout my body.

"I love that fire in you, Hettie." I was speechless. Just as abruptly, he turned around saying, "Follow me."

Jason completely erased my irritation by offering me the inner tube throne while he stripped off his shirt, throwing it into my lap and plunged into the water, kicking his strong, short legs and propelling me back to the *Spit*. After climbing back into the boat, I reached down for the inner tube and tossed it to the floor. Jason scrambled aboard then, trembling in the cool air. I pulled his shirt from the pouch of my sweatshirt and handed it to him. He smiled and gave me a quick peck on the cheek before drying off and turning on the blower. It had been over an hour since we'd left the Bay. By now, the fireworks display had ended and only a few stragglers passed by as we made our way back to Fishers Landing, ahead of my curfew.

After docking, I asked Jason, "What do we do with this information?"

"What information?"

"We know the identity of one of the smugglers."

"We don't know his name."

"Maybe we should ask Clive."

"Then what?"

"We report the smuggling."

"Okay, hold on. One, who are we going to tell? Want your Dad to know where you were tonight?"

"You've got a point."

"Two, we don't have proof. You heard something. Did you see any goods exchanged?"

"No, but something went into the water."

"Are you kidding me? You think one of the smugglers dropped goods overboard?"

"Yes, that's my theory."

"Are you thinking what I think you're thinking? You want to go back and take a look?"

"Well, you're the one who said we needed proof."

"We're not doing that kind of scavenger hunting at night. I'm not sure how deep it is out there and we don't know if whatever it is has been anchored down. Maybe there's nothing at all."

"When can we go?"

"I don't have another day off till next Sunday."

I leapt at him and landed another kiss on his delicious lips. He held onto me for a few moments, there on the dock, under a sky with gathering clouds. We broke apart when we heard my brothers coming into the cove in the *Nevermind*.

Jason Larabie

I'd found the key to Hettie's heart. She was a girl who liked thrills, a girl with a passion for life. And she was smart! I was hooked. I doubted we'd discover any smugglers out there that night, but something had happened and the coincidence gave me another opportunity to spend more time with Hettie. The summer was off to a hopeful start for me.

The Fourth of July evening had ended just the way it'd begun—with Hettie's family giving me a hard time. "Did you two go to the fireworks?" asked Stuart after stepping out of the boat and onto the dock.

"We saw them," Hettie answered quickly.

"I didn't see you. Where were you?" inquired Josh.

"Out on the water."

"By the looks of it, seems you were in the water, not on it."

I was keeping my mouth shut, but Josh peered at me suspiciously. Stuart didn't stay; he walked on up to the house.

"Seen Clive lately?"

"What's it to you?" sneered Hettie.

"I know you're his friends and I haven't seen him. Just wondering if he's okay."

"I think he's away," I said, "over on Tar Island."

Josh pulled the boat canvas out from storage under the deck and began snapping it onto the *Nevermind.*

"Do you have to do that right now?" asked Hettie.

"Clouds are rolling in. Might rain and I don't want to come back out."

It was apparent that Josh wasn't going to leave us alone, so I knew it was time to call it a night. I looked back after pulling away from the dock to see my hot-blooded girl lighting into her brother. Yeah! *My* girl.

Sunday started off with a steady drizzle, but tapered off before I left the marina. Under threat of being grounded for the remainder of the summer, I had to give a solemn promise to my father to get off the water should a lightning storm brew up. Hettie was worth it. I placed two fishing poles in the *Spit* which now sat covered in its rain canopy. Hettie's mother dropped her off at my house, most likely unaware that her daughter planned to spend her afternoon out on the choppy River. Though I'd told my parents that I was going fishing with a friend, their surprise was obvious when Hettie walked into our house.

"Hettie Voss!" said my mother. "I haven't seen you in a while. My, you're growing up to be a beauty." *Way to go, Mom. Put some more points on my scoreboard!* Though Hettie blushed slightly, I could see she was pleased by the compliment.

Sniffing for the bull pucky, Dad asked, "Got much experience with fishing?"

"You can't live in the Voss house, Mr. Larabie, and not know about fishing. I've been going out with my father and brothers since I was four." I had to hand it to her; she was smooth.

"Good for you," said my mother, the mediator. "No gender bias in your house."

We walked out to the *Spit*, Hettie carrying a backpack.

"Got your gear in there?"

"Yeah, some extra clothing. Previous experience has taught me that boating with you means getting drenched."

"It's going to be hard to see anything in the water if the rain starts up again."

"Like hunting for a needle in a haystack or a fish hook in a river? We could just go fishing," she smiled. But I knew she wouldn't settle for that and gave her a quick kiss on the nose before we took off.

The wind and the rough waves slowed our trip, but we finally reached the location where Hettie guesstimated the smugglers had held their nighttime meetings. If we hadn't crossed the border, yet, we were most likely straddling it. I didn't want to draw the attention of any Customs agents, but the possibility added excitement to the adventure. So did the mounting thunderheads off to the west. After chucking the anchor overboard, the wind continued to toss the *Spit* about, making it difficult for us to hold ourselves steady while preparing for the sea hunt.

I tightened my snorkel mask and jumped into the cold, rough water. Hettie followed after me. "Don't swim close to the boat," I cautioned. I didn't want the wind to whip the boat over us while we were scanning under the surface. Ten minutes passed by before Hettie swam back to me.

"This is useless. If one of the smugglers dropped something out here, how would he even find it unless he'd attached a floating marker?"

That gave me an idea. "Brilliant!" I yelled. "Why didn't I think of it before? We'll use the fish finder!"

We swam back to the *Spit* and clambered aboard, wrapping ourselves in towels to warm up. I dug around in the glove box and in the storage under the hull until I found the gadget.

"Let's head downriver a little. Maybe what we're looking for was dragged by the current."

"Could be that the smuggler doesn't intend to come back for his booty."

"Not unless he's desperate for money," she said.

After showing Hettie how to set the auto-depth and read the display on the fish finder, I slowly edged the *Spit* toward Crossover Island Light. "Fish move; solid objects not so much," I explained.

"I think we're getting closer to a shoal or some rocks," she said. "Stay between the Light and the island we were on the other night."

I turned the *Spit* around and cruised slowly back upriver.

"Jason, I'm not sure what I'm seeing on the display, here. Looks like something solid, a box-like shape."

I let the engine idle while taking a look at the display screen. Sliding the cursor, I found the depth of the object.

"It's too deep." While Hettie stood staring down at the water to weigh the alternatives, I noticed that the wind had grown to gale strength and the enormous, charcoal-colored clouds had advanced in our direction like stealthy foot soldiers amassing for attack. And then it came. A brilliant artery of lightning parted the thick gloom over Grenadier Island, followed by a fierce clap of thunder. "Come on, Hettie! The storm is getting closer."

"Are we just going to leave it down there?"

"We don't have a choice. We aren't equipped to make a deep-water dive. Even if we were, now is not the time."

Within minutes, the sky let loose its torrential downpour as we scrambled to pull up the anchor and take cover beneath the canopy. The wind whipped the *Spit* about while we waited for the bilge blower to clear the fuel fumes. As soon as the engine turned over, we sped south into Blind Bay. After safely securing the *Spit*, we raced inside the small marina store owned by a friend of my father.

"Hey, Jason! What are you doing out in this weather?"

"Hello, Mr. Fortier. Yeah, I thought we could make it back home before the storm arrived, but I guess not."

"So, who's the pretty lady?" he asked while nodding over at Hettie whose lips had turned inky blue as she stood shivering and soaked to the skin.

"Hettie Voss. She goes to my high school."

He pulled a couple of beach towels from one of the store shelves and handed them to us. "Well, why don't you two make use of the restrooms to dry off and change out of that wet clothing. I can loan you a couple of sweatshirts." We thanked him for the offer. I took the sweatshirt and Hettie, the planner, changed into her extra set of clothes. By then, Mr. Fortier had poured us two cups of strong coffee.

"As soon as the lightning has ended, you can use the phone to call your father and let him know you're safe."

I knew this wasn't a question or a suggestion. Mr. Fortier had lost a son to the River a few years back in a boating accident. After another hour and a couple of turkey sandwiches, the rain had petered out to a light sprinkle and the clouds were beginning to break up. My father sounded relieved and grateful for the call and we thanked Mr. Fortier who continued the phone conversation with Dad while we returned to the *Spit*. Just as we were about to release the stern line, Mr. Fortier appeared, asking, "Got enough fuel in the tank, Jason?"

"Yeah, I should be good."

"Let me just top it off for you, at least. I'd never forgive myself if one of Cal Larabie's kids ran out of gas on the River. Your dad and I go way back."

"What a nice man!" said Hettie when we were on our way again. "Your father has some good friends."

"Yeah, they're both vets, but my dad likes to say they're both survivors."

"We've got to find someone who can help us bring up that

mystery stuff—what do you call the stuff smuggled in and out of the country?"

"Drugs?"

"No, oh, I know. Contraband!"

"Your brother is a certified diver, isn't he?"

"Josh? I don't want to bring him into this! He'll just start giving me orders and treating me like ..."

I looked over at her face, pink lips now pursed in a pout. "Like a little sister?"

She shook her head no. "Like a girl! I'm not any weaker than he is."

I smiled as I watched over the water ahead. "You don't have to convince me!" She rewarded me with a hug and a kiss.

"Thanks, Jason. I appreciate you risking your boat and your neck, today."

After I dropped her off, I knew that her analytical wheels would keep turning over the image on the fish finder to figure out a way to bring it to the surface.

Josh Voss

I was going to have to let it go, soon. I'd been burned up at Hettie for over a week, the longest rift we'd ever endured. Besides, I was leaving soon for Plebe Summer, so it was best to patch things up before I left. I knew the rest of the family was fed up with our stubbornness, too.

Hettie was at work. She was a lifeguard at Grass Point, a neutral meeting ground where I could catch her off guard, hoping she'd be less likely to spazz out in front of an audience. I made sure to bring along something to sweeten the pot—chocolate. There weren't many people on the beach, though, because the sky was overcast and there was a strong breeze kicking up whitecaps. Hettie was bundled up in her canopied perch, an eight-foot tall wooden director's chair, when I arrived.

"Not looking much like summer out here," I commented, startling her out of a water watch trance.

"Josh! What do you want?" She wasn't happy to see me.

"Brought you some lunch, including hot chocolate." She eyed me skeptically as I stepped up on the second rung of the ladder to hand her the aromatic peace offerings.

"Did Mom put you up to this?"

"No, but if you don't want that toasted meatball sub, I'll take it." She opened the foil and stuck her nose in to inhale. Her eyes closed for a few seconds before she looked down at me.

"Look, Josh, it's over. I didn't think things through, that's all. I didn't mean to ruin your campout."

"You're right, Hettie. That's over, but you're still my little sister and I'm always going to be your biggest brother," I smiled.

She took a big chomp out of the sub and moaned with satisfaction. "That's not entirely true. I think Stuart has already passed you up by an inch or two."

"So, tell me. Where did you go the other night? I know you weren't at the fireworks." I really only had a hunch, but I wanted to cut to the chase and avoid any lies by omission.

Hettie chewed slowly. I climbed up in the chair next to her. She scrunched over to make room for me. "Déjà vu," she said finally.

"What do you mean, 'déjà vu'?"

"Jason and I took a boat ride and came across the same two smugglers, again."

"Are you kidding me? How do you know they were smugglers?"

"This time, one of them was wigging out about some new guy who was moving in on the deal."

"Do you hear yourself? You need to stay away from these guys. They could be dangerous."

"But I can identify one of them, now."

"Someone we know?"

"Not exactly, but I did meet him."

"Where?" She bit her lip, a telltale sign that she'd let something slip. "Hettie?"

"Alright, but just listen without playing Dad." I let the mock go, anxious to find out what she'd been up to. "Jason took me over to Tar Island so I could apologize to Clive, only when we got there he had company. The man I'd heard out on the water when we were stuck in the Amateurs was there, asking Clive where his father was. I got the feeling that Clive and his girlfriend didn't like this man, but he's the one I heard out there again when we went back to the Amateurs during the fireworks. I'm sure of it."

"His girlfriend?" Hettie nodded, but I didn't see any tears.

"With her mouth full of meatball, she said, "His friend is beautiful and blonde. She's from Toronto."

"Don't do that, Hettie. Don't under-rate yourself. Besides, Clive's got some hang-ups of his own, things you can't change."

She finished the sub, wiped off her hands and climbed down from her perch with the cocoa in hand. She was watching the waterfront again. I hopped down and we started walking along the beach, Hettie stopping every couple of yards to look behind her for signs of trouble.

"That's not all. Jason and I spotted something in the River that might belong to one of the smugglers."

"You sure you're not letting your imagination carry you downriver?"

"I don't think so. I heard one of the men throw something over the side of his boat, but I don't think it was his anchor because he tore off in a flash when he heard me holler." She bit her lip again.

"Geez, Hettie! You're lucky he didn't come after you and Jason."

"You could help us look for the contraband. It's too deep for me, but you could dive down for us."

"You can't be serious," but I saw the determination in her eyes. If I didn't agree, she might be reckless enough to try it herself though she didn't have the experience and I didn't want to think about what could happen to her. Maybe it'd be better to check it out to prove her hunch right or wrong.

"If we do find something that's illegal to bring across the border, then what?"

"We'll turn it into the police or Customs or somebody who'll investigate."

"And that will be the end of it, right? No more skulking around playing Sherlock."

"No guarantees, Watson." My little sister had a thirst for adventure. Guess it ran in the family.

Hettie Voss

My brother, Josh, couldn't resist being my protector. It fit right into that superhero fantasy he was living. He was definitely ripe for the military life and he'd probably be first in line for the daring assignments. I was thrilled he hadn't scoffed at my quest to expose smugglers, but that didn't mean I wasn't having second thoughts, especially about that man we'd seen talking to Clive over on Tar Island. If he was a smuggler, why would he want to talk to Clive's father, someone who worked for the Border Patrol? Were we sticking our noses into the middle of some kind of sting operation?

The three of us had agreed that the best day for the dive would be Sunday since it wouldn't interfere with our work schedules and the weather forecast promised fair skies, as well. The trick was to stay out of range of my father's observant eyes (and my mother's sixth sense). No way would he approve of this dive, especially without his expert oversight. Like Josh, my father had begun his own underwater diver training before he'd joined the navy. My brother had been schooled and certified in diver safety under his careful direction.

While I distracted my parents at the breakfast table with a long conversation about my upcoming college search, Josh covertly loaded his gear into the *Nevermind,* after telling my parents that he was going out with a couple of friends to do some cliff-diving over on Mary Island. Well, at least the diving part was correct. As soon as I heard the engine start up, I informed my parents that I was going to bike over to Jason's for a visit. That was also true. Josh was meeting the two of us over there to avoid more questions and more half-truths.

At Larabie's Marina, Josh transferred his diving gear from the *Nevermind* to the *Spit*. Fortunately, the rest of Jason's male clan were too busy with customers to notice what was going on in one of the backside slips. The still air was infused with the heat of a scorching sun and mild mugginess. As we began our voyage of discovery, the calm waters boosted our hopes for success. We sped by other boaters enjoying a day on the glassy-smooth River, heading northeastward in the channel until we came within sight of the Crossover Light, just beyond the Amateurs. We circled the locale where the booty was last sighted, but the fish finder turned up nothing this time other than fish and rocks. "It must've drifted downriver," I suggested.

"Stay out away from the shoals up ahead," cautioned Josh.

We edged closer to the Crossover Island Light while our eyes stayed glued to the sonar instrument. "There!" I pointed to the rectangular shape on the display. "That's it!" Jason eased back on the throttle and circled in more tightly on the object.

"Put out the anchor," he said.

I threw it off the bow while he shut off the engine and Josh scanned the water before pulling on his mask and jumping overboard to scout out the locale. He dove underwater and after a long minute and a-half or so, he surfaced and confirmed that the dive would be manageable once he had properly suited up.

Josh took his time preparing for the dive. "If this thing is too heavy, I may not be able to surface with it. Do you have a couple of tow lines you can tie together?"

"Sure do." Jason prepared the lines and handed one end to Josh.

"This shouldn't take too long, but if you don't see me shortly after ... let's say 1:25, get help. In the meantime, try not to drift too far downriver or into the shoal."

My stomach flipped when he said this. Was there really any danger? "Maybe this isn't such a good idea after all, Josh. This might turn out to be a wild goose chase."

"Hettie, we're here. The water is calm and there aren't any other boaters thrashing about. Let me check it out."

After he and Jason synchronized their watches, he lowered himself over the side, swimming about on the surface for a bit before pointing out the direction in which he was going to move underwater. Curling forward, he disappeared beneath the surface. All was very quiet. We must have checked the time every thirty seconds, feeling every tick, as we kept an eye on the line which slowly descended with Josh. Suddenly, the line was being jerked more violently, redirecting our attention to the fish finder.

"Looks like he's trying to tie the rope around the box," said Jason.

"What if it doesn't hold?"

"It will."

We watched as Josh's shadow on the display started to spin around. Jason looked at his watch again. We waited. Five minutes of dead quiet passed. "You think he's alright?"

"It's not 1:25. He's got plenty of time left."

"Oh, no. The box has slipped off the line! Josh is diving after it." We watched in silence. That's when I heard a familiar bass sound in the distance. I looked up in terror as a large freighter crossed into the American Channel about a mile to the east.

"Jason! A freighter!"

Our attention was divided between two horrifying sites—my brother wrestling with the box again and the freighter bearing down on us.

"He's trying to hold onto the box and untangle the line at the same time."

"Give the line a good tug. Maybe he'll realize we're trying to send him a signal." Jason reached over the side to pull on the tow line, but he had to reel it in before it was taut enough. "The box has slipped away again! Josh is diving deeper. We've got to get him out of the way!" I stared at the surface of the water, willing my brother to appear. Cargo ships are massive floating warehouses, carrying as much as several freight trains. I knew that even if Josh could hear the freighter, that didn't mean he could figure out from which direction it was approaching.

Jason rushed back to the fish finder. "He's got a grip on it, now. Wait till he gets back to the line and I'll pull an SOS signal on it."

My brother was dragging the box by its handle as he kicked upward and over to reach the line. He slipped the end through the opening in the handle and tied it in a knot. Jason leaned over the side and gave it three quick tugs, three long tugs, three quick tugs. Josh tugged back twice in response, then began to climb.

"But he needs to take a rest stop to avoid decompression sickness." Just then, we heard a warning blast from the pilot house of the freighter. "What do we do?" I screamed.

"I could cut the line."

"No! What if he dives after it again?" I began to tremble. Another warning from the freighter reverberated over the water. I checked the fish finder to read Josh's depth level. "He's at fifteen feet. That means another three to five minutes before he can head up to the surface." By now the freighter was close enough for me to see the men standing on deck. I crossed my fingers, held my breath and closed my eyes while counting the seconds aloud.

Only two minutes had passed before Jason flipped on the blower. "I'm going to risk starting the engine. Maybe Josh will realize there's an emergency."

"He's headed up!" I shouted. The *Spit's* engine roared to life and Jason let it idle while he hauled in the anchor line.

As Josh surfaced, I immediately pointed at the freighter. He swam to the boat and I yanked him aboard where we both collapsed onto the floor. Jason shoved the throttle forward propelling us clear of the freighter's path. My brother tore off his dive mask and yelled. "Hettie, grab hold of the line and reel it in before the wake tears it free." As the *Spit* tossed up and down over the freighter's wake, the tow line was pulled aft. I struggled to lean out over the rear corner of the boat without falling overboard, but could barely pull up any of the line. Josh rushed over and grabbed hold of me. "No, not that way. Get behind me." He knelt down, pressing his chest up against the back of the boat and began tugging the line, hand over hand. I sat down on the floor, took hold of the loose end and propped my feet up next to him. We looked like one half of a tug-of-war competition.

"What's in this thing? A pile of granite?"

Jason finally killed the engine and the resistance from the submerged end of the rope lessened. "Be careful not to let it crash into the prop," he warned.

Slowly, one side of what appeared to be a blue cooler emerged from the water.

"Oh, please let it be beer!" Jason sang out.

Robbie Barrett

I cashed my first paycheck as soon as I got it and took Nick out to play some mini-golf. Even managed to score us a couple of brewskies without getting proofed. The money made me feel free, like I had power, the power to decide. I began to dream about what I'd do with it. Maybe I'd even open a bank account for myself and save up for my own car. Maybe I'd move out on my own after graduation next year. What would the old man say then?

After the Fourth-of-July weekend, my father's boat never left the marina. The *Footloose* was hooded underneath the canopy and tied up in her slip while my old man's mood grew nastier by the day. I kept a watchful eye for any sign of a bruising on my mother. She made sure to cook up all his favorites and keep the fridge stocked with beer. The rest of her time was spent cleaning, trying to avoid triggering his temper. There was hardly a word spoken aloud in the house. My sisters and I made ourselves scarce, either hiding out in our rooms or staying away from home as long as possible. It was just a matter of time before the SOB erupted or passed out. Seemed like my mother had more reason to drink than he did.

On Sunday, I had the day off from Jacobsen's, but I had to mow the lawn at home. That was also the day of the week when my old man slept in after his bartending shift, so I waited till mid-afternoon to begin cutting the backyard. The house stood on a half-acre lot surrounded by evergreens. The job took at least two hours, including weed-whacking under the trees. I took my time, though, so my father wouldn't be able to use a missed patch as an excuse to go ballistic.

Just as I'd refilled the lawnmower with gas and pushed it out to the front of the house, Josh Voss pulled into Clive's driveway. About a half-hour earlier, I'd been mowing in the side yard and spotted Clive taking off on his bike with his backpack, so I knew he wasn't home. Josh, Hettie, and Jason Larabie stepped out of the car and went around to the trunk to open it. The guys lifted out a twenty-five gallon marine cooler. I froze when I saw the green number written on the side of the cooler in the same large handwriting as the one I'd seen on the cooler my old man unloaded from the *Footloose*. The top of this one was held shut with a double layer of duct tape, just the same as his. Hettie slammed the trunk closed and all three walked up to ring the doorbell. I heard a loud belch from behind me and turned to see my father watching out the front screen door. Right away, I yanked the starter cable on the lawnmower twice to get mowing again before he could cuss me out. Another twenty minutes went by before the visitors came back out of the Tierney place without the cooler. They glanced over at my house; my father was still watching from the doorway. No one waved.

The mowing was finished by supper time, but I wanted to grab a shower first. When I came through the back door, Mom stopped me. "It'll be just the three of us for dinner, Robbie. Your sisters are out for the evening."

"Dad isn't working tonight?"

"He's got the night off," she said guardedly. I knew what this meant. My sisters had probably gotten themselves invited to sleep over at a friend's house. I noticed my mother's hands shaking as she sliced up a cucumber. "Are you going out this evening?" She'd tried to sound casual, but her voice cracked. I knew she didn't want to be left alone with my father. This was the calm before the thunderstorm.

I touched her shoulder and leaned down to whisper in her ear. "Don't worry, Mom. I'll be here."

Just then, my father stumbled into the kitchen. "You two whisperin' behind my back?" We didn't answer. There was no safe answer.

"Make sure you cleaned off my tools. I don't want to find no grease or grass on my tools, boy!" My father was itchin' for a fight.

"They're clean, Dad, and back where they belong."

"Want some lemonade, Robbie? How about you, Craig? Some nice lemonade over ice?"

"What are you, stupid? I don't want that pee water you make! When's the last time you saw me drink that stuff? How about you make yourself useful, for once, and pour me a real drink? Get me a whiskey!" Without a word, my mother poured him a double shot and went back to cutting up vegetables. I waited for him to get back to his chair in front of the fan and the TV before I went upstairs to take a shower. I hoped he'd stay put till I came back down.

Later, Mom and I ate out on the back deck; my father had dozed off inside. "Maybe we should go out for a ride in the car before he wakes up."

"I've got to clean up and besides, it won't be any better when I get back, Robbie. Never has been." She'd made up her mind to take whatever came. I couldn't stand the thought of her getting another beating. Somehow, I needed to get him out of our life. I kept her company for the rest of the evening by helping her with the dishes; then we played a few hands of gin rummy. In the meantime, my father had awakened and continued to guzzle his booze. He didn't touch a bite of food the rest of the night, but by the time Mom and I were ready to pack it in, he'd passed out in his chair, the TV still blaring. We didn't dare switch it off, afraid we'd wake the beast.

It was a little before midnight when the slam of the front screen door woke me up. I listened for the engine of my father's truck to start up, but heard the whine of the door to the garden shed instead. My bedroom was in the front of the house, with two windows, one facing the side yard and one facing the front yard. The cloudless night was lit up by a moon not quite full, but plenty bright enough for me to watch my father stumble down the driveway and across the street. He disappeared behind Clive's house. The house was dark and Mr. Tierney's truck wasn't in the driveway.

Bolting out of bed, I threw on some shorts and my sneakers. I knew what was on his mind—that marine cooler that Josh and Jason had carried into Clive's house.

Out in the hallway, my mother stopped me. "Where do you think you're going?"

"You heard Dad leaving?"

"Let him be."

"He went around back of Clive's house."

"Let him be, I said! Don't get yourself tied up in his troubles." I could see she wasn't going to budge till I gave in, so I went back to my room to wait. My mom was a smart woman; she went downstairs to stand guard so I'd stay put. I peered out the window again. The house across the street was still dark, no lights. I sat down on my bed, but knew that I couldn't go back to sleep.

Carefully, I cracked opened my door and slipped out like a cat. I tiptoed into the bathroom, locking the door behind me. I waited, listening for any movement from downstairs. Nothing. I slid the screen up on the window over the side porch and stood on the toilet to hoist myself out and onto the roof. Crouching down, I scooted to the edge, sat on my butt, and swung my feet over the lip before leaping down onto the lawn. I squatted to run alongside the house, underneath the windows.

Working my way around to the back of Clive's house, I checked for signs of my father. There was a slash in the screen door. When I slowly pulled it open, I felt broken glass underneath the soles of my sneakers. The window of the inner door had been shattered and the door was unlatched.

As I stepped into the dark kitchen, I heard a crash in the front room. I paused in the doorway and heard what sounded like someone falling to the floor. I stared into the room and suddenly caught the glint of a blade, followed by grunting and a rolling sound. Grabbing a kitchen chair, I swung it up over my head, lunged forward and smashed it down with full force.

Sylvia Barrett

The first time Craig beat me, I'd just turned twenty-two and only known him for about six months. Afterwards, I told him I'd lost the baby and he cried. I believed his drunken promises not to hurt me again. We got married the next year with Robbie already on the way. Craig repeated the same promises, over and over, year after year, until I told him I'd lost our last baby. That was after he'd cracked my pelvic bones by shoving the dining room table over on top of me. He said it probably wasn't his baby anyway and put the blame on me for telling him lies when I didn't, using whatever false excuse he could dream up. No more pleas for forgiveness; no more promises for good behavior. No more love. I stopped believing anything Craig had to say. I just didn't know how to get out or far enough away with my three kids so we'd be safe.

He'd always threatened to come looking for us if I ever left him. One year just passed into another while we all tiptoed around his moods, me always on guard, watching for the storm signs. Craig worked nights which meant he had to sleep during the day, leaving it up to me to keep the kids quiet. I couldn't go out to work. If I'd taken a job at night—like him—I'd need a sitter in the house. We didn't have visitors in our house, this tumble-down house we'd been renting for years from Craig's uncle. The few and in-between tender moments dried up as the drink took over and the pressure mounted. Craig was always looking for ways to make more money. I knew bartending alone couldn't have provided for our family, but I never questioned him about where that cash came from that he kept locked away in the safe nailed to our closet floor. As if he'd tell me the truth, anyway. I kept wondering why he didn't run out on us, hoping he would.

I knew something had gone wrong for him when he'd been drinking steadily for two days at home, his mood getting downright meaner by the hour. Maybe he'd gotten himself fired, but I wasn't about to ask for fear he'd light into me or the kids. To get them out of the house, I called a couple of PTA moms and gave them a tale about Craig being ill, asking if my girls could sleep over at their homes. Robbie refused to go to Nick's, though. He stuck close to me, like a bodyguard, which only served to intensify my anxiety. I didn't want to see him tangle with his father.

When I heard my husband go out that night I prayed he wouldn't come back or even better, drive into a tree, but I didn't hear the truck start. Instead, I heard Robbie stirring; I hurried out into the hallway to head off trouble. He told me he'd seen Craig go over to the Tierney house and I warned him to keep out of it. Seemed certain to me that a Border Patrol agent could handle a drunk without my help. Doubtful that my son would obey me, I went downstairs to sit in the front room in case he decided to go snooping after his father. I nodded off while trying to figure out what to do if Craig came back in a fit of rage. I didn't wake up until I heard the screech of a siren from the county sheriff's car roaring up our street. I peered through the front curtains and saw the bubblegum lights blinking like a pinball machine as the car pulled up in front of the Tierney house. Two patrol cars were already parked in the driveway. The house was all lit up inside. I watched the sheriff walk up the front steps and that was when I saw my Robbie standing in the front doorway! I bolted up from the sofa, my heart full of dread, and flew out of the house and across the street in my bare feet.

"Robbie! Robbie, what are you doing here?"

"Mom!" he croaked.

"Ma'am, stop," barked one of the officers as he put up his hand to stop me from entering the house. Another police car skidded into the driveway. "I'll have to ask you to wait outside."

"But he's my son!"

"He's not hurt, ma'am. I'll send him out to you as soon as he's had a chance to answer some questions. Please, just wait out here. Butch, can you wait with this lady?" An officer approached me as I stepped back in a daze. He asked for my name, Robbie's name, and our address, and wrote it all down in a tiny notebook. I stood in the darkness, waiting and waiting. Sirens sounded again in the village and soon an ambulance pulled into the driveway. I was frantic to know what had happened inside that house. Paramedics rushed past me without a word.

As the humid night closed in on me, my chest tightened and my head ached. It was hard to catch a breath of air. Panic was gripping me by the throat. Finally, a gurney was hoisted down the front steps, carrying Craig's unconscious body, his head wrapped in heavy bandaging. I stepped forward.

"What's happened to my husband?"

"Someone will be right out to speak with you."

A second gurney was brought into the house. Shaking uncontrollably now, I was about to let loose with a scream when Robbie came out next, escorted by two officers.

"Robbie! What's going on? Are you alright?"

"Is this your son?" asked one of the officers.

"I told you that already!"

"We're taking him over to the sheriff's station. We need to get more information before we can release him. There's been an altercation."

We were interrupted by the paramedics again. As the next gurney was carried out of the house, I was stunned to see that it was Clive covered up to his neck in a cotton blanket. His right hand, wrapped in bandages, rested motionless on top of his chest. "Where's his father?" No one answered me.

The officer I'd been speaking with looked at my shoeless feet, then slid his eyes up over my bathrobe. "Why don't you get yourself dressed. You can follow the emergency vehicle to the hospital or meet us at the sheriff's station."

He wasn't asking; he was telling me what my choices were.

I yelled over to my son as he was helped into the back seat of a patrol car. "Robbie! I'm on my way." My mind was racing. Was Craig seriously hurt? How had Clive been injured? Who could I call in the middle of the night for legal advice? I decided it was best to get to the sheriff's station as quickly as possible to find out what had happened.

Sheriff Cy Froehlich

Craig Barrett had been in my sights before, once for a DUI offense and a second time for a domestic dispute which was called in by a neighbor. The wife had declined to file charges against him. When we found him lying face down at the Tierney place, he was drunker than my Aunt Mamie's rum cake. His son was there, too. Robbie told me he'd followed his father over to the house and witnessed his attack on young Clive. That's when he grabbed a chair and broke it over Barrett's head. From the look of Craig's skull, there was more packed into that wallop than saving a classmate's life.

Clive's story revealed that his father had gone out earlier in the evening and he'd been asleep upstairs when he heard glass breaking and thrashing about downstairs. When he'd gone down to investigate, he was jumped and stabbed by his neighbor.

I asked Robbie why his father had broken into the Tierney home.

"I think he was looking for something that belonged to him."

"Like what?"

"I don't know for sure, but I saw some of Clive's friends drop off a blue cooler at his house, one like the kind my father carries on his boat."

"Lots of people have coolers, son. What makes you think this one belongs to your father?"

"His cooler was numbered and duct-taped shut, like tight enough to keep out air or water. The one that went into that house today had a number on it, too."

After Robbie left the station with his mother, I sent some officers out to find Jeff Tierney. His vehicle wasn't spotted until almost dawn over in Rockport. That's when we woke up old Heinz Gunther to find out if Tierney kept a boat at his marina. He took us on down the hill where we found the slip unoccupied.

"It's always here 'less he's over on Tar Island. Want to ring him up?"

Heinz pointed to the phone in the corner of his cluttered office. We called the operator and waited for her to connect us with the other line. No answer. I notified the O.P.P. and the Coast Guard, requesting that someone check out the cottage. Tierney's boat was found adrift, downriver from his place. His body wasn't discovered for another several hours. Now, we had an American Border Patrol agent drowned in Canadian waters while his home was broken into by a neighbor. The ripples were widening.

Tierney's body exhibited a bullet wound through the artery of his upper right arm. His own holster was empty, the gun not recovered. We'd know more after the coroner had a closer look at him. Border Patrol had no knowledge of Tierney's activities and stated that he was off duty for Sunday, not due to report till

Monday morning for a day shift. So, why was he out on the River, north of the border, late at night? And who was looking after the wounded boy in the hospital, the motherless boy who'd just lost his father?

Gary Stanton

I was in a dead sleep when the phone rang just after two in the morning. A female voice asked if I was Gary Stanton. "Uh-huh." And went on to explain that she was calling from Bayview Medical Center.

I wasn't fully listening until she said, "He's been injured."

"Who's been injured?" I switched on the bedside lamp to clear the fuzz out of my head.

"Clive Tierney. He gave me your name as an emergency contact."

"Well, isn't his father with him?"

"Not yet."

I don't remember hanging up. I searched for clothing, wallet, car keys, as if in a trance.

The sun peeked over the horizon just as I arrived at the hospital. When I gave the intake nurse Clive's name, she asked for my identification. That seemed odd to me, but to save time I didn't balk, at least not until I was met with the same request from the officer stationed outside his private room.

"What's going on here? Why the need for security?"

"The patient asked for you, sir. We haven't been able to locate his father, yet. The boy has suffered a deep stab wound to his right hand. That's about all I can tell you at the moment, sir."

My mind was spinning in all directions. *Where was Jeff?* "Stabbed, you say?"

"Yes, sir. I don't have any of the details myself. I'm sure someone will be speaking with you later."

Clive was asleep when I walked in, so I sat down in the chair beside his bed, selfishly hoping he'd wake up soon to tell me what had happened. The heavily bandaged hand rested on a pillow, looking like a white boxing glove. Clive's pale face showed no sign of pain while he slept.

A doctor entered the room around six-thirty and introduced himself as Dr. Basil Matusik, an orthopedic surgeon. "Are you a relative of this young man?"

"No, just a close friend of the family."

"We've been trying to locate his father or another relative. Do you know anyone we can contact for permission to operate?"

"Sorry to say, no."

"Well, guess we'll have to hope his dad will show up soon. I'm going to confer with a colleague of mine in Boston and I'd like to get the boy into surgery right after that. The knife tore across the middle of his hand slicing through the tendons and ligaments. We think that the wound might have been caused during a fall."

"Will there be any permanent damage?"

"Can't say for sure until after I get in there." Dr. Matusik's somber expression held steady. He stopped to read Clive's chart and then, disappeared down the hallway. I sat down to wait.

I dozed off a bit before Clive awakened. "Hey, Gary," he said drowsily. "Thanks for coming."

"Don't mention it."

"Have you seen Dad?"

"Not yet."

Clive looked worried. "I don't know where he is. He said he was going into work and then he and a couple of the guys were going out for a beer."

"Did he tell you why he was going into work?"

"No and I didn't ask because I was practicing. Something's wrong, isn't it Uncle Gary?"

"Don't jump to conclusions. Maybe he had some car trouble." I was worried, too. This wasn't like Jeff, at all. He'd always kept Clive informed of his whereabouts and was never out late. *Where was he?*

We were interrupted by a quiet knock on the door. A registered nurse ushered in a county sheriff and another officer.

"Hello, Clive. I'm Sheriff Froehlich."

"I know. I've seen you at the high school."

The sheriff glanced over at me. "Yes, well, this is Officer Banks." Again, the sheriff looked at me. "I'm sorry. I don't believe we've met."

"Gary Stanton, friend of the family."

"I'm going to have to look at your ID."

I showed him my passport.

"You're an American citizen living in Toronto?"

"I own a restaurant there."

"May I ask who called you?"

"The hospital staff. I'm the emergency contact."

"Not a relative, though?"

I shook my head.

"Do you know how we can reach any of the boy's relatives?"

"I'm the nearest he's got." The sheriff looked at Clive who nodded in agreement.

"Afraid we have some bad news." Sheriff Froehlich hesitated and looked tenderly at Clive before continuing in a low voice. "Your father's boat was found adrift downriver from Tar Island. I'm sorry to tell you, son, that he drowned some time during the night."

I heard a sort of primal wail begin, then coughing, then sobbing. It wasn't only Clive. It was both of us coming apart. I moved to the bed and gathered Clive about the shoulders in an embrace. The officers tried to look away. The nurse stood by.

"How? What was he doing out there?" I whispered.

"We don't know much, yet. We're trying to figure out if the attack on Clive was connected to his father's mishap."

"Attack? *Mishap?* We're talking about an experienced Border Patrol agent. This all sounds like much more than a mishap, Sheriff." I wiped the wetness from my face, becoming incensed.

"We've been informed that Agent Tierney was not on duty last night."

"Eddie," croaked Clive. "That guy Eddie has something to do with this." The mention of my brother-in-law's name shot through me like electrical current. Had Jeff gone out to make some kind of arrangement with Eddie to prevent him from claiming his son?

"Who's Eddie?" asked Officer Banks.

"My sister's husband." I could have sworn I heard a distinct creaking sound in the room as the lid of Pandora's box snapped open. I wiped my face on my sleeve and stood up near the window to stare out, trying to compose myself.

"Why would this Eddie person be a problem?" asked Sheriff Froehlich.

"He's sneaky," cried Clive. "He's been showing up in odd places lately, trying to see my dad."

"You know anything about this, sir?"

I nodded toward the door before leading the way to the hall. The nurse and Officer Banks remained behind with Clive.

"This is complicated."

"Not sure I know what you mean."

"Clive doesn't know that Jeff isn't his biological father. Recently, Jeff told me that when he'd married Clive's mother, she was already pregnant, pregnant by Eddie Cox. Eddie started showing up a couple of weeks ago and all I know is that he wanted something from Jeff in order to keep quiet."

"Mr. Tierney's death may not have been totally accidental. There's a bullet wound in his arm. It's possible he fell overboard after being shot. Clive was attacked by a neighbor, a man named, Craig Barrett. Did Tierney ever mention having a problem with Mr. Barrett?"

"He told me the guy has some domestic issues, but never spoke of a personal conflict with him."

The sheriff paused as if he was waiting for me to say more. I didn't. "Looks like you're the one to keep watch on the boy for now, but he's going to need a legal guardian."

"As far as I know, that would be me. Jeff had documents drawn up a few years back and asked if I'd be willing. I'm sure I have a copy at home."

The sheriff was shaking his head now. "You were right when you said this situation is complicated. Gotta warn you there could be one heck of a legal battle if this Eddie Cox wants to claim custody. Same goes for the boy's mother."

I stood there, aghast. *Was it possible that I could lose Clive, too?*

"We'll get back to you, Mr. Stanton. I'll be talking with someone in our social services department while I send my officers out to question Mr. Cox. Do you know where I might find him?"

It sickened me to give the sheriff my sister's contact information. Samantha didn't even enter my mind.

V. Wake: a V-shaped trail of water behind a moving boat

Samantha De Haven

It was a little after one in the afternoon when I went to my mother's bedroom to tell her that there were two police officers downstairs asking for Eddie. Fortunately, she was already up and dressed in a long, pastel linen shift. I watched as she swallowed a pill, applied heavy eyeliner and lipstick, and slowly floated down the stairs to the front foyer in complete composure like some passé movie star making a grand entrance into an even more passé movie. Unaware of how gaunt and painted up she looked to her audience, my mother threw herself into the act, appearing unruffled and pleased to receive the unusual visitors, almost as if she'd expected their arrival.

"Eddie doesn't spend a lot of time at home, Officers. You mind telling me what this is all about?" I waited on the bottom step.

"We just want to ask him some questions about an acquaintance of his."

"Eddie has lots of acquaintances. Anyone I might know?"

"Jeffrey Tierney."

An involuntary gasp escaped from my lips and I felt my body go limp. The officers glanced in my direction as I slumped down on the stairs.

"Tierney? The name is familiar."

"Do you know if your husband has had any contact with him?"

"Why don't you men come in and have a seat. Can I get you something to drink?"

My mother casually sipped her cocktail while obliviously tearing apart my life. She spilled out her discoveries with a vengeful arrogance, informing the officers that my stepfather's son, the boy I loved, was living with Jeff Tierney. She was so proud of herself for unveiling Eddie's secrets, as if they were any more sordid than her own. My heart broke in two when she uttered Clive's name.

"That's not all, Officers. I don't believe there was ever any legal adoption. It's probable that this boy's mother received payment in return for handing over her son. I'm sure Eddie reaped a share of the profits. He's that type, not the fatherly type."

"Do you know where he might be now, ma'am?"

"No idea. As I've said, he isn't home much." I listened while my mother named a few of Eddie's favorite casinos and pubs, the places she claimed not to frequent herself.

When the officers left, I flew up to my room to call Clive. There was no answer. I tried Uncle Gary next, with the same result. The police never said why they wanted to question Eddie about Jeff, but the sudden chill icing up my spine signaled that some sinister force had cracked open the locker bearing the putrid flesh and fragile bones of secrets.

Trisha Cox

I hadn't seen my philandering husband in several days and I wasn't about to look for him. The police could do that. I called Felix, though, to see if he'd been following Eddie.

"As a matter of fact, I have. He rented a boat out of a place called, Rockport, which is about a three-hour drive east of Toronto.

"Rockport? What's he doing there?"

"I didn't follow him out on the River, so I can't be sure. The marina owner didn't know, or claimed he didn't, but said he was often out on the water at night so he must know his way around."

"Rockport. I think that's where my brother goes on the weekends. He owns a cottage on ... what is it? Samantha! Samantha! Hang on a minute, Felix." I put down the receiver and walked to the bottom of the stairs. Samantha opened her bedroom door and reluctantly trudged out to the landing. Seems like she's always pissed off at me lately. When I asked her for the name of the island, she flinched and questioned me with suspicion.

"Who are you talking to, Mom?"

"Nevermind that! Answer my question."

"Tar Island," she mumbled, running back to her room and slamming the door. I picked up the phone again.

"Tar Island, Felix, that's it. I'll give my brother a call and ask if he's seen Eddie in the neighborhood. In the meantime, though, the police are looking for him. They want to know if he's had any contact with Jeff Tierney."

"They say why?"

"No."

Gary didn't answer his phone at home and when I dialed his restaurant, I was told he'd been called away on some emergency. They suggested that I try to reach him at a hospital in Alexandria Bay, New York. I had no idea where that was. Who did my brother know over there?

The operator connected me with Bayview Medical Center and the receptionist informed me that Gary was not on the patient list.

"I know that. I think he may be visiting someone, perhaps someone in emergency." I waited on hold, watching the clock. After what seemed like twenty minutes instead of two, she came back on the line.

"I'm sorry, ma'am. I haven't been able to find your brother. If you leave a number with me, I'll have someone get back to you when he turns up."

"Ma'am!" I slammed down the phone. "Samantha? Have you finished packing? The movers will be here in the morning!" There was no answer from the upper floor as I went out to the kitchen to fix a drink, a mini-celebration. I'd be back in Manhattan by the time the police began to interrogate Eddie. *Hope he chokes on his own lies.*

Sheriff Cy Froehlich

I took the elevator to the third floor and walked down the hall looking for the officer stationed outside of Craig Barrett's room. "Is he awake?"

"Yeah, the aide just checked on him. They're trying to make sure he's lucid."

"Lucid? Craig Barrett? Not if he's sober!"

I walked into the room to find Craig sitting up in bed, sipping water through a straw. There was a turban of white bandages on his head, some bruising under his eyes, and he was rearranging some ice packs on his tray with one hand. I informed him that he was under arrest for unlawful entry and aggravated assault; then I read him his rights.

"That boy jumped me from behind! I was defendin' myself when he knocked out my lights," he whined.

"That's not how the accounting adds up. The two boys involved say you jumped young Clive. He has a serious stab wound to prove it. Oh, and the victim doesn't recall extending an open invitation for you to enter his home."

"I was just tryin' to get my belongin's back."

"What belongings are you referring to?"

Craig went silent then and turned to stare out the window.

"Look, Barrett, this isn't going to get any better. There's a young boy downstairs who's been badly injured and his father's body has turned up in the River. Know anything about that?"

Craig jerked his head back in my direction, eyes wide and bulging like doorknobs. "Dead?"

"Dead. How did this Border Patrol agent, your neighbor, turn up dead on the same night you broke into his house?"

No response.

"You'd better start talking or call your lawyer, Barrett. You're in this up to your neck." I started to leave when he called me back.

"Sheriff, you need to talk to Eddie Cox."

"We're already out looking for him. How's he involved?"

That's when Craig spilled out a convoluted story about smuggling. He said he'd been double-crossed when Eddie cut him out of any future deals, replacing him with someone else on this side of the border.

"I saw them kids deliver my goods to Tierney. Maybe he was pullin' a sting on Eddie. Or, maybe he was the new partner."

"What made you think these goods belonged to you?"

"Looked just like the cooler Eddie dumped overboard the same night he gave me the heave-ho. I think the kids found it."

"What were you moving?"

He paused before answering, looking about as comfortable as a rabbit with its neck caught in a wire snare. "Hash, cocaine."

No surprise to me. Law enforcement on both sides of the border had been attempting to gather evidence on what we thought to be an organized ring of drug traffickers, but Barrett couldn't give us any other names than Eddie Cox. "By the way, who were these kids?"

"Ask my son. He knows their names."

Hettie Voss

"Josh? Hettie? I need you both down here." I'd heard the doorbell ring so I hustled downstairs when my father bellowed, but stopped short when I saw Sheriff Froehlich standing in the hallway. Josh was right behind me.

"Let's go into my office, Cy." By the look on my father's face, I could tell this wasn't a friendly visit. I glanced over at my brother who was probably thinking the same as I was—Clive's father had turned the contraband over to the sheriff.

Dad sat down behind his desk, but the sheriff declined the offer to sit while Josh and I hesitated near the door. "It's been brought to my attention that you two visited the Tierney house yesterday. I'd like you tell me about the reason for your visit."

I held my breath while a menu of responses rolled through my brain, but Josh took the lead. "We found something suspicious floating in the River and decided that Mr. Tierney would know what to do with it since he works for the Border Patrol."

"What did you find?"

I was still holding my breath in, wondering if we were in some kind of trouble, either from Sheriff Froehlich or from my father.

"A cooler, sir," responded Josh. "A cooler filled with drugs sealed in plastic bags."

"What the blazes …?" my father blustered, but the Sheriff held up his hand in a stop motion to stifle him. I knew this would only be temporary.

"What did Mr. Tierney say to you?"

"He said the cooler could've been dumped overboard by smugglers and maybe someone was planning to return for it. He was going to take it into work with him today."

"Did he say who the smugglers might be?"

We both shook our heads.

"How did you find this contraband?"

This time, Josh looked at me to speak. I hesitated, contemplating how much to tell, but quickly decided that stating the obvious was the safest way to begin.

"With a fish finder. My friend has a boat with a fish finder attached."

"Is your friend Jason Larabie?"

How did the Sheriff know that? And how did he know about the cooler? He must've been speaking with Clive's father.

I nodded.

"So, you were just out fishing and noticed something unusual?"

"Uh-huh, we saw something unusual on the fish finder," I hedged.

"And where did you find the cooler?"

"Near Crossover Light," answered Josh.

"You were out there fishing?"

My father was glaring at me now.

"More like scanning."

"And how did you manage to bring the cooler to the surface?"

I crossed the room to plunk down in a chair, stalling for time to compose an answer, one which wouldn't flip my father's ignition switch, but Josh stepped up again.

"Hettie told me about the mysterious box, so I offered to dive down and get it."

My father pounded the desk with his fist, shouting in exasperation. "Josh, I've explicitly forbidden you to ..."

"Do you know who owns the cooler?" interrupted the sheriff.

"Not really."

"And by 'not really' you mean what exactly?"

That's when I knew that the whole story had to be told including the visit to Tar Island and the two nights in the Amateurs where I'd overheard the smugglers. I finished with, "The man we met at Tar Island had the same voice as the man I heard out in the Amateurs." Dad stared at me, eyebrows arched and mouth opened. He was speechless.

"I'm sure Mr. Tierney can give you more information," suggested Josh.

"Or Clive. He knows the other man's name," I added.

Sheriff Froehlich stared down at the floor for a minute, as if deciding what to say next. "I've spoken to Clive. Your friend is over at the hospital. Seems he was attacked and suffered a hand injury."

Josh and I were horror-struck. "I don't understand," I said, my voice rising. "Who attacked him?"

"We're checking all the details. We've arrested a man we believe broke into his home, a neighbor by the name of Craig Barrett."

My father couldn't contain himself any longer. "Blast it, Cy! What's going on? First we're talking about contraband, now we're talking about an attack on a teenager. Is Jeff with the boy?"

"No, no. He wasn't home at the time of the incident, but you'll probably hear the news soon." He stopped, looking at my brother and then at me. I shook in sudden dread. "Jeff Tierney drowned sometime during the night. We're still investigating."

I jumped out of my seat. "I'm going to the hospital." I hadn't forgotten how Clive had scoured the family portraits on the walls of our home during his first visit. "He doesn't have any other family. He needs someone."

Dad's temper was instantly cooled by this news. I could see a visible shift in him as he stepped into his professional role. He escorted the sheriff to the door, asking if would be alright for us to visit Clive. Josh gave me a shoulder hug while I blinked back tears. When my father returned, he spoke quietly.

"I'm not pleased with the recent course of events and the shenanigans you two have pulled, but that has to be set aside for now."

"Do you think Clive was attacked because we recovered the drugs?" asked Josh.

I hadn't thought of that! Instantly, my trembling intensified and then the sobs poured out. "Daddy, I didn't mean to get anyone hurt. Not Clive, not Mr. Tierney! He's dead?"

My father softened, enclosing me in his arms. "I know that." He pushed back from me to look down into my eyes. "And you're right. Your friend needs you."

Dr. Jack Voss

I'd turned the A/C on max, but it did little to lighten the heavy atmosphere inside the car as we headed down Route 12 toward the hospital. The children were stone silent. I chose to bite down on my own tongue until I sorted out my emotions. I was equally jarred by the revelation that Hettie and Josh had recovered contraband (narcotics, no less!) as I was by the news of Tierney's death and the attack on Clive. Had my children been foolhardy or bold? Josh's dive could have led to dire consequences and Hettie had been out prowling around during the night looking for smugglers! This was real life, not some school-girl detective mystery. Yet, underneath my fear flowed a strong current of fatherly pride.

I knew that the three teenagers in the back seat were also astounded by the attack on their young friend, wondering if they'd played a role in the chain of events which had led to the death of Clive's father. Clive's prior history of unhealthy coping tendencies left me with little doubt that the tragic events of the last twenty-four hours could lead to further detrimental behavior. Knowing that he and his father had few, if any at all, family or friends in the area, I wanted to ascertain that he was getting the help he needed. I used my position as an employee of the hospital and my acquaintance with Clive as his former physician to make inquiries. I learned that he'd been admitted to surgery for an acute wound to his right hand. One of Clive's recurring nightmares had become reality.

"Has anyone been contacted to advocate for the boy?"

The patient liaison directed me to a corner of the waiting area where a tall man was seated. We approached him and he rose to his feet as I made the introductions. "Mr. Stanton? I'm Dr. Voss and these are my children—Hettie, Josh, and Stuart. They are friends of Clive."

"Dr. Voss? Oh, Jeff has mentioned you." His voice was a hoarse whisper.

"First of all, let me begin by saying that we're deeply sorry to hear about the horrific situation surrounding Clive's injury. He's been a frequent guest in our home and we'd like to be of help. I'm also employed here at the hospital, so if there's anything I can do for you, please let me know."

My impatient daughter cut in. "What does the doctor say? Is Clive's hand going to be okay?" She ignored my frown.

Gary Stanton studied Hettie's face for a moment. "The doctor is uncertain." He turned to my sons, tenderness warming his gaze. "Are you the boys who took Clive camping?"

They nodded.

"And which one of you helped him build those muscles?"

Josh smiled and raised his hand.

"Clive has told me how much he's enjoyed spending time with you. His father is ... was grateful, too." The reality was sinking in. It seemed incongruous that passing from life to death could simply be condensed to a change of verb tenses. I sensed that this man was closer than a friend, confirming a suspicion I'd held since my early counseling sessions with Clive. This man not only loved the boy; he loved Jeff. Pulling my wallet from my pocket, I took out my business card and presented it to him.

"We're sorry to hear the news about Jeff."

Gary wiped a hand down over his face before he spoke. "Thank you. I suppose, at some point, I'll need to make arrangements for Jeff's ... I mean, after the police ..." He faltered.

I touched his arm to steady him. "Let me grab some information from my office. I'll be back in a few minutes." He and the children sat down to wait, to figure out how to fill the awkward moment with conversation. I needed the excuse to make a quick phone call. I wasn't about to let the hospital assume that this stranger was a legal custodian for Clive, no matter how sincere his grief appeared to be. Why wasn't an aunt, an uncle, or a grandparent here? If my intuition was correct, I knew why.

Cy assured me he was on top of things. He'd already run a background check on Gary Stanton who, as it turned out, was the owner of a popular restaurant in Toronto and came from a wealthy Manhattan family. "So, that qualifies him as an upstanding citizen?"

"You know me better than that, Jack. I don't buy the designer labels. The boy requested that we call Stanton, so for now, he's clear to visit." Cy finally got around to the point by telling me that social services would be handling the issue of Clive's custody until he could eliminate Stanton from the list of suspects.

I nearly dropped the phone. "Tell me you're not serious. My children are sitting with him as we speak!"

"Standard procedure, Jack. Let's just say I've got questions waiting for answers. Since you've spent time with the kid counting his marbles, maybe you can fill in a few blanks." Cy enjoyed teasing me about my profession.

"Ah, ah, ah. How many times have I had to explain that confidentiality clause in my code of honor?"

"Just hear me out a sec, Sir Gotahead. You think this guy and Jeff were more than friends? Dancing partners, possibly?" Cy was perceptive.

"Anything's possible, Cy, but not necessarily worth knowing."

"I've assigned an officer to be stationed near the boy at all times. Even though we've apprehended the attacker, there's another matter of concern."

"The other smuggler?"

"Stop doing my job for a minute and let me ask the questions. Clive appears to have older wounds, lots of them, but no hospital record of abuse. You know anything about that?"

"Cuts, you mean, on the upper thighs?" I wasn't revealing anything Cy didn't already know.

"There are wounds on his chest, too. Can I ask about the origin of these injuries?"

"You can, but let's just say this to prevent obfuscation of your inquiry. The wounds were self-inflicted, as far as I've been told by the patient himself."

"Ob-fussy-tarnation! Why, Jack, I daresay your pedigree is showing."

Samantha De Haven

Early Tuesday morning, I heard knocking at the front door. I slipped on my robe and dashed down the stairs, having spotted him from my bedroom window. "Uncle Gary!" I sighed as I hugged him. "I hoped it would be you."

Looking unusually haggard, he said, "Is my sister up?"

"Are you serious?"

He didn't smile. "Good. I need to talk to you alone." He hurried me into the kitchen and asked where we kept the coffee. I pulled out the canister and he began to prepare a fresh pot while I sat at the counter, watching him. "I have something to tell you, Sam, something which you're going to find difficult to hear."

"I know already. That's why I've been trying to reach you."

Uncle Gary put down the coffee measure to look at me. "What do you know?"

"That the police are looking for Eddie. They were here asking Mom lots of questions."

"Did they say why they're looking for him?"

"Something about whether or not he'd been in contact with Jeff. After they left, Mom talked to that detective she hired to find out where Eddie might be. She's connecting the dots, Uncle Gary! She's going to ruin everything. The detective will find out about you and Jeff and the cottage." I covered my face with my hands and Gary grabbed my wrists to pull them away.

"Look at me, Sam. None of that matters, now, and none of it was your fault. You have to listen to what I have to say."

I stared up at Uncle Gary through my tears, swallowing my sobs. He came around the counter to hold me.

"Clive's been injured, Sam. That's why I didn't answer your calls, yesterday. I was at the hospital in Alex Bay. A person broke into his house and Clive was stabbed. He needed surgery on his hand."

"What? I don't understand. Where was Jeff?"

I saw Uncle Gary's eyes moisten. He swallowed hard. "His body was found in the River, drowned."

"Drowned?" I looked at him as if I'd never heard the word before. I knew that Jeff Tierney was all about safety when it came to being out on the water. It was in his training. He was a Border

Patrol agent on the seaway, for crying out loud!

"It may not be accidental."

I was overwhelmed. *How could I move back to Manhattan, now?* "Who's going to take care of Clive?"

"I know that Jeff named me as guardian in his will, but we'll have to see what the court says since, in truth, his parents are still alive."

"This is all Mom's fault! She married that loser. She forced him on the rest of us. I can't stand the sight of her anymore!" I wanted to break something, hit someone. All of my buried thoughts and feelings suddenly boiled up to the surface, ready to spew like hot magma. I picked up the nearest object, the ceramic coffee canister, and tossed it across the room. My uncle ducked as the coffee grounds and pieces of pottery scattered through the air and then I heard the familiar doped voice of my mother.

"What's going on in here?" She stood in the doorway, in a transparent nightgown with her eye shade propped up on the crown of her head. I wanted to slap her!

"I'm going to Alex Bay with Uncle Gary, Mom." I didn't look at either one of them for permission. "You've managed to destroy another life."

I raced upstairs to change clothes while my mother and uncle argued. By the time I came downstairs, my mother was slumped in a chair by the kitchen table looking old and confused. "Samantha and Clive?" she asked quietly, "and you and Jeff Tierney? Why didn't you tell me all this sooner?"

Storming up to the table, I bent over her. "And then what, Mom? You would've listened? You would've protected us? You would've *cared?* I don't think you know how." I stomped out and waited by the curb for my uncle to appear.

We reached the border by way of the Thousand Islands Bridge. While waiting in line to go through Customs, my thoughts drifted. It seemed so long ago that the four of us took that trip to Kingston to visit Uncle Gary's colleague. Thinking back, I remembered the look on Jeff's face when he spotted Eddie, a brief look of guardedness, the kind that had darkened my father's face when I was little after I'd wandered away from him in Central Park to talk to a strange man with a pet cockatoo. Clive, too, stared hard at Eddie as if he recognized something, perhaps a facial expression. I pressed my eyes closed, trying to focus on Clive's face, trying to erase Eddie's. Uncle Gary and I spoke very little during the drive.

When we reached the village of Clayton, Uncle Gary turned down a residential street of clapboard houses and tidy front yards as he said, "I want to go by the house." I think my uncle was hoping to find him alive. Or maybe he just wanted to pick up something Jeff had touched, something which might hold some tangible connection to his lover a little while longer before he slipped off into the ethereal world. Instead, we were caught off-guard by the harsh reality of the yellow police tape which cordoned off the front door. Bypassing the driveway, my uncle drove us to the end of the block and turned the corner.

We parked by the village shops and got out of the truck. While Uncle Gary went to find us something to eat, I walked down to the River. A cold front had cut through the humidity, whipping the current into rough waves which beat against the dock. The air was tepid, but I shivered. I suddenly felt lonely.

The food seemed to revive Uncle Gary's desire for conversation while we drove to the hospital. "I want to stop in the gift shop and find something for Clive. Got any ideas?" I could think of no *thing*, no single object which might make him smile. There was no magic wand to resurrect Jeff or erase the fresh wound of grief.

"Which hand is it? Will he be able to perform in the competition?

"His right hand and it's doubtful."

When we arrived, he was sitting up with his wrapped hand resting on a pillow. He smiled immediately, genuinely happy to see familiar faces.

"Sam, you're here!"

I bent down to give him a brief kiss before Gary presented him with a stuffed Labrador puppy and a pound-sized chocolate candy bar. "Just in case you're missing Spike. You two visit and I'll see if I can find a doctor to get some information."

"I'm so sorry about Jeff," I whispered. "The police are looking for Eddie, too."

"This whole thing is connected somehow, I know it. Why did Eddie stop by the cottage to see my father? And then, a couple of days later, my neighbor breaks in and this happens," he said as he raised his injured hand. "And then, then ..."

"The worst happens," I answered, knowing that Clive had not yet heard the worst, that Jeff wasn't his father.

Sheriff Cy Froehlich

Win Crow was one of the best social workers in the business, if you can call that line of work business. She could sniff out a line of blarney faster than my hound dog could sniff out a raccoon in my backyard. She and I both knew there were some people with kids who should've never had any. Win told me once how she'd been the oldest of ten and by default, she'd been another parent to most of them. You might say she'd been in social work all her life and claimed that she had no desire to come home to more of it. She'd stayed single, but it wasn't on account of her looks.

Win was a tall woman, with smooth mocha skin, wide chocolate eyes, and a loud laugh that could be heard all the way down the hall. She most always wore her hair pinned up and I don't think I ever saw her in a skirt, but I spent more time than I'd admit imagining the long, slender legs that moved like a fashion model on a runway underneath her perfectly pleated slacks. Thoughts like that had earned me a divorce. Or, maybe it had something to do with my job.

She sashayed into my office in a cream-colored linen suit with a coffee in one hand and an overstuffed leather tote bulging with papers in the other. After setting her coffee down on my desk, she magically whisked just the right document from the disorderly heap without even searching for it, then slapped it down in front of me, tapping it with her glossy red fingernails. I waited for her to sit down and cross those legs with the stiletto heels attached, red open-toed heels with bare toes polished to match, I might add. "What am I looking at?" I asked, knowing very well what I shouldn't be looking at.

"Well, I think what we have here is a falsified birth certificate claiming Jeffrey Tierney is the father of Clive Tierney. It was found in the victim's home, but the one on record includes only the name of Veronica Wallace." A long, red nail pointed out the name as she said it.

"Have you made contact with her?"

"When I spoke to her on the phone, she tried to do a little story dance around my questions. You know what I'm saying? Tried to say she and Tierney had a shotgun wedding, but I put the end on that fable when I let her know there was no record of the marriage."

"How about the information we received from the interview with the wife of Eddie Cox? Did you speak with that Detective Silva?"

"Yes I did. He's a character, that one, but there's no moss growing between his ears. He reported that Eddie Cox is most certainly the father, so I asked the Wallace woman about her relationship with him. She started sidestepping again, but I instilled the fear of small, confined spaces in her by explaining the serious consequences of obstructing a murder investigation. That left her gasping for air for at least two whole minutes. I thought I'd have to put in a call to the paramedics."

"Did she fess up?"

"Now, Cy, how many times do I have to remind you that I'm good at what I do? *Very* good." Win flashed all of her pearly whites in a big smile between those cherry-red lips. "Of course, she fessed up! Admitted the boy was conceived by allowing Eddie into her knickers, but didn't admit to any money exchanging hands. She said she'd have to speak to her attorney."

"Did she ask about her son?"

"More than once, I stressed that he'd been the victim of a violent attack, but she seemed more concerned about her own skin and keeping any knowledge of Clive's existence from her current husband. That's not likely, but that's her problem. I think this case is going to need review from higher up before the boy is released into the custody of any adult."

"Who's going to break the news to Clive?"

"Well, I sure hope it won't be left to me and I hope it won't be that heartless mother of all mothers, if you know what I'm saying. You mentioned a family friend who may be a possible guardian. What about him?"

"We're checking him out. In the meantime, how about you and I get a bite to eat?"

"I'll get back to you, Cy." She hefted her filing bag and waved at me over her shoulder. Her empty coffee cup remained on my desk. I picked it up and stared at the lipstick print on the rim before pitching it at the waste basket. *Missed!*

The phone rang then and brought in some good news for a change. Eddie Cox had been detained for questioning at the Toronto airport prior to boarding a plane for the west coast. I made arrangements to meet the Ontario investigating team there and let my staff know I'd be out of the office for the rest of the day.

After the long, dull drive, I was eager to get right down to business. I began the interrogation to determine Eddie's whereabouts during the past thirty-six hours. In short shrift, his lies were sorted out with a few references to the information obtained from Detective Silva and the marina owner who rented him a boat.

"I didn't rent any boat in Rockport. Where's your proof says I did?"

"Oh, right. You're the smart guy who didn't use his own name. When we showed your photo to the marina operator, he remembered you. Here. Here's the photo. Sure looks like you. Maybe you didn't know about the detective who's been following you. Takes pretty good photos, wouldn't you say?" Cox shut down, visibly upset. I explained that we had reason to believe he was involved in the illegal transport of goods across the international border and asked where he was on a number of dates scribbled in a pocket calendar found in the glove box of Craig Barrett's truck.

"Can't recall," was his only response.

"So, you're going to play it like that, eh? I just want you to know that these dates also correspond with the boat rentals for the same Peter Simon who rented a vessel this weekend, the one who matches your physical description. Can you see me lining up the ducks, now? And we haven't even gotten to the good parts, the illegal sale of a child and the murder of a U.S. Border Patrol agent. You might want to reconsider some of your statements if you have any plans for retirement."

He was placed under arrest and allowed to call an attorney while I headed back to the States. Cox would be up late calculating what plea bargain might get him off the hook with the justice systems of two countries without risking retribution from his partners in crime. But I knew this was no open and shut case—not yet.

Gary Stanton

"What happens next? Can I go home? Will I be moving in with you?"

"I'd like nothing more than for that to happen." I stood near the windows instead of drawing close to his bedside in part to appear stoic, but mostly to prevent Clive from smelling my own panic. Ms. Crow had informed me that there was some legal uncertainty surrounding the guardianship of Clive which meant he'd be placed into foster care until the matter was settled. Jeff was gone and I was facing the possibility of losing the boy I considered to be our son, my son. "We have to wait for a legal review to determine who has the right to act as your guardian."

"What does that mean? Dad's dead! I don't have any other family except for you."

Clive's eyes filled up. There was no way around the agony. "There are some things you need to know, things I've only just learned myself. Your father recently made a confession to me. He told me that your mother had already been pregnant when they married, pregnant by another man." I watched for his reaction, but he simply stiffened, as if holding his breath while waiting for the other boot to drop. "That man, your biological father, contacted Jeff because he wanted to make a deal."

"Eddie!" he rasped, clenching his left fist.

I was flabbergasted. "How did you know that?" I knew that Sam hadn't told him.

"Out of the blue, this guy turns up three times in a month. He knew where to find Dad on Tar Island. It's him, isn't it?"

I couldn't speak.

"Was Dad ever planning on telling me? Would you have ever told me if ... if ..." He stared at me with resentment in his eyes.

I doubted it. Eddie was a vile man. We would've fought to keep Clive away from him.

"I won't have to live with him, will I? Sam hates him."

"Not if I have anything to say, but it may not even be a possibility at this point. He's been arrested in Canada on charges of smuggling and the authorities are questioning him about his interaction with Jeff."

Clive's eyes widened and I saw the tide of realization swell through him. He was catching up quickly. "You think Eddie killed Dad?"

The tears fell freely, now. I sat beside him on the bed, opposite the wounded hand, and held him tightly. "I'm not going to leave you alone, no matter what." I couldn't promise him that things would get better, that he'd wake up some morning and feel whole again. I couldn't even tell myself those things. On top of that, I hadn't told him the entire truth.

Andrew Zey

The news about Jeff and Clive sucked the air out of the community like napalm. The locals were talking about it at the post office, the diner, in the grocery store. "Hey, hear about that Tierney kid and his father? A terrible thing, that." Everyone was stunned. Clive had been stabbed and his father was dead. Some local guy, Craig Barrett, was involved. He was a known drinker, but a killer? Quite a shock for this little town. Another man had been arrested over in Ontario. This was playing out like some thriller movie. Maybe Jeff had been killed on some undercover assignment. He didn't seem like a bad character, but what was the deal with Clive's adoption? This story grew a new tentacle with every news report. Clive was like a man without a country. The question of his guardianship was all over the headlines. His whole life had been transformed overnight.

It was no news to me that Jeff was gay. Why else would he have been in *that* club with Gary the first night I met him? Gary knew I was gay, too. He'd seen the customers hitting on me when I played those gigs. Back home in Clayton, though, I kept pretty much to myself so I had little inkling whether or not any of the locals suspected my own predilection, but it was kind of a don't ask, don't tell climate. They didn't ask and I didn't tell. Living in New York City was different, though. More people, more variety. I'd had my share of bad relationships that lasted too long and a couple of good ones that didn't last long enough. It couldn't have been easy for Jeff trying to live his life in disguise. And the guy worked for Border Patrol, to boot! He must have been held together with cement.

Anyway, it bothered me that Clive might be sitting over in that hospital trying to chew on all of this by himself. I thought I should go see him, but called Gary first to see if it was a good idea. He gave me the thumbs up. The last time I'd seen Clive was the afternoon before he was attacked. He was feeling confident about his competition pieces and excited about going away to music camp.

He looked years younger lying in that hospital bed. "Hey, Clive. How are you feeling?" *Ouch! Why did I say that?* Just a reflex, I guess, but if you're in the hospital, you can't be feeling good and this kid had layers of rotten piled on top of him. "Sorry, dumb question."

He sat up a little straighter and I looked down at his right hand, wrapped in a cloud of white dressing. I wondered about the prognosis.

"Andy." No smile, just acknowledgment.

I tried to joke. "So, they giving you the hard drugs?"

He smiled. "Yeah, they're legal in here."

"I brought some of your buddies to keep you company." I laid some CDs on his bed, selections from his favorite composers like, Chopin, Mendelssohn, and Mozart, but I couldn't resist adding in Gershwin and the Monk, too. "Thought you might want to branch out a bit." He sorted through them with his left hand. I noticed a tear slide down his cheek.

"Sorry, man. I didn't mean to make you feel worse. Want me to take them home till ..." *Till what?*

"I don't think I can play them in here."

"Oh, snap! I almost forgot. Let me hook you up, man." I pulled a boombox and headphones out of the oversized shopping bag I'd carried through the hallways. "Even brought batteries in case they had you plugged into all the outlets in the room. Glad to see you're not."

The smile grew back.

"Would you like me to load one of the CDs for you?' Clive didn't look offended by my offer of assistance and I was amazed when he chose the Monk. I unwrapped the album and inserted the disk into the player, turning down the volume. We sat quietly through the first piece.

"Thanks, Andy. I needed a break from Chopin and his friends."

I was afraid to ask, but did it anyway. "So, what's the doc got to say about your hand?"

Clive stared at the dressing while he answered. "I think the thumb and index finger have a chance, but it's not looking good for the rest of the team. I'll need some rehab, but I can't … I mean, I won't … I can't do the competition this Fall. Sorry to let you down, Andy."

"Let *me* down? What are you talking about? This isn't about me. You shouldn't worry about me at all, but I'm worried about you." I was getting a little choked up. "How are you handling all this bullshit?"

He listened to the first few measures of the second tune before he spoke. "It isn't real to me, yet. I don't think it will be until I go … until I get out of here."

I thought I was going to lose it right then and there. I grabbed one of the cheap, thin tissues from the box on his nightstand and faked a sneeze. Oh, was it ever going to get real after they let him out of this place. It was going to hit him like a wall of concrete! I didn't know what to say. "If there's anything you need, maybe some pizza, a chocolate shake, whatever, just let me know." We were interrupted by sudden movement in the doorway. "Looks like you have more visitors." I was a little relieved that our conversation was broken off. I was beginning to sound stupid.

Jason Larabie

After Hettie finished telling me what had happened to Clive, we cried and then we argued. She had a freighter load of guilty conscience weighing her down. "It wasn't our fault, Hettie! How were we to know that the other smuggler lived right across the street?"

"Me and my big ideas! If I'd just kept out of it, Clive wouldn't be sitting in the hospital."

"You don't know that. Robbie's father might have gone looking for Mr. Tierney anyway. Besides, you weren't smuggling the drugs. You weren't the one who got this ball rolling down the wrong alley."

She let me hug her, then. I loved being close to her. It was like sitting in the sun after a cold dip in the River. "What if he can't ever play again?" she cried.

"I've thought about that, thought about if I were in his shoes. I know that I'd find a way to make music, one way or another. Clive is smart; he'll find a way."

We showed up at the hospital just as Mr. Zey was leaving. "Wow! Where'd you get the cool boombox?" I asked.

"Why, yes, I'm feeling much better. Thanks for asking," Clive remarked sarcastically.

"Sorry, the music distracted me." I had to look, then, had to look at Clive's right hand and wondered if I'd be able to look after the bandage came off.

"Well, I, the thoughtful one," Hettie said as she sneered at me, "made you some of my mocha chip brownies. You can decide whether or not you want to share." She leaned over and kissed Clive on the forehead. A brief pang of jealousy struck my heart. *Did embers still glow for Clive?*

We all munched on the brownies, joking about the crumbs that we dropped on his sterile, clean sheets, an almost typical conversation, until Clive said, "Yeah, I'm out of the piano competition. Don't know when I'll start playing again." Hettie and I glanced at each other, then down at his hand. We couldn't find words to fill the void.

"I figure if I say it often enough, I'll get used to the idea. Sure will free up a lot of time for me." He giggled softly, but we couldn't even manage a smile.

Hiding her own doubts, Hettie played the optimist. "It's too early to talk about forever, Clive. People do defy the odds sometimes."

Feeling more uncomfortable, I attempted to change channels by saying, "How about that Robbie? Came to your rescue, eh, and took out his own father!" Looking bewildered, my friends stared back at me while my words just hung in the air. I was about to apologize for my lack of tact when they broke up laughing. It felt good to laugh despite all the crap that had gone down, almost as if we could dam up the runoff headed our way.

"Robbie, my hero," he said while lifting his bandaged hand in an almost natural way and placing it over his heart. "Wouldn't have predicted that, but I should probably thank him. I don't mind saying that his father scared me out of my mind and might have finished me off if Robbie hadn't shown up."

There was another audio pause before Hettie asked, "So, when do you get out?"

"The red tape has some knots in it. My father's will names his friend as guardian, but he lives in Toronto. That would mean moving out of the country."

I couldn't stand seeing Clive unhappy, so I had to joke. "But you'd get a chick-magnet accent, eh?"

He smiled, but added, "As it turns out, I'm part Canadian anyway. Like you."

"Really?"

"Yeah, my real father is Canadian." I sensed a slow burn in Clive's tone.

"Your *real* father?" echoed Hettie.

"Yup, news to me. But wait. Here comes the best part. My biological father just happens to be the guy who might've been smuggling with old man Barrett. How's that for a happy ending?" He wasn't smiling.

"You mean that guy we saw you talking to over at Tar Island?" Hettie was bowled over by this news. "This can't be. You're nothing like him! Someone has made a serious identity mistake here."

"That's the one. Eddie Cox is his name. I'm sure they've taken enough of my blood to confirm it, so I doubt it's a mistake. My case is being sent to family court."

"Shit uphill, Clive!" I blurted.

"Jason! Keep your voice down," whispered Hettie through her teeth.

That's when we told Clive about our trip to the Amateurs, finding the smugglers and the cooler full of drugs. Clive hadn't known about the contraband.

"It's beginning to make more sense, now. If Robbie's dad was one of the smugglers and saw you bring that cooler over to my house, then that would explain why he broke in."

"We thought we were doing the right thing. We didn't think turning it in would put you in danger."

Silence followed as we each tried to swallow the huge dose of new reality. Clive's life was being rewritten right in front of us. Hettie's eyes began to tear up as the engines of the Guilty Conscience freighter churned louder. A few more seconds and we'd all be washed overboard, so I jumped into rescue mode by challenging my friends to a game of hangman. The nurse's message board was covered in scribble and my friends were smiling by the time Clive's dinner arrived. The attendant asked if Hettie and I would like a beverage, but I couldn't get an ice cream float, so I passed. Hettie busied herself with opening Clive's milk carton and cutting up his meat, then lowering the bed tray and propping him up with pillows. I was beginning to wish I was the one in the bed; then again, not.

Just before we left, Hettie asked, "Why do you think Robbie showed up at your house?"

"Haven't got a clue." said Clive.

Hettie Voss

Clive's name had been in the local news before, back when he was a child prodigy. That type of publicity promotes interest in the Thousand Islands area where most business owners depend on tourism to make their living. The piano competition is a major annual event that attracts people and performers from all over the world, so the river rat community had been Clive's biggest fans until their hopes were trampled by the daily barrage of headlines like, *Violence and Scandal Taint River Wonderland.* The gossip pipeline burst open, spewing muck all over Clive's father and his relationship with a man named, Gary Stanton. It had never occurred to me or Jason that Mr. Tierney was a homosexual. I can't say we were shaken, maybe just surprised by the truth when Clive confirmed it. There was a tinge of bitterness in his voice when he added, "Just goes to show that gay guys can live in your neighborhood, go to work, and raise kids just like other parents." Clive hadn't been totally shut off from the offensive commentary about his father. Desperate to set things right, I pleaded with my parents to officially become Clive's foster parents.

"Hettie, I cannot in all good judgment see that as an appropriate avenue. You and Clive have some history which the court may not view as favorable for family co-existence."

"Dad, we're only friends. There's no romance going on between me and Clive."

"That's not entirely my meaning. You also stumbled upon the smuggling net which snared both of the men considered to be his father."

Was Clive blaming me for his father's, that is, for Jeff Tierney's death? Dad seemed to read my mind.

"Now, I wasn't trying to imply that you placed Clive in harm's way or that Clive will harbor any resentment toward you."

"But that's exactly why I have to help him. Please, Dad, let's give him a home and relatives and a place to be safe, without secrets."

"I know you think that would be lovely, but it's not that simple. I've acted as his doctor, the kind of doctor that helps people deal with all kinds of secrets and mental anguish. To switch roles, from physician to parent, may not be what Clive wants. In fact, he might prefer putting more distance between himself and all the spurious chinwag." I rolled my eyes at his ridiculous choice of words.

"Can't we ask him, at least?"

"I'll think about it."

Meanwhile, as the public nosed around in all the nooks and crannies of Clive's life, Jason and I set aside time every evening to visit him. I brought up the issue of where Clive would go after leaving the hospital.

"So, you would prefer to move to Toronto and live with your father's friend?"

"Absolutely. Better to be in a place where no one knows me than to be around people talking behind my back. Gary's always been a second dad to me."

"Well, what's the hold up, then? Sounds like he's a great guy and he's got lots of bucks," said Jason who was nibbling from the box of assorted chocolates left by a previous visitor.

Clive smiled. "He is and he does, but the courts still don't favor homosexuals over straight couples when it comes to adopting children, at least, not this court."

"Why? Are they afraid you'll turn out gay?"

"There's some mumbo jumbo about being concerned for my welfare. In other words, yeah, they're afraid Gary's some kind of pervert."

"How's it okay for a beast like Craig Barrett to raise kids, but not a kind and loving person like Mr. Tierney or his, ah ... his friend?"

"Hettie, are you going to run for office after you get that law degree?" joked Jason.

Molly Larabie

The news was staggering. A stabbing in Clayton? We didn't have those kinds of goings-on here. In fact, I had friends who didn't lock their doors unless they'd left the county. And Jeff Tierney drowned or murdered? Then came all kinds of sordid innuendos about his personal life and whether or not Clive was his son.

It was Jason who first brought it up one evening when we all sat down to dinner. "Clive could live with us, couldn't he?"

"I'm sure there must be other family to take him in," I answered.

"He's always said there's no one else except his father's friend and Clive says the court probably won't allow a gay guy to adopt him."

I think we all dropped our forks at once. This wasn't our typical dinner table talk.

"Is Clive gay?" asked Christopher.

"No. Shut up!" Jason was agitated.

"Taking Clive in isn't like adopting a pet. Children have to be provided for."

"He can sleep with you," said Chad with a grin.

Jason punched him in the arm.

"That's enough!" When Cal barked, the boys obeyed.

"Well, how about it. Mom? Dad? You can't let Clive go to some foster home with strangers. He knows us."

"What I think is that this is a decision for grownups, not for you." With that, Cal ended the discussion until after the boys had gone to bed.

"Four is a nice even number," I suggested.

"Molly ..."

"Remember how we felt when we first learned we were having twins? We wondered how we were going to cope with a two-year old and two newborns, but we got through it."

"This is different than having a baby. Clive will be towing a lot of baggage."

"I seem to remember you shouldering a bag or two when we got married." We'd planned a quick wedding following Cal's discharge from the army after learning that his father had been diagnosed with stage four lung cancer. He passed away while we were on our honeymoon in Montreal. Cal and his older sister assumed responsibility for looking after his mother and making sure his two younger brothers walked the straight and narrow. On top of that, he was still wrestling with the demons that followed him home from the war.

"That was me, Molly. Not someone else's kid. And we're not sure whose kid this is, when you think about it."

"We may be the only other adults Clive knows. He's been in our home and he's best friends with Jason."

"Next, you'll be telling me that this is part of God's plan."

"Now that you mention it ..."

Cal agreed to meet with Clive's social worker before making a final decision. In the meantime, we'd submit an application to be his foster parents which, if accepted, would give us temporary custody and offer Clive a familiar place to call home. When we told the boys, Jason cheered. Christopher, as usual, was quiet. Chad simply asked, "Can we get a dog, too?"

Ms. Crow's earthy voice and her loud laugh put me at ease when I called to make the appointment with her, but I hadn't expected the tall, gorgeous bombshell who greeted us in person. I could tell by Cal's bashful blush that he was astonished, too. He didn't dare look over at me because he knew I was watching his reaction and it almost made me laugh aloud. I've often wondered if people with her looks know the impact they have on the plain-faced. She ushered us into a tiny room cluttered with stacks of files. There was barely room for her to squeeze her long legs around the metal desk in order to sit in a battered, wooden swivel chair. Cal and I settled into the metal chairs facing her. I noticed the name plate sitting on top of her desk. "Win Crow," I read. "Sounds like a strong name."

"Short for Winona, meaning first daughter."

"Beautiful name. How did it get shortened?"

"I have five sisters and four brothers. Whenever we played sandlot games, I out-ran, out-jumped, and out-batted all of them, so they started calling me Win. I didn't mind. It just made me work harder."

"Guess we should've tried that name on one of ours," joked Cal. I knew he was thinking about one of the twins.

"Oh, I didn't know you had a daughter." Win winked at me.

"No. Guess he would've been a Winston," Cal replied.

"You must know a lot about growing a family," I interjected to get us back on track.

"The stories I could tell ..." She asked that we tell her something about ourselves, our boys, and how we knew Clive. When we'd finished, she looked us in the eye and said, "I want you to know what you'll be taking on if you agree to become guardians for Clive." She continued by explaining that Clive had been through the simultaneous traumas of a violent attack and the murder of the man he'd called, Dad, all his life. Both had resulted in irreparable loss, yet there were other complications. Clive's biological parents were still alive and facing criminal charges. As if that weren't enough, Clive had a history of self-harming. Cal and I looked at each other, our brains buzzing louder than our hearts, now. My husband spoke first.

"You definitely haven't sugar-coated this undertaking, Ms. Crow."

"Win will do just fine."

"Could we have a few days to think things over?"

"Of course, but I have to inform you that Clive is going to be discharged from the hospital the day after tomorrow. He'll be sent to a residential facility for boys until a home is found for him. Given his background and his age, that will probably take some time. He'll be assigned to a counselor immediately."

"Have any other relatives been asking about him?" I wanted to confirm what Jason had told us.

"None that I know of, but Jeff Tierney did appoint a man named, Gary Stanton, as guardian. Since Clive wasn't legally adopted, this request most likely won't carry any weight with the court, but I do want you to be aware of the situation."

Cal wanted to know if Clive had voiced a preference for a caretaker.

"I'm not going to lie to you. He'd like to live with Mr. Stanton whom he views as another father. For the time-being, Clive will only be allowed supervised visits with the man until the closure of the criminal cases involving his parents. It's possible that the court may not feel comfortable awarding guardianship to Mr. Stanton based on his relationship with Mr. Tierney or if evidence reveals that he had prior knowledge of the illegal purchase of Clive as an infant."

I noted that Ms. Crow avoided defining—or judging—the nature of the relationship between the two men in Clive's life. "Will Mr. Stanton accept the court's decision to place Clive with another family?"

"It will be difficult for both of them. In a case such as this, there is the possibility of flight or kidnapping across borders. Mr. Stanton is a man with considerable financial resources."

We thanked her for her time, but I needed to ask one more question before we left her office. "There are so many layers to this tragedy. Anyone would find it extremely stressful to get past it, but you mentioned that Clive had a history of hurting himself even before all this happened. Is it possible … what I mean is, do you think he'll try to ..." I didn't want to say *it.*

"Kill himself?" Her bluntness made me cringe. "I can't guarantee he won't. He'll be grief-stricken for as long as it takes and he'll be depressed. He's lost a parent, possibly the dream of becoming a concert pianist, his home, and to top it all off, his family life has been fodder for hungry news reporters. Who knows what will happen when he returns to school. Even if he goes home with you, he'll still need long-term counseling, but we could discuss home-tutoring with the principal of River High. From what I hear, Clive is an excellent student so the GED program may be another option."

On the drive home, Cal steered with one hand and held mine in his other. We didn't speak, but we each knew the other was mulling over all we'd just heard from Win Crow. After parking in the driveway, Cal leaned over and gave me a sweet kiss. "Let this simmer overnight and say your Hail Mary's, Molly. We'll know what feels right in the morning."

I believe that prayer is stronger when it's based on blind faith, acceptance that God will hear the prayer and answer it. While I asked Him for wisdom, I wondered if Clive was talking to God, too.

Gary Stanton

There were times when resentment overruled my grief. Jeff wasn't around to clean up the mess he'd left behind. A huge magnifying lens had been slammed down over my private life, intensifying public examination, especially after a story broke alleging that Jeff had paid money for Clive. Now I was struggling to defend my own innocence in the matter which was made more difficult by the fact that my sister was married to Eddie, the man whose seed had created Clive. The odds against my being appointed his legal guardian were stacking up.

Worse yet, I was the one who had to explain Jeff's lies to the seventeen year-old whose life had been turned upside down. Seeing Veronica's face in the news drove the dagger in deeper. Clive's eyes stared back at me from her face. He had her complexion, too, but the dimples must've come from the snake charmer. Veronica, a bottle blonde, had expensive taste. She was impeccably costumed from head to toe, highlighted hair worn in a short perm, polished nails and tailored suit. Details about her background were sketchy. She'd once been the secretary of her current husband, the owner of a luxury resort. He'd gone through a nasty divorce after the discovery of his affair with Veronica who, as it turned out, would eventually give birth to his son. This meant that Clive had a half-brother. Did he need to know all of this? I knew I couldn't shut off every source of information or rumor forever. Like Eddie, Veronica was now facing a criminal charge. This story wasn't going away any time soon.

I'd called in professional reinforcement this time by asking Win Crow to accompany me. During my phone conversation with her, she'd emphasized that it would be easier on Clive to hear the facts about his mother from me rather than a stranger, but I wasn't so sure. She met me outside Clive's hospital room, looking powder fresh in her white muslin tunic and white slacks while I perspired profusely—the air outside was a steam bath—with the early warning pangs of a migraine. I focused on her long eyelashes as she gave my sweaty hand a firm shake and imparted her sympathy for the difficult situation. "Take it from me. Don't skirt the issue. Clive needs to see all the cards laid out on the table. He's smart and he'll know if you're still holding." *Too late for that bit of advice. I was sunk.* My head throbbed.

I could see the questioning look in his eyes as soon as the two of us stepped into the room. He knew something was up. I tried not to show my cowardice when I spoke. "How are you feeling today?"

"Not much pain."

He looked sideways at Ms. Crow who picked up the slack. "Good to hear. Had lunch, yet?"

"Grilled cheese sandwich."

"Maybe you'd prefer a couple of chocolate croissants." I placed the consolation prize on his tray table. He reached up with his left hand to open the bag and I instinctively moved to help, but Ms. Crow grasped my forearm. I watched as Clive dumped the croissants out onto the tabletop. He picked one up, took a bite, and leaned back into his pillow to savor the chew. A lump rose in my throat. I shook my head at Ms. Crow, my tail caught between my legs.

She took charge. "Clive, I've been working on the snag in your living arrangements."

He set the croissant back down on the table. I handed him a napkin.

"Right now, I don't have a good answer for you. It'll be up to a court to decide what's best."

Clive looked over at me. "So, I can't go home with you." Not a question; just a realization.

"Gary wants to tell you what he's learned about your mother." Ms. Crow wasn't giving me a choice. It was my turn to speak.

"I … well, you already know that Veronica Wallace is your mother and Eddie, well … you know that part, too. Turns out that your mother was never married to Jeff and ..." My eyes pleaded with Ms. Crow, but she just waved her hand in circles, signaling for me to get on with it. "And she didn't die in a car crash. In fact, she's alive."

Clive threw his head back against the pillows and pounded the bed with his good hand, clenching his jaw.

Worried that Clive would feel betrayed, I omitted Sam's part in the discovery about his mother. "I didn't know this either, Clive, until a few days ago. If I'd known the whole truth all along, I don't know if it would've made any difference to me. I loved Jeff and I love you and I still believe he loved us both."

"So, where's my mother now?"

A wave of nausea from the migraine overwhelmed me and I ran to the bathroom. When the heaves subsided, I rinsed my face with cold water while Ms. Crow continued to explain the developing circumstances to Clive until I reappeared. They both turned to stare at me—accusation in his eyes, no surprise in hers. She offered to call a nurse, but I declined, wanting to end this episode of Sledgehammer Exposé as soon as possible. "I was just telling Clive about the dubious adoption situation and the subsequent legal charges against Veronica." *Hit him again, why don't you?*

I could think of nothing to say to soften the blow, so I walked to his side and reached down to squeeze his shoulder. "Stop. Stop." He brushed my hand away. "So, everything was bullshit from the beginning! What did it cost Dad?" His voice cracked and he took in a deep breath to stifle a sob. "What did Dad have to do, Gary? What did he have to do to keep me?"

I couldn't answer.

Jason Larabie

I cheered when my parents announced that they'd received the green light for Clive to live with us, but my brothers didn't say a word. My excitement was diluted when Dad implied that Clive might not be looking forward to moving in with us. "The events of one night changed his life forever. He was told a pack of lies by people he trusted and you boys know how we feel about lies in this house." My brothers and I exchanged guilty looks. Lies were unacceptable in the Larabie home where we were always taught to own up and clean up before the mess got any bigger. All three of us were still working on putting it into practice.

"And don't go bugging him with a lot of questions about all that's happened. If Clive wants to tell you something, he will. Eventually, he'll be expected to pitch in around here just like the rest of you, but that time will be decided by your mother and me. In the meantime, approach him gently or give him space."

Mom emphasized the temporary status of the custody. Permanent custody depended on what was best for all concerned and any legal wrinkles yet to be ironed out. "We hope you'll each try your best to make this work. That's all we ask."

My mother helped me rearrange my room and make up Clive's bed with the items he'd requested from his house. We brought in Clive's desk and placed it under one of the windows facing the River, but I kept my bed right where it was, under the other window because I liked to fall asleep listening to the River sounds at night. Besides, I did most of my studying in bed. After I cleared my closet of the clothing and clutter which hadn't seen the light of day since elementary school, Dad installed shelves to add storage space.

"What's going to happen to all the stuff in Clive's house?"

Mom continued laying down shelf liner as she spoke. "That still has to be sorted out. Technically, the house belongs to the bank since there's a mortgage, so it'll need to be sold or rented out. If Clive wants it sold, then the equity can go into a trust for him. As for what's inside, that's up to Clive."

"Do you think he'll keep his piano?"

"We'll find room for it, if that's what he wants."

It was beginning to sink into my thick head just how much disruption Clive was facing. I knew my friend had established routines and methods for doing things. He was also anal retentive and was now going to share a room with me! Clive wasn't the only one who'd have to adjust. It suddenly struck me that I'd be giving up the freedom to apply random order to my private domain. I wasn't sure if our friendship was going to withstand the strain, but there was no reneging now.

Mom and I helped Clive place his few belongings and the gifts from his visitors into a couple of duffel bags which we'd brought with us on the day of his discharge. The nurse explained the wound care instructions to my mother as we waited for the required wheelchair transport to arrive. Already nervous for Clive, I did my usual and tried to make light of the situation with my comical antics. Clive climbed aboard the chair with the new boombox in his lap and I immediately tipped him back on the rear wheels, screeching sound effects included, and sped out into the hallway slowing just as we reached the closed door marked, *Stairs.*

Pulling the door open, I edged him forward. "Going down?"

Clive smiled slowly and began to stand up. My mother gawked at me in alarm.

"Just kidding. Sit down and we'll go first-class instead." The old Clive would have had a great comeback.

Back at home, I carried his bags up to my room while he followed. My brothers and my father were busy with the marina duties, giving Clive time to unpack in quiet. While my mother prepared a lunch for us, I showed him what was what and where he could stow his personal gear, but stopped my blathering when I saw his tears.

"Look, man. This can't be easy. I'll just shut up, now, and leave you to it. Come on down for lunch when you're ready. If you need anything, don't be afraid to ask."

Clive sat down on his bed and smoothed the blankets with his left hand.

Molly Larabie

Taking on a fourth son—one nearly old enough to be drafted—was nothing like bringing home a newborn. We had a steady stream of visitors for the first week, those who hadn't made it over to the hospital for a variety of reasons. Work schedules, sad memories from previous hospital visits, the police officer stationed outside Clive's room; some people just can't handle seeing others in pain. I made sure to keep the coffeepot ready and the cookie jar full. I can't say the visitors lifted Clive's spirits, but they may have momentarily dulled the grieving ache. More than one of the guests had a sad tale of their own. Not all chose to share it, but one of our parts delivery guys mentioned to Clive that he'd been only fourteen when his father fell through the ice on the River while riding his snowmobile. Clive wanted to know who raised him after the accident. "Well, my mom, of course." I saw a little hardness float into Clive's eyes until the man added, "We lost my uncle that day, too. He was trying to save my dad." Maybe Clive was feeling like his troubles outweighed the troubles of others, but that was like asking, *Can you top this?* Or, if you'd rather be crushed by a ton of snow or a ton of granite. Exact same weight, both unpleasant experiences.

In the meantime, I'd been filling up my days with matters like setting up Clive's bank account, seeing to his healthcare, and running him to his counseling and rehab appointments. I looked forward to the car rides when I could talk with Clive alone, if he was open to it. I applied the same strategy I used with Cal and the boys—wait and listen. Three out of four of them will start to speak before I have to say anything; Christopher can out-wait me every time.

We headed back to the car after Clive's appointment to have the stitches removed from his hand. I noticed him staring at his fingers as he walked beside me.

"How does it feel?"

"I can still pinch, but the other three fingers aren't responding to my commands."

I chuckled lightly. "The nerves and tendons have suffered a major disconnect, but there's nothing wrong with the transmitter." The harsh reality of the permanent damage to his hand was becoming more glaring by the day. I gently reminded Clive that he had a very fine brain. When we reached the van which sat in the full sun on the asphalt, I unlocked the doors and immediately felt the impact of the toaster-like conditions inside. The steering wheel was too hot to touch. As soon as the engine turned over, we opened the windows and I turned up the A/C before my clothing melted into the upholstery.

"Molly?" Clive had finally begun to use my first name after I'd insisted that addressing me as Mrs. Larabie was much too formal for our family situation. I avoided the suggestion that he call me Mom, leaving it to him to decide when and if that would ever feel palatable. I secretly hoped that it would.

"Could we stop by my house in Clayton?"

The request took me by surprise. Cal and I hadn't discussed the house with Clive, yet. If it was going to be put up for sale, it would be best to do it before Fall when housing sales tended to drop. Once the colder season set in, the house would need more attention to make sure the pipes didn't freeze, the gutters were cleared, the driveway was plowed, and the walkways shoveled. We didn't think it a good idea for the property to stay vacant for long, but we didn't want to pressure Clive.

"We'll have to stop back home to pick up the key."

"No need. There's a spare under the deck." I made a mental note to make sure the key didn't remain there.

The little house on Marion Street felt stuffy when we stepped in through the back door which Cal had repaired as soon as we were given access to the property. I'd already cleaned the kitchen, removed the food from the fridge, and taken out the trash. The broken chair was gone. Clive went on through to the living room. He stared down at the distinct rectangular section of darker floorboards where once there'd been a rug—the one now stained with blood—to dull the sound of footsteps, voices, music. He walked over to the ebony upright piano located on the interior wall opposite the front windows. Tenderly raising the lid with his left hand, he ran the back of those fingertips down the lower keys. I watched as he attempted to play a scale with both hands. He stopped where the right three fingers would strike the next consecutive notes. He started again, the right hand alone. Stopping once more, he tried playing the notes by moving his forearm instead of the fingers. His aim wasn't accurate. Closing the lid, he headed upstairs. I didn't follow him, knowing he needed time alone with his ghosts.

I went back out to the kitchen to start an inventory in case we decided to hold an estate sale. I took a pen from my purse and a pad of paper from the counter underneath the wall phone which was no longer in service. Feeling like a sleuth and a snoop, I began opening cupboard doors, telling myself that it was a job that needed doing and easier for someone who wasn't attached to any of the possessions or the flashbacks they may have invoked. The dinnerware in the Tierney household consisted of plain, oatmeal-colored stoneware and included just four place settings. The glasses and coffee mugs were a motley collection of whatever had been gathered from local establishments. In striking contrast to these was an expensive set of stainless steel pans of Italian manufacture.

I lost track of time until I'd emptied out and refilled the last drawer in the kitchen. It was time to head home and start dinner. While climbing the stairs to look for Clive, I admired the gumwood moldings and handrail. The oak floors and stairway were in scratch-free condition, an appealing feature to home buyers. The top landing was a small pentagonal space separating three bedrooms and the one full bath. I peeked in the room directly ahead which I knew to be Clive's, but didn't find him there. The guest room in the front of the house was also empty. In the master bedroom, I found Clive fast asleep in Jeff Tierney's bed, curled into a fetal position, his healthy hand covering the one with the raw scar.

I whispered his name, repeated it, then gently brushed the hair back from his forehead. He stirred, rolling over onto his back and that's when I spied the dark, quarter-sized stain on his olive-green T-shirt, near the center of his chest. It was a claret-red spot, a spot I hadn't noticed earlier. I bent down and picked up the hand with the raw scar to examine it for leakage.

Clive woke. "What? Oh, Mrs. Larabie." He slowly came up to a sitting position, hugging his knees to his chest. "Sorry. I didn't mean to fall asleep."

I felt awkward standing over him, but didn't want to sit on his father's … on Jeff's bed, so I pulled up a ladder-back chair with a rush seat to sit beside him. I gestured toward the stain.

"Clive, what's on your shirt?"

He let go of his knees to pull the shirt away from his chest and take a look at it, but then dropped it quickly. "Bug bite. It must've bled when I scratched at it." His sheepish look gave him away, so I followed my intuition.

"We need to be able to trust each other, Clive. You aren't going to hear any lies from me and I'm not going to keep any information from you that you have a right to know. Can I count on the same from you?"

His eyes filled up with tears and he struggled to find his voice. "It hurts so badly, Molly. I can't stand it! I can't stop thinking about home and Dad."

I reached out to touch his shoulder. "That hurt comes from love."

"I don't want to wake up and feel anything. I can only see what's gone." He began to sob uncontrollably in loud, wet sobs. I moved to the bed and held him in my arms, letting him weep until he was spent and quiet.

"I know your life won't be the same, but you can build a new life, a good life, if you let us help. I need to know if you've hurt yourself today."

He nodded.

"Would you show me what you used?"

He opened the drawer of the nightstand beside the bed and pointed to a razor blade with a bloody edge. I hid my dismay in order to keep him talking.

"I … I used to cut myself a lot. In the hospital, I couldn't do it; too many people checking up on me." He paused to choke down another sob. "I started to cut myself today, but then I looked down at this scar. Cutting won't hurt enough now."

"Enough? You mean enough to take away the other pain? Are you feeling like you don't want to live?" I lifted his chin to look directly into his eyes.

"I don't know. I don't know if I'll ever feel happy again."

"Wouldn't you like to find out?"

On the way home, I told Clive that Cal would have to hear about this because he'd volunteered to care about him, to care all about him and that was the way it worked in our family. I promised not to bring it up to the boys unless it continued to be a problem because if he were ill or in danger, they'd need to know just as Clive would need to know if the tables were turned. "It's natural to worry about the people you love."

"I'm good at worrying, Molly."

Samantha De Haven

I avoided contact with my mother after moving in with Dad and Cecile. It was a matter of self-preservation. I'd had enough. She was toxic. I couldn't fix her. God knows I tried, but now it was up to Him if He was even there—here, anywhere—at all.

Throughout the rest of the summer, the news media in Manhattan dredged through the sludge of Mom's life. I couldn't bear to listen to the television reports, but I read every printed word I could sneak into my room. She was the daughter of a prominent financier and had married the man accused of multiple crimes, including the illegal sale of his son, smuggling contraband, and the murder of a Border Patrol agent. Even my father's name was mentioned. Reporters had uncovered her "bouts" with alcoholism. *Bouts? Who were they kidding?* Gary hadn't escaped unscathed, either. His relationship with Jeff was shaded with insinuations of indecency. The readers were left to conclude whether or not these men were lovers, whether or not Gary was involved in the unlawful purchase of a child, or if he had any knowledge pertaining to the death of Clive's father.

By the time I returned to school, most of my classmates had enough sense or compassion not to bring any of this up to me. I didn't tell anyone that Clive was a friend of mine, at least not right away. When it came to Uncle Gary, if I was asked, I didn't come out and say that he was gay. It wasn't my place, but I did tell them that my uncle was the one of the best men I knew. As for Eddie, a few nosy wiseasses wanted to know if my mother had married some kind of gangster. I gave them a glib answer. "Yeah, so you'd better be extra-special nice to me."

I loved coming home, now. My younger siblings were happy little people and I enjoyed playing with them. Cecile ran an organized household with established mealtimes, school hours, and quiet evenings. For the first time ever, I invited friends home with me. Home, order, tranquility. What a concept. Dad and I got up early on Saturday mornings and jogged to a coffee café for private time together where we came to know each other better.

When I thought about Clive, though, I felt a twinge of guilt. He was so far away and I wasn't sure when I'd be able to visit him again. Phone conversations were sometimes strained. It was difficult to talk about my new family life, one in which I grew more comfortable by the day while he was still grieving. Instead, I asked questions to keep him talking about what he was doing or thinking. One conversation was particularly disturbing.

"It's like the person I used to be evaporated into thin air and I'm floating around trying to reshape myself."

"Don't you like living with the Larabies?"

"It's not that I don't like living with them. I just don't know *how* to live with them, yet. I used to spend so much time alone and now, I'm hardly ever alone. I'm part of one big family, but it's not my family."

"Jason sounds pretty nice."

"They're all *nice.* I feel like they all want me to feel better, be happy, so they won't have to tiptoe around me. I don't want them to! It'd almost be better if we could argue about something so I could yell at someone or break something."

Then Clive began to talk about running away.

"But these people care about you. They'd be hurt and worried if you just took off."

"I need to be by myself for a while, in a place where I don't have to put up a front so people won't feel bad for me."

"People will look for you. Uncle Gary will come after you."

"I'm screwed! I want to control my own life!"

"Clive, don't do anything crazy, please. I'd be devastated if I lost you."

"Sam, I don't need anyone else watching over me as if I was on the verge of slashing my wrists. I won't have to; my fishbowl will run out of oxygen."

I wanted to talk to Clive face to face and it sounded like a change of scenery might help, so I made a suggestion. "Do you think you'd be allowed to come here for a weekend? I could show you around the Big Apple. Remember all those plans we made? It'd be fun. You could even visit a couple of campuses." I held out hope that Clive might come to New York for his college years so that we could be closer to each other. I crossed my fingers and waited for his answer.

"Maybe. I'll ask."

Trisha Cox

Though Eddie's arrest tickled me with the sweet taste of revenge, it was the kiss of death for my social life. My name, my soon-to-be ex-husband's name, my brother's name, or my father's name appeared almost daily in the news. I knew my so-called friends wouldn't risk being infected by the yellow press.

I was cut off from Samantha, too. Whenever I called, Tom provided an excuse. I accused him of deliberately denying me access, raged at him over the phone, and threatened to take him to court over it until Samantha finally called only to say she didn't want to speak to me. "Just get yourself clean, Mom. Maybe then we'll have something to say to one another."

"This isn't like you, Samantha. You've never treated me like this. I know your father and Cecile have turned you against me." Without another word, she hung up on me. In early September, I left New York to enter a rehab center in Arizona. I told no one except my brother.

Gary Stanton

I hung up the phone in disbelief. My sister only called me when she wanted something, like a meal or a place to park my niece, or a rescue. I hadn't spoken to her since that heated argument just before Samantha moved back to New York. I couldn't give a care what her complaints were; she'd married a murderer.

Her speech was slurred and slow. She rambled on about how everyone had deserted her since Eddie's arrest and that even Sam wouldn't speak to her. "I'm her mother! I've given her everything she has. Private schools, nice clothes, spending money." I could hardly stomach one more it's-all-about-me whining out of her mouth. She hadn't given Sam what she needed most—mothering.

"She told me I'd ruined your life, too. Is that true, Gary? How could I've known that Eddie had peddled his own brat?"

Her choice of words disgusted me. Had she totally forgotten that *the brat* was the boy I loved? "I need to hang up, Trish. Call your doctor or call an ambulance. I don't think your self-medication is good for your health."

Just as I was about to hang up, she blurted out, "I'm leaving." I remained silent, trying to discern whether she meant leaving as in going away or leaving as in checking out of life. I didn't think she had the guts for the latter and I wasn't sure I cared if she did.

"I'm checking myself into a rehab program. I haven't told Mother or Father. Don't let them hunt me down, Gary. If they ask, tell them ... well, tell them whatever you want."

"Have you told Sam?"

"Did you hear me? She won't talk to me unless I make it through this."

Trish told me she'd be in touch later with her contact information, saying she was waiting for a callback from a couple of places. I was certain this was one of her melodramatic diva moments to get some attention and I wasn't going to waste time getting wrapped up in it. I had enough on my mind.

The police had completed their unsuccessful search of the cottage for clues to Jeff's demise, so I made arrangements with a caretaker to close it up. My time was now divided between work, discussions with my attorney or Ms. Crow, and visits with Clive which were to be supervised until further notice. The initial visits at the Larabie home were brief and forced.

Clive wasn't happy. How could he be? He refused to discuss his counseling sessions with me and became more sullen as the trials for Veronica, Eddie, and Craig Barrett drew near. We'd been advised not to talk about the court cases since we'd each been called to testify.

"My life is over, Gary!" He hissed this with a vehemence I'd never seen in him.

"No doubt about it. Our old life is over." Yet, a specter of a life shadowed me daily. There'd been a few times when I'd picked up the phone to call Jeff and started to dial before I remembered. "There's no choice but to move on and start another life. That's what I did when I left the States."

"Yeah, but then you met Dad … I mean, Jeff, and he sold you a pack of lies."

"I've been trying to sort that out, too. Sometimes I'm angry with him, but in the end, I know he was trying to protect us from the truth."

"And look how that turned out!" He spit my words back at me. "'Protecting us from the truth!' How about protecting us from *lies?*"

Before I could answer, Clive jumped up and shouted. "I don't want to talk about him anymore! Got that? I don't even want to think about him anymore! And I want people to butt out of my life. Just leave me alone!" He stormed upstairs, leaving me feeling shut out and helpless.

I stood up from the worn sofa and began to pace around the compact living room while trying to work out a way to bridge the widening gap between us. The walls of the room were adorned with sports trophies and photos of Larabies. It was a room full of family memories where Clive and I didn't exist.

Molly's quiet voice interrupted my ruminations. "He's angry, but not at you. He wants to go to New York to visit your niece, but his counselor doesn't think he should go on his own. She doesn't think it's safe."

I knew at once what she meant. "You mean because Samantha is connected to me. They think I'll try to kidnap him."

Molly sat down on a small floral-print chaise, the single feminine piece of furniture in a room full of masculine pride. "That, as well as his mental outlook. She wants to be certain he won't be a flight risk or injure himself."

I didn't attempt to hide my aggravation. "And I can't do anything to help him."

"There may be another way." Molly proceeded to explain that her son, Jason, was beginning to fill out college applications, hoping to complete a degree in music. "We don't have the funds for school in New York unless he's awarded a scholarship, so Jason will have to audition." I began to see where she was headed. "I've tried to encourage Clive to begin the process, too, especially since you've offered to cover his tuition."

"So, you would need to take both boys on a college tour, am I right?"

"That's my plan."

I suddenly realized that this quiet woman was an ally, and a wise one at that.

Jason Larabie

Talking to Clive wasn't fun anymore. It was like trying to talk to someone underwater. I felt like I was doing most of the work, making the motions, trying to encourage him to reconnect to the human race, but he wasn't hearing me. He was floating around in his misery. He spent more time in his room—our room—pretending to read, sleeping, or listening to music. I didn't even want to step over the threshold; it was like stepping into Clive's burial chamber. My pity for him was fading, while my impatience was growing. I couldn't decide whether I missed my friend or if I no longer wanted him for a friend. It was hard to watch him give up on everything he'd cared about.

My brother Chad was more outspoken. He'd been the first to

turn in his tact-o-meter.

"Has the gerbil come out of his cage today?"

"When does the house guest get some kitchen duty?"

"How are things with the living dead?" That one earned him some extra boat-scrubbing time from Dad, but Clive never reacted. I think that's what my brothers and I were waiting for, a reaction. Chad was right. Clive was walking around, but he wasn't living.

But Dad had a strategy. He'd watched some of his army buddies chew themselves up after returning home. Guess he knew a thing or two about what it takes to shore up a broken spirit and get it moving again. "Well, look who's risen and it ain't even Easter," were the first words out of Chad's mouth.

Chris, the quiet one, is more frugal with his words. "It's about time."

We'd just arrived home from school to find Clive sitting on the ride-on mower in the backyard.

"How did that happen?" I asked my mother when I came through the door.

"Your father thought it was time and Clive didn't object. We've also told him that he needs to start thinking about taking his driver's test."

I'd already passed the test and was occasionally given permission to use Dad's pickup or mom's mini-van. I heard an opportunity knocking. "I'll take him out to practice."

My first and last lesson was given on a Sunday afternoon when I knew that traffic would be sparse along Route 12. After we'd buckled ourselves into Mom's van, I reminded Clive to adjust his mirrors and pointed out the controls for the headlights, the wipers, and the directionals. I hammed it up a bit by imitating my father in hopes that I'd be able to resuscitate Clive's sense of humor.

"Now, son, the first rule of the road is don't run into anything or anyone and don't let anything or anyone slam into this vehicle. You do and the only thing you'll be driving is a two-wheeler."

That one had frightened me as much as Dad's commandment

about doing three-sixties on an icy road. "You do that, son, and you'll be shoveling the driveway with a spatula for the rest of the winter." I hated shoveling snow, a job that could last six months out of the year up here.

Clive clumsily backed out of the driveway, just missing the mailbox and barely coming to a stop before shifting into drive. "Braking means stopping, son. And just like a woman, if I say, stop, I mean stop." That got a smile out of him.

"Take a right at the next stop, and I do mean stop."

Clive steered cautiously close to the right shoulder while proceeding to the stop at a snail's pace. When he braked, I suggested that it would be helpful to place the weight of all five of his toes on the gas pedal in order for the needle to rise above ten on the speedometer.

His eyebrows furrowed, he looked left, then right, then left again before patching out, swerving into the right lane and flooring it down Route 12 while screaming at the top of his lungs. I grabbed onto the door handle and propped my feet up against the glove compartment.

"What do you think you're doing?"

"Driving! Watch this." Clive spun the wheel and did an abrupt U-turn in front of a car approaching in the distance. Stomping on the gas, he tore off again and took a right turn at the intersection without braking.

"Okay, Clive. Not funny. Slow down! You're driving a mini-van not a race car."

"What, no k-turn practice?" He swerved into the shoulder and braked, then adeptly demonstrated the signaling, mirror-checking, and the turn while smoothly shifting with a two-fingered grip and little hesitation. We sped off back toward Clayton, only slowing as he pulled into the village; then it dawned on me where Clive was taking us.

"Give me the keys," I demanded when he'd finally turned off the engine.

"What's the matter? Don't trust the handicapped to get you home safely?" he mocked as he slammed the car door and stomped off toward the back of the house, his house.

"What's wrong with you? I'm just trying to help."

"I don't want your help!" He was yelling now. "You can't help!" He pulled a key out of his pocket and unlocked the back door.

Angry now, I followed him inside.

"Look, my parents are doing everything for you. Maybe it's time you think about someone beside yourself!" I regretted the words immediately, suddenly aware that we were standing in the room which held reminders of all that he'd lost. Clive stood staring at his piano, clenching his jaw and blinking back tears.

"I can't," he whispered.

I looked around the room while sorting out what to say or do next until I spotted the answer. I walked over to a corner cabinet and began reading the labels. Without saying anything, I grabbed two glasses and mixed up a couple of concoctions. I had no idea what I was doing, but figured one drink couldn't hurt.

Before we knew it, the afternoon had slipped away into a fog created by a variety of alcoholic libations. We'd grown much louder, too. Clive was now pounding the ivories, performing a one-fingered accompaniment to Beethoven's *"Moonlight Sonata"* which blared from the stereo system. Meanwhile, I was using two large pots as a poor substitute for timpani, though Beethoven hadn't written a part for the pasta pan drums, when our facetious concert was unexpectedly interrupted by a voice calling from the back deck.

"It's Robbie!"

His bulky frame filled the doorway. "I heard the music." A look of disappointment crossed his brow as he glanced at Clive's hands and then at the stereo.

"Hey, Little John!" The alcohol had tickled Clive's funny bone at last. "Care to join us for afternoon ale in the forest?"

His eyes floated over the nearly empty bottles. "No, thanks. Just saw the car in the drive and wanted to see how you're doing."

"The car!" I yelled. "What time is it?"

"Almost five," answered Robbie.

"We've got to go! Dad will have my hide, I mean, my keys. Where are my keys?" I tried to stand, but nearly fell over the arm of the sofa and plopped back down into the cushions.

Clive laughed and laughed.

"You two aren't driving anywhere," said Robbie.

"I can drive home blindfolded," I answered.

Robbie stooped down to pick something up off the rug as he approached me. "Yeah, you're definitely blind, but you're not driving." Robbie stood over me, now, waving my keys in front of me.

"Watch out, Sir Wasted. You may be thwarted by the Large One."

"Look, you two can call someone and tell them you'll be home when you sober up or I can drive you home."

"When did you grow up? We can't tell my parents we're skunk drunk."

"Oh, I don't think we'll have to tell them," Clive giggled.

In the end, Robbie drove us home and my father met us at the door.

"Driving lessons are over. He's an ace," I quipped as I staggered up to him, tossed him the keys, and fell over the threshold. I knew I was in deep shit.

Molly Larabie

Oct. 1, 1989

Sunny with mild temps; the geese still linger on the grassy riverbanks and the deciduous trees are aglow in sepias and scarlet. Autumn is Nature's proud peacock moment, rebelling in loud color before reluctantly submitting to sleep for the long months of winter. "Remember Me, Remember Me," cry the trees.

I'd been keeping a journal since the day before I married Cal. Like hand-stitching a quilt, I meticulously penned the details of our family landscape as we evolved alongside the ever-changing River, at times in harmony, at times in discord. By his third month with us, Clive's emotions swelled in steep, unpredictable waves, cresting in kinetic anger and pitching him back down into a trough of lethargic grief. Our boys were tossed about with him, either riled by his tone of resentment or brought down by his gloom. I saw the looks on their faces when Clive sulked, or turned down their invitations to join in some fun, or when he left the room while they laughed over something that had happened at school. They gradually stopped bringing their friends to the house, instead spending more time away from home. I worried that our family wouldn't be enough ballast to keep Clive from sinking into irreversible despair.

Cal, on the other hand, was the voice of calm. He didn't view the boys showing up drunk as a matter of concern.

"They're doing what any teenager would do, something typical, Molly. Not exactly the word anyone we know would use to describe those two."

"Maybe so, but we have two younger teens watching everything they do and what happens afterward."

"Well, if that's the case, Chris and Chad also saw them puking out their insides for the rest of the night."

"That's not what I mean."

To show support for my point of view, Cal grounded Jason and Clive. They spent the next weekend scrubbing boats in preparation for winter storage. Clive, unable to hole up alone in his room, forgot his angst for those hours, and managed to put both hands to good use.

Whenever Jason and the twins were in school, Clive retreated to his room or pedaled off on his bike after his tutoring sessions. Cal and I agreed that the exercise was better than sleeping away the hours, but there was always the nagging doubt as to whether or not he'd return, especially as the length of his disappearances grew. I stopped him one afternoon on his way out the back door.

"I'd appreciate it if you'd tell me where you're going and when you'll be back."

He stared back at me, but didn't answer.

"That's what we do in a family. It eliminates worry."

"Or trust," he said flatly. "What's the curfew?"

There wasn't any belligerence in his tone, but I took it as a challenge nonetheless. Clive had been careful not to directly offend me, but he was beginning to try my patience. The days were growing shorter so we managed to agree on a half-hour before sunset or a maximum time of two and a half hours without contact unless he was at a social gathering. The likelihood of that was slim since Clive didn't attend school or participate in any extracurricular activities. This was something I intended to address once the legal matters were off his plate.

The prosecutor in the case against Craig Barrett had already spoken with Clive regarding courtroom procedures. On the morning of the trial, he and I dressed in what my mother used to call our Sunday best; he in a suit he'd previously worn for recitals and I in a blazer and long skirt. Clive rejected any offers for breakfast, his sensitivity barely held in check.

We arrived outside the courtroom twenty minutes prior to the appointed time. I took a seat on a bench and indulged in people-watching. This was my first visit to the Jefferson County Courthouse. Clive paced up and down the hallway, stopping more than once at the drinking fountain. As I glanced up at the clock on the wall above the elevator, the doors opened and Robbie Barrett stepped out with his mother close on his heels. He noticed Clive wiping his face with the cool water and waited for him to turn around. Robbie held out his hand and Clive stepped forward to shake it with his awkward grip while mumbling something that sounded like, "Sorry."

Robbie, dressed in pressed slacks, a shirt and tie, stood up tall, looking resolute and older than his years. "No need. I owed your dad. Tell them everything."

Just as Sylvia began to say something to Clive, the bailiff appeared in the doorway and called Robbie's name. Mother and son scurried into the courtroom.

When Clive was called to the stand by the prosecutor, he approached slowly, looking neither left nor right. After taking the oath, the questions began with that same hand, the extent of the injury and how it came about. Clive's voice cracked and he chewed on his lower lip, the terror of that night gurgling at the back of his throat. He explained how he'd been awakened by the sound of breaking glass and someone stumbling about downstairs. Thinking it had been Jeff, he'd gone down to check on him, but had been unexpectedly knocked to the floor as soon as he'd reached the last step. When Clive was asked if the intruder was in the courtroom and if so, to point him out, he complied by raising his scarred hand. I watched the eyes of the jurors move from Clive's fingers to the face of Craig Barrett who sat staring down at the table in front of him. The prosecutor's final questions underscored the forfeit of Clive's dream to become a concert pianist.

"And this dream is no longer a possibility due to the injury inflicted upon you by Mr. Barrett, is that correct?"

The attorney for the defense objected, the question was rephrased with similar meaning but less dramatic impact. Clive whispered, "Yes, it's gone," then was asked to repeat his answer so that the court reporter could hear him.

Mercifully, the defense attorney's examination was brief, but he attempted to cast doubt by suggesting that Clive had attacked first, forcing Craig to defend himself. That left an obvious question, more like a gaping hole in a sinking skiff. What was Craig Barrett doing in his neighbor's house?

We left the courtroom immediately after Clive's testimony. A cold front had descended on the area and a raw wind cut through us, bringing tears to our eyes. I reached for Clive's hand and held onto it as we made our way through the parking lot. I knew that closure wouldn't come today. There'd been no burial service for Jeff; his ashes remained with Gary Stanton. And Clive had yet to testify in the trial of Eddie Cox, his birth father.

Robbie Barrett

I was set free the night I broke that chair over my old man's head. He was a no-good son-of-a-bitch who didn't love one living thing on earth. Having him locked up was like being cured of cancer; the deadly tumor had been cut out of our lives. Mom took an office job over in Watertown and signed up for a computer class at the community college. My sisters hung out with their friends at our house—yeah, our house instead of theirs—and I kept working for Jacobsen and banking my paychecks.

The night before my father's trial, my older sister, Shelley, came into my room. She wanted to know what I was going to tell the court. I told her I was planning on telling the truth. She chewed her lip, looking nervous.

"Are they going to ask you about the bomb scare?"

"Why would they ask me about that? I had nothing to do with it."

She got all weepy-eyed then and told me something I wish I'd never heard.

"Dad was always drinking, you know. I was afraid of him when he was drunk, Robbie. So were Mom and Denise."

"We were all afraid of him."

"He came into my room one night, smelling like liquor. He woke me up with his bad breath and then ..." Her voice broke and so did my heart. I knew right then what awful truth was coming next.

"He said if I didn't let him, he'd go after Denise." She started to sob. "It made me sick! I was afraid he'd make me pregnant."

"Shelley, you should've told me. I would've made him stop."

"It was just that once. I told him I wouldn't tell anyone if he left me alone."

"Did he?"

"I had to do other things for him. It was me, Robbie. I called in the bomb scare and some other false alarms. Dad didn't tell me why, but I knew he was doing something illegal. He wanted the police out of the way. Will I go to jail?"

I hugged my sister, forcing down the vomit rising in my throat. "The only one going to jail is Dad. They'll lock him up, Shell. We're going to be safe."

Cal Larabie

After my tour in 'Nam, I needed to scrub out every stain of inhuman atrocity I'd witnessed. I only knew two ways of accomplishing that. One, I'd marry Molly and love her until the day I died. Two, I'd return to the River. I knew what Clive was going through. He'd been dropped into the middle of a minefield that had annihilated his perceptions of reality and blown holes in every one of his beliefs. He'd most likely been asking himself, or God, why he'd survived. The next question would be whether or not he wanted to keep surviving. He needed a reason to try.

The trial of Eddie Cox laid smack dab in the middle of that emotional minefield. One father was accused of killing another and their son was a prime witness for the prosecution. We left Clayton a little before sunrise on Halloween to make the drive to Toronto. Clive hadn't eaten anything before we left and he'd refused my offer to stop for something on the way. He slept, or pretended to sleep, for the first couple of hours. During the last leg of the trip, I asked him how he felt about seeing Eddie in person again. His face took on a pained expression. "I know he's the one, the man who killed my … he killed Jeff. I want him put away for life and I want him to know that's what I want." I recognized the thirst for revenge in his voice, but knew that retribution wasn't a cure for grief.

The prosecutor asked Clive a series of questions about the specific locations and dates of his encounters with Eddie Cox, especially at Tar Island a week prior to Jeff's demise. I watched Eddie while Clive answered. His eyes were dead. He stared straight ahead at the paneled wall behind the court recorder. Clive's yes or no response was barely audible. *Yes, Eddie had visited the island that day. No, Jeff hadn't been there, at the time. Yes, Eddie had specifically asked that his visit be mentioned to Gary Stanton who was there the same weekend, but not there when Eddie stopped by.*

"And what were the reactions of Jeff Tierney and Gary Stanton when you mentioned the visit?"

"Dad ..." Clive stumbled, "I mean, Jeff wasn't happy and Gary was even more upset. They didn't want me speaking to Eddie." Clive didn't look over at the table where his indicted father sat.

"Did they say why they did not want you interacting with Eddie Cox?"

"No, but I got the feeling ..."

"Objection!"

Clive wasn't permitted to conjecture as to the reason. The defense attorney turned attention to the firearms owned by Jeff Tierney and where they were stored. Clive admitted that his father owned a service revolver and one other, plus one hunting rifle.

"No revolver was recovered, not from his boat, not from the River, and not from your home on Marion Street. The rifle was found, unloaded, in the back of your father's closet. Do you know of any other place where he may have kept a firearm?"

Clive looked confused, then asked to have the question repeated before answering. "At work, I guess. Maybe in the cottage?" He seemed to be making a suggestion, rather than stating a known fact.

"None was found in the cottage."

"Did your father take a revolver with him on the night he disappeared?"

Clive looked frightened as he answered. "No, I mean, I don't know."

"Which is it?"

"I don't know."

"Where did your father tell you he was going that night, the night of July ninth?"

"He said he was going into work for a while and then out for a beer with a couple of the guys."

"Who were these guys?"

"He didn't say. I think he meant guys from work."

"Where were they going for a beer?"

"I don't know." Clive appeared more nervous, now. "I didn't ask him."

"Did your father take a blue cooler with him?"

"I don't think so. I didn't watch him leave because I was practicing, practicing at the piano."

"Did some of your classmates come to your home with a cooler of contraband they'd found in the River?"

"I wasn't at home, then. I was at a piano lesson. They told me about it later, after … after ..." Clive looked down at his injured hand. "After I was attacked by Mr. Barrett."

The attorney showed Clive a photo of the cooler and asked if he'd seen it in the house and Clive said he hadn't. The subsequent questions were posed in a sharp, accusatory tone of voice.

"Did you know your father was smuggling drugs across the border?"

Clive recoiled as if he'd been slapped across the face. *"What?* What are you saying?" His voice was louder now.

The question was repeated.

"No! That's not true!" Clive was visibly upset; his voice cracked.

"Didn't you indeed see your father take a revolver and a cooler full of cocaine out of the house and place it in his truck?"

"Objection!"

When Clive was finally dismissed from the stand, Eddie's cool eyes didn't flicker from their frozen forward gaze. Clive, in tears, rushed to the exit. I followed him into the hallway.

Immediately, someone called out to him. "Clive?"

"Sam!" A pretty teenage girl rushed forward to hug him. Clive squeezed his eyes shut, trying to hold back tears.

Gary Stanton stood behind her and reached out to shake my hand. "Sorry to see you under these circumstances, Cal."

"Same here, but it can't be helped."

Stanton looked sympathetically at Clive. I knew that their last visit hadn't ended harmoniously, but when Clive turned in his direction I saw a brief look of gratitude. "Gary," he said softly. Stanton stretched his arm across the back of the boy's shoulders to give him a sideways hug. Clive didn't resist. We were interrupted by the bailiff who announced that Samantha had been called to the stand.

"We'll wait for you here," I told them as they entered the courtroom.

Afterwards, the four of us went to a nearby pub, but avoided talking about the trial. Stanton talked about his restaurant business and asked me how I came to own a marina.

"Well, I leveraged every connection I could. Borrowed from family; used my vet benefits to earn a business degree and get a loan. Molly and I bought the marina when it was in sorry shape, but made improvements little by little. Seems to keep enough food on the table."

"There is something about the River that just gets into my veins and slows down the blood flow, or the blood pressure, I'm not sure which. I always feel at home when I'm there," he admitted.

"Can't disagree with you. That's what brings back my repeat customers."

Meanwhile, the teenagers had been sitting in a separate booth and speaking quietly with each other. I looked over at Clive. Color had returned to his face, but I don't think it was solely due to the oxygen flowing in and out of his heart.

He fell asleep on the drive home and we arrived just as the front doorbell rang with the first trick-or-treater.

Sheriff Cy Froehlich

As I've said, Halloween is on my list of holidays which should be obliterated from the calendar. Wrapping little kids up in outfits that they trip over and masks that make it impossible for them to see where they're going seems more like abuse than fun. I remember driving through town and hitting the brakes in front of a walking cardboard box. When I asked the little fellow what he was doing, he said, "I'm a TV." I walked him back to his parents who were chatting it up with other parents and politely suggested they monitor their TV or pull the plug on the costume.

And stupid reaches a whole new level when it comes to the adults—dressed up like zombies, witches, ghouls, or more appropriately, clowns—who spend the evening drinking before they get back behind the wheel of a car. The occasion brings out the grumblers, too. We're inundated with calls from crabby pain-in-the-rump, fuddy-dud homeowners who call to complain about masked children cutting across their lawns, stepping on their chrysanthemums, or climbing onto their front porches. "My front lights aren't on. That means no candy here. So why do these darn kids keep ringing my doorbell?" Others call because they left their cars parked in the drive in front of their empty garages and someone soaped up the vehicle's windows. Go figure. Then there are the calls about the stolen pumpkins—as if those darn pumpkins were pets! Trying to teach these people not to use the emergency number for petty grievances is like bowling uphill.

Meanwhile, more serious matters required immediate attention—the disappearance of a child, a hit-and-run accident, a drowning. This one night could result in more destructive vandalism than any other time of the year. I never saw any saints turn up at the station the next day, either. Just irate residents or penitent drunks or grieving parents.

One of the few people I didn't expect to call the station on Halloween night was Cal Larabie.

"Clive's missing."

I'd just finished clearing off my desk, ready to head home. I sat back down. "You've checked with your boys?" Knowing that Cal was astute, I was certain that this had been his first line of attack.

"He testified today, Cy, in Toronto. He was exhausted afterwards and went right up to bed when we got home. The other boys were out most of the evening."

Apparently, with all the comings and goings at the front door, no one had checked on Clive till Cal's oldest boy was ready to retire, sometime after 11:00, only to discover that Clive wasn't there or anywhere else in the house. No one had seen him go out.

"I checked the Marion Street house. No sign of him there."

Cal put Jason on the phone to provide me with a list of Clive's friends and enemies. He explained that Clive had had some previous run-ins with Robbie Barrett, but that had changed since the night of the attack. It sounded as if Clive had few friends other than Jason and Hettie Voss.

Given the trauma this boy had been through, I alerted my officers to be on the lookout for him along the roads, near the waterfronts, and in the usual locations for teen mischief. Next, I placed a call to Jack Voss who woke his daughter so I could ask her some questions. Hettie was more willing to share information this time than our last go-around.

"Clive's missing? Oh, no. The trial was today."

She confirmed that she hadn't seen him all night. In fact, she hadn't seen him in several days and explained that he'd been depressed. I asked her if she knew of any place he might go, other than the Marion Street house.

"He doesn't go many places and I don't know where he would go at night unless ..." Hettie began to cry. "Sheriff, he might want to hurt himself."

This thought had already occurred to me, but I didn't want to alarm the girl by pressing her any further.

"Let's not get ahead of ourselves. He may simply want to get away."

"Tar Island!" she blurted. "That's where he'd go."

I hung up with Hettie and refilled the coffee-maker. There'd be no sleep tonight.

Gary Stanton

Growing up in my father's house was prep school for facing men who considered themselves tough and powerful. Attorneys didn't make me nervous, but I wanted justice for Jeff. Sam, on the other hand, was wearing the stress of the day from head to toe. She'd managed to get through her testimony at Eddie's trial without shedding a tear until she left the courtroom.

Then it was my turn in the box. Eddie's attorney probed my relationship with Jeff and attempted to imply that I'd known about the illegal purchase of Clive from the beginning. The prosecutor took a different tactic and focused on Eddie's attempt to blackmail Jeff into aiding his smuggling ring in return for staying out of Clive's life.

"Did Jeff Tierney agree to this deal?"

"If he had, wouldn't he still be alive?"

"Please, Mr. Stanton. Just answer the question."

"Not that I know of."

"Did Mr. Tierney tell you what he planned to do in order to resolve the situation with Mr. Cox?"

I'd spent many sleepless nights pondering how I'd answer this question. "He planned to arrest him." Jeff had told me this, but at the same time, he'd left a dark thought hanging in the air. *Maybe Eddie will choose to resist.* I'd begged Jeff to let other agents handle the arrest, but he'd insisted on seeing it through himself.

My answer led the defense to attack on the re-direct. "Didn't Mr. Tierney indeed tell you that he planned to kill Eddie Cox in order to permanently shut up the birth father of Clive Tierney?"

"No." I doubted that I'd ever know the truth about what happened out there on the River that night.

As I left the stand, I heard my sister's name. The prosecutor began to explain to the judge that he was unable to depose the witness who'd been judged mentally incompetent. A fair call, I'd say.

Afterwards, Sam and I met up with Clive and Cal Larabie. The teens hadn't seen each other since July and were soon absorbed in their own conversation.

"He looks thin and tired," I observed.

"It's been rough. He's been dished an overdose of heartbreak. Not easy for a kid to accept."

"Not easy no matter what age. I appreciate what you and your wife are doing for him, though."

After a burger meal at a nearby pub, we said our goodbyes to Clive and Cal and headed back to my place. Sam had an early return flight booked for the next morning, but a phone call from Cal in the middle of the night delayed her departure. Clive was missing and Cal thought he might be on his way to Tar Island.

"Look, Gary, it would be faster for me to get there by boat than for you to drive down to Rockport."

"How's he getting across the border?"

"One of my tin cans is missing."

"He knows the River, Cal."

"I've notified the Sheriff, but I'm not sure how much of a headstart he's got on us."

I made sure Cal knew where to find the cottage and told him I was going to head over to Rockport anyway. There was no way I was going back to sleep. After hanging up with him, I dialed the number for the cottage phone. No answer. I dialed again and then one more time before waking Samantha.

Cal Larabie

Molly handed me a bag of sandwiches as I left the house. I think the food was less about our stomachs and more about giving her something to do while she worried. Jason was waiting in the boat when I stepped onto the dock.

"No, absolutely not."

"Come on, Dad. Clive's my closest friend. He'll listen to me."

"We don't even know if he's over there." More than that, given Clive's volatile state, I didn't know what kind of condition he'd be in if and when I found him. If he'd harmed himself, or worse, I didn't want Jason around to see it.

"Dad, I'm not a little kid. I can't sit home and do nothing."

As I stood on the dock looking down at the determination in my son's face, it struck me that I hadn't been much older than Jason when I was called up to fight a war, a war of disillusionment. "Okay, but you need to stay calm and do what I tell you to do without question and you're going to be the one to march back to the house and tell your mother where you're going." I zipped up my down jacket, pulled on the hood, and started up the bilge pump. It wouldn't be long before our own boat would be pulled out of the River for the winter months.

The ride across the water was cold and dark, but smooth. There was a fingernail of a moon in the sky and clouds were beginning to move in, but no wind to stir up the whitecaps. I directed the *Spit* down the channel past Alex Bay, turning north near the Summerland Group. Most of the cottages were deserted now, closed up until next Spring. We passed no other vessels. I didn't like boating at night. The shoals of the St. Lawrence were treacherous even for experienced boaters. In less than a half-hour we curved around the western end of Grenadier Island, slowing to follow the shoreline, in hopes that Clive wouldn't hear our approach. That is, if he was there at all. When Jason pointed out the cottage, I steered across the channel and throttled back before turning into the cove at the bottom of the hill. The tin can was secured to the dock.

After we tied up the *Spit,* I grabbed the flashlight from the glovebox, taking care to keep it pointed at the ground till we reached the bottom of the steps. I switched it off, then handed it to

Jason. "Don't click on the flashlight unless it's absolutely necessary. You circle around the other side of the deck and I'll head up to the back door."

Light spilled out onto the front deck from the open sliding doors. Traces of wood smoke floated in the air while classical music poured full volume from a stereo system. When I reached the top of the hill, I saw that Clive was seated in a chair in front of a glowing woodstove, his back to the doors. The music helped to cover the sound of my footsteps on the deck as I made my way up the stairs to the back door and found it unlocked. Slowly, I turned the knob praying the door wouldn't creak as it opened. I lifted it slightly, moving inch by inch, until I could squeeze through the gap. I crept down the hallway, through the kitchen towards the front of the cottage. I backed up against the wall to take a cautious peek around the corner. Movement out on the deck caught my eye and I spotted Jason as he crouched down to the right of the sliding door. Clive was rocking up and down in a pedestal chair, one foot resting on the knee of his opposite leg. It was then that I saw it, the gun.

I quickly drew back against the wall to avoid his notice. I could only think of one reason that Clive would bring a loaded gun to this empty cottage. I knew I had to act before anyone got hurt. If I rushed at Clive, would he shoot? Jason wouldn't be able to see the gun from his position out on the deck, not unless ... I took another peek.

Clive suddenly got up from the chair, opened the screen door and stepped out onto the deck. Jason was out of sight now. Bending down to lean his elbows on the top of the railing, Clive gripped the gun in both hands. With his left index finger on the trigger and using his injured hand to steady the weapon, he aimed the barrel toward the water. BLAM! He fired and then stepped back. Fearing he would turn the gun on himself, I dashed forward. Just one, two, three long strides and I dove through the open door, catching him in a bear hug from behind and pinning his arms to his body.

"Drop it, son. Drop it!"

Clive struggled against me, spinning us around until I was backed into the corner of the railing. Suddenly, we fell forward onto the deck, sending the gun skittering over the edge.

That's when I heard Jason scream.

Samantha De Haven

My uncle and I didn't reach the cottage until almost four in the morning. We'd hardly spoken during the long drive, both of us worried and deep in dark thoughts. The air was crisp when I climbed out from under the boat canopy to tie the lines. As we climbed the hill with Spike at our heels, we could hear voices coming from inside the cottage. When Uncle Gary opened the back door, we were hit in the face with an acrid odor which brought tears to our eyes and forced us to cover our noses. Spike began to whimper and backed away, choosing to follow the deck around to the front of the cottage. We found Clive, Jason, and his father seated at the dining room table, eating sandwiches. It appeared as if nothing out of the ordinary had happened, as if they'd been out on a fishing escapade, except for that offensive fog hanging in the air.

"Whew! Who got hit?" asked my uncle.

Jason, whose wet hair clung to his head, raised his hand and smiled. I noticed that he was wearing clothes much too large for him.

"Must've been one mother of a skunk!"

"I didn't hang around to take a look."

"Nope. He headed right for the River and dove in." Cal patted his son on the back. "We tossed him some soap before he went back for a second dip, but it's like spraying cologne on a garbage truck."

"Guess I was premature in having the caretaker put the plumbing to bed for the winter."

Clive looked sheepish when his eyes met mine. Uncle Gary took the empty seat next to him, but I stood still.

"So, what did you do, order out for some sandwiches in the midst of all the excitement?"

"Help yourself," said Cal as he pushed forward a plate with one and a-half remaining sandwiches. "It's Molly's homemade ham salad."

"Sounds like something I may have to put on my restaurant menu."

The banter irritated me. It was simply an evasion of the obvious—what were we all doing here in the middle of the night? Having lunch? I was out of patience and upset. Most of my life had been spent living with a person who created a lot of drama and avoided accountability. I thought I'd put an end to playing that game, so I wasn't about to munch on a sandwich like nothing had happened! While the joking continued, I slipped out the back door.

Spike joined me as I strode down to the dock to climb back aboard the *Escape*. I crouched beneath the canopy and curled up in the front seat, covering myself with the woolen blanket my uncle had brought along for the cold River crossing. Spike snuggled into the seat behind me. I waited. Clive would come find me. I was sure of it.

About fifteen minutes passed before I heard footsteps, but then, I smelled him. It was Jason who came looking for me.

"Hello? Anyone home?" A beam of light broke through the window flap of the canvas. Spike's nose went up in the air and he began to whimper again. I unzipped the canopy and climbed up on the dock to avoid polluting the small interior space of the *Escape* with eau de skunk.

"I brought you a couple of cookies," he offered. He seemed to be reading my face as he handed them to me. "He's okay, you know. No injuries."

"Thanks. I mean, thanks for letting me know."

"I think seeing Eddie and testifying just put him over the edge."

"I didn't enjoy it, either."

"You had to testify, too?"

I nodded. "So, what happened?"

Jason recounted the events, beginning with the discovery that Clive was missing.

"A gun? Where did he get a gun?"

"When the police searched his house, they didn't find the two revolvers owned by Clive's dad and figured he'd taken them with him the night he died. It turns out that one of the revolvers was hidden in a steel box bolted to the underside of the back deck. Clive dug it out on one of his visits to the house."

"What did he intend to do with it?"

"We didn't get that far. He fired one shot out over the hill before my dad tackled him. I was hiding under the deck, so I popped up and reached through the railing to grab Clive's ankle. When they fell over, they startled the skunk that nailed me.

I didn't laugh. "Do you think he's giving up?"

"Hard to say. Your uncle is having a chat with him, now."

Our conversation was interrupted by Spike's bark to announce the arrival of Mr. Larabie, but my canine guardian didn't emerge from the warmth of the boat enclosure. Even Spike had had enough for one night.

As he stowed a large, black trash bag aboard the *Spit*, Jason's father informed him that the clothing he wore on the way over would never see the light of day again. I was thankful for the slight breeze which had kicked up as the sky began to lighten. "We're going to head home as soon as Clive is done talking with your uncle. I'm sure he'd appreciate a couple of minutes with you."

I could see he was recommending that I not let an opportune moment pass, but I wasn't sure that I could offer Clive the comfort he needed.

"I don't know if he'll like what I have to say."

Mr. Larabie looked directly into my eyes. "But it may be something he needs to hear."

With that blessing, I returned to the cottage. The fire had died out, been smothered, and dampened. Uncle Gary discreetly withdrew and busied himself securing all windows and doors before our departure.

Always perceptive, Clive read my thoughts. "Sorry, Sam."

"For what?" I wasn't going to let him off easy.

"I know I've let you down."

I was trying to choose my words carefully. "I'm not sure how to help you. I … I know it must be hard to get up every morning with the same tragic reality hitting you in the face, stuff that can't be erased."

"One day changed my entire life, washed it away."

"But it hasn't been washed away! You were rescued, more than once." I stopped myself as my voice rose, lowering the volume. "You've got to give us all a chance. Uncle Gary, the Larabies … we all care about you, but ..."

"But what, Sam?"

"Well, I know how I feel and they probably feel the same."

"What are you trying to say?"

"Just that, well … we need to know that you care about *us*." I held my breath, praying I hadn't over-reached. I was no psychologist, though I'd had a lot of home-schooling in the field. Clive stood up and embraced me then, kissing me with a needy passion. I surrendered and began to cry.

"Sam, I didn't mean to ..."

We were both crying, now.

"Just try. Try to move on and make some sense out of losing Jeff. He took a risk to be a father to you. I don't think he'd want you to throw your life away."

Hettie Voss

My nerves were on edge as the court dates approached and to say that I had mixed feelings about testifying as a witness for the prosecution in two separate trials in two separate countries would be an understatement. A guilty verdict would mean prison time for the father of a classmate; an acquittal would leave unanswered questions. How could we feel safe with either culprit walking around free? I wasn't thrilled about seeing my name in the news either. The seventeen year-old who went looking for adventure in the Amateurs wanted all of this to be over. I couldn't look at Clive without feeling guilty or searching for signs of hurt.

In the end, Craig Barrett was found guilty of two crimes—smuggling and the violent attack on Clive—and was sent to prison for a long time. Eddie Cox also received a guilty verdict for the smuggling charge due to my testimony as the sole eye witness to his meeting with Barrett on that Fourth of July, but we were outraged to hear that he was acquitted of two other charges for lack of direct evidence. Prosecutors had attempted to prove that Clive's mother, Veronica Wallace, and his father, Eddie, had conspired to sell their child to Jeff Tierney although only Veronica's name appeared on the birth certificate. Eddie had claimed to know nothing about the birth of his son, let alone the sale of his child. It came down to what we called, "He say, She say." Since Veronica had confessed to the sale after hearing about the murder of Jeff Tierney, her attorney had argued that she'd been too young to offer a stable home to a child and that Eddie had cooked up the idea to sell the baby. There might have been some truth in that, but her claim that she'd been too young and gullible wasn't good enough for the jury especially since she hadn't shown an ounce of personal remorse, so she alone was convicted of the offense.

As for how Mr. Tierney died, there was no clear answer. No weapon was ever found and neither was the infamous marine cooler full of drugs. A boat rental receipt under a false name and a few public contacts with the victim weren't enough to eliminate the shadows of doubt. My friends and I were certain, though. Eddie Cox was the killer and he'd slipped off the scale of justice. For Clive, this was devastating. One guilty father was alive; a second, a devoted father, was dead.

Jason hadn't told me what had happened over on Tar Island during the wee hours of the first day of November. At first, I was hurt by this until I came to the realization that he was a friend to be trusted. After all, he wasn't keeping the kind of noxious secret which could expose others to harmful repercussions once the truth was revealed. He was keeping a *confidence,* a privacy, which belonged to Clive. I knew then that Jason would do the same for me.

Jason Larabie

Thanksgiving week was a turning point for Clive, for all of us. We had a real family vacation, away from the River, in the Big Apple of New York City, thanks to Gary Stanton who put us up in a hotel near Rockefeller Center. After touring college campuses on Monday and Tuesday, we were itching to take in the sites. Clive's friend, Samantha, joined us while we explored the Empire State Building, the Met, Central Park, and Times Square. On Thursday, we got up early to join the shivering crush of spectators filling the sidewalks to watch the parade. Later, Mr. Stanton took us to one of his favorite restaurants for a turkey feast which left me more stuffed than the bird.

The next day, Mom wanted to walk up Fifth Avenue in the Black Friday crowd of Christmas bargain-hunters, but we dragged our feet when it came to shopping. She got a kick out of looking at the holiday decorations, though.

"Everything is so big, the Christmas tree, the street ornaments, the ..."

"Skyscrapers?" my brothers said in unison.

Clive was invited to spend the evening with Samantha and her father's family before our departure on Saturday morning. The return trip was quiet. Mom and Dad chatted while the four of us snoozed in the back seats of the mini-van.

I think the trip opened Clive's eyes to possibilities beyond life at the River, though I don't know how you can ever get the River out of your blood if you've been raised there. During the following weeks, we filled out college applications and wrote our essays together. By the time Christmas arrived, all the paperwork had been mailed out and we began the wait.

In the meantime, my father and Clive had been remodeling the upper floor of the boathouse. My brothers and I were drafted (Dad doesn't like that word, but we like to razz him with it) to help out on weekends. My father's ulterior motive soon became obvious. As the subzero temperatures of winter forced us to spend more time indoors, we needed more physical space between the generations. While the bros hung out in the boathouse, peace and quiet reigned in the main house.

After the boathouse remodel was completed, my parents found other ways to keep Clive busy while the rest of us were in school. Mom gave him lessons in oil painting, her favorite hobby. She showed him how to use a broad brush to apply the paint to canvas. He could grip the brush with the two bendable fingers of his right hand, but eventually taught himself to use his left hand, too.

Clive had resurfaced. After he showed up at a few basketball games, Hettie managed to coax him into auditioning for the school musical, *"Bye, Bye Birdie."* It was more like she dared him into doing it, telling him that if he auditioned, so would she. I'd never tell her to her face, but that girl could not carry a tune. She ended up working with the set-building crew. No surprise there. Clive, on the other hand, not only got a part; he got the lead role—Conrad Birdie. I took up my usual gig in the orchestra. At first, Clive just showed up after school for his voice rehearsals with the chorus teacher. Who knew that Clive could sing? No one. We'd always known him as the piano man. No way any of us would've pictured him as a fifties rocker type. His first performance for his costars was a show-stopper. Seemed like there was a dramatic pause of two long minutes before the applause started and then another two minutes before it ended. I hadn't seen a grin that big on Clive's face since the day we got drunk together.

Molly Larabie

Winter is the season for repair. Cal does his inventory, orders parts, makes boat repairs, cleans up the shop, and reviews the books for his annual evaluation. He gets together with other local business owners to discuss marketing the Thousand Islands. Together, we attend meetings on environmental issues which impact the River and its shores.

The grass doesn't grow in winter; tulip bulbs lie dormant underground. Garter snakes and chipmunks sleep through the cold. Winter on the St. Lawrence brings bitter winds that bend the tall evergreens and crack off dead limbs from leafless trees while piling up deep snow drifts in the open fields. The River runs free from cargo traffic, its swift current hidden beneath a layer of ice. Temperatures hover near zero or below, but despite the cold outside, the Larabie household felt warmer that winter Clive lived with us. Clive spent less time in his room, less time asleep, and more time with the family. He was the grafted limb which took to our rootstock. The tree had become whole.

That didn't mean his grief had been permanently erased. There were moments when I caught a brief look of sorrow in Clive's eyes as a memory walked through his heart, but he recovered more quickly than in the early weeks of his mourning. One particularly difficult day was the day we returned to the Marion Street property to sort through Jeff's clothing and personal possessions in preparation to rent out the house. Gary Stanton had paid off the mortgage so that Clive could keep the house.

The clothing was set aside for donation, the photo albums boxed up for storage, and Jeff's hand-carved decoys were wrapped in layers of newsprint. Tools were added to the boxes of keepsakes and picked up the following weekend by Gary. The sponsors of the piano competition graciously accepted Clive's donation—his piano—for use in one of the practice rooms.

"It's my way of being there."

The rest of the items were sold, but Clive wasn't there for the sale. He was singing his heart out at dress rehearsal for the school musical. His performance for the public brought down the house. The audience jumped to their feet to reward him with an enthusiastic ovation, but I suspect they were recognizing more than his talent. The Spring thaw had begun.

Gary Stanton

In late June, Clive graduated. It was difficult to believe that the young man who walked across the stage amidst the loud applause of his classmates and their families had been the same tormented boy who, less than a year ago, had struggled to find a reason to live. He smiled and waved his battle wound at the crowd. No one noticed the scar. They stood and applauded the success of his recovery, a recovery which may never have been accomplished without the help of many who sat in the audience that night.

The next morning was a busy one on Tar Island. My catering crew was already hard at work setting up the luau for the graduation celebration when Sam and I boarded the *Escape* to pick up Clive in Rockport. Molly Larabie had dropped him off at the dock where he was waiting for us. After he hopped aboard and sat down, I handed him the urn which he cradled in his arms as we turned about and headed upriver. We'd decided to take Jeff on one of his favorite rides past Hill Island, Ivy Lea, and out beyond Wellesley Island until we found a deserted cove. After all these months of grieving, Clive and I chose only a modicum of words to sum up our feelings.

"You'll always be my father. Thanks for loving me, Dad." He passed the urn to me.

"And for loving me. Till we meet again, Jeff."

While leaning over the leeward side of the boat and turning the urn upside down, I carefully removed the lid and set him free. A gentle breeze whisked some of the ashes skyward while the rest floated on top of the current that would transport the precious dust downriver and past our beloved cottage. Reaching overboard, Samantha released a small bough of white pine dotted with white violets gathered earlier that morning on Tar Island. We held hands in silence as we watched the tribute drift away.

Hettie Voss

Jason, Clive, and I stood on the pebble beach near the Larabie marina. The boys were competing in a skipping stone contest. They were discussing techniques and counting out the skips. Last summer seemed more distant than a year ago. The ripples from that tragic day in July couldn't be washed away. Instead, they left indelible impressions and imposed involuntary changes, but not all the changes had been detrimental. Clive wasn't an outsider anymore. He wasn't teased about how he dressed. He wasn't bullied. He'd gained weight, cut his hair, and worked outdoors under the sun with his bare hands at the marina with his family. He'd lost a father, but had melded into a larger family and for the first time in his life, he had nothing to hide.

The three of us were celebrating more than our high school graduation. We were moving on, past the sadness, and looking forward to new experiences. Jason would be attending Potsdam in the Fall to study music. He hadn't received a sufficient scholarship offer from schools in New York City, but even if he had, I doubt he would've have been able to tear himself away from the River.

"This is going to save my parents a heap of money and I can come home on weekends to work." Needless to say, the Larabies were a close-knit family.

As for me, I'd decided to trade in my snow boots for a bikini to study marine science in Florida. Guess I couldn't get the River out of my veins, either. I was looking forward to living the beach life and considered myself the bravest of my friends for choosing to wander so far from home, at least that's what I thought. Clive had been accepted into NYU, but two days after graduation, he stunned me with the news that he was deferring his acceptance until the next semester.

"I finally convinced Gary and the Larabies to let me go to Europe instead. I'll be staying in hostels or with Gary's friends, all chefs, of course."

My mouth dropped open and I looked at Jason, knowing that he'd withheld this information from me. Reading my thoughts, Clive continued. "I wanted to tell you myself."

I couldn't help but wonder what would happen if Clive were to sink back into the sea of grief and depression. "But, you'll be so far away from all of us."

"Don't worry, Hettie. Gary has scheduled stops and contact times for me. If I don't show up or make the call, he'll come looking."

It made sense, though. Maybe Clive would have a better chance of finding out who he wanted to be in a place where no one knew about his past. I was feeling less happy, though. We'd each set a different course for the future and I was already missing us.

VI. Water: a renewable, life-giving liquid resource

Twenty Years Later

Samantha De Haven

Clive Larabie to Perform in Local Piano Competition. I smiled at the headline in *The River Ragg.* I could still picture him sitting at his electronic keyboard in the back bedroom of the Tar Island cottage. We'd come a long way since then.

The call of the geese from across the road near the water's edge woke me from my reverie. Wellesley, my black Labrador, barked at the birds, reminding them that he ruled this side of the road. I put down the paper to finish the chores of dusting the last of the spiderwebs from the wicker chairs and watering the potted chrysanthemums that lined the porch steps. I'd bought the inn with some of my inheritance after my mother died and loved sharing the beauty of the River with new faces, but tonight there would only be two guests at Chopin's Inn—Uncle Gary and Clive.

After giving Wellesley my final instructions, I locked the front door while he complained from behind the oval window of leaded glass. "I always come home, Wellesley, always." I walked down the front steps and along the sidewalk lined with maples and oaks waving their red and golden leaves in the breeze. Hugging my wrap about my shoulders, I looked out at the water. Before its nighttime plunge into the River, the blood-orange sun blazed with promise that tomorrow would be a warm, Indian summer day.

Jason and Hettie met me in the lobby of the Cape Hall. "Are they here, yet?"

"Already seated, third row on the right."

I peeked through the doors into the small auditorium. Uncle Gary and Clive were seated next to the grandparents, the Larabies, and the Vosses. "You must be very proud."

"Jason hasn't been able to sleep for the past two nights. He's more nervous than Clive."

"Looks like your son may have inherited your musical talent, but I think his confidence comes from the maternal side of this family."

"More than likely, the talent was inspired by his namesake." Jason had named his only son after his best friend. Clive Tierney had also acted as best man when Jason and Hettie were married, just days after their college graduations. Jason had gone on for a master's degree and now taught music at River High, while Hettie worked as a freelance writer and photographer, frequently writing articles about environmental issues impacting the St. Lawrence River.

"Hey, Rob. Long time no see," Jason called out to the burly man who had just picked up a program. "Didn't know you were in town."

Rob Barrett walked over to greet us. "Yeah, I'm in the process of moving my mother down to Florida to live with us. We've just listed her house with Samantha." I'd acquired a license to sell real estate shortly after I bought the inn and discovered that I enjoyed helping others find home almost as much as I did finding my own. Sylvia was ready to let go of the house she'd only been able to afford after her children were out on their own and she was looking forward to being, in her words, "a full-time grandmother." As for Rob, he'd recently retired from the army.

"So, how do you like Florida?"

"More water, more sun, more warmth." His deeply tanned face lit up with a toothy grin. "I'm running a landscape business most of the week and fishing with Darcy and my kids the rest of the time." Our conversation was then interrupted by the flicker of the lobby lights, signaling for all to be seated. "I'd better go in and find Mom. Talk to you later."

We were about to follow when Senator Voss entered the lobby with his wife. "Looks like your brother has arrived just in time." Jason escorted me into the auditorium, leaving Hettie behind to speak briefly with Josh before they joined us. When I stepped into the aisle, Uncle Gary and Clive stood up to embrace me. I stared into the eyes of the tall thirty-eight year old, dressed in a gray suit, whose dimples were hidden behind a dark beard. He smiled and took my right hand in his left as we sat down.

While the young performers poured all of their energy into their selections, my mind buzzed with thoughts of Clive. The cross-currents of pernicious secrets had nearly drowned him when he'd been set to step onto this stage all those years ago. But he'd been salvaged, salvaged by a community dedicated to preserving whatever is redeemable, whether it be a wooden skiff, a castle, or a broken heart. For the past decade, Clive had been producing documentaries about contemporary composers from all over the world. Hettie, ever the crusader, was hoping to convince him to change direction for a while to focus on the ecosystems of the St. Lawrence River, a River which endlessly continued to imitate the music of life through a diversity of natural movements and moods. I'd long ago surrendered to its therapeutic lure which soothed my worries and filled my soul with gratitude.

On our way back to the inn, we walked along the waterfront and sat down on a weathered wooden bench. Clive held me close as we rested quietly under a cloudless sky sequined with a myriad of stars. He rocked me gently back and forth while humming ever so softly, as if to himself only, but it wasn't Chopin he was hearing. It was the mystical lullaby of the River.

ACKNOWLEDGMENTS

It's true; the greatest gifts are faith, hope, and love. These attributes, or the lack of, frequently define a character and influence the course of action. At the same time, these gifts are what kept this writer writing. I would like to thank all of those who had faith in the project, who loved me enough to offer words of encouragement, or shared their time and skills. You gave me hope that I could realize yet another dream.

Linda Hunt-Nelson, Brian Quinn of Alfred State College, Colleen Kelley and her fellow book club members—you donated your time and critical reading skills to give me your valuable editing suggestions and reactions to this work. Without you, this story may have remained in the bottom drawer of my desk.

John W. Richardson—you shared your writing experience, software skills, and showed great patience in helping me transfer this work from my laptop to a world of readers.

Noel, my son—you used your creative eye and graphic design skills to enhance what would have been a so-so cover design.

Last, but never least, Allen—it was you who questioned why I wasn't writing, you who said, "What are you waiting for? All the obstacles have been removed." That was the key turning in the ignition. Thank you for being my constant example of faith, hope, and love.

Made in the USA
San Bernardino, CA
26 April 2016